M000039209

ONE OF A KIND

Dexter hadn't counted on meeting one special woman . . . a woman he could genuinely care about. A woman he cared so deeply for.

Gradually, Anthia had become an essential part of his life. She had reached into his heart in a profound way. He closed his eyes against the despair of tears burning his throat, filling his chest. Tears that he did not dare let fall.

Just who was in need of protection? Himself or Anthia? Was that what this was all about? Was he afraid of caring too much . . . risking it all? Was he afraid he might fall in love again?

He looked down into Anthia's lovely eyes. He covered her mouth with his. The kiss was not soft or gentle. It was stark and heavy with even deeper emotions, ones she couldn't begin to comprehend.

She opened her mouth beneath the onslaught of his driving hunger, allowing his tongue to move slowly, seductively against hers. He groaned deep in his throat, gathering her even closer.

Dexter was absolutely sure of one thing . . . he could not bear to lose Anthia. He could not even bear to think about it. He would do anything . . . anything to keep her with him.

BOOK YOUR PLACE ON OUR WEBSITE
AND MAKE THE ARABESQUE
ROMANCE CONNECTION!

We've created a customized website just for our very special
Arabesque readers, where you can get the inside scoop on
everything that's going on with Arabesque romance novels.

When you come online, you'll have the exciting opportunity
to:

- View covers of upcoming books

- Learn about our future publishing schedule (listed by
  publication month and author)

- Find out when your favorite authors will be visiting a
  city near you.

- Search for and order backlist books from our line cata-
  log

- Check out author bios and background information

- Send e-mail to your favorite authors

- Join us in weekly chats with authors, readers and other
  guests

- Get writing guidelines

- AND MUCH MORE!

Visit our website at
http://www.arabesquebooks.com

ONE OF A KIND

BETTE FORD

ARABESQUE

BET BOOKS

BET Publications, LLC
www.msbet.com
www.arabesquebooks.com

ARABESQUE BOOKS are published by

BET Publications, LLC
C/o BET BOOKS
One BET Plaza
1900 W Place NE
Washington, D.C. 20018-1211

Copyright © 1999 by Bette Ford

All rights reserved. No part of this book may be reproduced
in any form or by any means without the prior written consent
of the Publisher.

If you purchased this book without a cover, you should be aware
that this book is stolen property. It was reported as "unsold and
destroyed" to the Publisher and neitherthe Author nor the Publisher has received any payment for this 'stripped book.'

BET Books is a trademark of Black Entertainment Television,
Inc. Arabesque, the Arabesque logo and the BET Books logo
are Reg. U.S. Pat. & TM Off.

First Printing: February, 1999
10 9 8 7 6 5 4 3 2 1

Printed in the United States of America

My first hero:
In loving memory of my father
James R. Ford
You are truly loved and dearly missed
and
In memory of my
dear, sweet cousin
Kathleen Porter-Melton,
who's loving and caring
spirit lives on.

ONE

Anthia Jenkins could not stop smiling as she looked around her combined studio and office. She couldn't believe her good fortune. At thirty-four she was finally her own boss. No more waking to an alarm clock or having to deal with rush-hour traffic first thing in the morning and late in the evening. Her business suits were pushed to the back of her closet and her work clothes consisted of jeans, sweats and T-shirts.

Had it only been a little more than two years since that horrible day when she thought her world had come to a tragic end? Her son, Jeffery, had been unconscious in the hospital in critical condition after having been shot in the back. It had been days of not knowing if he would live or die, weeks of not knowing if he would ever walk again, followed by more than a year of intense physical therapy and rehabilitation.

She had to leave her job as a legal secretary because of the time she had to devote to Jeff's recovery. With time on her hands as she watched her son's progress, first at the hospital then later at the rehab center, she indulged herself by pouring her heart into her lifelong hobby of doll-making. She smiled as she remembered the large tote bag she carted around with her filled with doll paraphernalia that needed to be hemmed, stitched or embroidered. It kept her from biting her fingernails off on those bad days when Jeff was in so much pain. Who would have guessed that that indulgence would lead to a highly successful business venture of her very own. It had all started when one of his nurses was so impressed with her work that she bought a doll for her mother's art gallery. It mushroomed from there.

Thank goodness, the horror of that time was behind them now. Her boy was away at college, preparing for the future. Anthia could feel herself swelling with pride because he was doing very well.

Anthia managed her doll-making business out of her home. A home she was able to purchase because of her own efforts. She could not prevent the lovely smile that enhanced her amber skin tone as she lovingly smoothed her hand over the scalloped edged lace hem of the pink doll dress she had been putting the finishing touches on. It was a dream concoction of ivory and pink ruffles. It would be perfect for the one-of-a-kind doll she was close to completing. She was so proud of her individually sculpted dolls, from their hand-painted eyes, molded open mouth, satin smooth natural colorations, thick natural-looking wigs to their exquisitely handmade costuming.

Her work was shown in a private gallery in Birmingham, Michigan, as well as several prominent galleries across the country. She had more orders than she could possibly keep up with and more coming in daily. Things were definitely looking up.

There was only one area in her life that was painfully empty: She didn't have the one special man that she had cared for for some time now. Love was something that had to be given freely. Unfortunately, she had learned that lesson the hard way.

When the doorbell sounded, Anthia carefully folded the tiny dress before placing it in her sewing basket. Her window-lined studio was situated on the side of the modest size house between the garage and the large, combined living and dining room.

"Coming," she called. She absently smoothed her shoulder-length black hair that had been pulled back into a ponytail—not very original but comfortable.

Anthia was surprised to see the tall silhouette of a man with his back toward the sun thus throwing his face into shadow. But she would have known his large muscled frame anywhere. He was a throwback to the strong warriors who could run for miles without tiring in the hot African sun.

"Dex . . ." she said around a sigh, with trembling fingers she unlocked and opened the door. "Good morning. How are you?"

Dexter Washington was the director of Detroit-based Malcolm X Community Center, which sponsored a mentoring program geared toward saving black teenage boys from life on the streets. He was a broad-shouldered, lean-hipped man with bronze coloring. At six-one, he topped Anthia's petite frame by a foot. He let his dark brown eyes caress her small, brown features before lingering for a moment on her seductively full, lush mouth. He was smiling when he gazed down into her pretty ebony eyes.

Swallowing with difficulty, he said, "Mornin'. It's been awhile. You look well." He allowed himself one all-too-brief hug before he pulled back, his hands clenched at his side.

He devoured her through his veiled lids, enjoying the way her jeans clung to her shapely thighs and her lemon-colored knit top caressed the lush swells of her small breasts. His memory hadn't been playing any tricks on him. She was just as beautiful and tempting as he remembered. He suppressed a hungry groan, acknowledging his private struggle to keep her out of his thoughts . . . out of his dreams . . . from beneath his skin.

The trouble was she was never truly forgotten and always somewhere in his thoughts. Desire would not control his life. He had made that mistake once when he lost control and learned the sweet taste of her luscious mouth . . . never again. He was one man who learned from his mistakes.

Recognizing she was staring, Anthia blushed. "Come on in. Sorry, it took me so long. I was in the studio."

Dexter's slow, easy smile caught and held her interest. "Thanks. Hope, I didn't call at a bad time?"

There was no such thing as a bad time when it came to Dexter. "A friend is always welcome," she laughed. Oh, she knew what was missing from her life . . . Dexter Washington.

She had been forced to accept that without his cooperation there was nothing she could do about her undeniable attraction and tender feelings for him. It was a painful situation that she had no alternative other than to live with it.

Her feelings for him had blossomed so gradually that she

hadn't been aware of the change until it was too late to do anything about it. It was not as if she suddenly woke up one morning and realized that she was indisputably in love with Dexter. It had happened over time, stemming from his support and consideration throughout her son's lengthy recovery.

His kindness and thoughtfulness over the last few years had proven to be invaluable, which was surprising considering that he was such a private, self-contained man. Dexter was not what she would call an easy man to get to know. He kept so much of himself hidden. Very few people could honestly say they knew him well.

When Dexter stepped into the foyer where a dark oak table stood with a framed mirror above it, sharing the small space, his strong male presence seemed to dominate his surroundings. No woman could fail to take note of his masculine appeal, Anthia rashly decided. He was all man from his close-cut black natural to his keen even features. His strong angular bone structure reminded her of the Ethiopian people. He exhibited a natural strength and arrogant grace that was a throwback to the desert nomads of old.

It was a cool, crisp spring morning, the sun framed by fluffy white clouds. Even though it was April, the possibility of a spring snowstorm was still a real threat, especially in Michigan.

Anthia slowly closed the solid oak door. "Come on into the kitchen. Keep me company while I put on some coffee. I made a caramel and walnut coffee cake. Would you like a slice?"

She knew she was babbling, but she could not seem to stop. She was a mass of nerves, which was silly, considering they were such good friends. She had so much to be grateful to him for.

When she was ready to purchase her and her son's very first home, it was Dexter who had taken time from his busy schedule at the community center to go house hunting with her. He had also made sure she was making the best deal. He proved to be very knowledgeable about architecture and design as well as the real-estate market in general. He had been with her when she closed on the house. Most importantly, he had shared the most glorious day of her life when she and Jeff moved into their new home in the Detroit northwestern suburb of Southfield.

Unfortunately, she hadn't seen him since that day last fall. The funny part of it was that she had no idea why. Had he been spooked by that kiss they shared? It was a warm, triumphant kiss they'd exchanged at the end of that long day. She could not deny that she had been giddy with happiness and overwhelmed now that the dream of owning her own home was real. Sharing her excitement, Dexter had picked her up and whirled her around the room. Laughing, she had hugged him tight.

The next thing she knew, he let her petite, curvy frame slide slowly down his long, muscular body then lower his head to press his mouth against hers. That kiss had been so wonderfully sweet, yet sizzling hot with desire. She knew then that she had done the unthinkable, that she had fallen in love with him.

"Sounds wonderful," he grinned. He would be the first one to admit that he enjoyed her down-home-cooking. The girl knew her way around the kitchen. She also knew how to fill a pair of jeans.

He tried his best not to take notice of the way the denim hugged her soft, round behind as she walked ahead of him but failed. His nostrils flared automatically as he tried to catch her sweet woman's scent. She didn't wear heavy perfumes, yet her body always smelled seductively sweet.

He often found himself remembering how she tasted on his lips . . . against his tongue. She had small plump breasts, that he could not stop himself from imagining how they would feel in his mouth, his tongue slowly licking her nipples until they were little peaks hard with desire . . . desire for him alone. He swore beneath his breath, impatient with himself as his body prepared itself to join with hers.

"Did you say something?" she asked.

"I like what you have done to this place." His eyes fondly took in her special touches that made her home uniquely hers, from the small, black, sculpted clown doll on the table in the entrance way to the pretty black rag doll dressed in corals on the mantelpiece. On the window seat was a row of one-of-a-kind dolls. She used her dolls as decorative artwork. "This place looks like you."

She had used warm tangerine tones to decorate the house from the deep tones of the oversize sofa and love seat, to the pale peachy beige on the walls and carpeting throughout. It was a place of beauty, comfort and relaxation.

"Thank you." she said, recalling that he hadn't been here since she moved in. "So, how have you been? How are things at the center?"

Dexter was a hard worker and devoted many hours to the center. Most of the boys he worked with didn't have the benefit of a father or man in their lives like her own son. Dexter, along with a host of male volunteers, worked to combat the situation. They were determined to save a whole generation of males. A huge undertaking to say the least.

"Busy," he grumbled, taking a seat at the small kitchen table against the far wall of the sunny room. He rested his hands on the table relieved that his arousal was hidden.

"Oh!" she jumped as a coffee mug dropped to the mosaic orange and yellow pattern floor tiles. Luckily, it didn't break and shatter as she expected.

"Here, let me get it." He quickly crossed to her and squatted to retrieve it. The firm muscles in his taut thighs and buttocks flexed bringing her eyes to his muscular frame. He was all male, beautifully made and so darn self-contained that she wanted to shake him.

She never knew what he was thinking or feeling. She saw no more than he wanted her to see. It was disturbing what she didn't know about him. Goodness, she didn't even know if he was involved with another woman. The mere thought of it tore at her tender heart. She forced herself to turn away from him, furious with herself for wanting him.

"Thank you," she said, careful not to touch his warm bronze skin. She was trembling as she placed the mug in the divided sink, and busied herself by getting another one and collecting the dessert plates, utensils and napkins.

Dexter touched the pretty tangerine mushroom-shaped

creamer and sugar bowl that decorated the top of the small kitchen table, hoping to distract himself.

"You look tired," she couldn't help saying. "I don't know how you have time for a private life. You spend so many hours at the community center."

He shrugged. "It's important work. The two things we never seem to have enough of at the center are money and volunteers."

Dexter had been at the center during the three years he'd been back in Detroit. What he had done before that was a mystery. Other than the fact that he had grown up in Detroit, but had a faint Texas accent, she had no idea what he had done with his life. He didn't talk about himself. He kept his thoughts to himself. Outside of the center, she had no idea what his personal hopes and dreams were for his future. She often found herself wondering if it was just her he didn't trust.

For a time, she had firmly believed he was not involved with anyone. But lately she had decided that was very naive. The man was gorgeous. There was certainly nothing wrong with the eyesight of the women in the Motor City. He had no reason to be alone or celibate for that matter. It had nearly driven her crazy trying to figure out without asking who the woman in his life was. Why did he keep her hidden from his friends? Perhaps, if Anthia was forced to meet the woman, she could get over this childish infatuation with him.

But Anthia knew what she felt for Dexter was not a schoolgirl's crush. Her feminine desires for him were quite real. She craved his strong arms, yearned for his tongue-thrusting kisses and hungered for his lovemaking with a woman's appetite. He had no need to prove his virility to her. It was as much a part of him as his fingers and toes.

"We've been especially flooded since Charles proposed adding the year-round sports camp. We have so much going on these days with martial arts classes, computer classes, plus the GED classes. There is not enough time in the day to keep it all running smoothly while trying to get the fellows off the streets and out of trouble."

Dexter referred to their mutual friend, Charles Randol. He

was a wealthy backer who believed in the center so strongly that he had been willing to put more than his money into the effort, but also his time. It was Charles' fraternity brothers who had initially sponsored the community-center-based project. He had been the one to hire Dexter as director of the center. Charles had not stopped there but had recruited men with expertise, like pro basketball player Donald Williams.

Anthia watched Dexter closely, when she said, "Did I hear a catch in your voice? Aren't the new programs going to work out?"

He smiled, glad he had finally come. He could talk to Anthia. "Oh, yeah. All we have to do is find additional funding for the year-round camp and a security guard, not to mention funding the new centers needed throughout the city." His shook his head wearily. "Anthia, we still have so many kids that are falling through the cracks. That really gets to me. There are too many black boys to count who are being lured into gangs. Damn it, it happens every single day because of their deep need to belong, to be part of a family, even a substitute one."

His concern was genuine, for it was in his eyes, his frustration in his voice. "It never seems to stop. Who's going to be there for them? Who's going to keep them from becoming just another causality of the streets? Somebody has to care."

Dexter knew what it meant to be alone. He lived and breathed that life each and every day. But he was an adult able to take care of himself. He had met just such a boy this past week while speaking at Kettering High School. He'd asked around and learned that the kid was a loner. He had no one. He lived in the rooming house with no family to call his own, another casualty of the foster care system. How long did they have before he was swallowed alive by the streets? Maybe this time they could reach this one.

"You take it very personally when you lose a kid. Dex, you are but one man. Even you have to rest and rejuvenate."

Dexter tensed, he didn't know how much Anthia really knew about his past. He'd never had the guts to ask. She was a friend, someone he treasured. In truth he hoped she didn't ever find out his personal history. He knew he could not bear to see the disapproval and horror on her lovely face. He did not want to even think about losing her friendship. He had been very careful not to let her get too close or let his own male hunger overwhelm him. Their friendship was essential to his well-being.

"I'm too stubborn to quit," he shrugged.

"Are you concerned for a particular child?" she asked, trying to read his face.

"Yeah," he said gruffly, shocked by her insight. Were his thoughts written all over his face? He frowned, not liking the concept. "I met him while I was speaking at one of the high schools this past week. One of our kids pointed him out to me. I only spoke to him briefly, but I didn't like what I heard about his life."

His tireless devotion to helping black boys was only one of the things she admired about him. He put his heart into what he was doing. She had never known him to give up on any kid. He tried and tried, unwilling to leave anything to chance. Dexter quite literally had committed his life to this cause.

Anthia could only imagine what it would feel like to have this man's devotion directed her way. Shivers raced down her spine from just the possibility and her nipples pouted against the soft fabric of her top. Although, she wore a bra, her breasts ached as if they were exposed, eager for his attention. Was he a hungry, intense lover? Or was he slow and meticulous when it came to giving his woman pleasure? Goodness!

She quickly turned away, pretending an absorption in putting the coffee cake on a plate. Just what was her problem? Was she letting one kiss shared months ago cloud her thinking? In another minute, she'd be throwing herself at a man who was only interested in her friendship.

So why had he kissed her? Had it simply been a wild impulse? Perhaps a momentary lapse? It was a question that had been rattling around inside of her head for months. Unfortunately, she didn't have the nerve to voice the question.

Curiosity got the better of her, she couldn't stop herself from asking, "What brought you out this way? I haven't seen you in quite some time," she smiled, hoping to keep the hurt out of her tone. He had been so good to her, she didn't want him to think that she was ungrateful.

More nights than she could count had been spent with him, as they shared a late-night meal after she had spent long hours with Jeff at the hospital and he at the community center. The last thing she wanted was for him to think she was making any demands on him. He'd even been a real sport and volunteered to help her load the van and drive Jeff down to Georgia for college.

Anthia would have been shocked if she could guess his thoughts. He knew he should have called first. He knew he should not have come. He could not help himself. He simply had to see her. He'd purposefully withheld that pleasure as punishment for his pitiful lack of control. He should not have held her close and most certainly should not have kissed her.

He had to keep himself on a very short leash when it came to Anthia. He had done so for several months now out of necessity. Even though, he knew he was all wrong for her and that she deserved much better than an ex-con, nonetheless, he could not go another day without seeing her.

He had needed to look into her pretty brown face and indulge himself by viewing her petite curvy figure with deep masculine yearning. He was painfully aware of her. He was rock-hard with longing. He took a deep fortifying breath, hoping to calm himself. He should not have come. She was too damn tempting.

Any man would be lucky to call this woman his. She was warm and caring yet, she was a fighter. He admired the way she had raised her son alone and made no apologies for it.

"Yeah, it has been." Dexter frowned. He hadn't been the one she called when she needed a picture hung or a piece of heavy furniture moved. Was she seeing someone new? Or was that jerk Doug Henderson back in her life? He ground his teeth in frustration. It was none of his business.

At least they talked once a week or so, but she was not the one initiating the calls. She had not dialed his number since the day she moved into the house . . . the day he kissed her. Had his loss of control ruined their friendship and made him just too dense to notice?

"How's business, boss lady?"

She giggled. "Great. I've got so many orders that I was forced to seek help with the sewing. Dana Gray. Do you know her? She lives in the old building." Anthia was referring to the apartment building that she grew up in.

Dexter frowned, not liking the area, It was close to the center and had some serious gang activity going on. He, too, had been raised not too far away. "No, I don't know Dana. Glad to hear you're not working yourself into the ground."

Anthia shrugged her shoulders. "I admit I overdo some things, but it doesn't feel like work because I love what I'm doing. Because of Dana's help I'm able to concentrate on sculpting and designing these days and less and less on sewing."

Her one-of-a-kind dolls were in demand. The word was getting out about not only the high quality of her work but the individual nature. Her mail was filled with photographs of people who wanted either their likeness or a family member's captured. And they were willing to pay the staggering prices necessary to produce such an elaborate piece of folk art.

"I found the perfect name for the company, One of a Kind."

He grinned, "It fits. Your work is first-class."

Anthia blushed. "Thank you. I had no idea there were so many collectors out there and not only in the states, but from all over the world. I've been very lucky." Handing him the tray, she said, "Let's have this in the living room. I hardly ever sit in there with Jeff away at school."

"How is he?" Dexter asked as he carried the tray. He placed it on the wide marble coffee table before he sat adjacent to her on the love seat while she settled on the sofa. That particular sitting area was positioned in front of a brick fireplace. Across from them was a big picture window that was flanked on both sides by twin taupe high-back armchairs. The round marble table separating the chairs held Anthia's collection of family photographs. Her skill with a needle was evident by the needlepoint and embroidered pillows scattered about.

"He's doing well. He's keeping up with his physical therapy and his grades are high. I am so proud of that boy," she beamed as she filled their cups from a silver pot.

"Jeff is why I'm here. I thought you might persuade him to stop by the center when he comes home for his next break. Give a pep talk to the fellows."

TWO

Anthia schooled her face, careful not to let him see her disappointed that his reason for coming had nothing to do with her. She handed him a slice of the coffee cake before she said, shaking her head, "I don't know Dex. He's still so self-conscious since the accident." She preferred to call it an accident even though, he'd been shot during an armed robbery.

Jeff had made the horrible mistake of being in the wrong place at the wrong time. He had made the near fatal mistake of taking a ride from an friend from their old neighborhood. Eddie Walker and Jeff had grown up together. Anthia and Jeff had moved away into a better area, which meant on her salary a one-bedroom flat. Jeff's bedroom had been the sofabed in their living room.

Anthia had made a point of enrolling him in the community center. While Jeff had worked hard getting good grades in school, going to the center and being influenced by men like Dexter and Charles, Eddie had done the opposite. He had indulged himself in the street life . . . fast money and gangs . . . a brotherhood of crime and drugs.

On this particular day, Jeff had been led like a lamb to slaughter as far as Anthia was concerned. He had been left in the running car waiting for Eddie while he went inside the convenience store.

Unknown to Jeff, Eddie was using him to keep the car running while he robbed the store. Jeff had grown impatient with the delay and walked right into Eddie's mess. Eddie had tossed the gun at Jeff before going to collect the money. Jeff had caught it without thinking, demanding to know what was going on. When Jeff turned to leave, the outraged store owner had found enough courage to shoot Jeff in the back. He had wound up in the hospital fighting for his life while Eddie had vanished, leaving Jeff to take the rap. Anthia shuddered at the hateful memory.

"Don't you think he has hidden himself away long enough? He had friends at the center. Besides, he can help others, if he's willing to tell his story to the new guys, the next time he's home on break. Tell them what he has lived. He can show just by being there that guns and drugs go hand in hand. The most innocent situation can prove deadly."

Anthia, thoughtfully sipped her drink watching as Dexter seemed to savor the coffee cake. The accident had left Jeff, first in a wheelchair for close to a year, and now finally he was able to walk with the aid of crutches. It had been a long, painful ordeal that still unfortunately wasn't entirely over.

She could never forget that long agonizing night of the shooting. Dexter, Charles and Diane Randol and Doug Henderson, the man she was dating casually at the time, had all been there with her.

Dexter and Charles had eventually found Eddie. With the legal help of Quinn Montgomery, prominent criminal attorney, Jeff had eventually been exonerated while Eddie had been convicted for armed robbery. Their later civil suit against the store owner had paid the mountain of medical bills not covered by their insurance as well as Jeff's college expenses.

"Jeff's had a few difficult years, but he has bounced back."

"I'll give him a call and let you know what he says."

"Thanks," he smiled coming to his feet. "I have to be going. Thanks for the refreshments. That coffee cake was good, girl."

Disappointed, she said, "I'll wrap a piece for you. You don't have to rush off, you know."

"I've kept you from your work long enough."

Anthia shook her head. "No problem. I can always use a break. I'll get that cake." She excused herself. In the kitchen she consoled herself that at least he had come to the house for a visit as she cut another large slice of cake.

"Anthia, you don't have to go to any trouble," he said, having placed the heavy tray on the counter.

"All done." She smiled, handing him the foil-wrapped treat. As she walked him to the door, she said, "Thanks for coming by. It was good seeing you. It's been a while."

She was tempted to tell him that he didn't need a reason to visit. She enjoyed his company, but at the last minute decided against it. She did have a little pride.

"You take care of yourself," he said, one lean brown finger caressed down her cheek ever so gently.

Anthia trembled from the brief contact, but she tried to hide it behind a generous smile. She would not let herself think of a more intimate, deeper caress. There was no point in daydreaming about a man who did not want her.

"You, too. 'Bye." She waved, refusing to watch him walk to his car parked in the driveway. Quietly closing the door, she let out a thoughtful sigh. It was a ridiculous waste of time to find herself wondering how long it would be before she was lucky enough to see him again.

When Anthia returned to her workroom, she decided to tackle something she had some control of, such as the problem of duplicating a fifty-year-old christening dress for a baby doll. The doll would resemble a treasured old photograph. She had no doubt that it could be done. She had done it too many times to worry about the outcome. Her dolls were as unique as the likeness she painstakingly duplicated.

But her thoughts continued to slip backward. She'd been so young when she met Jeff Johnson. She thought she was deeply in love with him. He was only a few years older than she was and very handsome. He said all the things her young romantic heart had craved to hear. She had never had a boyfriend. At five-one, she considered her hundred and twenty-seven pound frame too short and overweight to be appealing. She looked nothing like the fashion models in the *Seventeen* magazine she loved. Her hair was unfashionably long and her clothes plain and simple because her mother oversaw everything Anthia made on the sewing machine. She'd been fifteen at the time.

Anthia almost laughed. Jeff was no fool. He sensed her vulnerability. He said the sweet words repeatedly until she could no longer withhold her love from him. She made love with him with all the sweet yearning she possessed, certain that her feelings were returned. Once was enough for him, then he moved on to the next girl. Once was also enough to prove how foolish she had been. By the time she was sixteen, she was disillusioned, brokenhearted and pregnant.

Anthia recalled how difficult it had been to tell her mother. It had been the hardest thing in the world because she knew how much her mother believed in her. Her parents had dreams of their daughter having an easier life, a prosperous life. Her father had been killed by a stray bullet when Anthia was only a toddler, leaving her mother to raise her alone. Her mother, naturally, wanted her to be in a position to have advantages and opportunities that she as a day worker didn't have. Anthia had been bright and was doing so well in school.

Even today, Anthia could remember her mother's face when she broke the news to her. She had put off telling for as long as she dared. She was sick every day and she didn't have the faintest idea how to care for herself.

Yet, as she looked back on it now, she realized that she knew deep inside that her mother would never turn her back on her child. That love and support was what had given Anthia the strength to get through the most difficult time of her young life.

That shattered look on her mother's sweet brown face brought tears to Anthia's eyes even now. It was a look of overwhelming hurt and disappointment. It had been painful for them both. That night, mother and daughter had cried together. Yet, there had been no question of Anthia keeping her baby.

Thank goodness, she was not alone. Her mother was there for her and supported her throughout her pregnancy. She had managed to finish school and start college while taking care of her son, only because of her mother's love and support. Anthia and Jeff had shared a roomy two-bedroom apartment even after her mother died from a stroke. Anthia missed her still.

Unfortunately, the neighborhood had changed drastically over the years. Gang violence and crime were too common. Anthia felt that it was not the place to raise an impressionable boy. Jeff was just starting those vulnerable teenage years and she feared for his future without a father's guidance.

She and her son moved into a small one-bedroom upper level of a two family flat in a much better low-income neighborhood. It had been crowded to say the least, but they had managed. The sofa bed in the living room became Jeff's bedroom in the evenings. It wasn't ideal, but it was the best she could afford. She had to give up her own schooling and work full-time as a legal secretary in order to afford the new place.

The smartest thing she had done after the move was enrolling her son in the Malcolm X Community Center where he was under the influence of strong black men like Dexter and Charles determined to make a difference. And it made a world of difference to both Jeff and Anthia. They had both made endearing lifelong friendships.

It was a shame she no longer possessed the confidence with Dexter that she had when she was first attracted to Charles. She had been so sure of herself . . . so full of it. Her thoughts flew back to the night she first met Dexter Washington. As she prepared for the evening ahead, her thoughts had centered on one man, Charles Randol. She had been floored by him from the instant Jeff brought him home to meet her.

He was everything she thought she wanted in a man, tall, handsome and extremely wealthy. He headed the family-owned Randol Pharmaceutical. And he had shown a keen interest in her son, a huge plus as far as she was concerned. Suddenly he had become not only her son's mentor but her black knight. She saw him as the answer to her hopes and dreams for a secure future. It didn't register that he had shown her nothing more than his friendship.

She had no idea that Charles' romantic interest and desires were focused on one beautiful woman . . . a woman from his past. So when he invited both Jeff and herself to attend a charity dinner-dance, a fund-raiser sponsored by Charles' fraternity to raise money for the community center, Anthia had been thrilled, certain that this was her chance to show him how perfect she was for him. She knew she could fit into his influential world.

She was just as pretty as those chic, well-educated women that were so much a part of his life.

She found the perfect dress, took extra care with her hair and nails. She had worked so hard, making sure that their tiny flat was spotless. She chuckled at the memory. She could afford to do so now. That evening had been a disaster. She had made a complete fool of herself. Charles had not come up to their door as she expected but had waited in the car. Her son had let her know he was there and not alone. Her feelings were crushed . . . all her fanciful daydreams vanished.

Jeff held the door while she slid into the backseat. When Charles had smiled and introduced his bride, Diane, Anthia wanted to sink beneath the floorboards. If it hadn't been for Jeff, she would have gotten out of the car and spent the evening nursing her injured pride.

She told herself on the ride downtown that it was a mistake. There had to be some type of mistake. Charles could not actually be married to this drop-dead gorgeous, sister. Diane Rivers Randol was everything Anthia was not. She was tall, flawlessly beautiful and was well educated. She had it all.

As the evening progressed, Anthia, seated at a large table, vaguely remembered being introduced to yet another man. He, too, was tall and attractive but unlike Charles, his eyes often move toward Anthia. He had a quiet strength that was so much a part of him that Anthia hadn't realized it at the time. That man was Dexter, someone her son depended on for male guidance, someone who would prove to be a true friend that she could call on time and time again. He had never stepped over the line . . . never asked for anything from her other than her friendship.

Anthia had foolishly looked to a man for financial stability while she should have been focusing on her own natural talents and creativity. Those inner resources were eventually what had changed her life around professionally and financially.

She had not known it then, but it had been Dexter's quiet strength that had gotten her through her son's ordeal. He had stayed that entire endless night of the shooting.

Anthia sighed recalling how badly she behaved that next

morning. Jeff had still been in critical condition. Dexter hadn't agreed with her readily enough that her son was innocent. She had lost her temper—demanded that he leave. She had been shaken from grief, fatigue and fear that her baby might not recover that she took it out on Dexter.

He had not said one word in his own defense. But he hadn't walked out of their lives. He kept coming back. He had weathered that first emotional storm and many others, offering whatever she needed. He was always willing to listen when she needed to talk or provide a strong shoulder to lean on during months and months of uncertainty.

Anthia found that she had absolutely no defense against that kind of generosity and kindness. It was only after much of the long ordeal was over that she recognized that her feelings for Dexter went far deeper than friendship.

He had become her rock. All the way through, not only for her but also for Jeff. How could she not care about him? There was no other man that she wanted to spend time with or that she cared for so deeply. There could be no other man that she could long for the way she longed for him. She ached to lay close to his heart, deep in his arms, and know his lovemaking. There was no need for her to try and impress Dexter. She didn't have to be anyone but herself around him.

For so long she'd been caught up in the struggle to survive. She had no time or energy to worry about getting or keeping a man. It was only recently that her worries about money and Jeff had eased. Suddenly she was able to fully examine her feelings for Dexter. She loved him with her whole heart. He meant the world to her. She treasured his friendship so much that she would never do anything to risk losing it.

Dexter groaned as he reached for the telephone yet again. He'd been locked in the office most of the day and was growing impatient with the arrangement. The community center needed another full-time secretary but was forced to make due with untrained volunteers.

As director of the community center it was his job to make

sure everything ran smoothly. The trouble was he didn't have the time to recruit and devote to the teenage boys that so desperately needed the center's assistance. More often than not, he was forced to leave the mentoring to Charles and other black men willing to volunteer not only their time but their money to the cause. He swore impatiently, his martial arts class had to be canceled yet again.

The aim of the community center was to get as many black men involved in the lives of the boys without fathers or uncles, or strong men in their lives willing to show them the right way.

The problem didn't start or end with the Million Man March. There was no end to the lure of the streets. The longer Dexter was chained to the desk and this small office the more frustrated and useless he felt.

The center was housed in a run-down neighborhood, surrounded by boys looking to gangs for the closeness and support of the family. Dexter was extremely proud of the center's efforts to make a difference. It had many successful young men that had gone on to make a better life for themselves. Some even came back willing to offer a helping hand to those left behind.

"Hey, Washington. You spending the night?" Guy Malone asked from the doorway of the small cramped office. Like Dexter, Guy was single. And that was where the similarity ended. Guy had a special lady in his life. Dexter had no one.

Dexter grumbled, looking up from the budget report he'd been working on. The figures were heartbreaking. They had to find a way to get two new computers for the computer lab. And a security guard to provide a reasonably safe haven for the kids. If he had to go out into the community and beg, then so be it. There were too many kids at risk for him to ease up. His job was important to him. It was all he had left.

"It's the only way to get anything done around here. What's your excuse?" Dexter said looking pointedly at the clock mounted on the wall. It was close to midnight.

Guy waved, good-naturedly. "All clear. The guys have all gone home. Night, man. My lady is expecting me."

The only thing waiting for Dexter was an empty house. There would be no hot meal on the stove, more important no tender kisses to welcome him, no sweet loving to ease the long hours of the night. He lived alone, ate alone and slept alone. He told himself that was how he preferred it, caused very few complications.

"See you," Dexter called. He stared down at the notes he'd been making on a legal pad. His life came down to the community center and nothing more. It was all he needed.

All too soon, the late night sounds settled around him. Eventually, he began his nightly tour of the building, double-checking all the locks. There were plans in the works to expand the facilities into the east, north and south side of town. The need was there, there was no doubt about that. The trouble once again was money. And there was also the problem of staff. Dexter was the only paid director and they had no funds to hire others. Was the board of directors expecting him to be in four different locations at once?

The building had been provided by the Poindexter Foundation. The late John E. Poindexter had set aside money, upon death, to help the poor and downtrodden. He had amassed his wealth in the stock market and in real estate. The prominent black man had been a self-made man. He had no one to help him as he was growing up. He had lost both parents at such an early age. Although, he had prospered, he had never forgotten his humbled beginnings. Poindexter's story was not an unusual one. It happened over and over. It was Jeff Jenkins' story.

Thinking of Jeff brought Anthia to mind. Who was he trying to kid? Anthia was never far from his thoughts. He had gone to her home this morning because he could not wait an instant longer to see her again. Months without even a glimpse of her had taken their toll on him.

He was beyond alone . . . he was emotionally stranded on a deserted island without any means of escape. Anthia represented the glimmer and beauty of the moonlit sky. She had the most wonderful smile and a warm, loving spirit. And she had been very generous with her sweetness and her smiles. For a time, she had lost that smile because of worry over Jeff and his extensive recovery and later during the trial. Thank goodness that was behind them now. The trouble was Dexter didn't see nearly enough of her.

He had fought his hunger as long as he could bear it, then he had started driving by her house at night, unable to sleep until he knew she was safe. This morning had been different. This time he had stopped and rang the bell. Although he'd been annoyed with himself because of his display of weakness, he had a reason for being there. That knowledge soothed his wounded ego.

When Dexter finished his rounds, he collected his things, set the burglar alarm and locked up. The parking lot was empty except for his somewhat battered old Buick. The Rivera had certainly seen better days, but then again, so had he. He and the car had been worn down and beat up by the ravishment of time and life.

He was almost out of the parking lot when he realized it would be days, maybe even weeks, until emotionally he had moved beyond seeing Anthia, again. It brought back sweet memories of the taste and feel of her. Her petite form had fit perfectly against him and left him hungry for her.

Only once had he pushed the boundary of their friendship. He had lost his head and kissed her. That kiss had been a huge mistake that could never be repeated. He had risked what he valued, in that careless moment. And he'd been lucky she had not pushed him out of her life for good.

Thank goodness, that mistake was behind them. Sexual involvement was no longer a part of his life. He had nothing left to offer a woman, nothing for her to believe in or trust in, nothing to build a relationship on.

He had failed at love. His marriage had been a dismal mistake. Even if by some miracle Anthia decided to trust him with her tender emotions, he didn't have anything to offer her in return . . . not love, not a commitment, not even the truth about his background. He had considered telling her, then had lost his nerve. Convincing himself that his past had no bearing on their friendship.

As long as it remained a friendship he could live with his secrets. He had closed and firmly locked the door on his past.

It was over. Not for anyone, including Anthia would he open that wasteland of disillusionment and despair.

There were very few people here in Detroit who knew about him. So few he could count them on one hand. When he had left prison, he had put all of that behind him. He had no intention of ever looking back. He had to be honest with himself if he were to survive heart whole. No woman in her right mind would willingly accept him and the baggage he carried with him.

"Enough!" It was close to one in the morning when he pulled his car to a stop in front of the all-night diner a few blocks from the center.

"Hey, Dex," Jan was the only waitress on at this time of night. She waved him toward the rear booth he preferred. "What will you have?" she asked, filling his cup with coffee.

"What's on special?"

"It's Tuesday. Meatloaf, mashed potatoes and peas."

"Give me the special," he said, barely aware of her leaving, his gaze on the steam rising from his cup. The diner was as familiar to him as his own place. Today had been no different from the day before or the week before except for one detail: He'd seen Anthia.

Refusing to dwell on what could not be changed, he opened the newspaper and began reading. It was not until he had finished both his meal and the paper that he looked around the diner. It was littered with people that looked as lonely and empty as he felt. Coming to his feet, he mumbled his thanks to the waitress, paid, giving her a generous tip then quietly leaving as seamlessly as he'd entered. No one really noticed, no one cared.

The night felt as dark and endless as always. His mind was not on the traffic as he drove through the silent streets. He didn't bother to question his behavior as he drove to her house. Once he was satisfied that everything looked secure, he felt free to go home.

He didn't even glance around the darkened living room of the small two-bedroom house he rented near the community center. He did not own it. He did not care enough to consider buying it. He bypassed the easy chair placed in front of the television and continued on to his bedroom. He turned on the light, uninterested in his drab surroundings as he stripped down before heading for the soothing warmth of the shower.

He let the hot water ease the tightness from his tired muscles while massaging the tautness from his neck and shoulders. He did his utmost not to think, not to remember. There was nothing to question . . . nothing to examine. He had already filled enough years with regret.

Anthia's amber features were as pretty as he remembered, her smile just as welcoming. He could have easily lost himself inside of her warmth. Her smiles were dangerously seductive. There were no two ways about it, he wanted her, badly.

He swore beneath his breath, then impatiently turned off the spray before stepping over the rim of the bathtub. This room was like the rest of the place, done in shades of beige and brown. It was a place to sleep. The place where he hid his anguish from the world.

Dexter paused long enough to brush his teeth and empty his bladder before he settled his long, lean body in the center of the king-size bed. No reason to even consider taking either side. No reason at all. It had been more years than he cared to count since he'd shared a bed with a woman, held her through the night.

Over time a man could grow use to just about anything, even empty arms and a pulsating erection. Why had he done it? He groaned impatiently, knowing a hard penis was just what he deserved. He should not have gone near Anthia, at least not until he knew for certain that he had himself under control.

It had been so much easier to be near her while Jeff had been recovering. Dexter had often gone by her place before coming home. They were friends. Friends were allowed to do for each other, see each other, share the good and the bad.

Now that Jeff was away at college Dexter had no reasons to stop by her place. He had racked his brain for weeks before he came up with a valid reason to see her. That reason could not be remotely personal.

He was like a man on the edge. He better not look down. He couldn't harness his natural male attraction or hunger for Anthia. But he would allow nothing, not even his sexual desires to interfere with their friendship. That friendship was far too important to him . . . necessary to his well-being. Quite frankly, he needed her. Yet, Anthia was the one person, he didn't want to know how susceptible he was to her. Or how vulnerable he was to her soft, petite frame or how much in need he was of her generosity or how badly he craved her feminine heat. Even though he knew he would never make love to her, his male instinct warned him that she alone would fit him like a hot, wet glove . . . perfection.

Dexter swore harshly, furious with his lusty thoughts. He grumbled punching his pillow. He'd never get any sleep at the rate he was going. Anthia could never be more than what she'd been these last couple of years to him: a dear friend. Lately, he had to constantly remind himself of that fact.

Rather than the peaceful sleep he craved, Dexter thrashed on the bed, twisting the sheets into tangled heap at the foot of the bed.

"Stop it! Damn it! Christine! Stop . . ." he muttered, then issued a painfully shouted, *"No!!!"* as the gun shot roared. He was so shaken that he instantly awakened.

Dexter was drenched in sweat, his breathing fast and uneven. He switched on the bedside light, running his hand over his damp, close-cut natural. His long bronze feet hit the floor as he fought the encumbrancing tendons of the dream. His legs were unsteady as he slowly made his way into the bathroom. He splashed cold water over his tear-streaked face and sweaty chest in a meager attempt to clear his head.

No amount of water could ease the pain of the past nor could it change the harshness of his reality. His wife, Christine, was gone as was their baby she carried inside of her. She had died, killed by his gun and according to the judge who sentenced him and by his hand. There had been no way to prove his innocence. No way because he didn't even know the truth himself.

All he knew was that he felt responsible . . . he felt guilty. And he had served five years of a ten-year sentence on a manslaughter charge. Dexter was still shivering by the time he returned to the bedroom. The pain, the grief eating at him never went away. During the long hours of the night, he remembered . . . relived the shooting over and over.

It was only during the day he could put it aside. He lost himself in the work that had become his reason for living. He had worked hard to control his thoughts, not to look back. He had years to think about it. Years to do nothing but remember. He had been locked away like an animal . . . a wounded beaten-down animal. Yet, somehow he had survived.

That night had changed the course of his life. He was no longer an expectant father, a husband, a man. He had lost everything that night . . . everything that held any meaning for him. Nothing he'd done since could make up for that disastrous ending.

He had no memory of pulling that trigger . . . only of trying to stop a suicide that was happening right in front of him. Yet, as her life's blood surrounded them, as it poured from the fatal wound, he could do nothing but hold her and cry . . . cry for them all.

THREE

The telephone rang as she worked the soft clay. Anthia's skilled fingers were bringing to life the small child's high-sculptured dimpled cheeks. The photo of Dorthea Turner's grandbaby was propped on the small easel.

Sighing, Anthia carefully covered the model with a damp cloth before she hurried to answer the telephone. Using a clean cloth, she wiped her hands before she reached for the receiver. "Hello?"

"Hey, darlin'."

"Jeff! How are you, sweetie?"

"Fine. Just fine. Are you busy?"

"Never to busy for you, son. I was just working on a doll for Mrs. Turner.

"From church?"

"That's the one. She's been heartbroken since her daughter and son-in-law moved across the country. Her husband wanted to surprise her with the doll for her birthday."

"He paying?"

"Yes. Why do you ask?"

"Ma! You're too kindhearted. Even though, you spend countless hours on your work, for a friend you would give the doll away.

"That's not quite true," she hedged, "But, I admit to doing this one for cost. Mrs. Turner took such good care of Ma-dear when she was so sick. I didn't have to worry about her during the day. She fixed her breakfast and lunch every day without fail." Anthia brushed a tear away.

"Yes, I remember. You're not working too hard are you?"

"I'm fine. How are your classes going?"

"Exhausting."

"You're not overdoing, are you?"

Jeff laughed. "Not in the way you mean. Next week are midterms. My head can't hold anymore."

"How's your back? Your legs?"

"I'm okay, Ma. Stop worrying. I'm not overdoing."

"Good. Don't worry, you'll do well on all your exams. Oh, Dex stopped by."

"Oh! First time I've heard his name in awhile. What's he been up to?"

"Busy at the center. He had a message for you. He wants you to stop by the center and speak to the guys the next time you're in town. When will you be home, son?"

"Next weekend. But I'm not making any promises. You didn't tell him I would do it, did you?"

Anthia thought she heard real fear in his voice. "No, of course not. Although, I must admit I'd hoped you would agree. It will be good for both you and the boys at the center. Think about it, baby, before you say no."

"Ma . . ."

"I just said think about it."

Jeff sighed loudly. Anthia knew what he'd been through. She knew how long and difficult the road back to good health had been for him. He'd made a mistake in going with his so-called friend Eddie, even after she had warned him to stay away from Eddie.

"Okay," he finally agreed.

"Made any new friends?" she asked carefully.

"Don't start!"

Anthia sighed heavily. Her normally outgoing son was developing into a recluse. Other than his college roommate, Sean, he had made no friends at college. Anthia suspected he was self-conscious, embarrassed by the lingering effect of his injury.

Anthia didn't like the change. She worried because he hadn't dated since his accident. What kind of life was that for a young man? She wanted him to be whole again, emotionally as well as physically.

"How are you getting home? Is Sean giving you a lift?"

"Yes, it's been weeks since you've mentioned Dexter's name. I didn't know you two were still seeing each other."

She swallowed with difficulty. "We've always been friends if that's what you mean."

"He likes you, Ma. Got to go. See you late on Friday. Don't wait up, we probably won't get in until late. Love you."

"Love you, too. Good luck with those midterms. 'Bye, baby."

Anthia wasn't aware of the frown on her face as she replaced the telephone. Jeff had come so far in such a short time. She was so proud of him. He not only carried a full class load but was able to live independently. She didn't want him to lack for anything, including friends. Anthia sighed. She was probably overreacting again. She'd done a lot of that since his accident.

She tried to catch herself before she went off the deep end. Being both mother and father was not easy. That was one of the reasons she was so grateful to Dexter. He lent his ear whenever she needed to talk about her son. Helped her to realize when she was overdoing. Lately, they hadn't done as much talking as they used to.

Wearily, she got to her feet and began straightening her workroom before she turned off the light and moved toward her bedroom. More often than not Anthia worked in the evenings. Work filled the lonely hours so when she finally was ready for bed she could sleep.

As she relaxed in a tub of the warm, scented water, Anthia remembered what Jeff had said to her about Dexter. Sure he liked her. They were friends, Jeff knew that. It was true that he had often stopped by during the evenings throughout Jeff's long recovery to check on his progress. That had ended when Jeff left for college. Well, that was not quite true. He had helped her find the house and settle in. To her disappointment his visits had never been romantic, except for that single kiss they shared on moving day.

With Jeff away, Dexter felt he no longer had a reason to stop by. Anthia tried very hard not to notice just how empty her evenings had been without his visits. A lone tear slipped down her cheek. Impatiently, she brushed it away. Enough of this. She had no reason to feel sorry for herself . . . sorry because of what could not be.

Seeing him after such a long time had been wonderful. She sighed, recalling how good he looked. He was just as dark, muscular and lean-hipped as she remembered. No, there had been a difference. He looked tired, somewhat drawn as if he were not taking proper care of himself. Unfortunately for her, his dark eyes were just as intense as always and his full lips were just as tempting. She would not recall how it felt to be in his arms, with her body pressed against his hard male length. What purpose would it serve, other than to remind her of what she could not have?

It was not until her bedroom was plunged into darkness that she allowed herself to focus on how badly she wanted to see Dexter again. She'd missed him. Perhaps she could stop by the community center one evening, bring him some of her home-made pound cake and tell him Jeff's answer? He would have no reason to suspect how badly she wanted his company. None at all.

Dexter was on the telephone when Anthia walked into his office. The second and third line were flashing as he handled one call right after the next. His mind was not on what he was doing. His gaze focused on the petite beauty with the shapely legs. He watched as she removed her wet black raincoat and hung it on the hook near the door. His interested gaze moved over her cream-colored, long-sleeve blouse and knee-length slim black skirt. Her thick curls had been pinned up in a French roll, small sterling button earrings sparkled in her ears, drawing his eye to her slender neck and throat. Her hose and shoes were also black.

"Hi, it is really pouring out there," she said with a smile.

"Hi," he responded. Dexter recovered enough to answer, "Yes, we will be open until eleven," into the telephone. For a moment he'd forgotten everything outside of this beautiful woman. She was all sweet curves and very female, more than enough for any man to want to handle or die from the pleasure of trying.

He swallowed, following her movements over to the steel-frame padded chair in front of his desk. As soon as he ended one call, the free line flashed signaling another one. He wasn't getting a thing done. It had been like that since he'd done the television interview with Emery King on the Channel 4 evening news.

Covering the mouthpiece, he said, "I'm sorry. It's just plain crazy around here." It was impossible for him to even have a simple conversation.

Anthia shook her head in amazement, but rather than settle back to wait until he was free, she went around to the desk across from his and began taking calls with the efficiency of the professional legal secretary she had once been.

"What classes do we have on Tuesday nights?" When she paused, to look over at Dexter, he was grinning as he handed her the schedule. "Thanks," she mouthed, unaware of the way he studied her red-tinted lips.

It was quite some time before things settled down. He leaned back in his chair, beaming at her. "Thanks, I appreciate the help."

"No problem. I used to manage an office, you know. Some things come back as easily as riding a bike. Is it always so hectic around here?"

"Lately, yes. That interview on Channel 4 did the trick. But it also generated some much needed income."

"How do you get anything done?"

He shrugged, "I don't. I've been trying to make sense of this new computer system. I have considered throwing it out the back door, but the company that donated the new system might object." Running his hand over his close cut natural, he hissed, "Gees, just when I get used to the old word processor."

Anthia laughed. "Play with it. I'll handle the telephones while you get used to it."

He'd like to play all right, but with her sweet mouth on his.

What he said was, "You didn't come around to answer our phones."

"It will keep," Anthia smiled, warmed by the sparkle in his dark eyes. How had she stayed away from him for so long? He was so utterly male and attractive. He, no doubt, had his pick of any number of women. Was that why he never looked her way? Obviously, he didn't find her attractive.

There could be no other reason why he never even considered offering her more than his friendship. He had to be seeing someone else. Who? He certainly kept her well hidden from his friends.

What choice did she have but to accept that he wasn't attracted to her? So why, then, had he kissed her? Even after all this time, she could not forget the sheer pleasure he had given her. His mouth had been hot and hungry, his tongue like rough velvet against hers. She had felt his arousal against her. He had wanted her. He had! Yet, the kiss had ended so abruptly, leaving her weak with longing. That kiss had to mean something.

"Are you sure?" Dexter said, breaking into her thoughts.

"No problem." she said, reaching to answer the telephone.

There was not an opportunity for a private word with him. Anthia did her best not to stare at him, especially when he was absorbed in studying the computer manual. With so many interruptions, she was amazed that he got anything done. By eleven, she felt as if the telephone had been surgically glued to her ear.

"Closing time," he grinned down at her, taking the telephone out of her hand, then saying into the receiver, "Sorry, we close at eleven. Please call back tomorrow between eleven A.M. to eleven P.M. Good night." Hanging up the telephone, he asked "Hungry?"

She laughed, "I could manage a bite. What do you have in mind?" She stretched stiff shoulders and neck muscles before collecting her things. "Oh! I almost forgot." Searching through her tote bag, she handed over a foil-wrapped package. "Pound cake."

"Oh, sugar. Thanks, I can't wait," he grinned. "There is a

little diner around the corner where I usually have a meal before I head home."

"Are you still eating dinner in the middle of the night?"

"Yeah. Come on. Keep me company."

Anthia blinked a warning to herself not to see anything in the invitation. It was all right to come here and spend time with him. It was not all right to lose touch with reality. "Okay. I want to talk to you about Jeff."

"Great. I sure appreciate you helping out tonight. Give me a second to make the rounds, make sure the doors and windows are locked and the building is empty. Then we can get out of here."

Anthia could have told him she was willing to wait for as long as it took if it would guarantee spending time with him. She genuinely enjoyed his company. It was amazing how quickly she had gotten used to being around him.

Often, he had brought a take-out meal with him when he would visit after he finished at the center. He was so easy to be around . . . too easy. He had never seemed too tired to listen nor had he been too caught up in his own problems to bother with hers. He had such a generous spirit.

Somehow, sometime during those long, painful months of uncertainty, she had done the unthinkable . . . she had fallen deeply in love with the man. He had touched her heart as no man had ever done, not even her son's father.

"All set?" he asked, holding out her coat for her to slip into.

"Yes," she said, "Thanks. Looks like the rain has finally stopped. At least my rosebushes should he happy."

"Mmm," he said absently. His eyes scanning the area beyond the door before he stepped out and locked up.

Dexter escorted her to her car in the side parking lot, making sure she was inside with the doors locked before he jogged to his own car at the rear of the lot. He drove slowly, careful to keep her car in his rearview mirror.

He caught sight of himself in the mirror and laughed as he realized he was grinning like a fool. He couldn't seem to help himself. He was so pleased that she had agreed to join him.

Anthia was like a ray of sunlight, taking away the gloom inside his lonely heart.

"Pretty night," he mumbled, as he opened her door and held his hand out to help her out.

"Yes," she shivered in the crisp night air. "We've been lucky to have such a mild winter. Don't you have a young woman answering the telephone and filing in the office?"

"Uh-huh. Tina Douglas. She works until six. It's the only time lately I have been able to get out of the office," he went on to say, "She's young, just finished her GED. I've been trying to talk her into taking some classes at Wayne County Community College."

"No luck?" she asked as he held the door open.

"Not much. All she wants is to work for the center. The kid's got her whole future ahead of her." Cupping her elbow, he ushered her toward the rear booth.

"Hey Dex. Got company tonight. Need a menu?" The late night waitress asked.

He smiled. "Hey, Jan. Meet Anthia."

The two smiled at each other as she handed Anthia the well-worn menu.

"What's on special?" Dexter didn't so much as glance at the menu.

"It's Wednesday. Beefsteak, mashed potatoes, peas and carrots," she rattled off clearly bored.

To Anthia he said, "They have great chili fries."

"No, thanks. I want to sleep tonight, not walk the floor with indigestion. I'll have a hot turkey sandwich and lemonade if you have it."

"Got it. Dex?"

"I'll have the special. And coffee."

"Sure thing."

Once they were alone, Anthia asked, "How can you eat so late and then drink coffee at night and sleep?"

He controlled his natural inclination to scowl. He rarely slept an entire night without nightmares. A couple of dreamless hours and he would consider himself lucky. It wasn't the food or the coffee keeping him up. He shrugged in answer, "Cast-iron stomach, I guess."

Anthia lifted a brow but she didn't comment. "So what's the problem with Tina?"

"What do you mean?"

"I saw your expression when you mentioned her name."

"Nothing really. It bothers me that she has no ambition . . . no hopes for the future. She is too content with her job at the center." He shrugged, "With our budget who knows how much longer we can afford the roof over our heads. We've been blessed lately with two new computers for the computer lab, and money for a security guard. There are so many other things that we need or want to do for the kids."

"How old is she?"

"Who?"

"Tina."

"Oh, she's a kid, barely twenty."

"If anyone can get her to change her mind about college, it's you." She didn't have to be told how he took his work to heart. He was determined to change lives for the better. When it came to the center, 'no' was not in his vocabulary.

"Thanks," he smiled genuinely thrilled by her compliment. "Let's not talk about the budget. It will never stretch to include hiring someone in the evening. Whenever I have to teach my martial arts classes, I will have to leave the office unattended."

Dexter was doing his best to distract himself, not take notice of how luscious and soft her full lips were . . . pure temptation. Did she always have to look and smell so good? She had no idea of the sexual hell she put him through whenever she was near. Yet, he was like a sex-starved kid, eager to spend whatever chance he could with her.

His heart had nearly stopped beating when she walked through the door tonight, then sped up like a pounding drum, his pulse went wild while his sex pulsed as if he needed to be reminded how very long it had been since he had been inside a woman's body.

"So volunteers are welcome," she hedged.

He looked up then, his dark eyes collided with hers. "Have

anyone I know in mind?" His eyes twinkling with humor, a rare occurrence indeed for him. Most often they were sober while he remained extremely self-contained.

Anthia couldn't help giggling. "Yeah, me." Yet her heart soared with anticipation at the mere thought of seeing him almost daily.

"How? You have no free time. You have a business to run, lady."

"Not so busy that I can't make time for a friend. Besides, it would be my way of thanking you for all you've done for me throughout Jeff's recovery," she said softly as she reached for his hand, squeezing as it rested beside his glass of water.

Dexter felt a jolt of awareness race up and down his back as he briefly clasped her small fingers. His voice was rough, hoarse with emotion when he said, "There's no need. I cared about Jeff. I still do. Anthia, you have limits. What if you get a large order?"

"It's a waste of time trying to stop me. This is something I want to do. Let me help you." Her pretty black eyes pleaded for his acceptance.

Dexter, if asked, would be the first to admit that he was not made of stone. "Okay. Just until I can find another volunteer in the evening." He was relieved when his food was placed in front of him. Talk about desperate for a diversion. "I'm hungry. How about you?"

"Well, I don't often eat at midnight."

"Sure you do. You've done it many times with me, remember?"

Anthia laughed, "So I have. Looks good."

Dexter nodded as he picked up his fork. "So, how's Jeff? You said you spoke to him?"

Anthia nodded, having just taken a mouthful of her sandwich.

"Did you ask him?"

She nodded again, then shook her finger at him. He knew she wasn't going to answer until she'd finished chewing and swallowing. He was deliberately picking at her. "You are terrible," she scolded. "Jeff's coming along fine, but not as quickly as he would like. He resents having to use his wheelchair to get around campus and his crutches for that matter. We've been over this time and time again, but I can't get him to see reason."

Suddenly Anthia's eyes became sad. For like her son, she wanted him to walk unaided. She didn't have to tell Dexter that. They all wanted that for him. "Don't get me wrong. I'm thankful he can walk at all. The how is really not an issue," she ended softly.

"Absolutely. It's good to have him back on his own two feet, even if it isn't for long periods of time." He ached to hold her close, ease her worries. Instead, he changed the subject, "Mmm, this is good. Care for some?'

Anthia knew how much he enjoyed sharing his food with her. Rather than indulge him, she shook her head no. It was enough to be with him. And she wanted to share more than the intimacy of a fork with him. She wanted what any woman wanted from that one special man. She wanted his hot, wet kisses. She yearned to be in his arms and to experience the full force of his masculine lovemaking.

There was no doubt in her mind that he was a generous lover. He was too unselfish in his personal life to be anything less. Anthia blinked in dismay, recognizing how far astray her thoughts were taking her. If she was not careful, she would find herself fantasizing about what she longed for him to do to her with him right in front of her.

Forcing her erotic thoughts away, she settled on a much safer subject. "What bothers me the most is that my son hasn't made any friends at school."

"None? That's not like him," he hid his disappointment that she had not let him feed her. Something that should have been innocent had suddenly become arousing. He wanted her mouth. He wanted to once again sample the velvety softness of her tongue against his.

"My point exactly. His only friend is his roommate, Sean."

"Has he said why?"

"No. Dex, I'm worried about him. This isn't like him. He has changed so much since the shooting. He doesn't laugh or joke anymore. Sometimes, I don't recognize my own son anymore."

Dexter longed to ease her concern. He settled for taking her small, brown hand into his. Hadn't he indulged himself enough for one evening?

As she took a deep, consoling breath, he couldn't seem to force his gaze above her breasts. He could make out the outline of her large nipples against the smoothness of her blouse. Her breasts were small but so lush . . . enticing. He unwittingly wet his lips, determined not to let his imagination take wings. In another moment, he could visualize himself giving each peak a thorough laving with his tongue. He wouldn't stop until she reached a hot sweet climax. Had she ever come that way? He was as hard as a steel rod from the thought and had to force his hungry eyes away if he hoped to gain control of his need.

What was his problem? Lately, all he could think about was her feminine allure. He almost laughed aloud. Lately, was stretching the truth a bit far. From the instant he laid eyes on her at that charity dinner-dance he had wanted her. Only then she had eyes for the newly married Charles Randol. Thank heaven's her interest hadn't lasted long. Anthia and Charles and his wife, Diane were all good friends now.

Friendship . . . it was all he allowed himself to have with Anthia, no matter how desperately he desired her. Not that he thought she might be interested in more from him because he certainly had been given no clear indication of it. He reminded himself that friendship had to be enough.

His voice was so thick with desire that he was forced to clear his throat before he could say, "Jeff has a good head on his shoulders. He's had to make a lot of adjustments for one so young. Give him time. This is only his first year away from home. Everything is an adjustment."

"Dex, he's not dating."

Dexter could have added 'neither am I,' instead he said, "Jeff will when he's ready. I repeat, give him time." Dexter knew all too well the anguish of being alone. It was something he experienced day in and day out. Deciding to change the subject, he asked, "Did you have a chance to ask him about coming to the center and talking to the younger guys about his experience?"

"Yes. That's how I realized how completely he's cut himself

off from others." She was embarrassed, but she told him the truth. "He didn't refuse, but he didn't agree either. Jeff didn't take the time to even consider it."

Dexter's thick brows almost came together as he scowled. "I see."

"I'm sorry."

"Honey, it's not your fault." He decided to contact the boys Jeff used to hang out with at the center before the shooting.

"He tends to isolate himself even when he's home, Dex." Her eyes were clearly troubled.

"We're not about to give up on him. This may be a natural part of his adjustment to being disabled. I'll talk to a few of his old friends see what I can find out."

"Thanks." Anthia was grateful for Dexter's continued interest in her son and his problems.

"Are you finished?" he asked, watching the way she pushed her sandwich around her plate.

"Guess my eyes were bigger than my stomach."

He chuckled. "I haven't heard that expression in years."

He could see the worry she was trying to conceal. He yearned to chase the shadows away. Yet, he was keenly aware that he was not her black champion. He had no reason to think she was in need of his shoulder to lean on. After all, he had no right to her sweet smiles or her hot, sugary kisses. What did he have to offer her? Nothing, not even his battered heart. Love, devotion or commitment were no longer a part of his world. All that was behind him now. No matter how badly he wished things were different, he could not change his past.

So instead of reaching for her, he removed his wallet. "It's late. I'd better get you home. Tomorrow, after all is another workday."

Anthia nodded not understanding his sudden withdrawal. What had she done? Had she said something that had touched a nerve? Had she gotten too personal? It was always like that with Dexter. It seemed as if when they were just getting close, something would happen and he would quietly withdraw.

Why must he always keep her at a distance? Maybe, it wasn't him but her? Was she just too needy? Too eager for male attention? She evidently left him cold. They shared a friendship, nothing more. It was long past time she accepted that fact, no matter how much it hurt.

It was true that Dexter was a virile, self-contained man. Perhaps, it was time she concentrated on appreciating his friendship rather than wasting her time wishing for more.

"Put that away," he said when she pulled her wallet out of her purse.

"You're not expected to feed me, Dex. We aren't on a date."

He shrugged, knowing that she had no idea how deeply he longed to be in just that position. He wanted to do more than pay for her meal. What he wanted was the exclusive right to take her home with him. Instead, he muttered, "My treat," before he stood to help her with her coat.

Anthia hoped he didn't notice her shiver at the brush of his fingertips against the nape of her neck.

"Ready?" At her nod, he ushered her down the narrow aisle between the booths. He paused at the cash register where he paid their bill then urged her forward. He didn't speak again until they were outside.

"Anthia, stop worrying about Jeff. The kid is going to be fine. Who knows, he could decide to talk at the center."

Anthia considered that highly unlikely. "Jeff can be stubborn."

"I'll follow you home," he said while holding her car door open.

"That's not necessary," she insisted sliding behind the wheel and locking her seat belt in place.

"Humor me."

Anthia recognized the stubborn angle of his jaw. "Good night and thanks for the meal." She kept her hands firmly on the steering wheel while fighting the urge to touch him.

He smiled then hurried to his own car. He didn't trust her to wait for him. She was too independent, too much for her own good. Dexter followed a car-length behind until she slowed to turn into her driveway. He waited even after she closed the automatic garage door, waited until her lights went on and she waved to him from her front window.

Reluctantly, he put the car into gear and drove away. Depression seemed to settle on his broad shoulders, weighing him down. He should not have been surprised at his swift mood change. He had not wanted to say good night. He felt very much alone as the car sped through the night. Their evening had been more than pleasant. The idea of her working at the center suddenly did not seem like such a marvelous idea.

How in the hell was he going to manage to see her several times during the week without wanting her? How was he going to keep his damn hands to himself? He was not made of steel. He was a man, for heaven's sake. He wasn't a monk.

Yet, it had been a long, long dry spell for him. He had not been near a woman sexually since he realized how deeply he hungered to be inside a woman that he could care about. The trouble was he cared for Anthia . . . cared far more than he had cared for anyone in a good long time.

FOUR

"Jack Donaldson!" Dexter exclaimed rising from his desk with his hand outstretched.

There was nothing striking about the medium height, brown-eyed man except his carrot-red hair. But he was remarkable. He had believed in Dexter when Dexter had lost faith in himself. Those were dark, dreary days when Dexter was first released from prison and had been assigned to Donaldson's heavy case load. Donaldson was not an ordinary parole officer, he took a keen interest in his clients.

"How ya doing?" Donaldson grinned, his deep Texas drawl unmistakable.

"Great. Come in. Have a seat," Dexter beamed, indicating the chair in front of his desk. "What are you doing in this part of the world?"

"I took a few days off to visit with family. Thought I'd stop in. It has been a while."

Dexter's glance strayed to the young black woman who was clearly more interested in his conversation than what she was suppose to be doing, which was filing and answering the telephone.

"Uh, Tina. Will you please excuse us for a few moments? Why don't you have a late lunch at the diner on me?" Dexter reached into his pocket and pulled out a five-dollar bill.

Tina Douglas, with her thick, curly, short black hair and shapely figure was not used to men ignoring her pale brown beauty, which was the case with Dexter Washington. Her curiosity was evident but she accepted the money without hesitation. Her lingering glance caressed Dexter's bronze male features before she went out and nearly closed the door behind her. Yet, instead of continuing on she pressed her ear to the door. Dexter Washington may not agree, but everything he did was her business.

"How are the letters about the sports clinic going?" Dexter leaned over Anthia's shoulder to view the computer screen. He absently caressed her nape with his fingertips.

"No, problem. I'm halfway there," she said trying not to tremble from the brief contact. She was acutely aware of him every time he stepped into the small office. "It's a great idea inviting well-known athletes to take part. It's bound to influence the fellows." Her dark eyes were momentarily locked with his.

Neither was aware of the intense gaze on them. Tina looked on in disgust. She didn't like this new arrangement. Since Anthia had been working at the center Dexter extended too much attention her way. He seemed to be fascinated with her.

Dexter was the first to look away when he said, "I'll be in the gym if you need me."

"Karate?"

"Yeah," he nodded. He had adopted an interest in the martial arts while in prison, finding the discipline and exercises calming.

Anthia went back to what she was doing. The upcoming sports clinic was too important not to give it her full attention.

"Is there anything I can do to help?" Tina interjected a bit too eagerly.

"Answering the telephone is enough." Dexter said, but his eyes lingered on Anthia before he left the office.

Occupied, Anthia didn't look up from the computer screen when Tina hurried after him. Following him down the central hallway, Tina had to call his name in order to get him to stop.

"Yes?"

"I'd like to speak to you," she said somewhat breathlessly.

"Something wrong?"

"I can volunteer in the evenings if you need help. You don't have to impose on Ms. Jenkins."

He smiled, "Thanks Tina. But that isn't necessary. We're not trying to take advantage of anyone." She was one of the few paid employees who worked regularly at the center. He wouldn't dream of asking her to volunteer during her off hours in the evenings, unless it were a real emergency. "What we need is another volunteer trained to do office work to take up the slack."

"She's here every evening." Tina pouted.

"No, three times a week." Dexter could see it bothered Tina, what he couldn't figure out was why. "Is there a problem that I'm not aware of?"

Tina shook her head, before she said, "It's just that we never seem to have time to talk anymore."

Dexter stared at her in confusion. "What is it? Is it your mother? Is she still on you to get your own place?"

Tina beamed, it was the first personal inquiry that he had made in some time. "Some things never change.

"Tina, why don't you go back to school. I'll be glad to help you in any way I can, either by finding you a job on campus or setting you up for a loan or scholarship money. You have the brain power to go to college and work toward a degree."

Tina blushed thoroughly pleased by his encouragement. "I'll think about it. But like I've told you before I'm not sure what I want to do."

"If not college, there are also vocational schools. Focus Hope has some really great programs. You do have options. Tina, you shouldn't spend all your time here at the center. You have your future to think about."

This was not exactly going the way she would have preferred. "Ms. Jenkins volunteers and you're not encouraging her to leave."

"Anthia also runs her own business."

"You like her, don't you?"

Dexter shifted restlessly from one foot to the other. "Anthia is an old friend. I've got to go, but I really think you should start thinking about your own career goals."

Tina wanted to throw something as she stared after him.

Whether he was willing to talk about it or not, he was more than a friend to Anthia Jenkins. Tina didn't like it! She wasn't sure what she could do about it, but she was not about to hand him over to another woman.

"Mom! Will you quit! I can't eat another one." Jeff Jenkins referred to the three pancakes she intended to place on his plate.

Anthia laughed, giving him a kiss on his lean cheek. "You are so skinny. Don't they feed you at that college?"

Jeff grinned around a mouthful of food. It was good to be home. He'd come in so late last night that he tried not to wake her. She met him at his bedroom door with a hug and kiss then hurried him off to bed.

His roommate Sean had dumped his stuff in his bedroom before taking off last night. Sean like Jeff was from Detroit area, but unlike Jeff had his own car and came from a well-to-do family.

"I can't believe you guys didn't wait for daylight. It's such a long drive."

Jeff shrugged. "I tried not to wake you. But I'm not exactly the quiet type lately, got to much hardware."

He shared the same even features and amber skin tone as his mother. Jeff's hair was cut close to his scalp. He preferred the baggy look like most teenagers. He was six feet, while his upper body was strong and muscular his long legs since the accident were painfully lean.

Anthia saw his frown as he glared at his wheelchair propped against the wall in the back hallway. Jeff detested all the equipment that labeled him different from others.

"Anything could have happened between here and Augusta."

"We only have the weekend, Ma. It wasn't a problem.'

Anthia sighed. Both young men were very responsible. Since Jeff didn't have his own car and couldn't drive yet. He was lucky that his roommate and friend lived in the metropolitan area.

"How were your exams? Passing everything?"

He nodded, "Midterms. You better believe, I'm doing better

than passing. No problems, nothing to worry about." He grinned, taking a healthy swallow of orange juice. "You're not eating." He couldn't help noticing how much weight she had lost since his accident, weight she could ill-afford to lose on her petite frame.

Anthia glanced down at her own plate. "Not too hungry. Had a late dinner with Dex."

Jeff couldn't hold back his grin. "Are you two dating?"

"Stop meddling. We're still friends. He has been so swamped from telephone calls to learning a new computer system. I felt sorry for him. I've been helping out a couple of days during the week at the center. I don't know how he managed to teach his martial arts classes and work with the guys when he is stuck in the office."

"Something is up. Before the other day, you hadn't mentioned him in quite some time. Suddenly the last two times we've talked, his name is in the conversation."

"It had been a while since I'd seen him. Moving day in fact," she said taking a sip from her steaming coffee cup.

"That long. Why?"

She shook her head. She had no explanation. It had hurt knowing that Dexter felt he had no reason to come by since Jeff was away.

"Ma what gives? I thought you and Dex might have gotten something going by now. No, don't look at me that way. I know you care about him." He was watching closely. "I also know you're not seeing anyone else. Well, if you are, you sure are keeping it a secret from me."

"No secrets," she whispered.

"Then what gives with you and Dex?"

"I've already told you that we're friends . . . nothing more, nothing less. Why are you all up in my business, son?"

He chuckled, then took her small hand in his and squeezed. "I love you. You've been doing it all. You could use a nice guy like Dexter. You don't want to be alone forever. What if I decide to settle in Atlanta after graduation?"

Anthia didn't want to think about him not coming back home. Yet, more than anything she wanted him to be independent. She smiled reassuringly at him. "Wherever you move, you just remember to keep the sofabed ready for my visits, kiddo."

He laughed, then sobered. She had always been there for him. She had suffered along with him through his recovery. She deserved some happiness. "We're talking about you. Don't you want a man in your life?"

"Of course I do. But that doesn't mean Dexter Washington is the man for me. I'm fine just the way I am. In fact, I'm doing better than fine. You haven't asked about the business."

"You told me over the telephone, remember?"

"Yeah. I forgot. I've enjoyed volunteering in the office at the center. There is so much going on."

He nodded. "They can always use extra help. Dex will look out for you."

"I can look out for myself. I took care of you in the old neighborhood, didn't I," she said sticking out her chin.

Jeff roared with laughter. "No doubt about it. I know it was especially hard for you after Granny passed. Ma, I still have a lot of good memories about the old building. Granny taking me to the park. Hangin' with the fellows. It wasn't all bad."

"No, it wasn't. We had some good neighbors: Mrs. Rice, the Jones family. I stopped by to visit with Mrs. Rice last week when I dropped off some fabric at Dana's. You remember Dana Gray, don't you? Mrs. Rice's granddaughter?"

"I remember. Dana still sewing for you?" Dana was only a few years older than he was, a very attractive girl who could have any guy she wanted.

"Yes, I couldn't keep up with all the orders without her help. I can concentrate on the designing, sculpting and making the bodies."

"Your business is really taking off. I always knew you could make a go of it. But Ma, I don't want you going over there alone especially after dark. With me down at Paine who would know if something happened to you? It's not safe."

"I know my way around, kiddo. Besides I usually go over in the mornings. Dana is the best seamstress around. Her work is flawless. And she's even designing now. I'd be crazy not to use her." She speculated, "She should be in New York designing clothes for the runways. She would be if she hadn't gotten caught up with Eddie's brother, Jerome."

Eddie Walker brought back painful memories. Neither of them wanted to recall how close Jeff had come to losing his life because of Eddie.

"Is she still hooked up with him?"

"Yeah. With two sets of twins, she has no time for much of anything let alone design classes."

"Honey, it's not a problem for me to drop off or pick up her work." Anthia didn't mention that she had bought Dana a new sewing machine with all the modern conveniences. It was something they both benefitted from. Nor did she mention her run in with Jerome.

"Well, you be careful."

"Yes, son," she feigned a meekness that had them both laughing. After filling both their coffee cups, she asked, "What are your plans for the day?"

"Chillin', nothing constructive outside of computer games and laundry. Don't worry, I won't get in your way."

"I can't believe you dragged your dirty clothes through three states, kid."

He chuckled good-naturedly.

"And you have never, ever been in my way." She suggested as casually as she could managed, "Why don't you call some of your old friends? Go to the mall, catch a movie. I have a couple of extra bucks I can donate to the cause."

"Naw, but I can always use the cash."

"Why not? It will do you good to get out and see your friends."

He's mouth tightened when he insisted, "I don't have any friends."

"Honey, don't say that."

"Why not? It's the truth. Who can blame them? No one wants to hang around a cripple. I can't go any where without my crutches or the chair."

"Jeffrey Jenkins! Stop that right now. If Luis Bennett and Bob Howard cared about you before the accident then they care about you now. You are doing so much better. Have you forgotten there was a time when we thought you might never walk again? You've come a long way."

"I know, Ma. It's not that I'm not grateful."

"If you took your chair you could outdistance them."

"No!" he snapped. His eyes shooting sparks of impatience. "And it was not an accident. That store owner meant to shoot me. He thought I was robbing him, Ma."

"Don't raise your voice to me, young man." Her tone booked no arguments, when what she longed to do was hold him close like she used to do when he was a little boy, make all his hurts go away. Even if he was all grown up, he would always be her baby.

"Sorry." He jutted his jaw stubbornly when he tried to explain, "Things are not the same. I'm not the same kid who got into that car with Eddie. Nothing is the same. It's time we both accepted it." He got clumsily to his feet using his strong arms and hands to boost himself, reaching for the crutches propped against the kitchen wall.

"Don't Jeff. Let's talk this out."

"There is nothing more to say. I'm not a little kid anymore. In a few years I will be out of school and on my own. I don't need friends."

"Honey, you're wrong. Everyone needs friends . . . everyone." When he didn't speak, she sighed heavily, "Does this have anything to do with why you won't talk to the guys at the center?"

"We've already talked about this. I have my reasons."

"You can do some good there, son. Eddie got caught up with a gang and his life went downhill after that. He ended up using drugs and doing crimes to solve his money problems. Where did it get him but a guest room in a prison."

"You don't have to tell me about Eddie. I was there, remember? I know how drugs and guns can destroy a life. His brother, Jerome, is not doing much better for himself."

"Another lost soul. The kids at the center don't understand the consequences of that lifestyle. It's too attractive for them. There are still a whole lot of boys without fathers or male figures to give them direction. They can so easily be caught up in that trap of self-destruction. It happens every single day."

"If I thought I could make a difference then I'd go, but I know better. Nothing changes in the 'hood," he ended dryly.

"How can you say that?"

He shrugged, slowly moving toward the door. "Excuse me. I'll be in my room if you need me."

Anthia swallowed her frustration, instead she said, "Okay, son." She knew when she had hit a brick wall.

Unfortunately, that set the tone for the weekend. When she saw him off on Sunday, she hadn't been able to change his mind about talking to the guys at the center.

FIVE

To Dexter's exasperation on Monday, he didn't have a private moment with Anthia all evening. They'd been constantly interrupted. In addition to that, he'd been in and out of the center's office.

It was a relief when she joined him for coffee and dinner after they closed. Finally, he was able to ask, "How was the weekend? Did you and Jeff have a chance to talk?" He flinched, his voice was rougher than he would have liked, a clear indication of his need.

Anthia was staring down at the menu. Her voice was so soft he had to lean forward in order to hear her. "It was good to have Jeff home. I really miss him when he's away." Looking at him, she said, "I'm sorry. I tried, but he wasn't in a sharing mood. I don't know what's really bothering him."

"You okay?" he asked, taking note of the slump of her slim shoulders and the weariness in her pretty eyes.

"I was disappointed, Dex."

"What do you mean?"

"We had a nice visit, but he wouldn't tell me what is going on inside of him."

"Perhaps it's just tiredness? He does have a full class load on top of having physical therapy. That's a lot of pressure for a freshman."

He yearned to reach out and take her small hand into his own. He settled for a quick pat. He didn't dare linger. He was

too vulnerable, too needy when it came to this one special
woman.

"We've always been so close. Now suddenly, he's shutting
me out. I don't like it."

"He's growing up, Anthia. That's a part of being a man, learning to be in control of your feelings."

"That's part of being stupid," she shot back. "Men don't share
their feelings. They keep them locked inside."

Dexter blinked, "You can't mean that."

"I do. That's what's wrong with the entire male population.
You men don't share."

"Wow. Hold on. We're talking about Jeff, not me. What happened? Did you talk about the center?"

When Anthia looked at him, her eyes were troubled. He found
himself wondering what she could be thinking. He had to remind himself that this was not about him. It was about her son.

"Anthia?"

"Yes," she said wearily. He was right, this was not about him.
It was never about him. How could it be when he never allowed
her to get too close. He was a master at distancing himself from
others.

"Anthia?"

"I couldn't get him to change his mind. He isn't going to
speak at the center." She paused before she went on to say, "I
don't understand it. Jeff has never been a selfish person. This
is so unlike him. In fact, I couldn't get him to really even discuss
the issue. He also refused to contact any of his old friends while
he was home."

"Here we are. Soup and salad for the lady and a hot roast
beef sandwich and potatoes for the gentleman," their waitress
said, placing their plates in front of them. "Anything else?"

"No. Thanks, Jan."

While Dexter ate, he watched Anthia, concerned by her con-
tinued silence. Finally he asked, "There is more, isn't there."
Putting down his fork, he persisted, "Don't tell me 'nothing.'
It's all over your face."

Surprised, she hastily added, "I'm fine. Just a little tired. I
haven't been sleeping well. I wake up in the middle of the night
and can't get back to sleep."

"How long has this been going on?"

"Few weeks."

"Call me."

"Why?"

When his eyebrows shot up, she quickly added, "What I mean is, why would I want to disturb you?"

"You won't be disturbing me, Anthia. I rarely sleep through the entire night." He didn't add that the nightmares came so regularly that he hardly ever enjoyed hours of uninterrupted sleep.

"Dex . . ." Whatever she had been about to say, she didn't finish.

"Next time call me. By the time we get off the telephone you'll be exhausted."

"You're such a good friend. How did I get so lucky to have found you? Do you ever think about yourself? You just keep on giving and never seem to ask for anything in return."

Dexter stopped eating, nearly choking on the food in his mouth. He swallowed quickly before reaching for his water glass. She couldn't be more wrong. He definitely had needs. And they were all uniquely male and centered around his desire for her.

He only had to look at her pretty succulent mouth or her perky breasts and his sex hardened readying him to fill her tight sheath. He had no idea how he knew she would be tight and hot, but he was sure she would fit him like a wet silk-lined glove. She had been made for him, even though, he didn't have a remote chance of earning her love. Anthia was special. She deserved the best that life had to offer, much better than a man with no real future.

"Dex?"

"Stop," he said, gruffly unable to meet her gaze. "You're exaggerating."

"I'm not. Dex, how can I forget that you were there for me when I needed you the most?"

He interrupted, "We're friends. Let's leave it at that."

"If you ever need me, you only have to ask."

His large body quivered from the heat of his need as his

imagination took flight. The mental picture of the two of them locked in a lovers' embrace formed in his head. He dropped his hands to his lap to hide their trembling. Thank goodness his engorged shaft was concealed by the table. He wanted her badly.

Determined to redirect his thoughts, he said, "Thanks but you've already proven that by volunteering at the center." As far as he was concerned the subject was closed. "Finished?"

He was reaching for his wallet before she could answer. He had to put some space between them before he did or said something really stupid. He couldn't trust his self-control. All he could think about was the taste and feel of her. He had to get out in the air, revive what was left of his control. Anthia was off-limits. It was past time he remembered that.

It wasn't until they were outside on the sidewalk that he felt safe enough to touch her. He took her hand into his, then said, "Try not to worry about Jeff. He's been through so much in the past few years. He's bound to come around, soon."

"I wish I could be as certain as you are."

"If you want me to talk to him, just say the word." He genuinely liked Jeff and it was not because he was Anthia's son.

"Thanks. I'll keep that in mind. I suppose I keep hoping the old Jeff will come back."

"I'd be glad to try and help," he offered sincerely.

Anthia surprised him when she slid her arms around his waist and gave him a warm squeeze and kissed his lean brown cheek. "Thanks, Dex. Good night.'

As he followed her home, Dexter could not stop wondering if she would call tonight. Just the thought of a long late-night dialogue eased the emptiness that seemed to wait for him. Even if he were lucky enough to be asleep when she called or rather if she called, he'd gladly sacrifice more sleep in order to enjoy the pleasure of listening to her soft feminine voice in the night. There was a feminine huskiness in her voice that he found incredibly sexy. Everything about her appealed to him in some way.

Dex found himself breaking into a sweat, his body throbbed from the intensity of his need. It was like a nagging toothache. What exactly was his problem? He had nearly lost it in the

restaurant. All he could seem to focus on was Anthia. Her sweetness seemed to be chipping away at his self-control.

He swore heatedly. He had to put a stop to this nonsense. Was the strain of celibacy wearing on his nerves?

Yet, he had never been one to embrace casual sex. Even as a young man it had never held any particular appeal to him. There was no true fulfillment in it for him, only a shallow, empty kind of release. Afterward, he felt more alone than before. After five years in prison, he vowed never again to do without life's most basic pleasure. Yet, he quickly learned that unless his emotions were engaged, there was no genuine satisfaction for him.

Time nor distance could not erase how it felt to be in love and be loved in returned. There was nothing like it on the face of the earth. Unfortunately, there was no place for love in his shattered life . . . no room at all.

What he could not comprehend, as he absently watched her flick on her inside lights signaling all was well, was what was going on deep inside of him since Anthia entered his life. He cared so deeply for her. He could not stop it or even control it. It was just there. He was left with no choice other than to deal with it.

At least he had the good sense to stop fighting it. What else could he have done? His sexual awareness of her continued to escalate, no matter what he did to curb it. He was at the point where he had no choice but to accept it. He valued what they had too much to do anything to jeopardize their friendship. For as badly as he wanted her, he knew he would not be good for her. He had too many demons in his closet.

Anthia watched until his taillights faded into the darkness before she moved from the window. She fought back tears. What could it hurt? What would it help? Tears couldn't change the hopelessness of the situation she had gotten herself into. It was time she accepted the truth of her actions.

When she decided to volunteer at the community center, it was partly to help the center, but mainly because she wanted

to see Dexter. What she hadn't planned on was that exposure hurting. And that was exactly what she was experiencing. It was a big mistake. She had not thought beyond being able to spend time with him. It hurt! It hurt so badly. The problem was it was much too late to back out of the decision. Dexter was counting on her. What a mess.

"You can't make him want you," she whispered to herself. She acknowledged that he did value her as a friend, as she made her way to her office in order to check the answering machine. She stopped suddenly. Nothing that couldn't wait, she decided changing direction to her bedroom at the rear of the house. There were no easy solution to her dilemma. She couldn't help caring so deeply for him, but she could help making a fool of herself over him because of it.

Would it matter to him if he knew how she felt about him? Could that make a difference? Just as quickly as the idea entered her head, she rejected it. There was no way she could tell him that she was in love with him. Just the thought of it was terrifying.

Seeing him every day, being around him on a regular basis was just not working the way she had hoped. She had been volunteering at the center for such a short time but she was the one affected by his nearness. What if she slipped and did something really stupid like ask why he couldn't love her back?

By the time she showered, prepared for bed and brewed a cup of tea, Anthia was much calmer. She had been going off the deep end for a moment there. She would be fine. Suddenly, she remembered how he suggested that she call him, no matter how late it was if she could not sleep. The thought of calling him made her heart pound erratically. There was something about the suggestion that was almost intimate. Yet, intimacy was the one thing they did not share.

For a few moments, she did not remember what she had said to him. She had been so rattled, she stammered out some stupid reply. Hopefully, she had not revealed too much. For a few wild moments there, she had felt her hopes rise, then reality set in. She had been afraid to believe that he was encouraging her to share her late night thoughts and fantasies with him . . . share

herself with him. For an unguarded moment she'd thought he meant he wanted her.

She caught herself, forced herself to think. Thank goodness, she had used her head. She had been dangerously close to confessing her innermost feelings for him.

Anthia swallowed, the tears lodged in her throat. Thank the Lord she had stopped herself in time. She could have ruined what they had with just such a confession. He didn't share her feelings. His knowledge of those feelings would only make him uncomfortable.

After finishing her tea, she turned off her bedside light, plunging the room into darkness. Anthia vowed that there would be no late-night calls. Dexter wasn't interested in her innermost emotions and she was unwilling to make a fool of herself by sharing them with him.

"Sorry, I'm late," was the first thing Anthia said when Diane Randol opened her front door.

"No problem," the clearly pregnant Diane laughed giving her a hug. "Come in. It's been months since I've seen you. I hope you don't mind having lunch here?"

Anthia returned the hug, careful of the long, peach-lacquered box with *One of a Kind* stamped in gold lettering on its top. "You don't have to feed me, you know."

"Of course I do. We never find time to talk face-to-face. There is always a telephone between us. I miss you. And now with your business doing so well, we hardly ever get together."

Anthia laughed. "I know. There's never enough time." She bent down to the beautiful toddler clinging to her mother's legs. "How are you, sweet Madelyn? Can I have a hug? Pleeeeease!"

The baby girl squealed with laughter and launched herself into Anthia arms where she received a hug and a kiss on her round plump brown cheeks.

"Sweet girl, you are so pretty. I love your dress. Is it new?" Anthia asked.

The baby nodded her soft, dark, fluffy curls, looking so much like her beautiful mother, her darling face wreathed in smiles.

Anthia gave her sweet-smelling plump little body another squeeze before she let her go. "She's getting so big. They grow so fast." She straightened and smiled at Diane. "I swear she looks more and more like you every time I see her."

Diane laughed, watching lovingly as Madelyn giggled at the attention. "Chucky thinks so," referring to her husband. "But I can't see it. Come on. We're in the family room."

"They are so sweet when they're this age. Too bad they have to become teenagers," Anthia teased.

Diane chuckled urging the baby along ahead of her. "What's this I hear about you volunteering at the community center? How do you find the time?"

Anthia didn't have to ask her source of information. Diane's handsome husband, Charles. How he managed to run his family-owned business, Randol Pharmaceutical and coach regularly at the community center while maintaining such a close relationship with his wife and daughter was a mystery to Anthia. Yet, she knew that after years of marriage, Diane and Charles were still very much in love with each other.

Anthia shrugged. "I'm juggling my time." She was too embarrassed to confess her motivation was Dexter Washington. The entire situation smacked of desperation.

Once they were seated on the sofa in the comfortably furnished room, Diane insisted, "How much longer are you going to make me wait?" She referred to the lacquered box resting on the coffee table.

Anthia teased, "It was my understanding this was not for you."

Diane said, "Don't be that way," shaking her finger at her friend. She had put Madelyn in the center of the floor on a soft throw surrounded by her toys.

"Charles told you I was volunteering."

"Who else? How is Jeff?"

"Good. He was home the weekend before last. I probably won't see him again until the end of the term." She didn't add that Dexter had volunteered to drive down with her at the end of the term to pick up Jeff and all his gear.

"Anthia, you sound like we're talking about years instead of a few months."

"I know. I miss my baby. Don't laugh."

"I know how you feel," she said absently patting her slightly rounded stomach. "We're hoping for a boy this time."

Anthia smiled, wondering with longing what it would be like to share the experience with the man you love. It had not been that way for her. Her teenage lover had no more been prepared to be a father than she had been to be a mother. If not for her mother, Anthia would have had to face her pregnancy and motherhood alone.

"Come on, Anthia. Let me see," Diane pleaded, eyeing the box.

"After lunch, okay? I don't think I can eat if you don't like it. I'd be so disappointed." Anthia knew she was overreacting but she could not help it when it came to her work. She loved what she did and put so much of herself into it.

"I'll like it. How can I help myself? Your dolls are wonderful." That was why she had given this very important commission to Anthia. They had both been through some difficult times.

Anthia had stood by Diane when Diane's marriage had almost dissolved because of the lies and secrets she had foolishly kept from her husband. While Diane had been there for Anthia when her son had been shot and others believed the worst of him. Now that Diane's life couldn't be better, she wanted that same kind of deep love and happiness for her friend. Anthia deserved to have her dreams come true.

"Well, since you won't let me peek then let's go in for lunch. I'm starving."

Giggling, Anthia remembered her own huge appetite when she was expecting. She reached down for the baby so Diane wouldn't have to lift her. Madelyn laughed and clapped her hands giving Anthia wet baby kisses on her cheek.

"She is such a happy baby." Anthia said nestling her neck. She loved Madelyn's sweet baby powder scent, thinking how much she would like to have a little one with Dexter's dark eyes and her own warm skin tone. Goodness! Where was her common sense? Quickly, she pushed that reckless thought away.

"Yes, she is. She is also spoiled rotten thanks to her dad. Chucky has a terrible time telling her no." Having settled the baby in her high chair between their chairs, Diane asked as casually as she could manage, "So, how long have you been volunteering at the center?"

"Charles didn't know that?" Anthia teased, lifting an eyebrow, then laughed at Diane's expression.

"No. He is sweet but he never asks the right questions."

"It's been a couple of weeks. Dexter stopped over to ask if I could arrange for Jeff to talk to the guys at the center, tell about his experiences. So when I dropped in to give him Jeff's refusal, Dex was swamped. I'm free most evenings, so I decided to lend a hand."

"Refusal?" Diane passed her the large salad bowl, thanking the manservant as he filled their glasses with iced tea and the baby's cup with milk.

"Yes," she answered in disgust. "Jeff wouldn't even consider it. I talked and talked but I couldn't convince him to change his mind. He better than anyone knows how drugs and guns can destroy someone's life."

"He'll come around. Jeff may need a little time to think it over," Diane said as she fed Madelyn.

"Thank you, "Anthia smiled accepting a thick wedge of vegetable quiche. Once they were alone she went on to say, "Jeff hasn't been to the center since the shooting."

"He's still healing. Be patient, I'm sure he'll come around." She paused before asking, "Soooo, how's Dexter?"

"Just fine," Anthia hedged.

"You two still tiptoeing around each other?"

"Charles didn't tell you that either?"

"Nope, claims he doesn't know," Diane grinned. She ate between coaxing the baby, who was more interested in playing with her food than eating it.

"Nothing has changed," Anthia couldn't keep the sadness from her voice.

"Well, don't you think it's time you did something to change it?"

Anthia didn't bother to respond. Diane knew how Anthia felt about him.

"Well?"

"There is nothing I can do short of telling him how I feel. And I am not about to do that. I don't want him to know how hard up I am."

"Chucky and I were friends for years until he got fed up with the situation. How much more proof do you need, girlfriend?"

"There is one major difference."

When Anthia didn't elaborate but concentrated on her salad, Diane prompted impatiently, "What?"

"You two were in love with each other."

"And you don't love, Dexter? Please! I know better than that."

"Dex doesn't love me."

"Sure he does. He's just too stubborn to realize it."

"When did you become such an expert on Dexter Washington? You know as well as I do that he's a loner."

"What he is, is lonely. He has to be with no one special lady in his life. He didn't seem happy the last time we had him over for dinner."

"When was that?"

"A few months ago while Donald Williams was in town." She referred to the Chicago Bulls superstar whose program with the black boys in New York and Chicago had proven to be highly successful. Both Charles and Dexter had been impressed with his year-round sports camp and were working on implementing it.

"Just how could you tell he was lonely?"

"The sadness was in his eyes."

Anthia had also seen that sadness which seemed to be a part of him. Yet, he never really discussed his personal life. "Diane, we have no way of knowing if he's involved with someone. Just because he doesn't talk any about one special lady, does not mean he's not in a relationship."

"Please! That man is alone in the world. He's also very fond of you."

"I don't want fond!" she snapped before she could stop herself. What she wanted was what Diane had with Charles. She longed for what every woman yearns to have with that one special man. A man capable of returning her love.

"I understand honey," Diane said, squeezing her hand. "Sometimes a woman has to be the one who takes the risk." Diane remembered how desperate she had been when she had followed Charles on a vacation cruise determined to win his love. "Tell Dex how you feel."

SIX

"No!" Anthia nearly shouted, putting down her fork. Suddenly, she wasn't hungry anymore. Just the thought of telling Dexter had her stomach queasy. "Isn't it bad enough that I'm volunteering at the community center because I'm desperate to see him? Must I also bare my soul? Give me some credit, Diane. I do have some pride."

"Anthia, pride doesn't hold you at night. You two can't go on like this."

"Why not?"

"Because you both are so miserable. I'm talking about a man who fully admits to caring about you," Diane encouraged gently. "Since you can't tell him, let me. His knowing may make all the difference in the world."

Clearly horrified, Anthia said, "Absolutely not!" Her hands were trembling so badly she had to clasp them in her lap.

"I want you to be happy." Diane, too, had a fatherless childhood. She knew firsthand about fighting her way out of poverty and despair, she also knew the joy and beauty of having a strong black man's deep love.

Anthia knew that Diane meant well, but she had no idea what she was asking. Dexter was not Charles and she could never be Diane. It was like comparing apples to oranges. Besides, she couldn't handle the disappointment of being in love with a man who could not return her love. It was too painful. She believed telling him how she felt to ease her mind would destroy the very friendship that they had both worked to maintain.

"I won't have anything, if I lose his friendship. Diane, I would risk losing everything. I don't think I can do that."

Diane nodded. "I understand. But I have this feeling it is going work out the way you want."

"I don't know. You may be right, but I need to think it over." Anthia changed the subject before she broke down and cried by asking, "What time is your mother coming by? You haven't told her have you?"

Diane beamed, shaking her head. "No way. I'm so proud of myself. You have no idea how hard it has been trying to keep my mouth shut."

Anthia chuckled, "So, did you tell her?"

"Not even a hint. She's going to stop by after she finishes at the bookstore. She should be here by two. Did I tell you she has gotten a promotion?" There was pride in her voice when she said, "She's the manager."

"Diane, that's wonderful."

Diane stared down at her plate. Her stomach was suddenly knotted with nerves. "I hope she likes it." Diane's relationship with her mother had always been strained. Only within the last couple of years had they been able to put the past behind them.

Anthia knew how Diane practically raised herself and had been on her own since she was a teenager. Anthia's relationship with her own mother had always been loving. She was thrilled that Diane's estrangement with her mother was behind them. This doll was a major gesture of love on Diane's part. She too, was hopeful that Diane's mother would recognize the love behind the gift.

"Ready to take a peek inside the box?"

Lingering over lunch was not even a consideration. Diane requested the apple cobbler and coffee be served in the family room. Madelyn fussed until Diane laid her down for a nap in the portable crib in the corner of the room.

When Anthia carefully placed the tissued-lined box on Diane's lap, she, too, was anxious. She was holding her breath with her heart racing just as she imagined Diane's was doing. What if she didn't like it? Anthia longed for her work to be loved and cherished. She put so much of her own heart into each doll she made. That was one reason why she preferred making one-of-a-kind dolls, for each one was so special, so unique.

Diane's hands were trembling where they rested on the lid. Just then the doorbell sounded. She smiled carefully placing the box on the sofa. "Excuse me. It's probably Mother."

Anthia nodded, unable to sit as she waited for them. She went over to admire the baby while she napped with her thumb in her sweet round mouth. As Anthia bent to gently stroke her soft cheek she imagined a little girl with her own features and Dexter's rich bronze coloring. A baby . . . her and Dexter's baby. She gasped in dismay realizing where her thoughts returned once more. There were no two ways about it, she longed to carry his child.

"Mother, you remember Anthia Jenkins, don't you?"

Anthia turned at the sound of her name. The two lovely women stood side by side. Their family resemblance was unmistakable. It was clear where Diane had gotten her toffee-tone flawless beauty.

"Yes, of course. Last summer at the family barbecue. How are you, Anthia?" Lillie Rivers said offering her hand.

"I'm well. It's good to see you again."

Although Lillie's face reflected the ravishment of a hard life, her eyes sparkled with pure joy as she gazed lovingly at her grand baby. "Oh, you've already put her down for her nap. I was hoping she would be awake."

Diane beamed. "She's exhausted, but you won't wake her by giving her a kiss. If you stay for dinner, you can have some time with her later."

Lillie didn't need any encouragement, she gave her granddaughter a tender kiss as she lovingly smoothed her blanket.

"Come on, Mother, sit down. Anthia has a surprise for us."

Anthia laughed, "Not from me. You commissioned it."

"What is it?" Lillie's eyes sparkled as she looked from her daughter to Anthia. "I love surprises."

"I hope you like it," Diane whispered, so much had changed between them. It had taken time, but they had finally put the past behind them. This special gift was truly a token of love meant to heal.

Lillie kissed Diane's cheek. "You are so sweet. I really don't need anything. Just being a part of your life has been enough to make me so happy. I love you."

"I love you, too."

"Sit down both of you." Anthia cradled the box in her arms. Once they were seated, she carefully placed the box on Lillie's lap.

"Open it, Mama," Diane urged.

Lillie smiled, before she carefully lifted the lid. As she brushed aside the tissue paper she gasped and tears filling her eyes.

"I hope those are happy tears?" Diane asked.

"Oh yes! It looks just like Madelyn at her christening. What a wonderful keepsake."

Diane slowly lifted the doll out of the box. The face was a perfect replica of her precious baby girl. "Oh, Anthia. It's beautiful," Diane cried. The dress was as elaborate and finely made as the original satin and lace christening gown. Carefully, she laid the doll in her mother's arms. "Mama? Are you all right?"

Tears of joy raced down her cheeks. "Oh, baby," Lillie whispered, hugging Diane. "You did this for me. It's wonderful."

"I'm so glad you like it," Diane said unable to go on. They smiled at each other in complete understanding.

Anthia felt as if she was intruding on a very private moment. When she rose and retrieved her purse and jacket, Diane stopped her.

"Anthia don't rush off. My mother and I are being sappy. Oh, I just love the doll. Madelyn will love it once she gets older."

Anthia was thrilled. She never tired of hearing how much her dolls were appreciated. "I'm so pleased you both like it."

"You are so talented. I've never seen anything so lovely, outside of my grandbaby," Lillie offered.

Anthia beamed with pleasure. "Diane is such a good friend. It was an honor to do this for both of you." She shook her head. "I really have to go."

"So soon. Stay for coffee."

"Yes, I must. Thanks for lunch." Anthia gave Diane a hug. "It was so good seeing you again, Mrs. Rivers. Take care."

"Excuse me, Mama. I'm just going to walk Anthia to the door."

"You don't have to," Anthia said after waving to the older woman and following Diane into the elegant foyer.

"Sure I do." Diane gave her another hug. "I want you to think about what we talked about."

"Okay," Anthia agreed. "Love you."

"Love you, too," Diane waved.

Anthia was wiping away her tears as she slid into her car parked in the wide circular drive.

She was so happy for them both. The doll would be cherished and loved for years to come. Anthia was thrilled that Diane's difficulties with her mother were finally behind her. She not only had the love of her life in Charles, but there was no longer anything from the past to cloud the future.

As Anthia drove home, she thought back to those few moments when she had watched the sleeping baby. Was it just a wayward thought? Or did she seriously want another child . . . Dexter's child? Not once in all the years since she had Jeff had she considered having another child. Now suddenly she was daydreaming about having Dexter's baby. The thought of it had her tingling with all sorts of emotions and fears.

"Hey lady! Watch it!" A driver yelled out his window as Anthia entered his lane. She was trembling by the time she guided the car over to the side of the road and stopped.

"Goodness . . . what is wrong with me?" she mumbled aloud. She could not seem to keep her mind on anything these days except Dexter.

He consumed her thoughts. She sat there on the side of the road concentrating on nothing but breathing as she fought to gain control of herself. She could not go on like this. Emotionally, she was falling apart because of that man. A man who didn't want her body or her heart. It was all so pointless.

What if she took Diane's advice? What if she told him how she felt about him? What then? Nothing! If he wanted her in the sensuous way men have wanted women for centuries, then surely he would have said or done something by now. They'd been friends for years! No! No! No! She was not about to make an absolutely fool of herself.

She'd been too ashamed to tell Diane the unvarnished truth. Even early on, Anthia was certain that Charles had been attracted to Diane, while Dexter had simply never been attracted to her. It was painful but real. She had no choice but to accept it.

Dexter was a grown man who knew his way around women. He wasn't an untried boy. It would be downright silly to believe anything else. There was nothing shy about Dexter Washington. He was a man in every sense of the word.

Telling him how she felt would only jeopardize what they had. It would be different if she didn't treasure their closeness. How could she even entertain the idea of risking their friendship? It had sustained her at the most difficult time in her life.

"Enough!" she scolded herself. Slowly restarting the car, Anthia paid careful attention to her driving. Once she reached home, she headed straight for the kitchen to brew a pot of coffee. She had no business feeling so isolated or alone.

She had a full and happy life. Her son was in college and getting stronger physically every day. She had close friends that she could depend and count on. Her business was growing so fast that it was all she could do to keep up with the demands. Financially, she was more secure now than ever before. She had no reason to feel like this.

If she really wanted to spend time with a man, there were several she could date. Doug Henderson was always trying to get her to go out with him. Her answers had been no for some time now because she knew he wanted more than a date from her: He wanted her sexually. If that was what she needed so badly, then why did she always turn down his overtures? But Anthia didn't want sex.

What she wanted was the emotional and physical intimacy with the man who owned her heart. The man who held her love in his large, generous, capable hands was Dexter Washington. Only, he was not interested in her that way.

Dexter was not Charles and it was time she did what she needed to do to keep herself grounded. As much as she loved and respected Diane, Anthia believed she was wrong about Dexter's feelings for her. There were no options open to her where he was concerned other than accept what she could not change. She had to start focusing on what they had and stop wishing and hoping for more.

"Deal with it, girl. Just deal with it," she murmured aloud.

"Hey! You're Jeff? Jeff Jenkins from Detroit?" The tall, slender young woman called as she raced from the education building. "I'm Cynthia Montgomery. Quinn Montgomery's daughter."

"Hi. Yeah, I'm Jeff. Your dad handled my case." Jeff had been extremely lucky that Charles Randol had arranged for Quinn Montgomery, one of the top criminal attorneys in the country to take his case. Quinn had managed to get him off armed robbery charges. He had also handled Jeff's civil case against the store owner. Due to his injuries, Jeff had received a hefty settlement that had cleared up the medical bills not covered by insurance and more than covered his college expenses.

"Daddy suggested I look you up. Heather, my stepmother and Diane Randol are good friends with your mother."

"Huh, you got railroaded into this." Conscious of the girl's good looks and friendly smile, he was forced to look up at her from his wheelchair. She was tall, but he was taller, at least he was when he was on his feet.

He had seen Cynthia around. She was a sophomore, popular and seemed to have her pick of the upperclassmen and frat brothers on campus. Why did she even bother to talk to a handicaped freshman?

"It wasn't a problem. Look do you have a few minutes?"

"Sorry, I'm on my way over to the library."

"Okay. I'll walk with you, if you don't mind. It's always good to see someone from home," Cynthia smiled easily.

"You don't have to go out of your way. Tell your folks hello for me," he said with a wave before he sped away. Jeff was aware of her confused gaze. She was pretty but she was no more interested in him than he was in her. She had done her good deed for the day and as far as he was concerned that was the end of it.

He knew he might seem abrupt but he couldn't help it. He didn't need her pity. A man, even a cripple one like him, didn't want a woman feeling sorry for him. He was better off without friends. He could not afford the heartache.

Evidently, his mother had talked to Mrs. Randol, who had no doubt spoken to Mrs. Montgomery. Women! Why couldn't his mother leave well enough alone? He was a grown man. He scowled in mute frustration. Didn't he have enough problems already?

That bullet in his back had taught him a valuable lesson. There were very few people he could trust in this world. He had seen the looks of pity many of the women on campus had sent his way. They might consider being his friend but none of them were willing to date him. That was fine with him because he wasn't looking for a lady. He was here to get an education . . . period. Most of the women on campus were after the able-bodied fellows with a car and money. No. He was not here to play their little games. He had learned to keep his distance, that way he would never be hurt.

"Malcolm X Community Center," Dexter said absently into the telephone. He'd been stealthily watching Anthia for some time now. She'd been especially quiet this evening. No. This had been going on for some time. She'd been markedly self-absorbed. Oh, she had gone through the motions of appearing normal but something was bothering her. What was it? Why didn't she trust him with her problem? Why had she suddenly felt the need for secrecy? What was it that she couldn't share with him? They were friends, damn it.

"Dexter. This is Donald Williams. How's it going?"

"Hey, Donald. Everything is going well." Dexter laughed. "We've contacted everyone. Hey man, we really appreciate the players you've gotten to take part in our sports clinic. It will be the biggest one around with both football and basketball players taking part. The question is are you going to be able to come?"

"Absolutely. I'm looking forward to it. Just don't change the date on me. I seem to be spending more time than even I imagined in your city." He laughed, "My lady is from Detroit. I think you might know her, Taylor Hendricks."

"Scott Hendricks' sister?"

"The same."

"You're a lucky man. Taylor's special. Not many single women are willing to take on the responsibility of raising a teenage brother. Congratulations."

"Thanks. And you don't have to tell me she's special."

Dexter smiled. "Thanks for agreeing to come. The fellows will be here in droves when they learn you're going to take part. Stop by next time your in the city. 'Bye."

He was grinning so when he put down the telephone that Anthia couldn't help asking, "What?"

"Donald Williams has agreed to take part in our clinic. He is the best in the NBA. We're going to go over the top with this one."

"That's great."

One of the boys chose that moment to stick his head inside the office. "Mr. Washington, come quick. There's trouble."

Dexter didn't hesitate. He was right behind the youngster. Anthia shot out of her chair and hurried after them. They went through the facility, passed the classrooms, locker room and pool area to the gym where a group of boys were congregated.

"What's going on?" Dexter asked pushing his way into the center of the crowd.

Charles Randol, who had been coaching the basketball game was right in the thick of things. At six-four he was no lightweight, more important he knew how to handle himself. His sarcasm wasn't lost on Dexter when he said, "These gentlemen have come for their boys."

There were five of them sporting their gang's colors on their leather jackets and bandannas, something which was not permitted inside the community center. Gangs and their turf problems were to remain outside the center. All the boys knew the rules.

Dexter and Charles stood side by side, presenting a united front. Both men seemed perfectly at ease.

Although the center tried to target younger boys before they faced gang recruitment, nonetheless they were not always successful. Sometimes, it felt as if they were engaged in an uphill battle. Even when they failed, they didn't turn any boys away, even when they were part of a gang. The idea was to show them a better way. They did not give up on any child easily. If black men didn't have time to save their own, who would?

SEVEN

"This is not the place for this kind of discussion," Dexter said evenly. "Anybody who doesn't want to be here is free to leave. You fellows are welcome to stay, only without the colors."

"We're leavin', man. Ain't got nothin' here we want. Carl, Todd you comin'?" A short, stocky boy spoke up, eyeing two of the younger boys they had apparently come to take with them.

"When you're ready to make a change stop back. We'll talk," Dexter said.

The stocky leader swore heatedly, "Stay the hell out of our business, man!"

No one said anything. Dexter ignored him, knowing that the choice was an individual one. Each boy had to decide his own path. Of course, the fact that they were at the center was a huge bonus as far as Dexter was concerned. As valuable as these boys were, the violence and crime was something they couldn't afford to let inside the community center, not if they wanted to survive.

"You heard the man," one of center regulars said. The other boys from the center crowded around the men. They were willing to stand with Dexter and Charles.

"You haven't heard the end of this," the leader swore hotly.

Dexter followed as they headed back down the central hall toward the front door, without the two boys they came to take with them.

"You okay?" Charles asked Anthia softly.

"I'm fine," she lied.

"Not to worry. Dex knows how to handle himself. We've been down this road before."

Anthia tried her best to hide her fears. "Thanks. You don't have to baby-sit me. The boys are waiting for you." She didn't move an inch until Dexter returned and she saw for herself that he was all right.

No, she wasn't all right. She wasn't even close. Seeing Dexter face those gang members had terrified her. She hurried back into the center's business office before her legs gave way. She'd been trembling so badly, she was not sure she would make it without collapsing. She couldn't bear if anything had happened to him. It took some time for her nerves to settle down enough for her to concentrate on the work in front of her.

When Dexter walked into the office, she nearly jumped out of her skin, her nerves were still so frazzled. She felt his dark, brooding gaze.

"What?" she finally said, unable to bear his pointed stare.

"Why'd you follow me?"

"I didn't know if you needed some help," she blushed, knowing it was ludicrous. After all, he was the one with the black belt not her. What could she have done? It didn't matter. All she knew was that she had to be there in case he needed her.

His dark eyes widen incredulously. "Were you planning to fight them off?" He slowly studied her petite, curvy frame, then lifted a thick brow doubtfully.

She jutted her chin stubbornly, before she answered, "Maybe."

He swallowed down the laugh bubbling in his throat while his chest swelled with joy. She cared about him. That realization seemed to touch his very soul. If only he could believe in that caring, hold on tight to it. Never let the wonder of it disappear like so many beautiful things disappeared. Dexter sighed wearily.

As badly as he wanted to touch her, he could not reach out to her. He had absolutely nothing to give a wonderful woman like Anthia. She deserved the best that life could offer.

"Why didn't you ask those two boys they were after to leave?

Wouldn't it be simpler in the long run? There is no way of knowing what could have happened? By letting them remain, aren't you putting the others and yourself in danger? What if those gang members take out their anger on you or Charles? They could have had guns. They are dangerous, Dex."

He took her hand and squeezed. "Calm down," he soothed, quietly stroking her hand as he went on to explain, "We can't ever forget our reason for being here. This center serves the community . . . all of it. We can't welcome some parts of it and overlook the others. The boys come here for a stable, safe haven and for the emotional support we can provide. We don't focus on what they have done in the past, but what good they can do in the future. The two boys those gang members were after have as much right to be here as the gang members themselves."

If she hadn't already known how strongly he felt about what they were doing here, it was written on his dark, handsome face. It was in the depths of his dark, intense eyes. He held the center and its goals close to his heart.

Anthia knew she was reacting on pure emotion, but she couldn't stop herself. She had been so scared for him. He was what mattered to her. Her voice was brimming with her feelings, when she whispered, "Those gang members are out to make trouble, either for you personally or the center."

"Perhaps, but if and when they are ready to come and join us, they will be welcome."

"But . . ." was all she had gotten out when the telephone rang. They both realized it was time to go back to work. Resigned, Anthia lifted the receiver saying, "Malcolm X Community Center . . ."

It was after the center was closed while they were walking to their cars that Anthia invited Dexter to her place for a late-night dinner.

His heart jumped, then he said, "It's late. Why should you want to go to so much trouble?"

She smiled, saying, "No trouble. Everything is done and waiting to be heated and put on the table."

"But why? It's not necessary." Dexter, who was looking around the area and not at her, was wondering how he could

get out of it gracefully. He couldn't very well say no because
he did not trust himself to be alone with her. His hands were
balled at his side, his whole body taut with tension.

Anthia needed to talk, wanted to be alone with him without
being constantly interrupted. Besides, the frightening incident
with the gang members had convinced her that Diane was right.
She had to do something about their situation. Her feelings for
him went too deep and she couldn't hide them any longer. They
could not go on this way.

Her voice was full of frustration when she snapped, "Suit
yourself." She got into her car, locked her door, started the
engine, and backed out of the parking space, all without giving
him a backward glance.

On the drive home she refused to look out of her rearview
mirror to speculate on him. "Damn that stubborn mule!" She
tried as hard as she could to concentrate on her driving. She
knew without looking that he was following her. He followed
her home every night that she worked at the center. It was nothing new.

When she turned into her drive and slowed to enter the garage, she refused to even glance his way. After flicking the automatic garage door closed, she hurried toward the side door.

Dexter managed to duck under the door before it closed.
"Hey, I thought I was invited to dinner," he said as she stepped
over the threshold.

She let out a soft breath, moving inside so that he could enter
behind her. "Welcome," she said trying to hide her annoyance.
Why couldn't he just say yes in the first place? He made everything remotely personal so blasted hard. He was always
pushing her away. Did he even realize what he was doing? Or
was that the idea?

"Thanks," he said softly.

He was so close that she could feel his warm breath against
her nape. She forced herself to move through her dark studio
into the living room where she had left a lamp on.

"Anthia . . ."

"Make yourself at home," she said, gesturing toward the wide
comfortable sofa. "Excuse me," she murmured, then hurried

down the hallway to her bedroom in the rear of the house. She dropped her purse, along with the jacket of the magenta pantsuit she had teamed with a cream silk blouse into the armchair before she went into the connecting bath and closed the door.

Anthia leaned on the counter because she was shaking so badly she could hardly stand. She was still stinging from his earlier refusal. She bathed her face with cool water gradually letting it warm. She was calmer when she patted her face dry and reapplied a light foundation and deep pink lip tone. She placed a fragrant rich drop of Cinnabar behind each ear.

Looking into the mirror, she reminded herself that he was here in her home. But it hurt knowing he didn't want to come. He clearly did not want to be alone with her. Why? They needed to talk. Why couldn't he see that?

It wasn't that she thought she could make him care about her. Life didn't work that way and no one had to tell her that. But what if their talk only made things worse? What then?

"Anthia?" Dexter knocked on her open bedroom door. "You okay?"

"Yes," she lied. "I'll be out in a minute. There's ice tea in the refrigerator. Help yourself." She had made it especially for him knowing he had a fondness for her mint-flavored tea.

"Okay." Dexter was reluctant to move away. He suddenly recognized that his hands were shaking. He didn't know what to do to make things better between them. He had hurt her feelings which was the last thing he wanted to do. Damn it! He could not risk losing control.

As his glance lingered on her bed covered with a cream quilted satin comforter and matching quilted pillow shams, he visualized Anthia in the center of it with her beautiful petite curves bare to his hungry gaze. His reaction was immediate, his sex hardened, ready to make her his. He swore beneath his breath.

Swiftly, he walked out, his hands balled at his sides. He should get his jacket and leave now. The knowledge that it would upset her more, kept him cooling his heels in the living room. He flexed his broad shoulders covered in a denim shirt, wiping his moist palms down his snug-fitting jean. He didn't bother to adjust the pulsating fullness crammed inside his jeans. What was the point? He hurt and there was only one way to ease that potent need. It was impossible. He could not have her! There was no way he could bury himself deep inside her wet, femininity and give her the hard loving he craved. No way!

He ground his teeth together, his heart heavy with grief. He couldn't stay. But how could he make her understand that his being here was tearing him apart? Their friendship meant everything to him. Yet, he'd been semi-aroused from the instant she had invited him home with her. It hadn't taken much and now he was erect and pulsating with need. Yet, he was damned if he stayed and damned if he left. There was no easy choice for him.

Dexter was trying to compose himself as he pretended to study the family photographs on the mantel when Anthia returned.

"No tea?"

"Later." He had no idea of the longing in his dark eyes as his hungry gaze studied her from the way her thick ebony curls clouded on her slender shoulders, almost hiding the oval faceted pink Rhodolite stones set in white gold in her ears, to her creamy amber toned skin to pause on her soft, pretty breasts. He inhaled sharply as he took note of the way her nipples beaded against the silk of her bodice. He swallowed with difficulty as he imagined himself slowly tonguing a dark peak before taking it deep into his mouth and sucking until she cried out from the exquisite pressure . . . only then would he even consider moving on to the other nipple to repeat the hot caress. He nearly swore aloud. His penis throbbed painful from the earthiness of his thoughts.

"Why don't you put on a CD?" she suggested, then moved into the kitchen, unaware of his dark eyes following the seductive sway of her round sculpted bottom. He was so long in answering that she glanced back at him. "Dex?"

"Good idea," he said around the constriction in his throat.

After Anthia placed seasoned rice and green peppers stuffed with crabmeat into the microwave to warm, she began putting together a green salad. She had prepared a deep-dish apple pie topped with caramel and nuts for dessert.

"Can I help?" he asked as he came to stand behind where she worked at the counter. He inhaled, filling his lungs with her womanly scent. His hands remained safely in his back pockets.

"Yes, you can get the tea and pour it into the glasses on the dining room table, unless you prefer wine?" The table, like the food, had been prepared ahead of time. It was set with her ivory fine bone china and sparkling crystal.

"Smells good," he said, grateful to have something to occupy his hands. Dexter worked alongside of Anthia carrying everything into the dining room. In no time at all, they were seated and sharing a delicious meal.

"This is so much better than the diner. You're a good cook, Anthia."

"Thank you. With Jeff away, I miss not having anyone besides myself to cook for."

"It's your choice entirely," he said quietly, sipping from his glass.

"Life isn't always so cut-and-dry."

"If you're not dating, it's because you chose not to," he said sincerely. "You're either too busy with your business or just not interested."

Anthia played with the pie on her dessert plate. "You say that as if I have men coming out of the woodwork to date me."

"It's the truth. You're a very beautiful woman. But you don't need me to tell you what's reflected in your mirror."

"I'm just not your type, right?"

Her bluntness shocked him. He'd been on his second slice of pie, suddenly he put down his fork. Eventually, he said gruffly, "I never said that."

"You don't have to, my dear friend. We both know your preferences. You favor my friendship over my lovemaking. Is that because you are involved with someone else?" she asked, praying her uneasiness didn't show. "Or is it that you just don't find me attractive?"

"Hold on!! Where are all these questions coming from?" Until then he had been able to relax and enjoy the meal, marveling over her many talents. Now he found himself on the defensive.

"Just curious. We've known each other for some time now. Yet, there is so much I don't know about you." She quickly hid her unsteady hands in her lap. "The way I see it, Dex, is that if we can't talk openly to each other then we don't have much of a friendship."

"All this because I didn't want to impose on you tonight?" he frowned, "Come on, Anthia. My sex life is not an issue between the two of us."

Anthia surprised herself when she said quite frankly, "I would have agreed with you earlier this evening. All that has changed after those gang members came to the center." She looked into his eyes when she said, "I was so afraid for you. It made me realize how much risk you face every single day."

His forehead had wrinkled into an even deeper frown. "What does that have to do with my sex life? Anthia, I don't get the connection."

She stared down, seemingly fascinated with her plate. To her horror her eyes filled with so many tears that they splashed down her cheeks. What could she say? How could she explain what appeared to him as a sudden change of heart?

"Anthia? What is this?" He reached for her small, slender hand. "Does this have anything to do with Jeff?"

She yanked her hand away, suddenly furious. "Damn your thick skull. This has nothing to do with my son."

"Then what?" Even as he asked the question, he felt as if he had stepped off a pier, right into the deep end. He was sinking fast and he knew it.

"I'm not dating because I don't want to be with anyone other than you, Dex."

He fought an overwhelming sense of relief along with an unexplainable joy. He had no rights were she was concerned. His selfish needs held no significance. Anthia's well-being was all that mattered. She apparently wanted the one thing he could never give her . . . himself.

She wanted him, his heart raced at the thought. She wanted . . . Enough! There would be time to evaluate his own keen disappointment later when he was alone. For now he had to concentrate on not hurting her.

"You should not be telling me this. I have no place in your personal relationships."

"And I have none in yours?" She questioned while her heart beat frantically in her chest. Her fear was unexpectedly palpable. She could see it, taste it, almost smell it, was overwhelmed by it. She should stop now. Couldn't, she tell that she was embarrassing herself? Why didn't she quietly wish him a good night and end this torment?

Dexter nearly stopped breathing for he could see they were on a collision course. Once it was said, they could not take the words or exposed emotion back, no matter how badly they wanted to forget what had been said. Why was she pushing this issue? Didn't she understand that they were headed for destruction?

"Aren't you going to answer?"

Unable to continue calmly sitting as if nothing was wrong, he pushed back his chair and rose to his feet. He went over to the fireplace, then retraced his steps before he squatted down beside her chair until he could see her beautiful black eyes.

He said softly, "I don't see the need to get into all of this. Anthia, I value you and what we have. It works for me. You're the one person I can count on. I can talk to you without any hassles." He waited for her response, but when none came, he went on to say, "I care about you. I care about your son. What we have is enough for me." What he didn't ask was why it couldn't be enough for her.

Her heart was in her eyes when she whispered tightly, "It's not enough for me, Dex. I'm a woman. I need more." She also rose to her full height, hand clenched. "I want a man who can really care about me. One who can accept the woman I was, having raised my son alone, as well as the businesswoman I have become. I need more than just a friend. I need so much more." She shook her head. "What I don't understand is how you can claim our friendship is so important to you, yet at the same time you look at me as a man looks at his woman . . . the one he desires . . . the one he longs to hold and make love to during the night. Dex I know you are a private man. I also know you're not shy nor are you a monk."

"Anthia!"

"If there is someone else, then do us both a favor and say so."

"There is no one else," he grated roughly. "There hasn't been anyone in a very long time."

"Then why can't we try? It just might be what we both have been looking for."

"I told you I'm not looking for a relationship."

She made herself ask, "Are you saying you don't find me attractive?"

The silky moan of Toni Braxton on the stereo in the living room was the only sound in the room as they stared at each other. When Dexter did not say a single word she grew impatient with his silence.

"Well?"

He recalled how badly he had wanted her when he'd stood in her bedroom. Hell no! He would not tell her how he felt about her. It should not be important. The fact that he was raw with hunger for her, was not her problem. Running his hand over his close-cut natural, he insisted tightly, "This entire conversation is going nowhere fast."

"If you don't find me desirable then why did you kiss me?"

She felt as if her back were up against a wall. She had nothing more to lose, for surely she had already lost her best friend. She might as well burn all her stupid bridges because when he left this night, he would do so with her heart shattered and her pride tattered. She consoled herself with the thought that at the very least there would be no secrets between them.

"Damn it, Anthia! How can you throw that in my face? It was a mistake! One thoughtless asinine mistake!"

She shook her head, pressing her folded arms close to her body as if she needed to hold herself together. "No it wasn't. It gave me hope. It made me wonder if it were possible for my feelings to be returned. It was not a mistake!" she almost screamed at him, realizing it had been all she had during the

EIGHT

"Aren't you ever lonely? Don't you ever long to be held?" she whispered, her voice betraying her own yearnings.

"That part of my life is over. I don't see any point in looking back." Nothing could change what he had done. No matter how he said it, he could not make her understand. He cared far too much for her. He cared so much in fact that he could not bear for her to push him out of her life because of disgust and horror.

"You've been hurt," she spoke her thoughts aloud. He looked so uncomfortable, she knew she had touched a sensitive cord inside of him.

"Hasn't everyone?" he hedged.

"Perhaps. I've made mistakes, too. I have a knack for picking the wrong man." She laughed, but there was no humor in the sound. "The first wasn't even a man. He was a boy looking to get laid. After he'd succeeded, he was gone. He left me with a male child to raise without benefit of a father." She sat back down, her eyes never leaving his face. "If not for my mother's help, Jeff and I would probably be homeless by now. I'm not sure I could have handled a teenage pregnancy, school and working part-time on my own."

"You've done well for yourself, Anthia," Dexter said in all sincerity as he returned to his own chair. "You have to be proud of yourself."

"Thank you." She studied him thoughtfully, before she went on to say, "Why is that part of your life over? I don't understand.

past few months when she had not seen him at all. She clung
to that sweet memory with all her strength.

Dexter needed no reminder to recall exactly what kiss she
was referring to. There had been only one in the two years they'd
know each other. It was a kiss he remembered well. He also
recalled what had promoted that hot, hungry kiss. They'd spent
the entire day together as he helped her move. At the end of
that day, he was so needy, so tied up in emotional knots that he
couldn't stop himself from reaching out for her sweetness, her
joy, her womanliness.

The kiss had started with a tender yearning as his lips brushed
against her soft delectable mouth yet that innocent caress was
not nearly enough. He needed more, so much more and he could
not stop himself from sliding his tongue into her sweet honeyed
depths and savoring.

Oh yeah, she had tasted good, so damn good that he had
practically devoured her before he recovered his common sense
and let her go. He had no idea if she had been hanging on to
him or if he had crushed her petite frame to his aroused length.
Her sweet plump breasts would fit his hands perfectly. He
ground his teeth in frustration as he recalled just how badly he
had wanted her. His body throbbed then—and now—with an
overwhelming need to be inside of her. He had no right to kiss
her that day or ever. None!

"We both should concentrate on forgetting it ever happened,"
he ended harshly.

You've clearly been in love before. Have you ever been engaged? Married? Fathered a child?"

Dexter hung his head, his entire body straining with dread. He knew this day was bound to come, but he had, with everything within his power, wished to avoid it for as long as possible. He never wanted her to know the truth about him. More than anything, he did not want her to hate him. That he could not stand. But he would not lie to protect himself. She deserved better than that.

"Dex . . ."

"My past isn't something I enjoy talking about."

"I don't mean to pry but how can we ever be close with so much of ourselves hidden? We'll always be strangers."

"There are things I don't want you to ever know about me. So much I detest," he snapped.

"I care about you, you know that. Nothing can change that."

"Anthia, you don't understand."

"My point exactly. You never even talk about your folks. If I didn't know better I would assume you raised yourself alone."

Anthia and Dexter were both on their feet now staring each other down. Dexter was the first to move. He pounded his fist on the table causing everything to jump including Anthia.

"You won't be satisfied until you've heard the worse, will you?" he accused. "Damn it, I'm an ex-con. Do you understand now why I didn't want you to know?" His tone was brimming with fury, yet edged with despair.

She focused on the last and reached out to touch his hand where it rested on the table. "Why didn't you tell me?"

Dexter moved away, unable to bear the sweetness of her touch. He demanded harshly, "How could I? What decent woman would want to associate with a man convicted of murdering his wife and unborn child?"

Anthia collapsed into her chair, her legs had given out on her. Her lovely, dark eyes wide with disbelief.

"You wanted to know, damn it!" His tall, muscular frame was tight with tension.

She stared soundlessly at him for a time, then eventually she said, "I don't believe you. You can't push me out of your life. You're just trying to scare me!"

He walked into the kitchen and return with the cordless phone. He dropped it into her lap. "Call Charles, ask him. He knows all about my past."

She slowly shook her head as she struggled to comprehend all that he had told her. Dexter a killer? Dex? How was it possible? It didn't make sense. It went against all that she knew about him. He was not capable of such an atrocity.

She dropped her head, absently moving her hands over her arms covered in goose bumps beneath her silk blouse. He said he killed his wife and unborn child. It couldn't be true. How could it be? How could he? How?

He paced the floor returning to stare at her tightly drawn small brown features. His heart ached with grief. His life had been destroyed long ago. He wasn't free to act on his impulses. He was not free to indulge his fantasy . . . his keen male hunger. Let her think what she liked. He could never tell her the entire truth because he didn't know what really happened himself.

"Dexter, I'm not going to call Charles. I don't want to speak to anyone but you. Would you please come over here and explain all this to me?" She sounded calm while her heart pounded with dread and fear. She had to understand. She just had to.

"I just told you . . ."

"No. You didn't tell me how it happened. How could you be convicted of murder? It just doesn't make sense. You aren't that kind of person." She knew this man. She knew him too well to believe what he had told her.

Dexter was quivering all over. He couldn't believe that this beautiful woman genuinely cared about him. That she hadn't screamed or tried to get as far as possible away from him. What had he ever done to deserve this kind of compassion? This depth of trust? She was incredible, wonderful.

He longed to take her in his arms and never let her go. Only his strong will held him where he stood in the living room near the fireplace. She deserved better than him . . . better than an ex-con. She was nothing less than a treasure.

He blinked in shock when she calmly went over to the oversize sofa and sat down. Her eyes never left him as she waited for his explanation.

Dexter was slow to join her even though she patted the cushion next to her. He was busy fighting to control his emotions, fighting to contain his need for her soothing warmth.

He was so raw with despair that he had to clear his throat in order to speak. "Christine and I met while we were still in college. It was an off-campus party. We both were into the partying scene then. We married right after graduation. Things were fine in the beginning, but after a few years we seemed to want different things. I desperately wanted a family, wanted to settle down. She on the other hand loved going out, socializing, partying each and every weekend. We kept trying to have a baby. After a few years, I couldn't figure out why we weren't pregnant. As far as I knew, we were doing all the right things."

He exhaled heavily, rubbing at his furrowed brow. "It wasn't until I found her birth-control pills that I realized I was the only one who wanted a family. She had what she wanted, a great career and me, the upwardly mobile husband. I blew up. We fought day in and day out. I refused to make peace with her, to even touch her until she finally agreed to try to start a family. I was so damn sure, certain that our baby could only make us closer like we had been when we first fell in love."

Anthia nodded quietly, a picture formed in her mind. Her hands were clasped in her lap.

"It took awhile for me to accept it, but eventually I realized that I was the only one who wanted the baby Christine was carrying. She hated the entire idea of being pregnant. As the pregnancy advanced, she still wanted to party every weekend. She didn't stop drinking or start eating healthy." Dexter accurately read the horrified disbelief on Anthia's face.

"The more I tried to convince her to stop the drinking, the more she drank. As she neared her final trimester, we were facing an underdeveloped baby with all the signs of fetal alcoholism syndrome. Suddenly, it was no longer a threat but our reality. Christine was so traumatized when she finally realized what she had done that she took my gun and tried to end her life."

Anthia's lovely eyes filled with tears. "I'm so sorry."

"I worked late that night. When I walked in, I found her with the gun in her hand. I didn't think, I grabbed her and tried to get the gun away from her . . . tried to pull her finger away from the trigger. The gun went off and in that instant I lost everything . . . my wife, our child, my life." He turned his face away as his eyes filled. Even the telling after so many years was excruciatingly painful. The hurt never, ever went away.

Anthia had never heard anything so heart-wrenching, so tragic in her entire life. She hurt for him. No wonder Dexter had been able to help her through the pain of Jeff's recovery and trial. He understood despair and pain because he had lived it.

She wanted to go to him, hold him, to share some of his grief. But she didn't move. She didn't dare reach out to him for she knew he wouldn't welcome it. He was so good at isolating himself. Hadn't he kept all of this inside of him for years? He had chosen not to share it with her, despite their friendship. He only told her now because she pushed him too far. He hadn't really trusted her with his secrets.

She found comfort in saying, "Thank you for telling me."

When he was able to finally look at her, his dark eyes mirrored his grief, but also an unexpected sense of relief. He took a deep, fortifying breath. His heart was startlingly lighter.

"You're wrong, my friend. You didn't kill your family. What you did was try to save them both. How could they have convicted you of murder?"

"I was convicted of manslaughter. Ten years in the Texas state pen. The judge was justified in doing so. I deserved the time."

"How can you say that?"

"How can I not? Anthia, I have gone over this hundreds of times in my head. I should have used my head and talked her out of it. Even to this day, I can't honestly tell you that I wasn't the one who pulled the trigger. I don't know." His throat burned from anguish.

"It's over. You've done the time and you've gone on with

your life. Don't you think it's time to look toward the future? You deserve some happiness," she ended in a whisper.

"If only it were that simple. Anthia, I care for you. But, I'm sorry, I don't have a damn thing to offer you," he said, then walked away. He paused long enough to grab his jacket from the hook beside the front door before he yanked it open and walked out.

Anthia had no idea how long she stared at that closed door. It took all her strength to go over and lock it. As if on automatic pilot, she cleared away what remained of their meal, cleaned the kitchen and then got ready for bed. It was only as she lay in bed, hugging her pillow that she allowed herself the freedom of tears.

She'd given in to the helplessness and misery she'd felt since watching Dexter walk out of her life. She cried for Christine and that sweet child that died with her. Anthia cried for Dexter. A man who felt he was undeserving of the love. His heart had been crushed and his dreams broken beyond repair. But she also cried for herself. It was so sad. He had no place in his life or in his heart for a new love. Most of all, she cried because in spite of all he had said, it did not change how she felt about him.

"Ma, are you okay?" Jeff scowled into the telephone while trying to decipher what he heard in her voice from hundreds of miles away. "Something wrong?"

Anthia held in a moan. It had been a rough ten days since that disillusioning dinner with Dexter. She'd done her best to contain her pain and disappointment during the interim. It hurt. It really hurt because things had changed drastically between them. She no longer shared an evening meal with him . . . she no longer shared anything with him. She missed him. Yet, it was her doing. She was the one who made excuses for not accompanying him after the center closed.

How could she calmly break bread with him when she knew there was no hope of them coming together . . . not ever. It was not that he did not love her. He could not love her. He had no

casualty

room in his heart for another woman. He was a ~~causality~~ to the
terrible tragedy that had taken both his wife and their child.

What she found most disturbing about the whole thing was
that she had discovered something within herself that she had
not known was there. She was unwilling to settle for less than
a full-fledge relationship. Their friendship was no longer the
issue. She wanted . . . no, she needed more. She longed for
what Diane had . . . one special man to love her with his whole
heart. How could she accept less? The problem was she wanted
Dexter to be that man.

"Mama?" Jeff said after a prolong silence.

"I'm fine," she said into the receiver. "You never told me
how you did on your midterms."

"All *A's*. No problem." He frowned because unlike the other
guys, he had no distraction to keep him from his studies. "Are
you sure, you're okay? You sound kind of sad."

"I am fine. I've been busy. What's new with you, kiddo?"

"Did I tell you I met Quinn Montgomery's daughter, Cynthia?"

"No. I forgot she was at Paine. Where did you meet?"

"She's a year ahead of me, but she's in one of my math
classes."

"How nice to have a friend from home."

"Come on, Ma. You set me up."

"What?"

"You heard me. You and Mrs. Randol told her to look me
up."

"I did no such thing," Anthia denied, sorry she hadn't thought
of it.

"Come on. Her stepmom is good friends with Mrs. Randol
and you two are friends. You can't fool me."

"So, do you like her? What's she like?"

"She's okay. Being nice to me because she has to," he insisted.

"Gee, you must have really turned into a jerk. I mean having
people forced to be nice to you. Poor thing," she teased.

Jeff burst into laughter. "Okay. Okay. Maybe I did exaggerate
just a little."

"Give her a chance. She might only want to see a friendly face from home."

"Yeah. More than likely she just needs help with the math."

"Then help her. We'd better get off."

"Okay, tell Dex hello for me."

Her heart had done a flip-flop at the sound of his name. She had to force herself to ask, "Did you think about what we talked about? Have you changed your mind about talking at the center?"

"No. I have not changed my mind. Love you."

"Love you, too. Don't forget your exercises. 'Bye."

Jeff slowly replaced the telephone wondering if she was keeping something from him. She just didn't sound like herself. The telephone rang again before he could move away from the desk.

"Hello?"

"Hi, may I speak to Jeff?" The soft feminine voice caught him unaware.

"This is Jeff."

"Hi, Jeff. This is Cindy Montgomery. Do you have a few moments?"

"Yeah," he mumbled, his curiosity peaked. What was she up to now? He thought he'd been pretty clear the last time they talked.

"Oh good. How have you been?"

"Fine," he said matter-of-factly, a single step away from being downright rude.

"I need a favor. Maybe, you can help a home girl out?"

"Such as?"

"I did really poorly on the math midterm. I need some help . . . a study partner. Would you consider helping me?"

Jeff's frustration quickly intensified. He'd made a point to not get involved with anyone. He didn't need friends. He didn't need anyone. But he felt like a traitor when he said, "I'm not really a tutor, Cynthia."

"It doesn't matter. We have a test next week. Can't we get together at the library or here in my apartment to go over the recent assignments."

"Cynthia . . ."

"Call me Cindy. I wouldn't ask, but I really need your help.

I've put off this class for more than a year. I'm going to need it to graduate."

Jeff knew he was wasting his time protesting. How could he in all good conscience say no to the daughter of the man who saved his hide. Without Quinn Montgomery's help, he would be behind bars.

"We can meet wherever you say," Cynthia insisted.

"Okay."

"Thanks," she laughed. "You have no idea how much I need your help. When it comes to math, I'm hopeless. How soon can we meet?"

"Tomorrow evening after dinner. Say seven in the library?"

"That's fine."

"Cynthia, I hope you're serious about studying because I don't have a lot of free time. I'm carrying a heavy class load this semester."

"And you're at the top of the class from what I hear."

Jeff was glad she couldn't see him flush with embarrassment. Her boast reminded him of how their professor used him as an example to the other students. It was embarrassing. He hated the attention. He had no choice. He had to keep his grades up. Both he and his mother had worked hard to get him back on his feet and in college. He was not about to let either one of them down by not doing his best.

"Thanks Jeff. See you then. 'Bye."

NINE

It took Dana Gray a few moments to release the series of locks lining her apartment door. She and her four young children lived in a low-income apartment building on the east side of Detroit. The once family-oriented area was now, unfortunately, a haven for gangs and street crime.

By necessity she worked out of her home, telling herself that she, too, was a small-business person like her friend and boss Anthia Jenkins.

"Hold on, Anthia . . ." Dana called just before she swung the door open. "Hi," she said, after returning Anthia's warm hug.

"How you doin'?" Anthia pulled back until she could look up into the younger woman's flawless clear copper-brown face. She wore her hair in a short natural that looked wonderful on her. Dana could have easily been a model, gracing the runways of Paris and New York with her sleek, long, slim frame and natural beauty.

Unfortunately, her hopes for a career in fashion had ended when she had fallen in love with Jerome Walker. After having four of his children in less than three years, the twenty-three-year-old Dana was forced to work out of her own home while she cared for two sets of twins, two-year-old and four-year-old girls.

She often stayed up late into the night sewing for her girls and trying to keep up with the workload. Their work was steadily increasing as Anthia's dolls grew in popularity. Dana was proud that for now, because of her help, Anthia felt she would be able to keep her head above water.

"Auntie Thia," the girls chorale racing for hugs and kisses.

Anthia held out her arms, laughing at their enthusiasm. She never came empty-handed and today was no exception. She had brought along caramel-covered popcorn treats.

"What did you bring us?" four-year-old Gina and Ginny asked simultaneously.

"Yeah!" Deborah and Deanna beamed.

"Let her sit down and catch her breath," Dana insisted.

The girls waited politely until Anthia was seated on the sofa, but the two-year-olds couldn't wait a second longer. They were in her lap offering more kisses and giggles.

Anthia kissed each one, laughing at their giggling and sweet-smelling wiggly forms. Sitting still was out of the question. Dana kept her apartment spotless and her babies smelling like baby lotion and powder. All four little heads were combed and braided every single day with ribbons and bows. Anthia had no idea how she managed the girls and kept up with the new sewing projects she gave her every week.

As she handed each child a carefully wrapped caramel corn treat Anthia said, "Don't yell, because I brought caramel corn, Dana. I brought fruit the last three times."

Dana laughed. "Okay. Just this once." She didn't like them to have too many sweets. "Say thank you and go into your bedroom. Gina and Ginny be sure and wash your hands and then help Deborah and Deanna wash their hands when you two finish."

Anthia adored their happy, pretty brown faces and watched as they ran off to their bedroom. "You're doing a great job with them, Dana." She went back to the door to retrieve the heavy tote bag filled with fabrics and variety of trims she'd brought with her.

"What did Mrs. Randol's mother think of her doll?"

"She loved it. Diane was also thrilled. She loved the christening gown. You did a wonderful job, Dana. You should see her sweet Madelyn. She is growing so big. And she looks just like Diane." Anthia beamed.

Dana was pleased. "I knew she would love that doll." Although, she had not met Anthia's friend she had certainly heard her name many times. Charles and Diane Randol often appeared in the society column of the newspaper. They were such a striking couple.

Anthia and Dana settled in the corner of the dining room that served as Dana's workroom. Spread on the cutting board were the four outfits that Dana had completed, waiting for Anthia's approval.

"Oh, Dana!" Anthia gushed, enthusiastically, "They are lovely. Exactly what I wanted. As usual you did an excellent job." Anthia pulled her checkbook out of the depth of her tote bag and quickly wrote out a check.

"Thanks. I'm glad you like them. I changed the lace on the beige dress just a bit from your sketch. I thought this ivory pleated lace would work much better."

"You're right." Anthia nodded, examining the lace. "The mixture of textures between the lace and the smooth satin of the pantaletts is marvelous, Dana. I love the lace accents you added to the socks. They are so sweet. I am sure Mrs. Durrent will be thrilled by the doll. Thanks to you, we will make our deadline. What would I do without you?"

Dana sincerely hoped it would never be an option. She loved working with someone as creative and skilled with a needle as Anthia. She was smiling as she carefully wrapped each small outfit in tissue paper.

Anthia began laying out the fabrics and trims she had brought with her. Then pulled the new photographs and sketches from her leather portfolio for their upcoming projects.

"I love this," Dana exclaimed running her hand over the white eyelet dotted with pink and yellow sprig flowers. "It will look perfect with this pink beaded lace, then with the matching eyelet trim pantaletts. I like it. Where did you find the fabric?" She asked while studying the sketch of the new doll.

"A tiny fabric shop in downtown Windsor. Isn't it fabulous? So many of their fabrics have a Victorian look to them. I practically bought the store out. I had to have most of it shipped. What do you think of this deep rose velvet?"

"I'd like to own an off-the-shoulder dress made of this." Dana chuckled. "I can't believe you're going to trust me to embroider the hem of the dress and underslip. Girl, I know how meticulous you are. Goodness, you won't even use a machine."

"Not on one of my dolls. The machine is much faster, but it lacks the warmth and intricacy of the detail of hand embroidery. What are you talking about? Your work is flawless. We're really creating gallery quality pieces at One of a Kind."

"But still . . ." Dana marveled.

Anthia preferred to put the finishing touches on her dolls, for her to give the task to Dana was high praise indeed. "Your work is exquisite. I'm lucky that you are available."

Dana shook her head. "I'm the lucky one. Working for you allows me to do what I love: designing and sewing while still staying home with my girls."

The two smiled at each other, before they painstakingly went over each new sketch and costume outlined by Anthia.

"Mommy, can we color now?" Gina came in followed by her siblings.

"Yes, sweetie. Share the crayon box," she warned.

Anthia only smiled, amazed at how artistic the children were, they clearly took after their mother in their flair and love of vibrant colors.

"What do you think if I add smocking here rather than inserts?" Dana asked as she studied yet another sketch.

Anthia nodded. "That might be interesting, especially if you pick up the green and yellow in the fabric. Okay. Let's go with it."

Dana not only respected Anthia's talents as a skilled doll artisan but also cared for her. Anthia worked hard to keep her work as flawless and exacting as the costly craft demanded. Dana had known Anthia and Jeff most of her life, having grown up in the same apartment building.

So much had changed for Dana since she was forced to give up her dreams of going to New York and making a name for herself with her designs. She had met and fell in love with Jerome before she was out of her teens. She had been so young . . . too young to get serious about anyone boy. She could see that now with perfect hindsight.

At least Dana had finished high school before she became pregnant with the older twins. Her mother was such a strict, God-fearing woman that she had put her daughter out of the house when she learned she was pregnant with no prospect of marrying the babies' father. Dana had no choice but to swallow her pride and go to Aid to Dependent Children for help. She had to eat and so did her babies.

Looking back on it, she could see how truly blessed she had been. Her grandmother had taken her in without question. She barely saw Jerome in those days. He was deep into the gang scene and ended up doing time for armed robbery. Dana frowned, pushing away the unhappy thoughts. Jerome had been back less than two months when she found herself pregnant again. After having four of his babies, he still didn't feel ready for marriage. Dana was so in love with him that she told herself it didn't matter. Told herself that his drinking and inability to find a job were not bad, because at least he was no longer on drugs.

Although Dana and her mother still lived in the same apartment complex, they saw very little of each other. Their relationship remained strained since she moved out. Even though they didn't agree on much, Dana was thankful that her mother allowed her younger sister to visit with her and the girls.

Now that she worked for Anthia, she was finally self-sufficient. She no longer had to rely on public assistance or occasional child support from Jerome to provide for her daughters. Things were definitely looking up. Only when it came down to Jerome, Dana turned into a marshmallow. He owned her heart. The one and only time she had ever stood up to him was after the second set of twins was born. She had insisted that he use condoms. She could not handle another pregnancy and provide for them all, nor could she be certain that he was not using drugs. She could not monitor his friends.

"Dana, I think this will be the prettiest doll ever," Anthia said fingering the material. She could not wait to get home and see Dana's handiwork on the nearly finished doll.

Dana laughed. "You always say that."

"I can't help myself. I love my dolls so much I hate to give them away."

"You okay?" Dana wondered if she'd heard a hint of unhappiness in her boss's voice.

"I'm fine. Why do you ask?"

"You look a little tired, as if you haven't been sleeping well. How's Jeff?"

"He's fine. I'm fine." Anthia said, eager to change the topic.

"Is it Dex?" Dana knew all about her volunteering at the community center and the reason behind it.

"Yes, like a fool, I told him how I felt about him. Major mistake."

"Why? You two have been so close," Dana whispered. "I'm so sorry." She didn't like seeing her friend hurting.

"So am I, but Dex has been hurt badly. He just doesn't want to try again."

Dana gave her a hug, offering what comfort she could.

Anthia thanked her, grateful for her support. She was fortunate to have such dear friends. When she glanced at the droopy children, she smiled, "It must be nap time."

Dana smiled. "Looks that way."

"Let me help," Anthia said lifting one of the younger girls.

"Thanks," she said rousing the two older girls. The two worked together tucking the girls into their beds. The room was small but neat. Gina and Deanna shared one of the two twin beds while Ginny and Deborah shared the other.

"Let's go over these last two designs," Anthia said glancing at her watch. Time was slipping away from them.

Late afternoon moved toward evening without either of them noticing. They were so engrossed in their work that they both looked up in surprise when Jerome unlocked the door and walked into the apartment.

"Hey," he said, but his hard angry eyes narrowed on Anthia. "What's she doin' in my house?"

Dana's dark complexion prevented her flush from showing, but her embarrassment was all over her small face. "Don't start," she said wearily. "You know I work for Anthia."

"I'm surprised you're slumming Ms. Boss-Lady," he jeered.

Jerome was Eddie Walker's older brother. He made no secret that he put the blame for his brother's incarceration square on Jeff and Anthia's shoulders. He didn't take into consideration that it was Eddie who offered Jeff the ill-fated ride . . . a ride that nearly cost Jeff his life. Eddie had involved Jeff when he purposefully robbed that convenience store.

Anthia stood up and began collecting her things. "I think I'd better be going."

Dana came to her own feet. "You don't have to rush off. You know you're always welcome, Anthia."

"We're finished here. Call, if you run into a problem." Anthia kissed the younger woman's cheek before she left.

Dana had barely closed the front door, when Jerome's voice thundered, "I know I told you about having that bitch come here."

Anthia couldn't help overhearing. She bit her lips in silent frustration as she hurried away. Dana was a sweet, loving woman. Why must she tie herself to a man like Jerome? Thank goodness, Anthia was wise enough to know that Dana would not welcome her advice when it came to Jerome. Dana's love for him was blind. To keep her friendship, Anthia bit her tongue and tried to mind her own business.

The hallway was dark because most of the overhead lights were lacking bulbs. Anthia took the stairs preferring them to the crammed elevator. She often wondered how long she would have stayed on in the building if she had not felt that her impressionable son needed to be away from the temptation of the gangs.

She hadn't forgotten how dank and depressing it could be living from hand to mouth. There was a sense of helplessness and hopelessness that seemed to permeate the air. Her mother had worked so hard to get out of this place and had never seen her dream of owning her own home come true.

Anthia's eyes swam with tears. She felt so sad that her mother had not lived to see her own personal success. It would mean so much to her. She would have been so proud of Anthia being

in business for herself and of Jeff being in college and making
A's.

Impatiently wiping away the tears, Anthia climbed to the fifth
floor and knocked on Mrs. Rice's door. Dana's grandmother had
been a long-time friend of Anthia's mother.

"Who is it?" Mrs. Rice asked from behind her locked door.

"It's me, Mrs. Rice. Anthia Jenkins."

"Well. Well," the older woman laughed as she worked to free
the locks lining her door. "Girl, come on in here and give me
a hug."

Anthia did just that. It was easy to see where Dana had gotten
her good looks. Even at seventy-two, Edna Rice was a good-
looking woman. She and Anthia's mother had often sat together,
talked and done needlework—from embroidery, needlepoint,
knitting to fine, delicate crochet. Both women had been excep-
tionally talented with a needle. They had passed on the talent
to both Anthia and Dana.

"You're looking good." Anthia said giving her a hug and kiss.
"You been taking care of yourself? Doing what the doctor
says?"

"Shoot! That doctor don't know no more than I do about
high blood pressure. He's a kid."

Anthia laughed. "He's old enough to keep your pressure
down if you do as he says and leave that salt pork and those
ham hocks alone. Now, tell me the truth. Have you taken your
pills?"

"Yes. Now come on in here and talk to me." She pointed to
the place beside her on the sofa. "You been over to see my
Dana?"

"I have. Those babies are getting prettier and prettier every
time I see them. Dana is a fine mother."

"Yes, she is, but when it comes to men, the girl ain't got a
lick of sense. Lord, Lord, Lord. Ain't no getting through to her
about that boy."

Anthia squeezed her hand. "Unfortunately, you're so right."
Hoping to lighten the mood, she said, "I brought you something." Anthia placed a foil-wrapped bundle in her lap.

"Brownies?"

"Yes, ma'am."

The older woman placed a loud kiss on Anthia's cheek. "You are so sweet. Your mama would be pleased that you haven't forgotten her old friend."

Anthia blushed at the praise.

"How's that boy of yours doing?"

Anthia happily chatted about Jeff and her business as the evening slipped away. Mrs. Rice wouldn't let Anthia leave without having a bit of dinner with her, which included collard greens, candied yams and fried chicken and Anthia's favorite banana pudding.

Anthia had just finished washing up the dishes in the small but tidy kitchen when Mrs. Rice said, "You modern, independent women. What you need is a good man."

"Uh-huh," Anthia said.

"I mean a good man. Like your daddy and my Russell."

Anthia teased, "Too bad they don't grow on trees. Then we'd all have one." Both women roared with laughter.

"You didn't run into that Jerome, did you?"

"Sure did. It wasn't pleasant."

"You'd think the fool would have the good sense to be polite considering that you are Dana's employer."

"Not him. He was his usual hateful self. All he thinks about is that I'm Jeff's mother and Jeff is responsible for Eddie being in prison."

"Eddie is the reason he's locked up."

"Don't I know it. I suppose he has reason to dislike me. I have made no secret of the fact that I don't think he's good for Dana or the babies. She is a lovely young woman and very talented."

"I try not to worry about that gal but it is hard. I just have to put it into the Lord's hands. I keep praying for her. That Jerome can't change the fact that she has a good head on her shoulders."

"You're right about that. Tell me about Mrs. Woods. I heard the family had to put her into a nursing home."

The two continued to chat about old friends and neighbors.

Before Anthia realized it, it was after dark and Mrs. Rice had long ago switched on the table lamps.

"Gosh, it's after nine." Anthia rose after checking her wristwatch. "I must be going. This always happens when I come to see you. I forget my way home." She smiled fondly at the One of a Kind bride doll prominently displayed on one of Mrs. Rice armchairs.

"We don't get to talk nearly enough," Mrs. Rice beamed, linking arms with Anthia as she walked her to the door.

"You take care of yourself, dear heart." Anthia said, giving her a hug and a kiss on her lined brown cheek.

"I will. You give that boy of yours a kiss for me. I thank you for all you've done for my Dana."

Anthia nodded. "Dana is a wonderful help to me. Love you." She waved. "I'll wait while you lock up."

"Okay. You be careful going to your car," Mrs. Rice warned as she clicked the locks into place.

Anthia hurried to the elevator, relieved it was empty. How could she have forgotten the time? She had to hurry. She knew better than to stay so late. It just wasn't safe. The gang activity was much too prevalent.

When the two young men got into the elevator on the second floor, Anthia normally would not have been alarmed, except they sported gang colors like a badge of honor. She nodded hello to them, unconsciously hugging her tote bag tight against her side.

"How you doin'? I haven't seen you here before. You just movin' in?" The taller of the two eyed her petite curvy length appreciatively.

"No, just visiting." Anthia said, suddenly aware of the eighteen-karat gold hoop earrings she wore in her ears and gold stampato bracelets around her wrists. What had she been thinking? She was getting soft. Why had she gotten on the elevator in the first place? But then she could have just as easily run into someone lurking on the dark staircase.

"This ain't exactly the new center area, baby. I'd be happy to walk you to your car." The taller one said, eyeing her smartly tailored pale yellow blazer and silk knit top that she wore with snug-fitting jeans.

"That won't be necessary."

"Hey mama, I'm just trying' to look out for ya."

"Yeah. My man is just trying' to be nice," his companion added.

"No, thank you."

The elevator doors opened then and Anthia stepped out prepared to rush out alone. Neither one of them looked too sober to her.

Anthia managed to clear the door and was down the sidewalk, but she could hear their taunts and footsteps behind her. She quickened her speed and had just reached the unlit parking lot behind the building when she felt a tug on her arm from behind.

"Let go!" she jerked away.

"Anthia," Dexter said from over her shoulder. "Something wrong?"

"Dex . . ." she gasped, barely stopping herself from throwing herself into his arms. "You scared me!" Her heart was racing and she was shaking from head to toe.

"Sorry," he said, spotting the two younger men. "Flemmings! Carter! You say something out of line?"

"Hey, not me, man," the taller one denied.

"Hell, we didn't know she was your lady, man."

Although, they clearly had been following her, neither was willing to mess with Dexter without backup. They knew his reputation for being able to take care of himself.

Dexter pointedly glared at one man. "Watch yourself!"

The younger man puffed up with anger, swearing softly but he didn't respond directly to Dexter. He kept on walking right past them.

"You know them?" Anthia whispered.

Dexter watched until they cleared the lot and kept going toward the next apartment building. "Yeah. From the center. Those two stopped in to make trouble. Said they were tired of the gang scene, but it was a lie. Neither one of them want anything better than what the streets have to offer," he grated harshly.

Anthia nodded, avoiding his intense eyes.

Dexter found he could not look past her petite beauty. It had been a rough couple of days. They had not really talked since he walked out of her place. The incident with the boys just brought home to him how much she meant to him. He couldn't tolerate the idea that she might have been hurt. He placed his hands on her shoulders cupping them gently.

"Thanks for your help."

"You're trembling," his voice was deeper, huskier than he would have liked.

She shrugged, moving away from his grasp. "I'm okay. What are doing here?"

"I need to talk with one of the fellows from the community center. I could ask you the same." Swallowing a curse, he detested the way she jerked away from him as if she couldn't stand his touch.

"I had business with Dana Gray. Then I stopped in to see an old friend of my mother's, Mrs. Rice, Dana's grandmother." She stopped abruptly, wondering why she was even bothering to explain herself to him.

They were not even friends anymore. He made sure of that when he walked away from the tenderness she offered. The only reason she continued to volunteer at the center was because she had given her word. Besides, her son had benefitted from the center. It was payback time.

"Why couldn't you have done this during the day? This is not Southfield," his tone was raw with impatience and hidden need.

Hell, he had thought his nights were empty before, that was nothing compared to what he had been going through since their talk. He missed her terribly. Damn it, they didn't talk anymore. She wouldn't even share a meal with him. She had totally withdrawn from him. And he detested it.

Anthia did not bother giving him an answer. She simply turned on her heels and walked away. The arrogant, boneheaded jerk!

"Anthia!" He took off after her. She refused to stop until she reached her car. She hastily disengaged the alarm and power locks. Dexter grabbed her keys before she could get inside. She was not going anywhere until she talked to him. "What's with you?"

"What concern is it of yours?"

"Is this about what happened the other night? Is that why you're treating me like a leper, because of what I told you? Is that it?" Dexter was shouting. He couldn't seem to help it. She was driving him nuts. She wouldn't even look at him at the center. She was steadfastly pushing him out of her life. Forget friendship, he didn't get a damn smile.

"Give me back my keys!" she hissed at him.

"Answer me!"

"I thought this was such a bad neighborhood."

"I thought we were friends," he countered.

"Evidently we were both wrong." Holding out her small hand, she persisted, "I'd like my keys, please."

"And I'd like things to be the way they were before I spilled my guts to you." He was in pain and didn't know how to stop it. "I knew it was mistake."

"How can one man be so dense?" she yelled back at him. "That night taught me that you're not the man I thought you were. I couldn't have been more wrong about you. You are not thoughtful and compassionate. You're secretive and shallow. I'm truly sorry I ever invited you to come home with me!" How dare he walk out on her and expect things to go on as they had before, she fumed. He had to be out of his mind!

Dexter's bronze, African features had gone hard as granite as he handed over her keys. "I'm sorry, too." He looked away, not about to let her see how deeply she had hurt him.

She surprised them both when she said, "Why did you tell me about your past when you clearly have no feelings for me?"

"No feelings? How can you possibly believe that?"

"You walked out on me, remember?" Her voice was bitter with hurt and unhappiness. Before he could respond, she slammed her door then locked it. She didn't even glance his way as she backed out of the parking space and drove away.

She was a block away before he recognized that he didn't know if it were the truth about him that made her turn away or if it was his leaving so unexpectanly that upset her the most. He didn't have a clue to what was going on in her beautiful head.

TEN

Anthia had just locked the door leading from the garage when her doorbell rang. She knew who it was. She still had not recovered from that awful scene in the parking lot. She could not believe she had said those cruel things to him. She had overreacted, focusing on her own hurt feelings. It was not like her to be so cruel to anyone. That was not her way. Hadn't they both already said enough hurtful things to each other?

"You shouldn't be here," Anthia said after opening the front door.

Before Dexter could reply, the telephone rang. Anthia mumbled a hasty, "Excuse me," before she turned and hurried to retrieve the cordless phone from a side table. "Hello?"

"Anthia, are you okay? I've been calling for hours."

"I'm fine, Dana. I stopped in to visit with your grandmother. What's up?" she said, trying not to notice the way Dexter filled her entrance way.

"I forgot to ask when do you need the new designs finished?"

"No particular hurry. I have three dolls to sculpt before I'll need them."

"Okay," there was a hesitation before she went on to say, "Look, I'm sorry about what Jerome said. I was not expecting him so early. If I had known I would have made arrangements."

Anthia noted that she said nothing about limiting Jerome's comings and goings in her life. Dana was hopelessly in love with the wrong man. No matter what Jerome said or did, he remained the love of Dana's life. What kind of example was she setting for her girls?

How could he possibly make her happy and provide her with the love and commitment she needed when his lifestyle was so unsavory? Nothing good could come from it. But Anthia knew she would be wasting her time telling Dana that. All she could do was be her friend and be willing to support her when she fell. In Anthia's opinion she would fall. It was only a matter of time until he broke her heart.

Anthia wearily recognized that her own feelings for Dexter were just as misguided, just as hopeless. She would be better served by finding a man who was capable of returning her feelings. Someone who would treat her the way she longed to be treated.

Unfortunately, it was too late for both of them. Anthia had given Dexter her whole heart, just as Dana had given Jerome hers. There was nothing either one of them could do but deal with it.

Anthia did not glance at Dexter. Yet, she knew he was waiting for her to finish her call. No, she didn't look because she was not ready to face him. She had made a fool of herself earlier. She had been mean and spiteful because she had been scared of how deep her feelings were for him. She was the one who ended up hurt and alone.

"Anthia?"

"No harm done, Dana." Unwillingly, her hungry gaze strayed to the tall, silent man. His full-lip mouth was bracketed by hard lines. "We both know that Jerome can't stand the sight of me and why. That does not affect our working relationship or our friendship. Stop worrying."

The relief in Dana's voice was evident when she said, "Good night, Anthia. See you soon."

"Good night." Anthia reluctantly hung up the telephone. She was not ready to face Dexter. But her options were limited. She had to face him and deal with her hurt feelings without resorting to nastiness . . . the nastiness went beneath her dignity. Besides, it was not the way she had been brought up. Her mother would certainly not approve.

Taking a deep breath, she said, "I suppose you heard."

He nodded, as he came to stand next to her. "Jerome was at Dana's?"

"Yes. I should have expected to see him. He's practically living with Dana these days. She's the mother of his kids."

"He doesn't deserve her or those kids." There was a touch of bitterness in his voice, plain jealousy. That part of his life was over. "What did he say to you?"

"The usual," she said vaguely.

"I don't like it."

"He is not a threat. He just has a big, foul mouth."

"If he ever puts a hand on you, I'll . . ."

"You'll what? Never mind! I'd rather not know. Look Dexter, you're not my black champion. I fight my own battles. Besides enough angry words have already been said between us tonight."

Dexter's emotions were raw, like an open, festering wound. He should have kept going. He was opening himself up for more pain. Yet, he had to be there. He had to talk this through with her. Too much was at stake. He could not give up what they had. Their friendship may not have meant anything to her, but it meant everything to him. It was all he had.

"We need to talk. Anthia, we've been fr . . ." he nearly stammered over the word *friends* and quickly changed it, ". . . close for some time now. Please, just listen."

"I'm not up to this," she swallowed down a sob. She was too shaky and wasn't prepared for this conversation. She reminded herself over and over that she could not cry now. She must not embarrass herself anymore than she already had.

"You were wrong, Anthia. I care about you. You are important to me." He purposefully kept his hands in his pockets, careful not to touch her.

"Just not enough to have a relationship with me, right?" she blurted out.

"Why would you want one with me? You know the truth about me."

"It was an accident, Dex. You didn't kill your wife and child. You're not some kind of monster," she stated emphatically.

"Funny, that's how I've thought of myself. I deserved what happened after that. I had no business touching that gun. If I hadn't, maybe I could have talked her out of it? I didn't even try. At the time, I merely reacted," he said, his mouth taut with emotion.

"Stop it! It's over. You've paid the price of that mistake. Years of your life were taken away from you. Years that you can never get back."

"It's not over, Anthia," he whispered hoarsely. "It will never be over for me."

"Dex, can't you see? You're refusing to let go," she said, with a sinking heart. She forced herself to face the bitter truth. Dexter was still in love with his late wife.

"That's not true!" His temper flared. "I lost my wife and child. I lost the only family I will have. My own father won't have anything to do with me. I had no one outside of my sister until I met you." He stared at her, his intense gaze caressed her pretty brown features. "Anthia, please. Don't turn your back on what we have." He suddenly recognized that when it came to her, he had no pride.

"What exactly do we have, Dex? We've barely said two words to each other in more than a week. All we had before that was a few late-night meals. For months we didn't even see each other, just talked on the telephone. How can that be enough for you? It's not nearly enough for me."

They stared at each other, looking deep into each other's eyes.

He shocked them both when he said, "Please, baby, don't do this." He reached out a hand to her, then let it drop before he could touch her.

Tears welled up in her eyes making them look like deep pools of sadness. One after the other they slid slowly down her smooth cheeks. Her soft, full lips trembled uncontrollably. "I need more."

"Oh, baby . . . don't cry." He touched her then. He pulled her soft trembling form into his arms to rest against his broad chest. "Please, don't cry. I can't bear it." He wiped awkwardly at her cheeks.

Anthia was shaking badly, choking on the tears that she couldn't seem to stop. They trickled like raindrops.

"No . . ." he rocked her, smoothing his large hands over her shoulders down her back to her tiny waist. He crooned softly in her ear, "Baby . . . don't."

Anthia really tried, but she could not seem to stop. All the anguish she had held deep inside for so long poured out. She sobbed out her fear . . . her unhappiness . . . her endless need for a love that could never be.

Dexter didn't even consider letting her go. He quickly lifted her and carried her over to one of the armchairs near the window. When he sat, he held her on his lap, cradling her against his chest, her cheek against his shoulder. "Anthia . . . please."

Gradually, she gained some measure of control. He used his handkerchief to mop her damp face. He tried to smile down at her, his fingers in the cottony softness of her thick curls. Anthia snuggled even closer to him, her soft breasts pillowed on his chest. Dexter's entire body stiffened, his nostrils filled with her clean womanly scent. His suddenly hungry gaze centered on her full, red-tinted lips.

He whispered, "Anthia . . ." He groaned an instant before he surrendered to his overwhelming need to taste her sweetness. Dropping his head, he placed tender kisses against her damp cheeks, her forehead, her chin. Oh, man, she felt so good, so right in his arms. He brushed his mouth over hers repeatedly, seeking the bounty within. When she gasped, parting her lips, Dexter lost his last small measure of control and dipped his hot, rough tongue inside. The kiss deepened even more, he moaned in his throat as he licked the inside of her lips then slid deep inside, savoring her sweetness. He was not disappointed. She was every bit as delectable as he remembered. Her tongue hot and velvety against his.

Anthia shuddered from the insistent brush of his tongue over hers, burning from the virility of this man. She moaned, melted even deeper into his arms. The tips of her breasts were tight and aching from her escalating need, she opened herself even more to his potent male need.

Dexter groaned low in his throat, his nostrils flared as he

took in the natural essence of her enticing scent. Her softness was his undoing. He gathered her even closer as he lost himself in her softness, the velvety texture of her tongue was impossible to resist. He found himself drawing her tongue into his own mouth and sucking. He had no idea that he was crushing her with the force of his long denied hunger.

Anthia quivered in his arms, uncomplaining. She had waited an eternity to once more enjoy the taste of his mouth and the feel of his body pressed against hers. She was not about to push him away. Her arms encircled his trim waist and she stroked beneath his leather coat to his broad back covered by a silk shirt. He felt so good, so strong. She could feel his body heat even through the layers of cloth that separated them. Her senses soared from his potent masculinity. He was so gloriously male. And for this special moment, he was hers.

Lost in a sensual daze of his making, she whispered his name, a deep throaty appeal.

Dexter was the first to recover, shocked at his weakness, his lack of control. He rose to his feet, lifting Anthia to her feet, but he also set her away from him. When it came to Anthia, he had no restraint. After weeks of being near her without being able to have her had nearly driven him out of his mind with hunger. Living without her beguiling smiles and gentle warmth these last few days had been pure hell. Evidently, it had taken its toll on his self-control. He was so damn needy he hardly knew his own name. It had gone far enough. It had to stop . . . now.

"I lost my head . . ." he said, his hands clenched at his sides as his eyes bore into hers. "The truth is I want you . . . badly." His body was so swollen with desire he couldn't think beyond his need. The way her soft bottom had been against his erection, there was no way she could have failed to notice his problem.

"I have no objections," she whispered softly.

"But . . ."

She quickly pressed her fingers against his full lips. "No buts." Her arms tightened around his waist. She stretched up enough to press her lips to the vulnerable base of his throat. "Make love to me, Dex. I want you."

He shivered in reaction to the lure of her femininity. How

could he fight himself and her sweet appeal? Had he ever
wanted a woman more? It was highly unlikely. He was so painfully aroused that his entire body felt like one huge ball of
aching need.

Just the soft brush of her mouth against his skin had him
throbbing painfully. She drove him wild with longing. His deep-
seated reservations had been at war with his burgeoning need
for some time. It had all come down to this agonizing moment.

His voice was gruff with emotions when he said, "How? How
can you even want me knowing what I've done?"

In spite of the inquiry, he held her with both hands wondering
if he could let her go. He had waited so long to have her like
this. He had spent so many empty nights filled with yearning
for her sweetness. In spite of her small stature, she felt so right
against him. He fought the overwhelming urge to lift her until
he could rub her soft mound against the hard ridge of his sex.

"You did nothing wrong other than try and save your family.
Why can't you see it was a tragic accident? You should have
never been punished."

"Thank you . . ." he said softly. If only he could believe, unfortunately he had lived too long with the harsh reality of it to
believe otherwise. When Anthia moved her soft breasts rubbed
against him, Dexter groaned, "Anthia . . . I need you so badly."

She needed no further invitation. Anthia lifted her mouth
against his. Her sleek, hot tongue slowly outlined the fullness
of his lips, exploring the upper curve thoroughly before moving
to the fullness of the lower one, then she sucked his bottom lip
into the warmth of her mouth.

Dexter groaned heavily as he lifted her to give him better
access to her mouth. He could not resist the hot wet honey he
found inside.

"Oh, baby," he groaned urgently, cupping her soft hips, urging her into the cradle of his muscular thighs. He did not stop
until her fleshy mound was flush against the pulsating length
of his erection. "I've wanted you for so damn long."

She quivered at the intimate contact, her mouth meshed with
his, each stroke of his tongue bolder, hotter than the last. Anthia
was the first to pull back doing so because of the need to

breathe. Moaning deeply, he allowed her body to slide down his body. They were both trembling as they studied each other. There was no doubt that the fierce need was mutual.

She was so tiny, so beautiful. She deserved a man who was free to love her. She deserved better than him. He had nothing to offer her, outside of his body. He was a man with a terrible reputation . . . a man who had ruined his own life. He was an ex-con, who had lost his good name . . . lost his own family . . . lost everything. But he was a man.

"Dex . . ."

He was trembling from the power of his need when he said, "You deserve . . ."

She pressed her fingers against his lips to hold back his refusal. "Let's think only of being together now. I want to feel you inside of me."

Dexter's heart raced with excitement. Her taste lingered in his mouth, the remembered feel of her soft breasts and large nipples against his chest, and imagining the heat of her wet sheath surrounding his sex was steadfastly eroding his self-control.

Her hands went to the base of his throat and she pushed his leather jacket away, then she began to slowly release the buttons down his shirt. In spite of her boldness, her fingers trembled as she stroked her hands beneath his shirt to the warm haven of his hair-roughened chest. When her soft hands moved over his flat nipple, he moaned deep in his throat trembling in reaction. Anthia didn't disappoint him, she worried the dark, sensitive disc with her nail. He groaned his enjoyment, his large frame shook with need.

By the time Anthia's hands caressed Dexter's flat, washboard stomach he was rock-hard, having nearly filled to his entire long, thick length. He stopped her sweet caresses at his waist before she could do more than release the snap of his jeans. She raised questioning eyes to his.

He caught her hand in his and pulled her along toward her bedroom. When he had helped her arrange furniture in this room on the day she'd moved in, he'd never dare hope that he might one day share the queen-size bed with her.

Dexter did not give her a chance to think, perhaps reconsider.

He reached for her with both hands and his whole heart. He wasn't satisfied until her soft breasts were cushioned on his wide chest and her small frame pressed tightly against his.

He pulled her blazer off, before his hands went to her silk top, then he released her belt before he unzipped her jeans and peeled them down her legs until she could step out of them. He slowly ran his hands over her soft arms, down her back to her hips. His mouth devouring hers, taking kiss after kiss. She whimpered in his arms wearing nothing more than yellow lace panties and a bra. Soon they, too, were gone, leaving her bare to his touch, his gaze.

She stammered, "I know my breasts are small but . . ."

"Shush," he murmured huskily, his long fingertips circling her perky breasts. "You're beautiful . . . perfect."

He was fascinated by her large prominent nipples. With unsteady hands, he cupped her softness in his palms before he dropped his head to tongue one dark brown nipple. He took his time licking the firm peak over and over, eventually he took it into his mouth to suck. Anthia was quivering so badly that she had to hold on to his broad shoulders to keep from falling.

"Dex . . ."

Relishing the enticement of her soft skin, he swept her up in his arms and carried her over to the bed. He loved the feel and taste of her against his tongue, but he needed more. "Anthia . . ."

She encouraged, while moving her hips against his, "I need you. Only you Dex."

She didn't have to say it twice. He stood up to undress. Her eyes locked with his when his hands went to his waistband. As he unzipped his jeans, he watched for the slightest hesitation on her part. He slid the jeans along with his briefs down his lean hips and muscled thighs. Anthia caught her breath at the size of his sex. She experienced a momentary hesitation.

It had been so long for her. There was no doubt he was ready for her, was she ready for him? When Dexter joined her on the bed, Anthia was a mass of nerves while his hot male body pulsed from the strength of his need.

"What's wrong?" he whispered, afraid to touch her in case

she changed her mind. He had never taken a woman against her will, he was not about to start now. Yet, he wanted her so desperately he was nearly out of his head from the longing.

Anthia was scared and she didn't know how to explain her unexpected reluctance. He lay stiffly beside her, his wonderfully bronze body on display.

"Nothing . . ." she said, unconsciously holding herself away from him.

Dexter ached to pull her against him, feel her pretty breasts on his chest while rubbing her silky thighs against his hair-roughened ones. He made no move to cover her petite frame with his. He ignored the demands of his body to bury himself deep inside of her, surrounded by her sleek heat.

"Something," He swung his legs down to the side of the bed, frustration battling with need as he hung his head. "If nothing is wrong, why did you freeze up? Anthia, I won't hurt you. Or don't you trust me? Is that why you changed your mind?" His voice was harsh even to his own ears. He couldn't look at her without needing to touch her, so he stared at his hands, clasped between his knees.

Anthia scrambled to her knees, her arms encircling his waist from behind. She pressed her soft lips against one powerfully muscled shoulder. "I'm sorry."

He gazed back at her, studying her lovely features, before he asked, "What happened?" He made no effort to touch her.

She didn't exercise the same restraint. Her soft hands stroked the firm muscle of his chest. Dexter shuddered in reaction.

"Anthia . . ."

"I got scared," she finally confessed with difficulty.

"I won't hurt you, baby. I couldn't. You mean too much to me."

She pressed her lips to a shoulder. "It's not you, it's me." She stroked down the length of his forearms enjoying the smooth feel of his bronze skin.

He turned until she rested against his chest. "I don't understand." His eyes searched hers while one hand cradled her jaw, lifting it. "You're so beautiful. I can't help but want you."

"It's been a very long time for me, Dex. When I saw your

body, I realized just how long it had been . . ." she blushed, "since I've been with a man."

He blinked in surprise, realizing she was referring to his size. Knowing it was none of his business, but wanting to know regardless, he asked, "How long has it been?"

She looked away. She couldn't tell him that she hadn't been tempted until she fell in love with him. Her only encounter had been with her son's father, more than eighteen years ago.

"Anthia . . ."

"Before my son was born," she finally admitted.

Dexter groaned, closing his arms around her, cuddling her against his chest. "I feel honored," he said an instant before his hot, hungry mouth descended on hers.

His kissed her again and again. He parted her lips with the bold thrust of his tongue, glided into that moist, sweet cavity. "Baby . . ." he moaned, kissing Anthia over and over. His hungry mouth devoured hers before he dropped to tantalize the soft silky length of her creamy brown throat. He tongued her ear before he suckled the lobe.

"You're so beautiful . . . so lovely," he said pressing soft kisses down her throat to the tender hollow.

"I never wanted to be with anyone until now."

"It's okay."

Anthia shivered at the rough heat of his tongue against her skin. She lay across his thighs. There was no way she could fail to notice the strength of his arousal.

"Can you feel how much I want you," he whispered, one hand cradled her breast, then he explored its softness, the satiny warmth of her skin. "You're wonderful, taste so sweet," he said, huskily as he thoroughly licked the plumpness of one breast before he favored the other with the same wet caress. "You are driving me wild with need."

Anthia's moans quickened as he continued to lick the dark circle surrounding the prominent peak. She cried out when he took a sensitive nipple in his mouth first to wash with the rough velvet of his tongue, then to gradually apply a hot suction that nearly drove her out of her mind. Dexter soothed her as she whimpered her enjoyment.

She wasn't able to catch her breath un... ...tention to her mouth, but only for a few... ...before he moved to her other breast. His h... eyes as he concentrated on giving her the utm... the continued hot wash of his tongue until he e... ...ucked the painfully engorged peak. His lean-fingered ... ...s explored her soft bottom and slender thighs.

When his caressing fingers smoothed from the outer curve of her thigh to the petal-soft upper portion, Anthia shivered from a spiraling pleasure that just kept on coming. By the time his large masculine fingertips brushed the thick curls covering her mound, Dexter found her damp with heat. He fingered her fleshy folds until Anthia gasped as he boldly slid a finger deep inside her passage. Her whimpers of pleasure accelerated as he slowly and steadily stroked her, not easing up until she cried out upon reaching a dazzling sweet climax. Dexter held her close, his face buried in her neck until she was calm and able to breathe easily.

Then his kisses started again with drugging intensity. Anthia did not have an opportunity to collect her scattered thoughts but responded without question to him. Dexter easily lifted her and positioned her in the center of the wide bed. His body covered hers as his hypnotic kisses went on and on.

"I want you . . ." she said breathlessly, "now."

Dexter studied her beautiful deep, dark lustrous eyes. She wasn't sure what he wanted to see, but evidently he saw what he needed to see because he slowly rose and retrieved his jeans from the carpet. At her curious look, he held up the foil-wrapped package, he said, "I always carry them to give to the fellows at the center."

She flushed as he prepared his body to join with her. This was all seemed so new to her. He was no inexperienced boy. He was all man. She tried not to stiffen or tighten her body as he slid between her thighs.

"Dex . . ." her hands gripped his powerful forearms. Anthia had to close her eyes in order to contain her fears.

As a protest rose in her throat, Dexter used the bold tip of his penis to caress her between the damp folds of her femininity.

no doubts about her readiness for him. Suddenly her
went wide from the sizzling hot pleasure he gave her with
each new caress of his body against hers.

"Anthia . . ." he murmured thickly. "Look at me . . ." he
choked out around a deep, husky groan. When she complied,
he said, "I won't hurt you, baby. Let me . . . let me show you
how good it can be." When she nodded her response, he let out
a deep sigh.

As carefully and slowly as he could manage, Dexter pene-
trated her exquisitely tight sheath. She was so creamy and so
hot he had to grit his teeth against the sweetness. He held himself back, determined to give her time to adjust to his steel-hard
shaft. Anthia gasped, clinging to him. Dexter's breath came fast
and uneven as he fought his body's demand that he stroke himself to a long-awaited release. With his mouth close to her ear,
he asked "Are you all right, baby? Did I hurt you?" Anthia
shook her head, unable to voice her feelings.

It took all Dexter's willpower not to thrust. She had only
taken part of his length and he was dying to be fully sheathed
inside of her. He dropped his head to lave a hard nipple then
took it deep into his mouth, when he sucked the tip, it caused
Anthia to cry out, quivering from the sweet pleasure. Her body
instinctively tightened around him.

Unable to bear the raw craving from that tantalizing caress,
Dexter moved until he filled her completely. She whimpered
his name. He slid a hand between their bodies to stroke her
clitoris. Anthia screamed as Dexter's stroking fingertips sent
her into a heart-stopping release that in turn caused her to
tighten around him, shattering his control and sending him into
a gut-wrenching climax.

ELEVEN

For the first time in more years than he cared to count, Dexter slept soundly. The sun filtered through the peach vertical blinds when he left the warmth of Anthia's side. He did not dare linger. He showered in the peach and warm beige bathroom surrounded by her things. He smiled as he sniffed her lotion. It smelled pretty, like she did.

Anthia drew him like a moth to a flame. It was her warmth, her generous spirit that had touched the emptiness inside of him.

"Dexter?"

"Hmm?" he came toward the bed, buttoning his shirt.

"You're dressed," she complained sleepily.

"Mmm, I overslept. I'm due at Redford High at ten." He sank down beside her, caressing her cheek with one long brown finger.

"Talking to a group of boys?" she asked unable to meet his gaze.

"Yeah. Tenth graders. How are you?"

"Good," she smiled.

"So why won't you look at me?"

She found herself blushing, acutely aware of the intimacy they had shared. She had no reference point. This was the first time in her thirty-four years that she woke with a man in her bedroom. Shrugging her shoulder, she forced herself to meet his gaze.

His dark eyes studied hers before they dropped to her full

pouty lips. "That's better. Did I hurt you?" he asked pressing his mouth against hers.

"No. I'm fine." Her smile lit her lovely eyes.

"Good. You have no reason to be shy with me."

"This is so new to me," she murmured barely above an uncomfortable whisper, but he heard.

When Anthia slid into a sitting position, she was careful to keep the sheet over her breasts. He was amused by her modesty. After last night when he had devoted so much time to her soft, pretty breasts, there should be no modesty or secrets between them.

But there was still so much darkness inside of him that Dexter could never share. Nonetheless, he found he wanted to yank the sheet away. He resented even her partial withdrawal from him. Although he knew they should not have made love, Dexter could not stop himself from reaching for her twice more. He could end up hurting her and that was the last thing he wanted to do.

Now he knew how loving her could be and how perfectly her small body fit his. He had been unable to get his fill of her tight heat. Even now as he studied her sleepy lids and tousled hair, he ached to be inside her yet again.

"There seems to be one big advantage to working out of your home. No clock to punch," he said, hoping to distract himself.

"Just longer hours," she countered.

"Will I see you later? At the center tonight?"

She blinked rapidly. "Do you think I should continue?"

"Naturally. Why would you ask?"

"Things have changed, Dexter."

"We haven't. We're still the same people who cared about each other before we made love. Why should what we've shared last night change that?"

"I don't know," but Anthia knew there was a difference. She wouldn't have believed it possible, but her feelings for him had deepened even more. And it hurt more than ever knowing that he remained unchanged.

He leaned over to kiss her deeply, his tongue caressing hers. "I'll see you tonight. Would you like to go out to dinner later? Somewhere special?"

The only thing she wanted was for Dexter to return her feelings. Nothing else seemed to matter. "We'll see. 'Bye," she said as he left her alone with her turbulent thoughts.

Unwilling to linger in bed, especially after what they had shared, Anthia hurried into the bathroom. Because of the unaccustomed soreness, she soaked for a time before she dried off and dressed for the workday ahead. She purposefully pushed aside thoughts of Dexter and what they had shared. She had toast and coffee before she quickly became absorbed in her work.

It was while she smoothed the clay brow of her latest doll head that she faced the tenderness of her emotions. She hurt deep inside because she had given Dexter all her love and he had not been able to return the emotions.

There was no doubt that he desired her because he reached for her several times during the night. And he made love to her with so much care that she received the utmost pleasure. Nonetheless, she doubted his heart was engaged.

How could he have room in his heart for her when she suspected that he was still in love with his late wife? Christine was gone. No amount of wishing on his part could bring her back. The important question was would he allow himself to fall in love again?

What he valued was their friendship. Recently, Anthia had not given him a choice if he wanted to maintain any kind of contact with her. Last night making love was what they both wanted. But it hadn't changed anything. How much more evidence did she need? And how could she accept less for herself? Evidently she had no pride when she decided above all else she wanted to make love to Dexter. Nothing had been more important than the expression of that love. It was much too late to look back and wish things were different. She had made her decision and regardless of the path she had chosen for herself, must go on.

Anthia wasn't sure what to expect when she arrived at the center later that day. No one would look at her strangely, as if they were aware of the changes between her and Dexter. She would be the only one to keenly feel the difference. It was disturbing how much she had changed within a few short hours.

Her feelings for him had grown to alarming proportions. Opening her body to him had been the same as giving her soul away. A tear slowly slid down her cheek before she hastily wiped it away. As much as she cherished their lovemaking, she suspected he would remain heart whole.

In fact there was not a doubt in her mind that this evening he would revert back to the way things were before they had made love. She was so certain of it that she was willing to bet her business on it.

As he dressed for his appointment, Dexter with a heavy heart accepted what a huge mistake he'd made by giving in to his desire for Anthia. He should have followed his instincts and kept his pants zipped. His instincts had kept him alive and relatively unscathed during his five years in the prison.

He had known from the very first that he could not have Anthia. Their lovemaking had only complicated an already complicated situation. He had no way of winning this one. His shoulders slumped wearily. He would hurt her if he allowed their intimacy to continue knowing he could not give her the love she so deserved. He would also hurt her if he withdrew from what they had shared last night in her bedroom. No matter what he did, he would end up hurting her.

He couldn't even allow himself to dwell on the sweet magic he had found in Anthia's arms. Had he ever experienced such deep satisfaction? Not likely. It should not matter one way or the other. Yet, there could be no comparison. Although, he cared for her deeply, he was not in love with Anthia. He didn't feel for her what he had once felt for Christine. Nonetheless, with Anthia he had reached dazzling heights of release. His climax had been heart-stoppingly powerful.

"Hell!" he muttered as he cut himself shaving. Not once in his adult life had he lost control of his sexual needs. Last night with Anthia that had all changed. There was no logical explanation. All he knew was that his body had taken control of his head. The instant he had touched her, he had stopped thinking. He was not aware of anything outside of what had happened

between the two of them. How he had wanted her . . . wanted her with an insatiable hunger.

Anthia pleasured him to the point of madness. He totally lost it. He could not stop himself from losing himself inside of her again and again. There was no excuse for what he had done. He had taken her again and again and still longed for more.

What was he going to do? How could he prevent hurting his best friend? The one person he valued above all others. His choices were not exactly unlimited. Should he walk away from what they had shared? Should he hope to continue as before and thus risk hurting her more?

He had to be truthful, for both their sakes. If he were not careful, he could become even more involved with her than he already was. The longer he permitted her to think they had some kind of a future, the more devastating it would be for both of them. He would not be the source of her pain. He couldn't! Somehow, he would make her understand that the romantic, committed part of his life was over.

He had messed up royally! He had no business touching a woman as loving and caring as Anthia. No right whatsoever.

"Hello?"

"Hey, short stuff," Jeff laughed at his own joke. "How you doin'?"

"Watch your mouth, young man. That's no way to talk to your mother." Anthia tried to sound ticked, but her soft chuckle gave it away. "How are your classes going this week?" she asked, switching the receiver from one ear to the other.

"I'm definitely living large. An *A* on my history paper, an *A* on math quiz and an *A* on my English paper."

"That's my baby! Great. I am so proud of you, sugar."

"Aw, Ma, don't get mushy on me. Thought I would be able to get a ride home on the weekend but that fell through."

"That's all right. Don't worry about it, you don't need to be on the highway for thirteen hours every weekend."

Jeff grumbled, not pleased by her answer. "Then you need to send me some food. I'm sick to death of this cafeteria stuff."

"You did not look like you were hungry to me."

"They don't have Vernors ginger ale or those homemade apple turnovers I love. Ma! I'm serious. I need some chocolate chip cookies with walnuts."

Anthia could not help laughing. "Okay, son. Now tell me how are you doing in physical therapy? Are you still working hard at your treatments?"

"Yeah. It's going so slowly. I want to walk on my own. I am sick and tired of these crutches. You know I absolutely hate the chair," he confessed then sighed, "Sorry, Ma. I'm just frustrated."

"It's going to happen. You can't give up. Okay?"

"Yeah. Did you set Cynthia Montgomery on my tail?"

"Not that again."

"Cynthia has talked me into becoming her study partner and tutoring her. She's failing math."

"What's so wrong with seeking help when you need it? And why are you so against helping someone out? Don't tell me you've forgotten it was her father who took your civil case when he really didn't have to."

"No, I haven't forgotten. My memory isn't that short."

"Then what is your problem? When have you gotten so good that you can't help someone else? I know I raised you better than that. It's bad enough that you won't help Dexter out with . . ."

"Okay . . . okay. I'm going to help her."

"Speaking of Dexter. I'm going to give him your number. I refuse to deliver any more messages between the two of you," she warned.

"Ma!"

"If you're not going to help him out and speak to the guys at the center, then you have to tell him why, not me."

"That's not fair!"

"That's life, my son."

"How is he?"

"Busy as usual. Other than that he seems fine," she said struggling to keep her voice even. She didn't want Jeff to read anything more into it.

"How are things going between you two? From what you've told me about him taking you out to dinner when you volunteer at the center, it sounds like you two are dating."

Anthia realized she was blushing as she struggled with how much to tell her son. It wasn't like he was a baby anymore. Yet, what happened last night was so private. She was not ready to discuss Dexter or rather her feelings for him with anyone, not even her own child.

"We're friends," she said as explanation.

"That's what's new?"

"For now, yes. You know I care for him. Honey, we'd better get off the phone. I'm self-sufficient, not independently wealthy."

"It's only a matter of time considering how well your business is going. You were featured in that doll collector's magazine last month, remember?"

"Yes." The interview had garnered several new wealthy clients who were interested in buying more than one doll. "Thanks for the compliment. Take care of yourself. And keep up your exercises. Love you."

"Love you, too, Ma. Don't forget to send food. 'Bye."

" 'Bye," Anthia laughed as she hung up the telephone. Jeff sounded well, but there was something in his voice. She couldn't quite put her finger on what it was. Did it have something to do with Cynthia asking for help? It was so unlike him not to be willing to help someone else. Or maybe that was the old Jeff she was thinking of. He had been through so much these past few years. And yet, he was a survivor. He was also a good, loving person.

Lately, he had gotten too good at isolating himself. Despite what he said, Anthia was glad that the Montgomery girl had sought him out. Jeff may not realize it, but he needed friends. Perhaps more now than ever before.

That question about Dexter had really thrown her for a moment. Had she been obvious? Was she wearing her feelings for the man on her sleeve? Could others sense her vulnerability where he was concerned? Worse yet, had Dexter guessed how deeply she cared for him? Anthia shivered uncomfortably at the thought. No she didn't even want to think about that right now. It was too unsettling.

Anthia kept herself extremely busy. In spite of the late start, she managed to get quite a bit accomplished. Even as she put the finishing touches on two new dolls, then prepared them for shipment, Dexter was never far from her thoughts.

Hurrying into her room to freshen up and prepare for her long night at the center, she realized that she was nervous about seeing Dexter. Her glance lingered on the freshly made queen-size bed. Her heart pounded with excitement as she recalled their lovemaking.

Nothing in her experience had prepared her for the intensity and thoroughness of Dexter's lovemaking. First he had aroused her to the point of madness, then he had given her such indescribable pleasure. He was so very male, so virile. Her pleasure often came before his. And when his release came, Anthia cherished those moments when he shuddered in her arms, his throaty shout thrilling because he'd called her name. That had to mean something, didn't it?

After only one night with Dexter, she recognized that she had had sex with Jeff's father but she had made love with Dexter. Finally she knew the difference and it was because of Dexter. They had truly made love.

Everything would be near perfect if only he could open himself up and let go of his painful past. It was true that he'd warned her that part of his life was over. Nonetheless, she could not quite make herself believe it. She could not seem to give up hope that things would, someday work out for them. It was all she had to hang on to . . . to believe in.

Oh, she realized that a part of him had died when he buried his wife and child. It was possible that someday he just might allow himself to grow close to another woman. More than anything, Anthia wanted to be that woman.

What if he had given all he had to give last night? What then? Was it enough? If she wanted him, Anthia had no choice but to accept Dexter as he was. As long as she kept her feet planted on solid ground, then she would be all right. Her common sense had to prevail. She could not afford to get carried away emo-

tionally because of one special night of loving. Now all she had
to do was figure out how.

As she studied herself in the full-length mirror behind the
bathroom door, dressed in ivory slacks and a long-sleeve, lace-
yoke and high collared ivory blouse, she could not stop her
heart from speeding up at the thought of being near him once
again. Gold citrine studs glimmered in her ears, while a citrine
tennis bracelet set in fourteen-karate gold encircled her slender
wrist, but as her gaze touched her left hand, Anthia couldn't
help daydreaming that Dexter's ring might one day be there

There was no doubt that he was firmly lodged in her heart.
A touch of mascara and a brush of cherry-red lipstick and she
told herself she was ready for anything. Even if he withdrew
into himself as he often did when he was disturbed, she could
handle it. Or if he tried to pretend nothing had happened between them, she was prepared. The one thing he had better be
prepared for was that she was not willing to pretend.

There was no way she was willing to go back in time. They
had been intimate last night. They were no longer just friends,
but lovers. Things were different between them. The sooner he
accepted that, the better it would be for both of them. She was
not the same woman she had been before she had laid in his
arms. She was unwilling to even entertain the idea of being
only friends. If that was what he expected of her, he was in for
a rude awakening. They shared too much.

TWELVE

"The prime rib not to your liking?" Dexter asked eyeing Anthia's plate. They were seated in a plush Southfield restaurant.

"Just not very hungry," she said taking a sip from her water goblet. It had been a emotionally draining evening.

Dexter had been away from the center most of the night. He and Charles Randol had been out in the community, trying to locate one of the two young men that gang members had come to the center looking for. Guy Malone had been left in charge to oversee basketball practice, computer classes and tutoring sessions that had been scheduled for that evening.

It saddened Anthia, knowing that some of the older boys were on their own. More often than not, they rented rooms from rooming houses. They had no family to speak of. No one to care if they stayed in school or became involved in the gang scene.

"You're not doing so well yourself." He'd barely tasted his own food. "You have to stop blaming yourself. You did everything you could," she ended softly.

They hadn't found the boy in the tiny one-bedroom apartment he shared with his grandmother but in Sinai Hospital. He had been badly beaten, shot in the side and left to die in a deserted alley.

"Craig was lucky. They could have killed him if they wanted. They were sending a message to the others not to try to find a way out," Dexter said with a scowl. "We have a proven method of help and support, yet too damn many kids still choose the streets. Why? I just don't understand it. There are ways out of poverty other than crime. Damn it, it doesn't have to be this way."

Anthia reached out to Dexter, squeezed his hand reassuringly. As he knew, there were no easy answers and she didn't waste their time trying to find one. It said a lot that he was willing to risk his own safety time after time again in order to help others. He was one of a kind, a rare gem, in her opinion.

"I just hope he pulls through."

"He will," Dexter said stubbornly. "He's young and he's strong. He's got to be all right."

Anthia could not help recalling the struggle it had been for her own son to recover from having been shot. She shuddered, remembering the agony and fear she had faced as she waited in the hospital for word.

Dexter turned his hand until their fingers interlaced. It was the first time he had touched her all evening. Her beautiful, dark eyes collided with his.

"We haven't had any privacy," he said softly. He couldn't stop himself from asking, "How are you?"

She blinked quickly in surprise before she said, "I'm fine."

"I hurt you last night. And I didn't stop with once. Are you terribly tender?"

Anthia's cheeks were so hot that she wanted to hide her face as she flushed with embarrassment. "I'm fine," she managed before she chose a less personal topic. "Are you going back to the hospital tonight?"

If Dexter was surprised by the question, he did not show it. "Yeah. His grandmother isn't strong enough to stay with him through the night. He needs someone."

"And he has you," Anthia smiled, feeling a sudden urge to press her lips to his. His compassion was only one reason why she cared so deeply for him. Dexter was a very special man who lived as he believed. There was no double standard with him.

She reached into her purse and handed him a peach note card. "Jeff's number. When you have some time, would you please talk to him about speaking at the center? I think he's making a mistake by isolating himself. He needs friends both male and female."

"Of course," his eyes lingered on her small African features. Her skin was so rich, flawless like a creamy brown chocolate. She was like that all over. He blinked trying to clear his head of the enticing memory. His voice was huskier than he would like when he asked, "All set?"

He had not been given a chance to say what was on his mind. In truth, he hadn't really had time to sort it all out himself. One night of this petite woman's lovemaking and he was hungrier than he'd ever been in his entire life. Could he walk away from what they had found in each other's arms? More importantly, did he even have the strength to try?

This thing with Craig was almost a relief, not that he wanted the boy hurt. Nevertheless, it gave him something to focus on outside of himself. He needed time . . . time to evaluate their situation with some prospective.

He was too close to it right now . . . too vulnerable were she was concerned. He almost laughed aloud. He certainly thought he knew what was best that morning when he left her bed, satiated for the first time since he'd lost Christine. Anthia made their lovemaking special . . . sizzling hot loving coupled with a powerful release.

"I'm ready," she said collecting her things before rising.

Dexter found his hands lingering on her shoulders even after he'd helped her into her tangerine swing coat. He had to force himself to focus on the obvious, like dropping a bill on the table and following her out without his interested gaze lingering on the soft, sexy sway of her hips. Hot damn! The girl knew she had a man-catching walk. She attracted men like flies to flypaper . . . without any effort on her part. He was as hard and randy as the next guy. For he never tired of just looking at her.

Outside in the restaurant parking lot, Anthia paused to say, "Good luck with Craig. I will keep him in my prayers." She reached up on tiptoes to briefly brush her soft mouth against his before she slipped behind the steering wheel of her car.

A muscle worked rhythmically in his cheek as he fought to control his natural urge to take her in his arms and never let her go. He closed her car door with a deceptive quietness. What he really wanted was to slam the damn thing as hard as he could.

Was that peck designed to appease him? Didn't the woman know the difference between a man and a boy? If she found it necessary to kiss him, why hadn't she opened her sweet mouth under his and given him the tonguing he craved?

As was his custom, Dexter followed her home. When she hopped out of her car, he was only a few steps behind her. His gaze dark and brooding.

"Dex? I thought you were on your way to the hospital?"

"I thought you knew how to kiss a man. I don't like being teased," he snapped, before he dropped his head, hungrily covering her mouth with his.

Legs spread, he lifted her into the cradle of his thighs. He moaned deep in his throat as he thrust his tongue between her full, perfectly formed lips into the honeyed depths of her mouth. His arms tightened around her until her sweet curves were pressed into his hard, aching length. She had not been teasing last night when she opened her soft thighs for him. How could she expect him to accept less now? His earlier decision temporarily forgotten as he indulged his senses.

After years of loneliness, Dexter could not deny himself this tiny bit of pleasure. Anthia was all he desired in a woman. She was petite, but she pleased him, pleasured him to the brink of madness. Last night, she had belonged to him.

"Dex." she whispered against his mouth, her hard-nippled breasts soft against the wall of his chest. He was driving her out of her mind with longing. The memory of his intense loving made her eager for more. He had driven his steel-hard length into her until she literally came apart in his arms. The experience had been breath-takingly wondrous. She'd never experienced a climax until she made love with Dexter. Talk about rocking her world! He had done that and more.

Dexter released her before she did something insane like rub her sex against his in plain view of her neighbors who might happen to look their way.

She whispered, "Let's finish this inside."

As the sensual haze cleared, he was disgusted with himself.
He'd gone against his own best judgment. He had allowed his
sexual hunger to do his thinking for him. Damn it, it never
happened this way with any woman, only Anthia.

Cupping her elbow, he silently urged her toward the door.
Using her keys, he was grateful for the space it put between
them. When she was in his arms, his brain stopped functioning
and his hormones went into fast-forward.

"Don't you need to disengage the alarm?" he asked hoarsely.

"Yes . . ." she answered as if coming awake from a deep
sleep. After punching in the code, she turned back to him. But
to her disappointment, he made no move to take her back into
his arms. "Must you go?" she whispered.

"Yeah."

She nodded, then said as she boldly moved back to where
she longed to be, "Why don't you stop over before you go on
home in the morning? I'd be glad to give you breakfast . . . a
back rub . . . whatever you need."

Dexter had no trouble reading the blush on her soft brown
face or the sensuous desire in her velvety dark eyes. What man
in his right mind could resist her? She was everything he could
want in a woman. He tried not to think of how much he wanted
her or how many ways he would like to make love to her, take
her until she screamed his name as she climaxed. He had to
remind himself yet again that there were other considerations.

Where Anthia's happiness was concerned, it mattered to him.
He didn't want to see her hurt and he couldn't bear the thought
of him being the source of that hurting. She deserved the best
that life had to offer . . . the very best. She deserved a man that
could give her his name and his babies, but most of all, his
heart.

He did not need to be reminded that he had completely lost
his head last night. He was still on the shaky ground. If he
continued to let his libido do his thinking for him, he would
end up hurting her a little more each and every time they made
love. How could he do that to her?

He had nothing to offer her . . . other than his friendship. He
had no choice but to tell her . . . tell her now.

"Anthia."

"Honey . . ."

Before she could move any closer, he grated harshly, "I was wrong last night. I lost control and took total advantage of the situation. I let my erection do my thinking for me. For that I apologize."

"Apologize . . ." was all that she was able stammer aloud. Her thoughts raced as she stared up at him as if her heart was breaking. It certainly felt as if it had crumbled into too many pieces to count . . . all piled in an aching heap at his feet.

"Anthia, if you could try to . . ."

"No! Don't say it," she said holding her hand up as if to stop the flow of his words. All she knew was that she had given him all she had to give and he was tossing it carelessly away as if it meant nothing to him . . . nothing.

"How can you say this now when you clearly wanted me last night. You can't even tell me that you didn't want me. We made love several times, Dexter."

"I never said I didn't want you. I had no right to take advantage of our friendship like I did. No, right at all!" he grated impatiently.

"I gave you the right. I welcomed you into my home . . . into my bed . . . into my body. What is this? Why was it so wrong? We were both consenting adults, not children." Her voice shook from emotion.

Dexter stood with his hands balled at his side, struggling with himself. What could he say? How could he explain it to her when he wasn't even sure he understood himself.

"That first time was so exciting . . . you shuddered in my arms, but the times after were so wonderfully sweet and satisfying. I had my first climax with you, Dexter because you took your time with me. You made me feel so special . . . so cared about, baby."

He swore beneath his breath, refusing to voice how deeply her revelation touched him. He was already semi-aroused just thinking about being inside of her. She turned him on big time. But he was more than a sexual being, he was a man who valued her as a person.

"Don't you think I was flattered that you let me make love to you?" He choked out past the constriction in his throat. "This is about more than mutually gratifying sex. This is about genuine caring. Anthia, we can't fall in love with each other. You know why it can't work."

Fury built inside of her to such proportions that she wanted to throw something, preferably at his big old head. How could one man be so blind? She knew he cared for her, but she also knew he flatly refused to let himself love her.

"We've been over this before . . ."

She interrupted, "And you know I think you're so wrong. You're letting what happened in the past destroy any chance that we might have for future happiness. We only go through life one time, Dexter Washington. Don't you want to feel whole again . . . complete?"

"Naturally, I do, but . . ."

"Well you're not going to have it as long as you let the past get in the way. Not with me, not with anyone!"

"I made a terrible mistake, Anthia. Nothing you or I can do will change what happened. Our being together was no little thing. I . . ."

"It was an accident. Christine's death was not your fault. Why can't you get that through your thick skull?"

"Because it may not be the truth. The fact remains that my wife and child are gone. Don't you see, as long as there's doubt I can't be free of it."

"You won't let yourself forget. You've decided to pay for it with the rest of your life by denying yourself any kind of happiness," she said candidly.

"That's not what I'm doing!"

"That's exactly what you're doing."

Frustrated by his inability to make her understand, he said wearily, "You deserve the best. A man who can give you his whole heart. A man without any emotional baggage constantly mucking the waters."

Anthia had been prepared for this. She knew him well enough to realize that he would not let himself be happy or celebrate what they had. She had suspected that he might regret their intimacy. It had been in his eyes that morning. In his voice at dinner. Nonetheless, she felt a keen sense of disappointment.

She had fought her own fears and tried to find the best way to handle the situation, without allowing it to hurt her. She'd failed. She felt as if he had constructed a brick wall around his heart and her hands were bloody from trying to pull them down one by one.

While she gained joy from their coming together, Dexter had experienced something entirely different. To Anthia it had been a natural expression of what she felt for him. Despite the fact that her sexual experiences were limited, she knew what they had shared was very special, something to be treasured.

His caring was in the determined way he put her needs ahead of his own. His tenderness was in the way he held her, cradling her close to his heart. His anguish was unmistakable.

"I don't want to lose you, Anthia."

"You'd rather I pretend that we didn't make love," she accused.

Dexter let out a deep, heavy sigh, after glancing wearily at his watch, he said, "Please, can we discuss this later. I have to get to the hospital. I gave my word."

The last thing Anthia wanted to do was postpone their discussion. She longed to say, "Right here, right now," but she wisely decided not to push the issue. What would it hurt to give herself more time to think it through?

"Good night."

Although Dexter studied her soft pretty mouth, he made no attempt to kiss her, again. He settled for squeezing her hand before he left. "Bye."

Anthia was surprised at how much control she exhibited as she closed the door and locked it behind him. She would like nothing better than to scream her frustration at Dexter. She was furious with him. It felt as if he had tossed her love right back in her face.

Did he have any idea how deeply he had hurt her? How badly it made her feel about them . . . what they had shared? She would have rather he kept the information to himself.

She couldn't ignore the regret she had seen in his eyes . . .

She had not wanted to accept it this morning or now. She had known going in that there was a risk. A big risk. It was not as if he had not always been open with her about his feelings. Nonetheless, she wanted to blame him. She needed to place her keen disappointment at his door.

It had taken years to find a man she could trust and believe in. Her mistake had been quite simple. She thought she could trust him with her love. How could she have been so foolish?

Evidently, he had shared only his superb male body with her. When their sexual encounter was over, he was also finished. He could walk away with a clear conscious. He had done what any man would have done. He had merely taken what had been offered.

"Dexter . . . why can't you give us a chance?" That was all she really wanted, a fair chance.

But she had known. She had known all along. What had she been trying to do? Had she hoped to trap him? Was that what all this was about? Had she wanted him so badly that she was willing to do whatever it took to keep him?

Anthia moaned in misery. Surely, she was not that naive, that desperate for a man. She walked into her bedroom without bothering to switch on the lamps, sank dejectedly onto her bed. It was nothing new. Women had been making fools of themselves over men since the beginning of time.

Slowly, she replayed their night together in her mind. Her hunger for him had matched his for her. Was he also denying that? How could there be any doubt that what they had done was make love to each other. It had been a mutually enjoyable experience that had left them both breathless from the sheer wonder of it. They had both been equal participants.

As she hugged her knees to her chest, Anthia accepted that she had nothing to be ashamed of. Dexter had made love to her through the night. When he had left in the morning he had been semi-aroused.

In spite of his own personal tragedy, Dexter had wanted her. That had to have meant something. It had to be a good sign. He was not as immune to her as he wanted her to believe. It had not been easy for him to tell her what he had told her tonight.

"Where's your backbone, girl?" she mumbled aloud. She had been the one who raised her son alone after her mother's death. She had been the one to turn away from a job that lacked creativity and fulfillment to finally do what she genuinely loved. She'd started her own business and she was making a success of it.

No, she had done nothing wrong by giving and receiving love from the one man she respected and adored. He was her best friend. The one who had stood by her through the most traumatic time of her son's life. With God's grace and Dexter's support, she had made it through. He cared deeply for her.

What he was doing was running scared. He was the one allowing the past to come between them. He was the one not able to admit to himself that he had strong emotions where she was concerned. No matter how vehemently he denied it, he was as needy for love as the next person. It was what he sought from her even if he were not able to admit it.

As much as he had hurt her, she instinctively knew that now was not the time to give up on him. Life was just too unpredictable to throw away that special magic that they shared simply because it made them vulnerable to each other.

Why couldn't Dexter see that? Why wasn't he willing to risk trying again? He had been hurt badly in the past, but so had she. Anthia had known the hurt and disappointment of loving someone who did not return the emotions.

It was true that she had never suffered a tragic loss like the one he had experienced, nor had she paid the ultimate price by giving up years of her life like he had. Somehow, she had to help him see that his personal life was far from over. He had no right to give up on his own chance at happiness.

Anthia was forced to acknowledge that no matter how badly she wanted things to be different for them, Dexter was not in the same emotional place as she was. He had endured more heartache that any one man deserved.

Maybe, she was the one asking for heartache. Nevertheless, she could not turn her back on him. He was such a compassionate man, who had dedicated his life to helping others. He was worth all the hell he was putting her through. He was worth much, much more. No, she was not quite ready to give up on them. She loved him too much. And she knew she had an uphill battle ahead of her.

THIRTEEN

"What are you scowling at?" Anthia kept her smile firmly in place when she walked into the center's office. She was determined to conceal her disappointment that Dexter had not stopped by on Saturday morning after his night at the hospital with Craig or Sunday for that matter. She had been forced to wait until Monday evening to even see him. "How's Craig?"

Dexter's dark gaze, tenderly glided over her smooth brown features, lingering on her generous raspberry-tinted mouth before moving down the slender slope of her neck to linger in the sweet-scented hollow at the base of her throat. He recalled how responsive she had been to him as he licked her there . . . she had let out a soft, sexy moan that had caused his senses to flare even more.

She had quivered when he cupped her soft breasts, gasping his name when he had gently squeezed her dark nipples between his fingers. They were a deep rich brown, the color of bittersweet chocolate. They had puckered even more when he'd taken each in turn into his mouth and laved each thoroughly before he suckled.

He frowned, her rose, long-sleeve blouse hid all her ripe beauty from his hungry gaze. Nevertheless his eyes caressed her softness, keenly aware of the sensitivity of those ripe peaks. He swallowed a groan as his sex surged painfully against his fly and his tongue came out to moisten suddenly dry lips.

"Dexter . . ." she said, as she attempted to ignore the heat of his blatant masculine scrutiny. She worked at settling her fluttering nerves as she sat down behind the desk across from his and stowed her purse in the bottom drawer. She wore a black knee-length skirt and high heels rather than her customary slacks and loafers, ". . . you're scaring me. Craig's going to be all right, isn't he?"

Dexter recovered himself enough to say, "He's in pretty bad shape. I spent most of the weekend at the hospital. He's going to make it. But his recovery time is going to be lengthy."

"His legs?"

"About the only thing that is working. His internal injuries are extensive."

"Thank heavens he's out of the gang. They won't hurt him anymore, will they?" she asked hopefully.

"Let's hope not." He dragged his gaze down to the engraved invitation in front of him.

"What is it?" she asked, her curiosity getting the better of her.

"Here," he got up and brought it over to her. His displeasure was written all over his bronze face.

Anthia read it, then said, "A wedding invitation? This has you scowling as if you've lost your best friend?"

Dexter winced, that was exactly what he had been wondering all weekend. Had he lost his best friend? Had he lost Anthia because of his inability to control his sexual desire for her? Just the thought of her not being in his life was almost too painful to consider. He had made a serious mistake when . . .

"Well?" she prompted bringing him back to the matter at hand. "Are you going?"

"It's not just a wedding, Anthia. It's my sister's wedding. She expects me to attend."

"I don't see the problem."

"First of all, it's in Houston. I haven't had any contact with my family in years. I'm not exactly an upstanding member of society. My father made himself clear at my trial. He no longer has a son." The sound of bitterness was evident in his deep tone.

"Because of what happened with . . ."

"Exactly," he interjected, not wanting to hear his wife's name.

It still hurt too much. Hell! He was sick and tired of hurting. The strained relationship between himself and his father was something he did his best not to dwell on. His late wife's death had ripped even the polite facade he and his father maintained over the years.

"Wait a minute. I thought you grew up in Detroit." She naturally knew about his faint accent but had attributed it to the years he spent in Texas while in college.

His nodded. "I did. Born and raised in Detroit until my mother passed. My parents met here while my dad was in college. She waited tables in a small restaurant near Wayne State campus. To put it bluntly, my father married her because I was on the way. They were together as long as he was in Michigan. When he returned home to Houston, he was traveling alone."

"How old were you when your mother died?"

"Thirteen. That's when I moved to Houston to live with my father."

"That must have been difficult for you especially at that age." Her sympathetic smiled was like a soothing balm.

For a moment, Dexter could not look away from her dark lovely eyes. Finally, he said, "It was."

"I'm sorry. Evidently your sister doesn't feel the same as her folks."

He smiled then, the first she had seen that day. It caused her heart to race in response. Handsome did not describe his hard angular, striking good looks. His brown features were keen, his lips wide and sensuous. Anthia hastily looked away.

In another minute, she would be begging for his sizzling hot kisses . . . his lovemaking. The last two nights without him had been unbearably lonely. One night of his lovemaking had her hungry for more. It was ridiculous considering she had been celibate for so many years.

"Stephanie doesn't let anything stop her from doing what she feels is right. She has stuck by me from the first. You might say, we adopted each other when my father married her mother."

"How old was she?"

"That was fifteen years ago. That would make her fourteen. She's twenty-nine now. I imagine my stepmother is putting on the dog for this one. No holding back. It'll cost the old man plenty." The thought pleased him.

"Are you going?"

Dexter stared at her as if he were weighing the matter. He was quiet for so long she wonder if he was going to ignore the question. Finally, he said, "I don't know how I can avoid it. Stephanie will be crushed if I don't come. I don't want her upset."

"You're a sweet brother," Anthia longed to touch him, but thought better of it.

"I'm a fool for even thinking about going."

"Don't say that. You're doing this for your sister. This is her day. It's only natural that you want everything to be perfect for her sake." Anthia encouraged.

"Yeah. She was the one who wrote to me while I was incarcerated, who came to visit me even against the family's wishes. She's what helped keep me sane all those years." He glanced at Anthia. "She is a lot like you, full of enthusiasm and understanding. Nothing ever gets her down for long." He said thoughtfully, "She deserves to be happy. I just hope she has found the right man."

"Have you met him?"

"No. All I have to go on is what she's told me."

"This will be your opportunity to check him out for yourself."

"As long as he treats her well, he and I won't have a problem."

"I think you'll be glad you decided to go."

"Come with me."

"Huh?"

"You heard me." His gaze collided with hers. "Anthia, I'd like you to come. It can be a long, leisurely weekend for both of us. Give us a chance to relax and enjoy a change of scenery."

"But . . ." she stopped abruptly because she would like nothing more than to be with him. Perhaps, it was what they both needed, some uninterrupted time alone. Time to really get to know each other. Could she shatter his defenses? Did she dare even hope? Was she willing to take the risk?

"Anthia, how long has it been since you've been on vacation? I've known you for more than two years. I don't recall you taking one."

"I'm always too busy trying to earn a living."

"Then it's time you had one. There is nothing like Houston in the spring. Say you'll come," he persisted unwilling to even consider going without her. He surprised her when he said softly, "I need you with me."

Unable to resist his appeal, she whispered, "I'll come." It certainly couldn't make things worse between them. It could only help.

He reached for her hand, then caught himself in time before he could brush her soft knuckles against his lips. He held it clasped in his own. "Thanks," he said somewhat gruffly.

"Excuse me . . ." Tina Douglas, stood in the open doorway awkwardly, glaring at the two of them. "I didn't mean to interrupt. Dexter, I brought you some homemade lemon cake."

"Hi, Tina," Anthia said, snatching her hand away from his as if they'd been caught in a compromising position.

Dexter had to force his eyes away from Anthia before he could acknowledge the younger woman. "That was nice of you. Thanks," he said, accepting the offering. "I didn't expect you back. Don't you have classes at Wayne County?"

Tina was all smiles when it came to Dexter. "Yes, just thought I'd stop in for a few minutes. Is there anything I can do for you before I take off?" She offered Anthia nothing more than a glare. She did not have to say the words, she clearly didn't like the idea of Anthia being anywhere near Dexter.

"No, thanks. Well, I better get back to the gym. The kids can't have a karate lesson without the instructor. 'Night, Tina," he said before leaving.

The silence was heavy between the two women as they studied each other. There was no doubt in either one of their minds that Dexter was the problem. He was seeing far too much of Anthia and Tina did not like it.

"Are you dati. . . ." the sound of the ringing telephone intruded on Tina's question.

Anthia was relieved. Her relationship with Dexter was not

open for discussion. Lifting the receiver, she said, "Malcolm X Community Center. How may I help you?"

A thoroughly infuriated Tina did not bother to wait for the older woman to finish, she turned on her heels and went out the door without so much as a backward glance.

Jeff was not only frustrated, but annoyed with Cynthia. For their first study session in the library, she had brought along her beautiful roommate Cora Denton. Jeff did not welcome the distraction. Cora was busy locating material for an upcoming political history term paper. Cora was hardly a stranger. It was a small campus and she and Jeff had taken a class together last term. There was no way Jeff could have forgotten the shapely beauty.

Cora had made an impact on him just by walking into the library. She, like Cynthia, came from a well-to-do family, only in Cora's case outside of Atlanta. The two girls shared an off-campus apartment. Both had pretty brown skin, that was where the similarities ended. Cora's blatant curves were enough to have caught and held his interest but her quick intellect and easy smile captivated him. Half the fellows on campus were trying to get a date with her. Yet, she didn't date, which was a real puzzle as far as Jeff was concerned. Why not when she could have her pick? The last thing he needed was this kind of aggravation.

"Jeff? Is it right?" Cynthia asked

He just grunted impatiently. "Why don't you get your roommate to tutor you? It couldn't be more convenient."

Cynthia laughed. "Believe me, she has tried but it's hopeless. Cora has no patience."

"The problem may not be hers," he said dryly.

"Jeff!" she wailed, then covered her mouth guiltily when others shushed her. She whispered with that teasing light dancing in her dark gray eyes, "Don't get upset. Just explain it one more time."

"Did I hear my name?" Cora looked from one to the other as she joined them at their table.

"Just telling the simple truth," Cynthia teased. Nothing seemed to get her down, she seemed to keep a smile firmly fixed on her face.

The next two hours moved painfully slow from Jeff's vantage point. He didn't make an effort to move when the girls began collecting their things. He hadn't gotten much of anything done. He'd been too busy dragging his gaze from Cora's lovely light brown eyes and soft peach-tinted lips.

"Aren't you coming?" Cynthia asked.

He shook his head. "I've got work to do." He didn't explain that he could have easily put it off. He was carrying *A's* in all his classes. He could have skipped one night, but he was also self-conscious. No way did he want Cora focusing on his awkward sometime jerky movements especially after sitting for so long. He'd really be stiff when he got up.

"I'll give you a lift to your dorm," Cynthia offered.

Jeff suddenly remembered he didn't have his chair outside waiting for him. His roommate had dropped him off before heading over to his girlfriend's apartment. Stupid! He'd never made it back to the dorm under his own power.

"Okay," he said gruffly. He was furious with himself. He did not need pity. He forced himself to look away. He hated being dependent on others. He hated everything about his disability. Right then he felt so disgusted with himself that he almost told them to leave him the hell alone. Common sense prevailed. He quickly packed his backpack and put on his jacket before grabbing his crutches.

The walk to the car was painfully slow. He made no comment whatsoever. The girls gave up trying to include him in the conversation after a few of his single word answers. He knew he was acting like a jerk but he couldn't seem to help it.

While Cora and Cynthia chatted in the front seat of Cynthia's sports car, Jeff brooded in the back. He was in a towering rage by the time he mumbled his thanks and clumsily made it up the walkway. He made a point to slam the outside door with all the force of the frustration he'd been holding inside all evening.

He was still on edge when the telephone rang at his bedside the next morning. He had a very restless night. He dreams were

full of Cora's continuous laughter. He woke knowing she'd been laughing at him.

"Yeah . . ." he grumbled into the telephone.

"Jeff?"

"Dexter?"

"Yeah. How are you?"

"Good. Nothing wrong with Mama, is there?" he asked anxiously.

"No . . . she's fine."

"Okay," he said, his heart rate returned to a normal beat. For a moment all he could think of was something was wrong. "What can I do for you?"

"Thought I'd check up on you. How are classes? Your mom said your grades were great."

"Yeah. I'm working at it. Are you and Mom dating?"

There was a hesitation before Dexter said, "We're friends . . . good friends."

"Are you sleeping with her?"

"That's between the two of us, but I think you know how deeply I respect and care for her."

"I don't want her hurt."

"Naturally. And I understand how you feel. Your mother means a lot to me, Jeff. She's a very special lady." Dexter cleared his throat before he went on to say, "So what's going on with you? Why won't you help us out at the center? We need you, man."

Jeff closed his eyes, giving himself time to think before he answered. Dexter knew him so well. He didn't want to reveal his innermost fears. "I wish I could, but I can't."

"Some of the new guys are really young. They're the ones most at risk."

"Look, there are others guys who've been shot before that you can ask."

"Yeah. And they're using those wounds like victory trophies, as if it's something to be proud of. They have that gang mentality so ingrained that they can't see what's really there. We don't need that kind of help. I need you, Jeff."

"I can't . . ."

"You won't."

Jeff clenched his jaw. "Let's drop it, okay."

"Think about it . . ."

He bit out harshly, "Drop it!" He could hear the other man's heavy sigh.

"There was a time when we could talk about anything. That wasn't that long ago."

"Yeah, I know. You've been a good friend. Mom and I both came to depend on you, Dex. Man, I can't stay in that same spot. I have to move on."

"Sure you do, but I hope that doesn't mean we stop caring about each other. If you need to talk, I'm here for you. As you well know there are things you might not be able to talk to your mother about."

Cora's pretty face flashed through his mind. Jeff scowled with indecision. He had so many doubts, questions that he hadn't asked the doctors . . . deep personal fears he couldn't share with his mother. Yes, he had missed Dexter . . . missed their closeness. "Thanks," he whispered his voice raw with emotion.

Dexter evidently sensed something, for he said, "I mean it. Your life has changed a lot in the past couple of years. Things you took for granted are no longer there for you."

"Uh-huh."

"You've handled yourself well, my man. I'm proud of you."

There was a prolonged silence as Jeff struggled to control his emotions. Dexter's opinion of him mattered. There was no getting around that.

"You seeing anyone?"

"Hey, I'm still in a wheelchair part of the time with no guarantee I'll ever be completely free of it."

"What does that have to do with dating? The last time I looked you weren't butt-ugly."

Jeff hedged, "I prefer not to get involved."

"Why?"

"What is this? It's enough to say I have my reasons."

"Teenagers can be insensitive. I know that. Come on, my man. You'd better believe there's some young lady down there who thinks you're good enough to spend your money on her. What's so complicated about a date?"

"It's more complicated than just dating," Jeff ended on a somewhat ragged tone.

"Such as?"

"Me! I don't need people feeling sorry for me, especially females. I can't handle that."

"You're a man. What's to feel sorry about? You're legs aren't what makes you a man. Your heart and soul have not changed. If some gal has a problem with your legs then it's her own problem. Let her own it. It's not your issue!"

"That's easy for you to say but almost impossible to do."

"You've already proven yourself. You've gotten through years of therapy without feeling sorry for yourself. Remember, how far you've come. You've been flat on your back, unable to do no more than lift your head. Have you forgotten?" Dexter asked.

"Not hardly," Jeff shot back, recalling the emotional and physical struggle he had endured. It was not over yet.

"With God's grace you have no limits, my man, except for those you put in your own way."

Jeff swallowed back the tears lodged in his throat. "You're right. I've learned that the hard way. How could I have forgotten?"

"You haven't. Its there inside of you. You just have to look for it."

"Yeah."

"Now about the center . . ."

Jeff laughed. "I'll think about it. Glancing at the clock he said, "Look, Dex, I've got class in an hour and I still have to go over my notes."

"Okay. We'll talk again soon. You know you can call me anytime.

"Thanks, Dex. 'Bye."

" 'Bye."

Jeff sighed, wishing he could verbalize his fears. Somehow the telling would make it too real . . . even more painful. His hands were trembling when he put the receiver down. Geez! Dexter had hit too close to the truth. He was running scared and did not think he could deal with even the possibility of rejection.

Cora was a very special young lady. From what he heard, she came from a very wealthy family and she was a year older than he. She was too popular. What chance did he have?

Then there were questions, personal questions that he had no way of knowing the answers to without putting himself in a very embarrassing situation. No, it wouldn't solve anything to share this with anyone, not even Dexter.

FOURTEEN

Dexter, having locked the center's rear door, had taken no more than a step away when someone stepped out from behind concealing shrubs. Without conscious thought, his body automatically went into the classic martial arts defense mode as he prepared to attack.

"Tina!" he gasped, forcing himself to relax and slow the energy force. "What are doing here? I could have hurt you."

"I need to talk to you."

"It's after midnight. Why didn't you come into the center? Why were you waiting out here in the dark?"

The crisp night air swept against his face forcing him to raise the collar of his leather jacket and shove his hands into his pockets. It was a cloudy night, even the moon was hidden.

"I wanted to talk to you privately. I never get the opportunity at the center," her mouth twisted somewhat bitterly.

"Is something wrong? Are you hurt?" His glance ran swiftly over her tall, slender length. There was no visible injury that he could detect.

"You're always so busy."

Dexter was tired and hungry, not in the best of moods. Anthia had refused his dinner invitation, yet again. She left earlier with the others. He'd hoped tonight would have been different, the first time he asked her out in nearly a week since she agreed to accompany him to his sister's wedding.

Despite his resolve, he had been without Anthia's sweet loving for too blasted long and he was feeling cheated. He literally ached for her sweetness, her warmth. Hell, he hadn't had a decent amount of sleep since the night she slept in his arms, her softness pressed against his side. His mood had gone downhill steadily. As time went on, it wasn't getting any better.

"What is it? A problem at home?"

She shivered inside her thin raincoat. "I want to know what's going on between you and Anthia Jenkins. I've seen the way you look at her. Are you sleeping with her?"

"What!" He stared at her. He couldn't believe her nerve. Swallowing down his temper, he said quietly, "My personal life is none of your business, Tina. As far as Anthia and I are concerned our relationship is not open for discussion . . . not ever."

He was clearly offended. He had always been a private person. Since he lost both his wife and child, he had been even more so. The mere thought of openly revealing his feelings for Anthia was unthinkable.

"I care about you! Dexter, I could make you happy. I know I could," Tina said. Her smooth light brown forehead was creased with agitation.

Dexter sighed wearily, shifting from one foot to the other. He did not have the patience to deal with this silliness. Tina was a sweet kid, but she was just that, a child in his estimation. She was barely twenty years old and had her entire life ahead of her. He had no interest in dating children.

Careful, not to hurt her feelings, he said cautiously, "I'm sorry, Tina. I don't think of you in that way. With all these young fellows around here, what do you want with an old man like me?"

"I love you. You're the only one I can talk to. You always listen." Tina's eyes filled with tears, but she quickly blinked them away. It was not the time for crying. She needed to think clearly . . . make him understand how much he meant to her. She wasn't a child! Why couldn't he see that?

"It's late, Tina. Do you need a ride home?"

"Yes," she nodded. "Please." It took all her resolve to control her emotions. He wasn't willing to even consider having a relationship with her. It hurt that he wasn't even taking her seriously.

As he walked with her across the deserted parking lot, Dexter kept up a steady flow of conversation, choosing the neutral topic of the center. He held the passenger door open for her before moving around the car and settling himself behind the steering wheel. He was weak with relief when they reached the small house Tina shared with her mother. They lived in the bottom of a two-family flat not too far from the community center.

"Dexter, please. You have not given this any thought. I know you care about me. You've taken time with me. If it were not for you, I would not have gone back to school and be working finished my GED. You gave me a chance to work at the center. I know you care. Why won't you admit it?"

"Tina. Yes, I care about you. I care about all the kids I work with at the center." Dexter had no patience for this kind of thing, but he didn't want to destroy her self-esteem. He said gently, "That does not mean I'm interested in having a relationship with you. I'm old enough to be your father." At forty-three, how could he think of her in any other way?

"But you're not my father. You're nothing like him. You would not have walked out on your wife and child for another woman. You would not have taken every penny out of the bank so your family would be left with nothing. You are not like that." She was practically wringing her hands in frustration.

"Tina . . ."

"No, let me finish. You have not given us a chance. You are so strung out over Anthia. Just because she's good in bed, does . . ."

Dexter had had enough. His relationship with Anthia was private. He scowled with impatience cutting her off mid-sentence. "This has got to stop. If you want to continue working at the center, we will end this topic now." He was adamant. "There's no you and I. We work together, nothing more. Good night." He leaned across to open her door. He made no move to get out. He remained only long enough for him to see that she was safely inside, then he drove away.

By the time he reached home, he had his temper somewhat under control. He was not proud of the fact that he had lost it for a moment there. He had wanted to be sympathetic and understanding with Tina's tender feelings, but she pushed him too far. He swore with disgust. He was not about to let anyone speculate about his love life with Anthia. Just the thought of that kind of speculation made his blood boil.

Oh, he knew there were plenty of people at the center who were naturally curious about their relationship. Thank goodness, they had enough sense not to comment on it in his presence. He and Anthia had made no bones about the fact they saw each other outside of the center. The intimate details of their time away from the center were no one's business. The idea that others might be speculating bugged the hell out of him.

"Damn," he muttered as he let himself inside. He couldn't have been more surprised if Tina had proposed marriage. Was she out of her mind? She was Jeff's age for heaven's sake. The whole thing had come totally out of left field. No way had he seen it coming.

Dexter wondered if he had handled it right? He just hoped that he hadn't made a bad situation worse because of his temper?

He wished he could talk to Anthia about this. She would know how best to handle this kind of stuff. But that was impossible. Anthia would not welcome a late-night call from him.

He was able to ignore his hunger for food, but not the other nagging hunger deep inside of him. He stared broodingly at the bedside telephone before he undressed and went into the bathroom. Even the heat of the shower didn't soothe his ragged emotions. He had promised himself that he would do nothing to further complicate their friendship. He had already strained the relationship to the breaking point by spending the night in Anthia's bed.

Just the thought of her sweet, wet heat caused his sex to thicken and lift, aching for her. He swore, gradually cooling the water temperature. He had messed up royally. What had possessed him to lose control like he had that night?

Celibacy should not have been a problem. He had done without for more years than he cared to count. Even after having survived years in prison without a woman, he had not pounced on the first woman he had chosen to have sex with once he gained his freedom. Yet, it had been a empty release because his emotions had not been engaged. In other words, it had been meaningless sex.

He'd been married, he knew the difference. And because of that, he had chosen celibacy long ago. After Christine, he didn't think he was able to care enough for another woman to want to bed her. He had been wrong.

Since he met Anthia, it seemed as if all the rules he held dear had been tossed out the closest window. Never had he been in less control of his male need. Nor had he ever enjoyed intimacy more . . . not even with Christine, the love of his life. That realization scared the hell out of him.

It had been totally unexpected. He had nothing to compare these new raw feelings he had for Anthia. She kept him hot and ready for more. When it came to Anthia, *excitement* seemed like such a meek word. She blew his mind! There was something so special about her that he could not even name it, but it was almost magical. She was so sexy, earthy and all sweet woman.

Man! He groaned as he recalled that night. Anthia had him so raw with need that he hadn't been able to see straight, let alone think. His brain had shut down and all he could do was feel. Dexter had been in sheer agony until he had joined his body with hers. And her tight, damp heat had caused a virtual firestorm inside of him.

Words failed to define the sheer beauty of their loving. His chest swelled with satisfaction as he dwelled on the pleasure he had been able to give her. Her first climax. It meant a lot even if he could not tell her how much it meant to him. Her sheath had gloved him to perfection, tightening convulsively as she climaxed triggering his own explosive release.

He scowled as he turned off the water. He was so erect, he hurt from it. The cold water had done nothing to ease his hunger for her. He was in for a long, uncomfortable night . . . another in a series of such nights where he laid awake while his sex pulsated from unfulfilled yearning.

How was it possible that he could want her more now than that special night, he wondered as he dried off. His need had not diminished but instead had grown with each passing day.

Get 4 FREE Arabesque
Contemporary Romances
Delivered to Your
Doorstep and Join the
Only Book Club That
Delivers These Bestselling
African American Romances
Directly to You Each Month!

4 FREE BOOKS

**LOOK INSIDE FOR DETAILS ON
HOW TO GET YOUR FREE GIFT.....**

(worth almost $20.00!)

ARABESQUE

WE INVITE YOU TO JOIN THE ONLY BOOK CLUB THAT DELIVERS HEARTFELT ROMANCE FEATURING AFRICAN AMERICAN HEROES AND HEROINES IN STORIES THAT ARE RICH IN PASSION AND CULTURAL SPICE...

And Your First 4 Books Are FREE!

Arabesque is an exciting contemporary romance line offered by BET Books, a division of BET Publications. Arabesque has been so successful that our readers have asked us about direct home delivery. Now you can start receiving four bestselling Arabesque novels a month delivered right to your door. Subscribe now and you'll get:

- ◈ 4 FREE Arabesque romances as our introductory gift—a value of almost $20! (pay only $1.50 to help cover postage & handling)
- ◈ 4 BRAND-NEW Arabesque romances delivered to your doorstep each month thereafter (usually arriving before they're available in bookstores!)
- ◈ 20% off each title—a savings of almost $4.00 each month
- ◈ A FREE monthly newsletter, *Arabesque Romance News* that features author profiles, book previews and more
- ◈ No risks or obligations...in other words, you can cancel whenever you wish with no questions asked

So subscribe to Arabesque today and see why these books are winning awards and readers' hearts.

After you've enjoyed our FREE gift of 4 Arabesque Romances, you'll begin to receive monthly shipments of the newest Arabesque titles. Each shipment will be yours to examine for 10 days. If you decide to keep the books, you'll pay the preferred subscriber's price of just $4.00 per title. That's $16 for all 4 books with a nominal charge of $1.50 for shipping and handling. And if you want us to stop sending books, just say the word.

See why reviewers are raving about ARABESQUE and order your FREE books today!

WE HAVE 4 FREE BOOKS FOR YOU!

(If the certificate is missing below, write to:
Zebra Home Subscription Service, Inc.,
120 Brighton Road, P.O. Box 5214, Clifton, New Jersey 07015-5214)

FREE BOOK CERTIFICATE

Yes! Please send me 4 *Arabesque* Contemporary Romances without cost or obligation, billing me just $1.50 to help cover postage and handling. I understand that each month, I will be able to preview 4 brand-new *Arabesque* Contemporary Romances FREE for 10 days. Then, if I decide to keep them, I will pay the money-saving preferred subscriber's price of just $16.00 for all 4...that's a savings of almost $4 off the publisher's price + $1.50 for shipping and handling. I may return any shipment within 10 days and owe nothing, and I may cancel this subscription at any time. My 4 FREE books will be mine to keep in any case.

Name _____

Address _____ Apt. _____

City_____ State_____ Zip_____

Telephone ( ) _____

Signature _____ AR0299
(If under 18, parent or guardian must sign.)

Terms and prices subject to change. Orders subject to acceptance by Zebra Home Subscription Service, Inc. . Zebra Home Subscription Service, Inc. reserves the right to reject or cancel any subscription.

GET 4 FREE ARABESQUE ROMANCES TODAY!

ARABESQUE

4 FREE
ARABESQUE
Contemporary
Romances
are reserved
for you!

(worth almost
$20.00)

see details
inside...

AFFIX
STAMP
HERE

ZEBRA HOME SUBSCRIPTION SERVICE, INC.

120 BRIGHTON ROAD

P.O. BOX 5214

CLIFTON, NEW JERSEY 07015-5214

HEALTH, FITNESS AND BEAUTY FOR AFRICAN-AMERICAN WOMEN

heart & soul

1 year (6 issues) $16.97 plus receive a FREE HEART & SOUL
Healthy Living Journal with your paid subscription.

YES! I want to invest in myself and subscribe to HEART & SOUL, the health, fitness and beauty magazine for savvy African-American women. I'll get a year's worth of helpful information that will inspire me to discover new ways of improving my body....my spirit...and my mind. Plus, I'll get a FREE HEART & SOUL *Healthy Living Journal* to keep a daily record of my wonderful progress.

Name _____

(First)   (Last)

Address _____   Apt #

City _____   State _____   Zip _____ | MABI3 |

☐ Payment enclosed   ☐ Bill me
  Rush my HEART & SOUL
  Healthy Living Journal

Please allow 6-8 weeks for receipt of first issue. In Canada: CDN $19.97 (includes GST). Payment in U.S. currency must accompany all Canadian orders. Basic subscription rate: 6 issues $16.97.

BUSINESS REPLY MAIL

FIRST-CLASS MAIL   PERMIT NO. 272   RED OAK, IA

POSTAGE WILL BE PAID BY ADDRESSEE

heart&soul

P O BOX 7423
RED OAK IA 51591-2423

NO POSTAGE
NECESSARY
IF MAILED
IN THE
UNITED STATES

He was so damn hard, he had to clench his teeth from the relentless longing.

"Forget about it," he mumbled to himself as he made his way to his solitary king-size bed. There was absolutely nothing he could do about it. The idea of spending yet another night with a hard-on did not sit well with him. There was only one woman who could ease the throbbing ache deep inside of him or soothe the savage need clawing at him. "Anthia," he groaned her name aloud.

He consoled himself with the reminder that she had agreed to accompany him to Texas for his sister's wedding. It was a victory, but a very small one considering how badly he wanted her tonight.

He tried to force his mind to safer channels as he turned on the television. But the all-night news channel could not begin to hold his attention. He hadn't seen his father or stepmother since the beginning of his trial. His prominent, well-heeled family had no place in their society life for a convicted felon. Yet, every single day his sister, Stephanie, had been in that courtroom, there to support him. Later she had visited him in prison, against their folks' wishes. She was the only real family he had left. As much as he hated the thought of returning to Houston, he knew he had no choice. He could not disappoint his baby sister by not coming to her wedding.

He knew he had been damn lucky that Anthia had agreed to come. He could face his folks alone, but he wanted her at his side. Anthia made so many things bearable for him. The past two years of having known her sweet smiles and warm laughter had come to mean the world to him.

He would be lost without her. So why had he been willing to risk their friendship because of an erection. He'd wanted her sexually for a very long time. It had been something he had been determined to ignore. Unfortunately his control had lasted only so long. Being near her at the center, seeing her on a regular basis had gradually worn him down to the point he could not think of anything but her.

Anthia's small body fit so perfectly against his long, lean one. He had totally lost it that night. He had reached for her

time and time again . . . needing nothing more than to be surrounded by her wet passage. She had been so wonderfully tight,
caressing his entire male length to the point of madness. It was
as if he had not been able to breath until he was buried to the
hilt . . . his shaft deep inside of her snug, damp heat. Only then
had he been at peace. He wanted her tonight just as much· as
he had wanted her that night.

Did she ever think of how good it had been between the two
of them . . . how right? Did she go over it in her mind as he
had? How could he get past the fact that she had experienced
her first climax during their long, sweet night of loving? He
couldn't seem to think of anything else.

As he used his hands to soothe the aching need so he could
sleep, Dexter fantasized that it was Anthia's soft hands stroking
him. It was only afterward that he accepted the bitter reality of
the situation. He would be lying to himself if he didn't admit
how much he was looking forward to having her all to himself
for an entire weekend. He sighed disgustedly, acknowledging
what was bound to be a major problem. How in the world was
he going to be able to keep his hands off her?

It had been two long, empty weeks for Dexter until he finally
had Anthia to himself for a time.

"All right?" Dexter asked as he gazed at Anthia. They were
buckled in their respective seats in the first-class section of the
aircraft as the plane taxied down the runway.

"Yes," she said softly, wondering why he had insisted on
buying first-class tickets. It seemed like such a waste of money.
His response when asked had been that he wanted them both
to be comfortable, then he'd cleverly changed the subject.

She had cautioned herself to take everything as it came and
not read too much into this trip. He asked her to accompany
him as a friend, nothing more. She continued to remind herself
that she had to get over her hurt feelings, if she wanted to be
a part of his life. Their lovemaking had clearly meant more to
her than it had to him. That realization had been painful to
accept. But she had no other choice. She had been trying her

best not to dwell on the past. Focusing on their single night of loving would change nothing, perhaps prolong the agony.

She could not help wondering if she was asking for more heartache by coming with him? Despite her poor judgment in sleeping with Dexter, her feelings for him had not altered. They were just as deep and powerful as before the night they became lovers. When it came down to Dexter, Anthia was downright pitiful. She longed to be near him and help him in any way she could. She simply had no pride where he was concerned. It was only because he insisted that he needed her with him on this trip that she had agreed. She had been unable to refuse. What she hadn't taken into consideration was what was best for her.

Although, she had been very involved with her work, needing to sculpt several new dolls and finishing up several others, it had not occurred to her to turn him down. Her business had suddenly taken a backseat. It had never been the most important part of her life, for her son held that place. Now Dexter's well-being and happiness were also a major concern.

"Anthia? Are you nervous about flying?" he questioned, having watched her move restlessly in her seat.

"Just a little. I took my first flight when I went down to Augusta during the winter to visit Jeff. I'm by no means a seasoned flier." She laughed nervously. "Oh, by the way, Jeff mentioned that you called him."

"Yeah . . ." before he could elaborate, the plane began moving swiftly down the runway gaining speed as it went. Dexter didn't hesitate to take her soft hand in his. He ignored the way his breath had quickened in his throat from the innocent contact. They continued to hold hands until the plane was in the air and had leveled off. Anthia was the one who moved her hand away from his and placed it in her lap.

"I appreciate you taking time to talk to Jeff. He seems, I don't know. Uh, more confident since you two talked. These days he's having a tough time opening up with me. He's keeping something locked inside and I don't know what to make of it." She lifted deep, dark troubled eyes to his.

Dexter's breath caught in his throat for a long moment. Then he said gently, "He is a man now. Men do not wear their feelings on their shirtsleeves. He'll talk about it when he's ready."

She pursed her lips thoughtfully, unaware of the way it drew his eyes to their red-tinted softness. "I know he's not a child. But I'm his mother. I can't help remembering the days when he came to me with his problems. I'd put him on my lap and we would talk."

Dexter teased, "He no longer fits."

She glared at him, then giggled unable to resist his humor. Dexter joined in her laughter, reminding her that he did not laugh nearly enough. The lines around his mouth and eyes were more pronounced since they had been estranged the past few weeks.

He looked as if he wasn't getting any sleep. She wanted to shake him and tell him that it was his own fault. His stubbornness was the only reason they were not together. He had turned his back on what they shared. Why couldn't he see that he was only making them both unhappy?

"Sooo, did my son change his mind about talking to the fellows at the community center?"

"I wish," he sobered. "He seems adamant about it. He wants to make it on his own in this world . . . without friends."

"That can be a hard and lonely path."

Dexter looked at her sharply wondering for a moment if she was referring to him rather than Jeff. But she was staring out the window and he couldn't see her beautiful eyes.

"One thing about planes, the view is breathtaking," she said softly. "Tell me about your family, Dexter."

"There isn't much to tell," his hands tightened on the arms of his seat. "No aunts or uncles still living, only my father, stepmother and Stephanie." His voice was filled with regret when he went on to say, "My mother and I were close. She worked hard to support us, not wanting anything from him. I often wondered how my parents ever got together in the first place."

He said bitterly, "I never really knew my father until my mother passed and I was forced to leave Detroit and live with him. We've never been close." His arrest for murder has been the end of their relationship.

"I'm sorry. It had to be difficult for you growing up."

He shrugged. "Forced me to learn how to depend on myself."

Anthia's tender heart ached sympathetically. Without thought, she reached over and placed her hand in his, giving his a gentle squeeze. She had no trouble reading the sadness in his eyes.

"In a sense you also grew up without a father." This compassionate man, who never hesitated to share himself with the kids at the center, had known suffering in his own life. It explained how he had grown into a strong, self-reliant man, yet with a tender core. In spite of the difficulties they were having, his pain suddenly became her pain.

"My arrest did not endear me to him," he candidly admitted.

"How could he not believe in his own son?"

"My father had no room in his life for failure. He had a lovely, exciting wife, a highly profitable business. There was no place for me in that mix."

"I can understand why your sister's support meant so much to you," Anthia said gently.

He nodded before saying tightly, "I have to go to this wedding. No matter what my feelings are for my father and my stepmother, it has nothing to do with how I feel about Stephanie." The fact that they shared no blood ties was a none-issue. He and Stephanie were brother and sister.

Anthia had no idea how she knew, but she suspected that when he gave his love, he did so with his whole heart. Would he ever stop yearning for the family he lost so tragically? Could he someday make room in his heart for a new love? If not, how would Anthia be able to bear the disappointment?

"How long has it been since you've been home?"

"My home is Detroit. There's nothing for me in Houston. Nothing at all," he ended tightly.

"Except for your sister?"

Suddenly he smiled. "Stephanie never once believed I was guilty. Not once. If it wasn't for her . . ." he stopped abruptly. "Let's just say she's worth any inconvenience."

"What hotel will I be staying in?"

"We," he corrected.

"Dexter . . . Your sister will want you to stay with the family."

A muscle jumped in his jaw for he hadn't considered the possibility. "And you'll be right beside me wherever I am. I need you with me, Anthia." His dark eyes locked with hers, before he decided to change to a less personal topic. "Craig is doing much better. I spoke to his grandmother this morning. He's getting stronger every day. He should be out of the hospital soon."

"I just hope he has learned his lesson about gang involvement. He came close to losing his life. Kids with guns are a volatile combination. I just wish my stubborn son would cooperate and share his experience."

"He's got a lot on his mind, Anthia."

"Such as?"

"Man things."

"What kind of answer is that?"

"I can't break his confidence. A guy doesn't tell his mom everything," he said suspecting the boy's doubts about his manhood.

Dexter laughed enjoying the spark of temper that caused her pretty eyes to flash and her mouth to pout provocatively. Did she have any idea how attractive he found her? Her knit top gently hugged the lush curves of her breasts. The prominent tips drew his eyes like a bee to a honeycomb. He recalled how good they felt in his mouth against his tongue. Hell! He was forced to swallow a groan.

"Is he seeing someone?"

"Can't tell," he said with a smile.

Anthia glared at him before returning her attention to the doll magazine in her lap.

He lifted a brow, then could not suppress a grin as she pointedly ignored him. He was far from being disturbed by her attitude. In fact he was on top of the world. Vastly different from the way he had been this morning as he prepared for the trip.

He woke with a throbbing headache, something he hardly ever suffered from since he'd moved to Detroit and started working at the community center. He had not slept the night before. He'd tossed and turned for hours, worried that she might change her mind, that she might not come after all. As the morning went on and no call came in from her, his anxiety began to ease somewhat. It wasn't until he had picked her up at home and she was settled in the car with her luggage in the trunk, that he was able to fully relax.

He didn't bother with weighing the issue as to why it was so important to him that she came. What mattered was that Anthia was here with him. He had made a promise to himself that he would do nothing to jeopardize the tentative peace they had established. He had learned the hard way to keep his hands to himself.

He wasn't going to do a thing about his sexual desires for her. He was man enough to admit that when it came to Anthia, he had very little control over his male hunger. It was there slapping him in the face time and time again. All he had to do was look at her and his body automatically prepared itself to join with hers.

Frankly, one night of her sweetness had not eased his unrelenting need. If anything, it had made it worse for now he knew what absolute pleasure she was capable of giving him. Naturally, he wanted more.

Yet, he knew that if he wanted her in his life he had to do his level-best not to jeopardize the parameters of their friendship. He had hurt her . . . badly. In so doing he had hurt himself. He cared too much for her to ever let that happen again. And he had been very fortunate. She had forgiven him once, he would be a fool to think she would do so yet again. As long as he kept his pants zipped, they would not have a problem.

"Tired?" he asked when she quickly covered a yawn.

Her lovely smile was never far away. She graced him with one as she shrugged her slim shoulders. She was dressed so prettily in a beige top and slim skirt. Her shapely legs and feet were encased in cream hose and cream stack heels.

"Why not take a nap? I'll wake you when we land. Here, I'll get you a blanket and pillow."

"Thanks," she sighed, propping her head back against the seat and kicking off her shoes to tuck her legs beneath her.

Dexter also let his seat back, content just to watch her sleep as her long, silky black lashes rested above her sculpted cheeks. She was a beautiful woman, but her beauty came from deep inside. She saw the best in him even after she knew the truth of his background. She had offered him her trust and faith without question. He treasured both as he treasured her.

When the small pillow slipped, Anthia shifted until her head rested on his shoulder. Dexter did nothing to retrieve the pillow for her. He found himself inhaling deeply, closing his eyes as he filling his lungs with the clean, floral scent of her thick black curls and soft petite body. She sighed, shifting once more until one soft breast was pillowed on his arm. Without conscious thought, he lifted his arm until it rested behind her slender shoulders and she rested on the wide expanse of his chest.

At this point, sleep was out of the question for him. There was no way he could relax with his sex painfully crammed in his slacks. He didn't move one muscle to adjust the thick ridge and make himself more comfortable. In spite of his good intentions, he was not taking a chance on waking her. He wanted her exactly where she was. As he held her, he reminded himself again and again that he was a thinking man. He was ruled by his head, not controlled by his erection.

FIFTEEN

Anthia had no idea what woke her, but when she opened her eyes, her cheek rested against the firm muscle of Dexter's chest. Her thick lashes quickly lifted and she sat up, looking away from his dark gaze.

"Have a nice rest?" His deep somewhat husky voice caused her pulse to race and caused her to flush with embarrassment.

"Sorry, didn't mean to use you as a pillow."

"No problem," he said, careful to hide his disappointment as she settled in her own seat once more. Yet again, he found it necessary to remind himself that *platonic* was the operative word where they were concerned. He might hate it, nonetheless, it made perfect sense considering how close their night together had come to destroying their friendship.

What the hell did it matter that he had never known such pure enjoyment and sheer pleasure with any other woman? Being with Anthia was magical. The nights since had been long and empty. The walls seemed to close in on him while he laid awake aching for her. Regardless, he would never again put them in such a compromising position. If there was a next time, he believed he would lose her for good. A risk he was not willing to take.

Dexter had waited a lifetime to find a woman like Anthia. She had a sincerity and warmth that no matter what happened seemed to keep right on giving. He didn't have to be told how fortunate he was that she had not turned her back on him. He had been so lucky. Damn lucky.

Somehow he would get through this weekend without touching her. She deserved his respect and so much more. If only he were able to love her the way she was entitled to be loved. If only . . .

"We are approaching Houston from . . ." the pilot's voice broke into his thoughts.

"I made a reservation at the Four Seasons," he said after stowing their luggage in the trunk of the rental car. "Do you want to check in, get settled first before we drive out to the house and let them know we've arrived?" he asked as he held the door of the roomy Lincoln Town Car.

Anthia looked thoughtfully at him as he made himself comfortable behind the steering column, adjusting the seat to his satisfaction. She suddenly realized that her stomach was tight with nerves. She couldn't help wondering what kind of sleeping arrangements he had made at the hotel.

She knew better than to think he planned for them to share a room. Just the possibility of them being together in the same room made her feel as if her heart had taken a giant leap. Why did she have to constantly remind herself that that first time had been a mistake?

She was here as a personal favor to him, moral support to ease his discomfort after such a lengthy estrangement with family. If only she could get her heart to go along with her head, then there would not be any embarrassing moments ahead for either of them.

"Well?" he asked, after starting the engine.

"Let's go on ahead. Your family may be expecting us. We can always call the hotel and let them know we will be along later."

"Okay." He had no trouble following the interstate out to the plush Houston suburban of Sugarland. The Washingtons' property was named Green Haven for its lush green grounds filled with large trees and sprawling lawn, and including a tennis court, pool and beautifully landscaped gardens. The house was set quite a distance from the road.

Anthia could not suppress a ⸏⸏⸏⸏ as the ⸏⸏⸏
story house came into view. "G⸏⸏⸏⸏⸏, ⸏⸏

"This is Texas, baby, everythi⸏⸏⸏ ⸏⸏ ⸏⸏⸏, ⸏⸏
could not hide the bitterness. H⸏ ⸏⸏⸏ ⸏⸏⸏⸏⸏⸏
came rushing back as if it had all ⸏⸏⸏⸏⸏⸏ ⸏⸏
left this place and his so-called fa⸏⸏⸏⸏ ⸏⸏⸏⸏ ⸏⸏
stances.

Those memories could not be eras⸏⸏. ⸏⸏⸏⸏⸏ ⸏⸏⸏ ⸏⸏ passed
since he had lived in Texas, eight sin⸏⸏ ⸏⸏⸏ ⸏⸏lease from prison.
While on parole he had lived in town, rather than impose himself on the parent who had turned his back on him during his
darkest hours.

Even though thirteen years had passed since that painful night
Christine had died, it did not lessen Dexter's sense of loss and
betrayal. Both emotions lingered deep inside. He needed to remind himself that he was here for Stephanie's sake. Stephanie's
happiness was all that matter. ✌

"This is the home my father designed and built for my stepmother soon after they married. Impressive, isn't it."

"That's a major understatement. Did you say your father designed it?"

"Yes. He's an architect. We jointly own Washington Connection, the family-owned firm."

"Jointly?"

"Yeah. We're partners, at least we are on paper. I have not
been an active part of the business since the trial." The bitterness
in his voice was unmistakable.

"I had no idea," Anthia said softly, her hand rested momentarily on his thigh until she recognized the inappropriateness of
the action, then jerked it away. "So when you said you lost
everything, you meant everything including your career."

"Yes, I was also an architect."

"I'm so sorry," she whispered.

Dexter's life here had been entirely different from the new
one he had made for himself in Michigan. He had obviously
been a wealthy man, with a loving wife and child on the way.
That had all been shattered when the gun went off that fateful
day, destroying all that he worked for . . . all that he loved. For

lost his wife and their child, he had also lost
ove and support.

been left with no career, no family . . . nothing but
pty future filled with regret. How he had survived and
me out on the other side of that dark, dark time in his life
was nothing short of a miracle as far as Anthia was concerned.

"Anthia?" he said softly.

"I'm beginning to understand how difficult this weekend will
be for you. No matter what anyone says, please don't forget you
have made a wonderful life for yourself. You're liked and well
respected." She did not want him to be hurt yet again by these
people.

"Thanks," he mumbled, his throat clogged with emotions.

He had barely pulled the car to a stop in the wide circular
drive when a young slender woman came running out of the
house.

"Dexter . . ." she cried throwing herself into his arms.
"You're here . . . you're really here." Stephanie Washington
laughed, giving him a loud playful smack on the cheek. She
was a tall woman with pale brown coloring and short, curly
dark brown hair cleverly cut into fluffy layers. Her features were
classically beautiful and her eyes filled with joyful tears. There
could be no doubt about the fact that she was thrilled to see
him.

Anthia stepped out of the car, glad she had worn a silk knit
suit as she quietly waited for Stephanie to let go of her brother.

"Who's this?" Stephanie asked, beaming up at Dexter.

Dexter reached out a hand and clasped Anthia around the
waist. "Anthia Jenkins, my sister Stephanie Washington."

"Hi!" she was all smiles. "Welcome. I'm so glad you both
could come. Let's go inside." She led the way through the wide
double doors into the pearl gray marble foyer. "I can't wait until
you meet Ken, Dexter. He's so wonderful. I still can't believe
we'll be married in a matter of days." She laughed. "You two
are going to be best friends."

Dexter laughed, pleased to see her so well and happy. He
reminded himself that she was worth the emotional upheaval of
seeing his father and stepmother again. He was dreading their

inevitable clash. He was also having second thoughts about asking Anthia to accompany him.

He had not brought Anthia here as a eyewitness to the results of the disintegration of his family, but that was exactly what she would eventually see. He had only been thinking about himself when he invited her. He had no business putting her in the middle of an emotionally charged situation.

He was not conscious of how taunt with tension his tall frame was until he entered the large foyer, at its base was a wide sweeping staircase.

"Mother!" Stephanie called, tugging Dexter along with her through the archway into the luxuriously furnished spacious living room.

Marian Washington was a beautiful woman, whom the passing years had been extremely kind. Her pale brown complexion was as smooth and unblemished as her daughter's. Her thick black hair, tinged with silver, had been swept up and pinned into a graceful knot. The smile she reserved for her only child was radiant. She was elegantly dressed in a sand-colored silk dress with a long strand of cultured pearls draped around her neck and large square-cut diamond and pearl studs graced her earlobes. Her left hand was adorned with a large emerald-cut diamond ring teamed with a wide diamond-encrusted band. She practically reeked of money and social grace.

"Hello, Dexter," her voice was soft, refined and cold. She made no move to approach him, but remained seated with her hands clasped loosely in her lap. The chilly smile she gave him fell far short of welcoming. "You're looking well."

Dexter nodded. "Marion."

His hand tightened around Anthia's so much so that she bit her lip to keep from crying out in pain. Anthia quietly took in the sheer opulence and cold beauty of the room. Never had she imagined that Dexter came from this kind of wealth.

"Isn't it wonderful, Mother? Dexter is finally home." Stephanie laughed nervously, looking from one to the other. "Oh, I'm sorry. Mother this is Anthia Jenkins. Dexter's lady friend from Michigan."

"Hello, Ms. Jenkins," Marion rose, holding out her hand.

"Welcome to our home. I hope your stay will be a pleasant one."

Somewhat embarrassed by the assumption, Anthia said, "Thank you. You have a fabulous home," and returned the handshake even though she was aware that it was more than Marion had done for her stepson in way of welcome.

Marian nodded and laughed, "We like it."

"Well, I see you made it in." The deep male voice, much like Dexter's, came from the archway. The similarities between father and son did not end with their voices. Damon Washington was every bit as handsome, tall and striking as his son. Good living had left a thick ridge around his midsection.

"Dad," Dexter said, quietly meeting his father's gaze. His mouth tight and unsmiling, his body perfectly straight.

"Have a good flight?" the older man asked, going to stand beside his wife.

"Fine," Dexter managed evenly.

"Oh, Daddy, this is Dexter's lady friend from Michigan. Anthia Jenkins, our father, Damon Washington."

"How do you do?" Anthia acknowledged, trying to hide her astonishment at the depth of this family's coldness. There was no warmth, no welcome home from either one of them. Dexter could be a stranger off the street, for all the interest they showed in him.

After the two shook hands, his sister said, "Oh, Daddy, I'm so thrilled to have Dexter home. Now the wedding will be just perfect." Stephanie's gaze went to her father's, her eyes pleading with him not to spoil this reunion for her.

Her father cleared his throat, "As long as you are happy that is all that matters, baby" He went over to the portable bar in the comer of the room. "Drink anyone?"

"Yes, dear," his wife requested. "White wine, please."

"Ms. Jenkins? Dexter?

"No thank you," both of them said at once.

"Please, won't you sit down. I'll call Margaret, our housekeeper, to bring refreshments," Stephanie invited. "Mother do we have any more of those lemon tarts. Dexter always loved them."

"Nothing for me," Dexter said stiffly, making no move to sit down.

"But . . ." his sister trailed off. Then she took a deep breath, "You two must be exhausted. Let me show you to your rooms." She didn't wait for a response but led the way back into the foyer, toward the central staircase.

Dexter stopped her before she could mount the stairs. "It's not going to work, Steph. I can't stay in his house."

"Yes it will." Her chin lifted defiantly. "I want you here. I've arranged everything. All the out-of-town guests will be at the Four Seasons in town." She took his hand. "Please, Dexter. It is only for a few days. Surely, you and Daddy can stay in the same house for three days!"

Dexter closed his eyes as he fought his inclination to refuse outright. Stephanie was pleading with him to stay. He didn't want to hurt her. He had missed her. They saw so little of each other these days. Soon she would be a married lady and he wanted her wedding to be just as perfect as she planned it.

"Please . . ." she whispered, squeezing his hand.

He glanced at Anthia and saw her nod her agreement. Finally he said, "Okay," he gave her a gentle hug. "I'll get the luggage out of the car."

Anthia was smoothing out a dress as she unpacked when there was a soft knock on the open door between the bathroom that connected her room with Dexter's.

"May I come in?" he asked.

Her ready smile was warm and welcoming, just what he needed. "Yes, please. Are you unpacked?"

Dexter went over to the floor-to-ceiling window overlooking the expansive gardens. The tennis court and pool house were visible from this angle of the property. He stood with his back to her, his hands shoved into his trouser pockets.

"Dex? Have you . . ."

"No. One of the maids will take care of it. Goodness knows Marian can't get along without a truckload of them. I can't imagine her washing her own dirty clothes like my mother used to do. He married her because of me and he never let either one of us forget it." He turned then, to look at her. "Dad has given Marian everything she wanted. But then she has the proper background. She was a debutante, daughter of a prominent Boston family of doctors, a Howard graduate and member of a sorority. My mother was none of those things."

"Oh Dex, you must not forget the most important thing. Your mother was a good, hardworking woman and she loved you. No one can take that away from you."

He looked at Anthia, touched by her thoughtfulness. "You're right. My father saw that I was taken care of, but he had no love for me. It wasn't until I met Christine that things started to change for me." He rubbed his hand over his hair. "Just a few more days then we can get the hell out of here."

"If you prefer that we not stay . . ."

He shook his head. "We're staying. It means too much to Steph." He looked around the lavish pale blue bedroom. "Do you have everything you need?"

"Yes. The room is lovely. But I can only imagine how stressful this is for you."

Dexter was not sure why he was surprised. Anthia was his best friend and knew him well. She understood him better than he understood himself. He was such a self-contained man that so much of himself was kept private from others.

"It's only for a few days. I can put up with anything for that long. It's amazing how down to earth and unpretentious Stephanie is considering Marion's influence," he marveled. "Stephanie seems very happy with this Ken."

Anthia's heart swelled with love. It took all of her self-control not to go over to him and show him how she felt about him. His ability to put others' needs before his own was only one of things Anthia adored about Dexter. Time and time again she saw firsthand his devotion to the kids at the center. He knew what it meant to have only himself to depend on. He had helped so many youngsters in the same situation. He was willing to risk his own life if it came down to it.

She had benefitted from his helping hand in her own personal life. What would those painful months while her son healed have been like without his support? She didn't want to even think of it.

There was no doubt about the fact that he had earned both Jeff's and Anthia's respect. Dexter Washington was all man, in every sense of the word. Any woman who was lucky enough to break down those walls he used to protect himself would be extremely fortunate. For so long Anthia hoped to be that woman. She felt it was unlikely, because he would not let her get but so close to him. He trusted her with his secrets but not his heart.

If not for this trip she would not have known he was a trained architect or his family's background or his estrangement with his sole remaining parent. He was an expert at keeping his private life private.

No matter how much he desired her sexually, he could not love her. He was still very much in love with his Christine. Why did the knowledge hurt so much? He had been very open and honest about his feelings from the very beginning. She was the one who had made the mistake of caring too much. She had opened herself up for disillusionment and heartache. Why didn't she have sense enough to keep some distance between them? If for no other reason than self-preservation.

"Ready?"

"Huh?"

"Dinner," he quirked a brow.

Anthia blushed. "Yes, of course. Let me run a quick comb through my hair."

Kenneth Jackson, Stephanie's fiancé, and his parents arrived just before dinner, easing the tension around the table somewhat. The engaged couple had met at the family-owned firm. Stephanie worked in the marketing department while Kenneth was an architect in management and design. The Washington's definitely approved of the match and Damon Washington didn't even try to conceal his fondness for the younger man.

Anthia was pleased to see that Kenneth clearly adored Stephanie. The conversation around the table centered on their upcoming wedding. Although it proved to be a festive evening, Anthia was relieved when it drew to a close. Mr. Washington had barely spoken to his own son. Anthia could almost feel Dexter's tension and she resented his father for it.

"Tired?" Dexter had been self-absorbed as he walked her to her door. He rested his shoulder against the doorjamb.

"Mmm, it's been a long day. I like your sister. She certainly loves her older brother." The comment brought a smile to his dark, thoughtful features.

"Yeah. Kenneth seems like a nice guy. It's good to see her so happy. I'd better let you get some rest. See you in the morning." He didn't offer so much as a kiss on her cheek.

Determined to hide her disappointment, Anthia said " 'Night," then slipped inside her room and quietly closed the door behind her. As she sank down into the deep cushioned armchair, she knew she had no right to his kisses. It was true that Dexter cared about her. Why else would he have included her in his plans? Nonetheless, his distancing himself hurt. She wanted him to at least share his feelings. But she didn't need to be told that she didn't have the emotional objectivity or the experience with men to evaluate the situation clearly. Her own feelings for him kept getting in the way.

Anthia didn't remember her own father because he had died while she was still young. As hard as she tried, she simply did not understand how a man could continue to be so cold and unemotional toward his own son. The two hadn't seen each other in years, yet the strain between them was almost tangible.

There was nothing she could do to help Dexter. He had already decided to keep her in a safe tiny little corner of his life. What they shared on that single night was over. It was as if he preferred to pretend that they had not become lovers. She took his regrets very personally.

"Just stop it!" she softly scolded herself. It was pointless to go over it yet again. She was here because Dexter claimed to need her with him. Yet, she still could not see how her being here was of value. He was a man accustomed to standing alone. Nevertheless he had asked for her help.

She was here to support Dexter during a rough time as he had helped her. As long as she kept that goal close at hand and forgot her own tender needs then it should not be a problem.

Anthia was soaking in the bathtub when she heard a knock on the connecting door. "I'm almost done," she called through the door.

"Take your time," was Dexter's deep throated response from the other side of the door.

She finished her bath, creamed her skin with scented body lotion, then slipped into a long pink silk gown edged with ivory lace before she called to let Dexter know she had finished. Returning to her room, she brushed her hair, then relaxed against the pillows with a novel. The low murmurs from the television let her know that Dexter hadn't gone to bed.

It was after one in the morning when she set her book aside and clicked off the bedside lamp. Despite her best efforts, she still couldn't sleep. She was too busy listening for sounds of movements in the next room.

It was close to two when the shower was switched on in the bathroom. She had not realized how closely she had been listening to him until his footsteps receded and the bathroom light was turned off.

Flooded by painful memories in spite of her best efforts, she ached for what she could not have. She knew what it was to sleep beside him, resting in his arms. She knew the sweetness of being held against his heart. It had only been a few weeks ago, but it felt like an eternity. "Dex . . ." she whispered. He had made himself clear. He did not want her as his lover, merely a friend.

On more than one occasion, he had emphasized how he valued her friendship. There was no place in his heart for more. Yet, there was no way she could stop herself from wanting him. He was so deeply entrenched in her heart. And she came with him knowing how he felt. It was too late for regrets. She could not have comfortably stayed home, knowing what he had to face alone. Thus she found herself in an impossible situation.

Dexter remained steadfast in his determination that there would be no intimacy between them. Their single interlude had been enough for him. How could it have meant so little to him while it meant everything to her?

She had never known the kind of enjoyment a woman could

find in a man's arms. She suspected it might be uncomfortable for her considering how long it had been since she had been with a man. What she found was an incredible pleasure because of his consideration of her. He had been so tender with her, so sensitive to her needs. He had delayed his own climax in order to assure her a heart-stopping release. Tiny shivers raced down her spine as she vividly recalled those wonderful moments in his arms. The pleasure seemed to go on and on.

How could she to forget that? She sighed heavily. A lifetime was not long enough to allow her to forget what it was like to join her body with his. It might not have been love on his part but it was nothing less on hers. Unlike Dexter, she had no regrets. He might be able to walk away from what they shared, but she could not. He meant the world to her.

She knew beyond any doubt that Dexter Washington cared for her. "Why Dex? Why?" she mumbled aloud, but she knew the answer. It was because of his lost love. There was no doubt that he had been deeply in love with Christine. When he lost her, he had lost everything that mattered to him.

To make things worse, there was no possible way that he could prove to himself that he was not responsible for her death. No way, he would allow himself to love again.

Finally giving up all pretense of sleeping, Anthia flicked on the bedside lamp. She quietly paced the confines of the bedroom as her head filled with troubled thoughts. The soft knock on the connecting door startled her.

"Anthia?"

She stood absolutely still as if she had been caught doing an unspeakable act. Eventually she said, "Yes?"

"I saw your light. May I come in?" Her response was so long in coming that, Dexter repeated her name a bit louder this time.

"Yes, of course," she said, before she remembered she was wearing nothing more than a silk nightgown.

He was in the room before she had taken a single step. "Can't sleep," he said, leaning against the doorjamb, his arms folded. He wore a dark green short toweling robe. He didn't look like he was wearing much under it for his broad hair roughened chest, long muscular legs and feet were bare. His dark brooding gaze moved over her thinly veiled frame.

Anthia picked up the pink robe from the end of the bed, quickly put it on and belted it at her waist. Unfortunately, the silk robe did very little to conceal her soft breasts and small waist and shapely hips. Her small toes painted cherry-red peeked out from beneath the hem.

"Little restless," she said, keeping her eyes concealed beneath long, silky black lashes. She did not want him to know how much she had been longing for him. "How about you?"

He shrugged making no move to come farther into the room. "It's normal for me. I turn the television on for company." He watched as she sank down to the side of the bed.

"It's been a long day," she said absently smoothing her hair which curled around her shoulders.

"Yeah," he murmured, curious as to why she would not look at him. "Does my being here make you uncomfortable?"

"No, why do you ask?"

"You haven't looked at me since I entered the room. What's going on Anthia? Is something wrong?"

"No."

SIXTEEN

"Why won't you look at me?"

Anthia shrugged, unable to find a ready answer.

Dexter was not buying it. He went over to her and lifted her chin until he could look into her eyes. The sadness he saw was unmistakable. Something was very wrong.

"I shouldn't have asked you to come."

"Doesn't matter . . ." she hedged.

"I should have done a better job of preparing you for meeting my stepmother and father. I'm sorry, baby," he said unaware of the endearment. "I knew what to expect."

"How can you stand it? Why do you have to be so strong all the time? If I didn't know better, I'd think you had no feelings at all."

"Anthia," he said, careful to keep put some space between them. Her soft breasts had been pillowed on his chest. He was having difficulty following the conversation. In fact, he ached for not only the feel of her, but the taste of her. He forced himself to breathe deeply in hopes of easing his problem, but he unwittingly inhaled in her sweet floral scent. "Damn," he mumbled.

"What did you say?"

"Nothing worth repeating." He was hard already. It did not take much for her to drive him wild with desire. Dexter wanted to touch her, longed for her softness, but he settled for placing his hands on her shoulders. "I'm sorry. I never meant to involve you in my family's problems."

"I know." Anthia risked looking up into his dark eyes. "It's not your fault. Your father may not realize it, but he has lost a wonderful son. I just hope he will wake up soon so that he can do something to change the situation before it's too late. Nothing in life is promised. He may need you someday." Due to his prolonged silence, she added, "I probably shouldn't have said that. I didn't mean to criticize."

"It's the truth. Every single word." As hard as he tried he had never gotten to the point were he did not care what his father thought of him. Even after so many years, Dexter was willing to put the past behind them if his father would do the same. He was not trying to fool himself. He knew it was nothing more than wishful thinking on his part. He had learned a long time ago not to depend on Damon Washington's goodwill.

"We can move to the hotel in the morning. Stephanie will just have to understand. I'm sure you will find it much more comfortable."

"No, Dex. One more night, then we can leave on Saturday evening after the reception. Maybe, you and your father can use the time that's left to just talk to each other?"

He shook his head. "He's completely closed himself off to me. It started before my mother died. When I came to live with him, I never felt cared about. My being charged with murder was the final straw." Dexter was saddened that he was his father's biggest disappointment. "I was happy to have Stephanie as a sister when my father adopted her after he married Marion. She has never let me down, not like him."

"Perhaps, if you told him . . ."

He interrupted, "No! He's not interested in my feelings. Hell, he isn't interested in me period," his voice was raw with anguish.

Anthia's arms automatically went around his waist, she whispered, "Oh, Dex . . ." She brushed her lips against the base of his throat. Intent on offering comfort, she smoothed a soft hand against his chest inside his robe.

Dexter's reaction was instantaneous and decidedly masculine. His sex instantly swelled to its full length while his arms momentarily tightened around her. He was not thinking, simply feeling as he lifted her until her feminine mound was against his throbbing erection.

"Anthia," he shuddered, "what are you doing to me?" he growled, his sexual frustration at war with his tender feelings for her.

Alarmed she tried to push herself away but he held her fast. "Let me go," she said.

His whisper was throaty, heavy with need, "I can't." His face was buried against the side of her neck.

She was just as painfully aware of him as he was of her. "Dex . . ." Clinging to his wide shoulders, she moaned, "I can't take anymore of this. You either want me or you don't."

He sighed with keen disappointment as he allowed her body to slide down his. He balled his hands at his sides, then said "This isn't about you and me, baby."

"That's exactly what it's about," she insisted, her bitterness evident. "Once and for all, please, be honest with me. I need to know how you really feel." Wild with frustration, she pounded her small fist against his chest. "I have a right to know!"

"Baby, I've never been anything but honest with you . . . painfully so," he added through his teeth as if it hurt him to admit his vulnerability were she was concerned.

"Stop lying to me and stop lying to yourself! You say you care about me as your friend, yet I'm suppose to ignore the erection I feel against my body. Dex, I can feel the strength of your desire for me. I see it in your eyes when you think I'm not looking. I feel it right now as I'm touching the pulse in your throat. Your heart is racing."

"What do you expect? Your breasts are barely covered by the lace on your gown. Your nipples are boring into my chest. I can smell your sweetness. I know how your skin tastes against my tongue. Damn it! I'm a man. I can't help but want you."

Anthia moved away from his hot male length, hugging herself as if she were cold. She nearly shouted, "I'm sick to death of your pretense, Dexter Washington. If you can't be open with me, at least, be honest with yourself."

"I don't want you hurt. If that means denying myself sexually so be it," he said between clenched teeth.

"Your sacrifice is not appreciated. Just go away," she snapped fighting tears. "I deserve to be with a man who's not afraid to admit he has needs. Since you're not interested in being my lover and I'm not interested in being your friend, we have nothing to say to each other."

He reacted if she had struck him. "Don't you think you're being unfair? Why now? Why tell me this when we're so damn far from home?"

"You know why!

His large hands bit into her shoulders refusing to let her turn away from him. He felt as if he were being torn in half. Her angry decision crushed his heart and accelerated his own anger while intensifying his sexual frustration. Hell, what he wanted was her, spread wide beneath him.

"Why don't you tell me , then we'll both know," he grated between clenched teeth.

"Because I can't bear being so close to you, knowing you regret what we shared. It hurts knowing you're on the other side of that door and I can't go to you or invite you into my bed."

"Anthia . . ."

"Don't 'Anthia' me! Didn't that night mean anything to you, Dex?"

"Of course it did," he said hoarsely. It meant the world to him. He could not get that magnificent night or her out of his head, no matter how hard he tried to bury it.

"Then please stop the pretense right now. We've become lovers."

He closed his eyes, trying to shut out her beauty and his undeniable hunger for her. He needed a clear head. Finally he said, "Anthia, I took advantage of the situation and by doing so, I hurt you. I won't deliberately do that again."

"What hurts is your continual withdrawal. I won't pretend that I don't want you. I'm sick of doing without our late-night meals and talks. I am also fed up with doing without your love-making."

"You know why we can't," he insisted, fighting the yearning deep inside.

"All I know is I want you. Dex . . ." her eyes locked with his, "I want you to make love to me. I want you to touch me, take my breasts into your mouth the way you did that night . . ." her voice was husky with feminine yearning. "I need you, baby, deep inside of me . . . loving me."

Dexter was visibly shaken by her seductive urging. He'd been aroused to the point of pain and had been so since he had entered her bedroom. Enchanted by the way her dark hair curled around her soft neck and shoulders, he tried and failed not to take note of the dark outline of her large prominent nipples that beaded against her thin-strapped nightgown. All of which kept his erection thick with need and pulsating with desire.

His hands were balled into fists at his side as he fought with himself, not to yank her into his empty arms. She did not have to tell him that he was capable of giving her the hard, deep thrust she craved. He knew just how he would have made love to her, if he could have her. That was not the problem damn it. Making love would solve absolutely nothing.

"No! We'll still be right back where we started. I repeat, I do not want you hurt."

"You've already hurt me because you won't give us a chance. We both deserve that much . . . a chance. Oh, what's the use. I've known concrete walls more flexible than you. I give up!"

She raced over to the closet, tossed out her empty garment bag and began flinging clothes on top of it.

Dexter stood frozen, staring at her for a moment. His entire body had gone tight with tension. He knew he could not bear her walking out of his life. He'd waited so long to find a woman he could really talk to, someone who knew about his past and could accept him regardless. He had lost so much during those empty years in prison, including his ability to dream. His mind told him that she was asking the impossible, while his body demanded he take what was offered and shut the hell up about it.

After his parole, Dexter left Houston for Detroit, unsure of just what he was looking for, of what he needed to feel whole again. He had created a satisfactory life for himself, doing what made him feel good about the man he had become. With time and hard work, he regained his own self-respect. What he hadn't counted on was meeting one special woman . . . a woman he could genuinely care about. A woman he cared so deeply for.

Gradually, Anthia had become an essential part of that new life. She had reached into his heart in a profound way. He closed his eyes against the despair of tears burning his throat, filling his chest. Tears that he did not dare let fall.

Just who was in the most need of protection? Himself or Anthia? Was that what this was all about? Was he afraid of caring too much . . . risking it all? Was he afraid he might fall in love again?

Dexter didn't know the answers . . . he honestly didn't have a clue. The bottom line had not changed. Anthia's well-being was too important to him. He would do nothing that would jeopardize her happiness.

He was so long in reacting that her buoyant, positive spirit sank like a lead-filled balloon. Tears blinded her, but she hastily blinked them away. She had no idea where she was going, but she could not stay here. She could not . . .

His bare feet were silenced by the carpet as he moved toward her, his lean dark hands tenderly caressed her shoulders before he encircled her small waist forcing her to stop. "Don't . . ." he said throatily.

"Let me go."

"No," he said. "You're not going anywhere without me." Turning her to face him, he whispered, "I don't know, baby. I just don't know anymore." All he was absolutely sure of was that he could not lose her. He could not even bear to think about it. He would do anything . . . anything to keep her with him. Finally, he whispered throatily, "Okay."

"What?"

He looked down into her lovely troubled eyes. "Whatever you want," he said before he covered her mouth with his. The kiss was not soft or gentle. It was stark and heavy with even deeper emotions, ones she couldn't began to comprehend.

She opened her sweet mouth beneath the onslaught of his

driving hunger, allowing her tongue to move seductively against his. He groaned deep in his throat, gathering her even closer until her breasts were cushioned on his hair-roughened chest.

"Yes . . ." he moaned, his hands pushed her robe away, then moved to the straps of her gown and pushed them down her arms. His large hands were far from steady as he bared her breasts and stomach to his hot hungry gaze.

"You're so beautiful . . . so perfect," he palmed her softness, gently squeezing the taunt dark tips between his thumb and forefinger.

Anthia threw back her head, trembling from the heated caress, but she shook her head. "Please . . . Dex. . . . please," she begged.

"What, baby? What do you need?" he asked, tugging each highly sensitive elongated peak. His mouth was hot against her delicate brown throat.

She moaned as if in pain, unable to verbalize her desires as she trembled all over. If she had not been clinging to him, she probably would have fallen. Her legs refused to hold her weight. He stroked her tongue against his, until they both were trembling from unfulfilled longing.

She pressed his hand against her breasts until he cupped it gently. "Please . . . I need your mouth."

Dexter did not require further urging. He dropped his head until he could lick the tight nipple until it stood up sweet and erect from his attention, only then did he take it into the deep warmth of his mouth and sucked. At first the suction was gentle but she moaned as she tried to push even more of her softness into his mouth, then he groaned, deepening the suction until he gave her the strong friction she needed.

She was on fire. Anthia pressed her aching mound against his thigh, wordlessly seeking his attention. She called out his name when he released her hard, sweet nipple. Dexter soothed her with a deep kiss before he moved to lick the other breast, not stopping until it too received the full force of his lips and tongue. He didn't ease up until her legs were so weak that he supported her petite frame.

Dexter lifted her, then carried her over to the bed. When they came down together, somehow she had lost her nightgown. It was no great loss, for his hands were hot on her bare skin as he smoothed over her slender throat, down her rib cage, flat stomach to the curls shielding her feminine mound.

"Hurry . . ." she begged, needing his long, blunt fingertips against those fleshy folds. Fortunately, she didn't have long to wait.

He caressed the cottony soft curls before he parted her dew-kissed heat. He spread the feminine petals open and gave her the full caress she longed for until she was a trembling mass of nerves. She wanted him so badly that she was beyond speech and could only whimper. He found her so gloriously wet with need. He whispered her name as he stroked her, paying close attention to the tiny heart of her passion.

His voice was thick with desire when he said, "Let me taste your sweetness. I want to feel you on my tongue, drink you in." Suddenly his mouth replaced his hand as he licked her with long, intense strokes sliding deeper and deeper into her feminine heat.

"Don't . . ." she whispered, once she caught her breath. How could he want her like this? She ignored the way her body trembled from head to toe.

He lifted his head until he looked her in the eyes. "I want you . . . this way. Let me make it good for you."

Anthia nodded, too embarrassed to meet his gaze. Dexter was not put off by her reluctance. His only thought was to drowning his senses in her feminine magic and giving her the utmost pleasure. His tongue was so gloriously hot and velvety against her as he laved her sweetness. He concentrated on her clitoris, laving her over and over before he applied a sweet suction. He didn't stop even when she called out his name. He didn't stop until her control shattered and she climaxed as waves of the raw pleasure rushed over her.

When she recovered enough to speak, she found herself cradled in his arms against his chest. Anthia pressed her lips against his while she caressed his chest.

Dexter was too far gone to wait for what he wanted. He

needed her soft hands on his body . . . now. "Touch me . . ." his voice reflected his hunger.

Anthia's hands circled his flat nipples nearly sending Dexter over the edge. He growled, his breath quickening as she explored his lower abdomen, moving through the thick crisp black hair surrounding his penis.

"Baby . . ." he whispered unable to bear the anticipation. He longed for her silky hands on his sex, cupping the fullness below then stroking his shaft. Their one night of love making had only made him wild with desire for her. He knew what deep pleasure she was capable of giving him. She had satisfied him so completely that he had nothing to compare it to, but he yearned for more.

It took his last drop of willpower not to beg for her loving. He had been fighting himself for so long, enduring endless, empty nights without her. Not once during all that time had he even considered replacing her with another woman. It wasn't even an option. Anthia filled his head, and warmed his heart. There was no room for anyone else.

His deep voice was rough with the rawness of his need when he said her name unable to disguise his hunger. "Stroke me . . . baby." He groaned heavily. "Oh, yes! Just like that." He was quivering from the force of his desire for her. He closed his eyes, unable to contain the pleasure . . . the utter bliss he found as her small hands caressed him from the broad tip of his sex to the thick base. Had he ever been so hard?

"Dex . . ." she whispered his name as she cupped him below and then gently squeezed him before she moved her hands along his hard length. She not only felt the swelling caused by her caressing hands but she heard his quickening response. When she bathed the satiny moist crown of his sex with rough velvet of her tongue his large frame shook in reaction.

"Baby . . ." he choked out unable to bear anymore, he growled his pleasure and pulled her up and beneath him, his mouth hot and insistent on hers. Dexter was not satisfied until she opened for him, allowing him full access to her mouth. He thrust his tongue repeatedly against hers.

One kiss lead to another and another each hotter than the

last. Unable to wait any longer, Dexter slowly parted her thighs, then pressed the tip of his sex against her softness stroking her before he slowly filled her to bursting with his thick shaft. The silky wetness of her body welcomed him as he pressed deeper and deeper into her tight sheath.

Anthia clung to him, overwhelmed by the hard unyielding strength of him as he thrust repeatedly. Without warning, her body tightened and sent sheer pleasure racing through her system as her world disappeared and seemed to shatter as she experienced yet another climax.

When she could breathe normally once more, Anthia pressed soft kisses on Dexter's throat. "What are you trying to do to me? Drive me out of my mind with pleasure?"

"Exactly," he said around a heavy groan. He lifted her legs to his shoulders, continuing to stroke into her again and again. He would have laughed if he had not been so painfully aroused. Thick black lashes covered his lids as he deepened his thrust while he moved his hand between their bodies. He didn't hesitate. He stroked against her clitoris. She trembled from head to toe, opening herself even more to his hard thrust.

"Anthia . . ." he whispered close to her ear, then licked the lobe before he took it into his mouth to suckle. "Finish with me . . ." he kissed the supersensitive place behind her ear. The hot wash of his tongue sent shivers racing up and down her spine. He waged a full assault on her senses as he continued to caress her slippery pearl while his repeated thrust intensified.

She was close . . . so close. Unable to bear the sensual torment, she licked his nipple. Dexter groaned thickly as he closed his eyes against the sweetness. He gave her what she needed, his body hard and persistent. His wet, warm kisses covered her throat as he pressed his face close to the place were her neck and shoulder joined, filling his lungs with her feminine scent as he urged them both toward completion.

"You feel so good . . . so hot," he moaned as he flexed his hips driving himself deeper still.

Anthia was beyond speech as her body instinctively tightened around him, giving him the heart-stopping caresses he hungered for. He cried out at the pleasure, intensifying his thrusts.

"Come . . . come with me," he chanted over and over again.

As she stroked her hands down his back, Dexter knew his control was slipping. He worked to give her exactly what she needed but it was his continued stroking of the tiny heart of her desire that led to her undoing. Her release was as swift and uncontrolled as a volcanic eruption. It rushed over her and triggered his long-awaited climax. His hoarse shout of completion mingled with her sobs. They clung to each other while their bodies gradually cooled.

Dexter marveled at the experience, such an incredible pleasure. He tended to lose himself within her glorious heat. He placed tender kisses on her cheek, her throat and finally on her kiss-swollen lips.

"Girl, you know how to drive me out of my mind with pleasure." The kiss deepened sweetly.

"Please . . . don't tell me you regret what we shared," she said pressing her face against his throat.

"I needed you too much to regret anything that has happened between us tonight," he said quietly as he caressed her nape.

Anthia rested on his chest, hoping with all her heart that this time, he meant it. She didn't think she could bear it if he turned away from her again. She cautioned herself not to worry about what tomorrow might bring. For this one night she was in his arms.

Dexter cradled her against him. His wide palm smoothing gently over the slope of her spine. He cupped the round fullness of her bottom, relishing her softness. His breath quickened as his lips moved insistently against hers.

"Anthia . . ." he said throatily as he coaxed her mouth open for the full thrust of his tongue against hers while he parted her thighs. All too soon his body lifted and thickened ready to once again claim hers.

It was sometime before either one of them got any sleep. Then, she slept so hard that when he whispered close to her ear, " 'Morning," she jumped.

"Sorry, baby. I didn't mean to scare you. Are you okay?" he asked pressing his lips to that tender spot behind her ear.

Anthia shivered in response. Then she stretched before slowly opening her eyes. "Good morning. What time is it?"

"Eight. Hungry?" His dark eyes slowly explored her fine African features. She was even more beautiful now than the day before, he decided rashly. Her mouth was so sweet, so alluring that he placed a kiss there.

She opened, eager for the brush of his tongue on hers. She was not disappointed, but he ended it much too quickly. "I'm starving. Did you sleep?" she blushed then, for neither of them had gotten very much sleep. They'd been too busy making love.

Dexter chuckled, "Not much. You?" he teased, knowing the answer as he caressed her cheek with a long lean finger. "Care to share a shower?"

Anthia was tempted but she was still too shy with him. Her experiences with men were so limited that she was afraid to let him know how the idea embarrassed her. She shook her head. "You go on ahead."

Dexter was clearly disappointed but he accepted her reluctance. They had taken a big step last night. Maybe they both needed time to adjust to the changes. "Breakfast in town, say twenty minutes?"

"Make it a half hour."

He grinned before swinging his legs over the side of the bed. He pulled on his robe before he padded across the room into the bathroom, closing the door quietly behind him.

Anthia sat up in bed hugging her knees. Her eyes lingered on the clothes and opened case in the chair, evidence of what she had done to make him change his mind. Had she gone too far? Would they both live to regret it?

What now? Last night had eased the loneliness and despair inside of her. The only thing missing was his love. A single tear slid down her cheek but she quickly brushed it away. What they shared had to be enough. It was all she had and she was grateful for it. She did not try and fool herself into believing that things had changed between them. Dexter was still very much in love with Christine. Anthia suspected she was the one who had to change, that's if she wanted Dexter in her life.

Anthia had put on a happy face by the time she joined him

for the ride into the city. They teased each other when they saw that they were both dressed in jeans and cotton knit sweaters, Anthia's was pale green while his was navy.

They ate a leisurely meal in one of the downtown restaurants, then later Dexter drove them around Houston, showing her the city.

Dexter flexed his broad shoulders restlessly. His eyes constantly going to Anthia. She'd been so quiet at breakfast. Finally, he asked, "Is something on your mind? Are you having second thoughts?"

"Not me," she answered quickly, then asked softly "Did you realize we overlooked something? You didn't use a condom, why?" She kept her gaze straight ahead unable to meet his gaze.

They were at a red light. He turned her face toward his.

"It was an oversight on my part. It wasn't until this morning that I realized it. Why didn't you say something?"

She was embarrassed, she couldn't meet his gaze. "I don't know. I wasn't thinking clearly. What if . . ." She couldn't finish.

"We'll just have a baby together. Don't worry. I'm clean. I don't have any STDs."

"It's not just that," she blushed. "I don't want to raise another baby alone. It's too hard."

"You won't be alone."

He was staring so intently at her profile and was disappointed when she wouldn't look at him. It was the blast from a car horn behind them that brought his attention back to the congested roadway. Accelerating, Dexter decided right then and there that if Anthia was carrying his child then they would get married.

Anthia stared down at her tightly clasped hands as she wondered what he meant. She was not sure how she felt. But one thing was clear, Dexter was nothing like Jeff's father.

"You haven't asked but I want you to know that I have not been sexually active in quite some time. And I used a condom then. It was a casual acquaintance. It was not repeated. I don't enjoy casual sex. I'm kind of old-fashioned to the extent that my emotions have to be engaged."

She nodded. "I appreciate you telling me. As you already

know, you are the first man I have been with since Jeff's father and we broke up after that one time."

"Once was all it took?"

"Yes," she whispered.

"Why, Anthia? Why haven't you been involved with anyone? What about Doug Henderson?" His voice was gruff with disapproval when he said, "I know the guy had the hots for you."

She looked at him sharply wondering if she heard jealousy in his tone. "Doug and I were just friends. We went out a few times but that was it. I never had strong feelings for him."

"We've been just friends for a long time," he could not help adding. A muscle jumped in his cheek.

"There's a difference and you know it."

"What's the difference? Why me? Why did you let me become your lover?"

"What do you mean why you? How can you ask?" She said unhappily, "You know I care about you." She wanted to throw something at him. She was not the one who had been reluctant to get involved. She was not the one with leftover feelings for someone else.

What he wanted was to hear that he was the only man she cared about. "I also care deeply for you." Then he said so quietly, she had to strain to hear him. "If I was able to love it would be you, Anthia. If we've made a baby together then we will raise it together."

Anthia's hopes sank as she slowly accepted the bitter truth. She couldn't settle for less than his whole heart. She wanted them to be together because of love not because of a child they might have made.

It wasn't until they reached Sugarland when they did not take the turn off but continued on, finally stopping beside a impressive ranch style home that Anthia became curious. The house was set back from the road beside a wooded area. It was lovely but in spite of the cared-for lawn, it had a deserted feel about it.

Dexter sat quietly with his hands tightly gripping the steering wheel, his jaw taunt with tension.

"It's a beautiful house. Did you design it?"

"Yes. Would you like to see the inside."

"What?" Anthia looked at him closely "I don't understand. How could you have a . . ." Suddenly she knew. "This was your home, wasn't it? The one you shared with Christine."

"Yes," he said with difficulty. "Her life ended here and so did mine." His hand was shaking as he moved it over his short natural.

For once, Anthia had no idea what to say. Nothing could change what had happened here. Nothing could ease his suffering. She wanted to drop her head in her hands and howl from her own sense of hopelessness.

This was why he could no longer love again. All his love, hopes and dreams had gone into his marriage with Christine. They shared so much more than this fabulous house. Now that Christine was gone, there was nothing left. A part of Dexter had died with her and their child.

"Why did you bring me here?"

SEVENTEEN

"I wanted you to see it. I want you to understand."

"I understand only too well. You prefer to live in the past rather than to look toward the future," she whispered.

How could she have been so certain she could deal with this? How? Right now all she could do was accept what was right in front of her face. She could never lose what she never really had.

"That's not what I'm doing."

"Really? Then why have you kept this house? And don't tell me you don't own it, because I suspect you do. Do you have plans to someday move back here?"

The look he gave her was a sharp, pointed one, but he didn't voice his thoughts. He put the car back into gear and set it into motion. Not once did he look back, but then he did not have to, Anthia decided bitterly. As long as he owned that house he held on to a part of Christine.

They shared a quiet dinner later that evening in a small steak house near the interstate where dress was not an issue. The music and good food seemed to ease the mood.

She surprised them both when she asked, "Have you considered having a talk with your father while you're here?"

"There's nothing to say. Our lives have moved in two entirely different paths over the years." Dexter did not want to remember the time after his release from prison. His voice was bitter as he told her how things were when he'd moved back to Houston.

For five years, he'd worked and lived in the city while on parole. His only contact with his family had been with his sister.

When he finished, Anthia asked, "How can you have nothing to talk about when you haven't seen each other in more than ten years?"

"We said it all before my trial. He no longer has a son and I have no father."

"I can see where he might not be willing to change. He's an old man, set in his ways. Dex, you're not. Can't you at least try to repair the rift between you?" Her dark eyes filled with concern.

"I was not the one who left his wife and child before the ink was barely dry on his degree. He left and never looked back. I never turned my back on him during the most difficult time of his life. He believed the worst. He believed I killed my wife and child in cold blood."

"It's in the past. Why can't you two leave it there?" Anthia said, pushing her food away. Like Dexter, she didn't have much of an appetite.

"You're wrong. It's still there between us."

Frustrated, Anthia sighed wearily. Dexter was a good man, but he could be stubborn. He deserved some peace in his life, some happiness. If he could repair his relationship with his father, perhaps that could be one step toward leaving his past in the past. Anthia was acutely aware that the only person in his family that genuinely seemed to have feelings for him was his sister.

"Honey, I do so admire you for coming back. I'm not sure if the situation were reversed I could find the courage to do so."

Dexter smiled, briefly taking her hand in his. She made him feel good about the changes he had made in his life. Perhaps she had a point.

"Look," she said, her eyes glimmering like an eager child, as the waitress approached with the dessert tray.

Dexter chuckled. "That chocolate cream pie looks good." His breath caught in his throat as he visualized a little girl with

Anthia's pretty features and petite stature. She was a wonderful mother.

"Nothing more for me. Thanks." She said pushing away her plate.

"Are you sure? We can share a piece . . ."

"Don't tempt me. No really, I've had enough." She smiled at him.

"Okay." He took it upon himself to order coffee for them both.

Anthia was not ready to end their discussion on his father. She waited until they were in the car, when she said, "If the opportunity presents itself, will you talk to your father? Tell him about the new life you've made for yourself in Detroit?" She still couldn't imagine a parent totally indifferent to his own flesh and blood.

It was dark as the car sped through the warm night. Dexter was quiet, seemingly lost in thought.

She said softly, "You have no idea how often I wish I still had my mother. Promise me that given the chance, you'll at least try to resolve you're differences with your father."

"We'll see," was all he was willing to concede.

"Hi, you two. Have fun?" Stephanie asked as she entered the foyer where Dexter was helping Anthia off with her denim jacket.

"Yes," Dexter smiled, returning Stephanie's hug and kiss. "How about you?"

"Busy. There is no end to the last minute things that have to be done."

Anthia also received a hug. "Getting nervous?"

Stephanie laughed, "A little jittery, with the rehearsal dinner tonight and parties afterward. In fact, I was on my way up to change. I know I won't get any sleep tonight and I want to look my best tomorrow."

"Stop worrying," Dexter encouraged squeezing her hand. "You're going to be a beautiful bride."

Stephanie laughed happily. "I'm so glad you're here. I know

how difficult it must be for you staying at the house. Dex, it has meant the world to me having you here for my wedding," she said wiping at a tear. With that said, she added in a conspiratorial whisper, "What do you think of my Kenneth? Isn't he wonderful?"

Dexter chuckled. "I won't say all that. Yes, he seems like a nice guy. As long as he treats you well, he and I won't have a problem."

"Remember, the bachelor party is after the dinner. Kenneth and his best man are scheduled to pick you up around ten. You're still going, aren't you?"

"Wouldn't miss it." Dexter hid his reluctance behind a smile. If his attending would make his sister happy, then he would be there. She was the best.

"Good. Anthia, my bridesmaids and I will pick you up around the same time. Don't worry, we won't be out too late."

"Sounds good."

"Everything is all set," Stephanie said cheerfully, heading for the stairs. She was halfway up when she paused, saying, "Oh, Dex. Daddy's in the study. He asked if you would stop in before you left for the party. See you two later." With that she hurried on ahead.

Dexter's entire demeanor changed in an instant. His easygoing manner had disappeared. Anthia did not try to conceal her concern. "Dex?" She touched his sleeve.

"Huh?"

"Say something."

"There's nothing to say. I'm not interested in what he has to say."

"Just listen. It can't hurt to listen to what he has to say."

"Okay," he muttered, "I want you to come with me."

"But why?"

"There is nothing he has to say that can't be said in front of you." When she was slow to answer, he prompted, "Well?"

"Yes, if that's the way you want it."

"Thank you." He brushed his lips against hers before he took her hand in his. "Let's get this over with."

Damon Washington's office was situated at the end of the

main hallway on the left. Dexter's knock was quickly answered with a gruff, "Come in."

Dexter urged her ahead of him into the plush masculine domain. The walls were paneled in dark cherry wood, the carpet was a rich mahogany. Oversize leather chairs were positioned in front of a massive dark oak desk. The walls were lined with plaques and honors for the highly successful family-owned architectural firm.

Damon Washington sat behind his desk with an open folder in front of him. "Good evening, Ms. Jenkins, Dexter. Please make yourselves comfortable." If he was surprised that Anthia accompanied his son, he didn't show it.

Although, Damon was a good head shorter than his son and a good fifty to sixty pounds heavier, it was easy to see where Dexter had inherited his keen African features and deep bronze complexion. Dexter's father was a well dressed, educated, charismatic black man, used to giving orders and having them quickly obeyed.

"Are you enjoying your stay with us, Ms. Jenkins?"

"Anthia," she smiled. "Yes, I am. You have a very lovely home, Mr. Washington."

"Is this your first trip to Texas?"

"Yes, Dexter has been showing me around."

"Wonderful. Wonderful," he said cordially. "You don't mind excusing us. I need to speak privately with Dexter. This won't take long."

Up until then Dexter had made no effort to make himself comfortable. He stood beside her chair, with his hand on one of her slender shoulders, thus keeping her seated. "That won't be necessary. Anthia stays. Say whatever you like."

Judging by his frown, Damon Washington did not approve of the arrangement, but he made no further objections. Apparently airing their family difficulties in front of guests was not to his liking.

He came straight to the point when he said, "Dexter, you have not been active in the company for some time." His voice lacked warmth and affection for the son he had not seen in years.

"It's a little hard considering the five-year vacation I was given courtesy of the State of Texas. Afterward, my services were no longer desired," Dexter said dryly.

"Neither one of us need reminding of how you failed yourself and your family."

Anthia managed to hold down the gasp rising in her throat. There could be no doubt of the man's disdain for his only child. It was in the cold, emotionless way he looked at Dexter. He obviously preferred to believe the worse in Dexter, believing that he deliberately killed his own wife and child. Anthia's body went rigid, horrified by his father's lack of love or faith in him.

"Incarcerated," Dexter clarified.

"There is no need to be so blunt."

"There is no need to sugarcoat it. Anthia knows the truth."

"She knows you're a . . ."

"Killer?" Dexter supplied. "Is that the word you mean, sir?" His broad shoulders were straight and his head was held high, yet his hands were balled into fists at his side, the only indication of his emotions.

The two men stood staring each other down. Neither willing to give an inch. Anthia was disgusted. How could the man have so little faith in his own flesh and blood? He did not know the sincere, genuinely kind man he had fathered.

There should be no way on earth that he could not believe in his own. No way!

Unable to remain silent a second longer, Anthia's voice revealed a calm she was far from feeling when she said evenly, "Christine's death was a tragic accident. It's time you accepted that. Blaming each other won't change what happened." She could not stand the way Dexter's father was deliberately hurting him. "Dexter could not have killed his wife. He's not that type of man. You above all people should know the kind of child you raised to manhood. We are talking about your son."

Dexter squeezed her shoulder, in an attempt to soothe her. He knew what a disappointment he was to his father. His father was well educated, but a self-made man. Dexter was supposed to be as an extension of Damon. What Dexter had done was to make a mockery of their family name. His involvement with the law had brought shame and dishonor down on all of them. That was what his father could not forget or forgive.

Dexter stated bitterly, "I stopped being his son the day I was arrested for murder. He was the first to judge me and find me guilty, long before the case came to trial."

"Look, I didn't ask you here to dig up the past. You and this young lady are guests in my home."

"Very reluctant guests. As you well know, the only reason I'm here is for Stephanie's sake. Her wedding will be perfect, regardless of how little we think of each other," Dexter ended coldly. Dexter considered Damon Washington a failure as a father as Damon considered Dexter a failure as a son.

Anthia persisted, "Will you two listen to yourselves? You're father and son . . . blood. That has to mean something? You're part of each other."

"You're wasting your time, Ms. Jenkins. Dexter and I haven't gotten along since his mother died."

"Ain't that the truth! I was a little upset when you left us to build a financial empire for yourself. You never looked back to the woman who loved you or the child that you fathered."

"I took you in when she died and I saw to it that you were well educated. You are the one who messed up your own damn life. I no longer have a son. He died for me the day he destroyed his life and our family's good name." To Damon's acute disappointment he had been unable to father another child with Marion.

Dexter had had enough. He said, "This entire conversation is pointless. Why did you want to speak with me?"

"It's time you resigned your vice presidency in the company and sold your stocks."

A muscle jumped in his jaw, but Dexter's voice was even when he asked, "Why? I've been a partner and stockholder since I earned my degree and joined the company. At one time, it was what we both wanted."

"You haven't worked for the company in over thirteen years. You partnership is on paper only. I see no point in it continuing."

"Why the sudden need to make a change?" Dexter asked

carefully as if he were holding on to his temper by a slender thread.

"Kenneth is an excellent architect. He deserves to be able to move up in the company. I want him to take over your position. As Stephanie's husband, he has the right."

"What if Dexter decides to return to the business?" Anthia couldn't help asking.

His father clearly did not appreciate the question, but his manners were impeccable. "After all this time, I think that is highly unlikely."

Dexter was amazed at how deeply his father's continued rejection hurt, especially after all this time. It was nothing new, but to offer his rightful place to someone else was too much.

"You have no right to offer my inheritance to anyone else, not even my sister's husband."

"I'm offering you a fair market value for your shares of the business. A small fortune by anyone's standards."

"Let me get this straight. What you want is to buy me out of this family so that Kenneth can take my place as your son? You plan to turn the business over to him one day I take it?"

"The business is mine. I say who stays and who goes." The two men openly glared at each other.

Dexter's keen disappointment and pain were hidden behind a cold countenance. "You stopped being my father a long time ago. There is no doubt about that. You'll probably go to your grave believing the worst of me." Dexter's face was marred by a scowl as he shoved his hand into his pocket. His voice was deceptively soft when he said, "There was a time when all I wanted in the world was for you to believe in me."

His eyes bore into his father's as he said, "Yes, I did not deliberately kill my wife and our baby. What I did was try to stop her from destroying herself and that is all I did. It was a failed attempt, true enough, but how could I have lived with myself if I had not tried?"

If he had looked at Anthia, he would have seen the tears of love that momentarily blinded her that she hastily blinked away.

Dexter's eyes were on the man he had loved and looked up

to for so many wasted years. The man he could not stop loving no matter how much it hurt to do so.

"Yes, my life is different now, different from the way you wanted it to be. I'm my own man. I live my life trying to help young men without fathers. It's something I find more fulfilling than working for profit."

He paused, swallowing down his disappointment. How he wished that he had never returned. "We both know that it's my choice what I decide to do about the position and the stock. At this moment, I don't want any part of you." He placed his hand under Anthia's elbow and urged her up and out of the chair. "Come on, Anthia."

They had reached the door when his father asked, "I'd like an answer."

Dexter had nothing more to say. He urged her down the hall-way. Their pace was so swift that by the time they mounted the stairs and reached her bedroom door, she was out of breath.

"Dex . . ."

He didn't open his mouth until they were inside of her room. "I'm sorry you had to witness that." He paced the confines of the room, moving to the patio doors and back again.

"I'm sorry, too." Anthia sank down into the nearby armchair. "I hate that you had to go through that. I pushed you into it," she sighed. "My father died when I was little so I never knew what it was to grow up with one." She felt so badly about the false hope she had given him. She had been so sure that if Dexter could bend just a little that he and his father could rec-oncile their differences. She could not have been more wrong.

"With an old man like mine, I'd say you didn't miss much. Thank God, I know men who are genuine fathers to their chil-dren. Men like Charles Randol and Quinn Montgomery."

There was a time when he wanted nothing more than to be the best father he could to his own child. Unfortunately, that had also turned out badly. He had learned to compensate for the loss. Helping fatherless boys at the center had gone a long way toward healing his own deep wounds. A child of his own was a lost dream . . . one he no longer consciously allowed himself to hope for.

Suddenly, last night's slipup with the condom flashed through his mind. That kind of mistake had never happened before. He was a careful man, not that he'd been sexually active in years. Now suddenly he admitted the truth to himself.

Fatherhood was something he secretly longed for. He hadn't considered the possibility until he met Anthia. Just the thought of a child with her sent a surge of sheer warmth through his entire system. He had to keep reminding himself that it was nothing more than wishful thinking. Thank goodness, reality had stepped in and prevented him from asking her to marry him the instant he realized what he had done.

He may not be a father, but he could still strive be a better man than Damon Washington. He could never even imagine himself hurting the woman who he claimed to love as his father had done without apparent remorse. And as far as Dexter was concerned, that kind of neglect had nothing to do with love.

Dexter considered his own father a hopeless failure when it came to parenting. That disappointment was as glaringly absent today as it had been years ago when he turned his back on Dexter during his trial. His father should have learned a long time ago that you can not buy and sell family. Love, trust and loyalty were the things that truly matter in life.

Even after so much time, it was still difficult to accept that his own father had found another to replace him. Damon did not think Dexter was worthy of the title . . . son.

"Damn it!" he fumed. It should not hurt this much.

"Are you okay?" she asked, close to tears. "I'm so very sorry that I encouraged you to open yourself to what turned out to be more disappointment."

"It's not your fault." He laughed, but the sound fell short of the humor it was meant to convey. "I haven't had any illusion about the man who fathered me for a very long time. I was the one who underestimated him, once more. I didn't think he could ever hurt me again because I didn't want anything from him. I was wrong." He swallowed past the constriction in his throat, "I wanted his respect. I realize now that's the only reason I've maintained the partnership and my stocks. It meant I was still, although limited, a part of this family. I see now that it was a wasted effort."

"Don't . . ." she was forced to clear her throat of the tears in urgent need of release. "For what it's worth, I'm on your side."

His dark eyes locked with hers for a timeless moment. When he spoke, his voice was a deep-throated whisper, "That means a lot to me. I'm sorry, baby, but I'm not fit to be with right now. Enjoy your evening with the girls. I'll see you in the morning." He was at the connecting bathroom door when he paused long enough to say, "Pack tonight if you can, so that when we leave this house before the ceremony, we don't have to ever come back to it." He closed the door between their rooms, not waiting for her to response.

Anthia was upset, resentful of the way Dexter had shut her out and furious with his heartless father. She suspected Dexter was experiencing a tremendous amount of pain. She was so disappointed that he felt he could not share this with her. He was one to keep his problems and his concerns to himself. He did not share himself easily with others. But she was not just anybody. She was his friend, as well as his lover. He mattered to her.

She'd been back from the bride's party a little over an hour when she heard Dexter's footsteps in the hall as he passed her door before continuing on to his own. He probably had as much fun as she had had tonight . . . which was next to none after the unpleasant conversation with his father. It had certainly put a damper on her evening.

"At least Stephanie had a wonderful time. That was something to be grateful for," she mumbled softly to herself as she glanced yet again at the bedside clock. Not fifteen minutes had passed since she last looked.

Having showered and changed into a pale green nightgown, she found she could not sleep. If only she could turn her thoughts off. After last night, how could he isolate himself this way? Sure, he was upset, but shouldn't they deal with this together? Why must he face all his difficulties alone? Why must he always shut her out? Couldn't he see that that was exactly what he was doing?

It had been an exhausting weekend. She was so thankful that the wedding was the next day. Tomorrow, they could fly home.

Oh, she had learned a great deal about Dexter's background. He had failed to mention that he had given up a successful career as an architect. Nor had he acknowledged that he had a partnership in the highly successful family-owned company.

More disheartening for her was to learn that he could not bring himself to sell the home he had designed and built for Christine. If she had any doubts about his ability to love again, this latest discovery had shattered the last tiny grain of hope that she had clung to.

She wondered if she should consider herself lucky that he had told her that after his release from prison while he was on parole he had chosen to work with juvenile offenders rather than go back to his chosen career. When he left for Michigan, he had put his past completely behind him, determined to never look back.

Now that she had seen with her own eyes the way his father had turned his back on his own flesh and blood, she had no choice but to accept the harsh, bitter truth that Dexter had lived with for years. In Damon Washington's view, there could be no margin for error, even for his own son.

Anthia considered his heartlessness and cruelty unconscionable. She, too, had faced the difficulties parenting can involve. Jeff had made a serious mistake, perhaps the most serious of his entire life. If she had turned her back on him then, their whole life would be different today.

Jeff would probably not be in college paving a solid future for himself, but in jail serving a sentence he did not deserve. His attitude about life and people would have certainly changed for the worse, if she had not supported him. His faith and trust would no doubt have been altered in a negative way. More importantly, she would have lost her son's love and trust.

In her opinion, Damon Washington had made a serious mistake and because of it he had lost the trust of a wonderful man.

Dexter was one of a kind. She could never forget that he believed in her before she was strong enough to believe in herself. He never doubted that Jeff would make it through a difficult recovery. Nor had he doubted that she could make a success of her business. He encouraged her at every turn. He was her number one supporter and friend.

Anthia suspected that Dexter still loved his father whether he was willing to admit it or not. In fact, she was sure of it. If Dexter did not love him, Dexter could not be hurt by him. He had been deeply hurt by his father's last heartless act. Why couldn't Mr. Washington see that he had probably severed the last bit of hope that the two of them had of ever reconciling their differences?

As Anthia rested on her side in the dark, she was oblivious to the lateness of the hour. Yes, she was tired but she knew her weariness came from more than lack of sleep. Her feelings were hurt because Dexter preferred his own company. He did not want to be with her tonight.

It was after three in the morning when she heard his hoarse, cry of anguish. Anthia did not weigh the wisdom of her going to him under the circumstances. She swung her legs over the side of the bed and hurried through the connecting bathroom. She paused long enough to knock lightly on his closed door.

"Dex? Are you all right?" His throaty shout had her rushing into the dark room to where he tossed on the king-size bed. "Dex . . ." she shook him trying to wake him. "Honey, wake up."

"No!" he gasped, then sat straight up in bed.

"Shush, it's okay. It was only a dream," she crooned to him, stroking his bare chest.

"Anthia?" he said groggily.

"Yes," her caressing hand moved soothingly over him. "I heard you moaning in your sleep. You okay?"

"Yeah," he said catching her hand and holding it in his own for awhile. Dexter pushed back the sheet and padded over to the patio doors that overlooked the garden. He was unconcerned by his nudity as he stared out into the night. Taking in deep fortifying breaths, and then letting it out slowly, he said, "Sorry I woke you."

Anthia crossed to him, wrapping her arms protectively around herself while telling herself that she had no business being hurt because he had moved away from her. "I was awake. Well, if you're all right . . ." she said before her voice trailed off.

Dexter turned moving swiftly across the room, blocking her path. "Don't leave. Not just yet." His large hands were balled at his sides.

She tried not to follow the powerful muscular lines of his shoulders with her eyes, but failed for her gaze moved on to the trim lines of his midsection, his sex heavy even when reposed, his long well muscled thighs and calves. He was like a dark bronze statue . . . gorgeous. She lifted her chin when she said, "I had the impression that you preferred your own company."

EIGHTEEN

"You're wrong. His head hung low as he struggled to get himself under control, to clear his thoughts.

She could see he was still shaken from the dream. She sat down on the edge of the bed crossing her legs primly at the ankles. She had overreacted. She had gone all emotional assuming he was rejecting her. This should not be about her but about him. He was the one in need of support.

Softly, she said, "A nightmare?"

"Yeah . . ." he sighed heavily. "They had been less frequent since . . ." he stopped abruptly having almost said since his absorption with her. It was true. Lately, he'd been almost dreamless. A real blessing for him after so many years of hell.

Since Anthia had come into his life, especially since she had been volunteering at the center, his dreams when he did have them were most often filled with sensuality, a reflection of his male hunger for her. All the emotion and raw need he felt after being around her came during the night and seem to feed on his desires to make love to her over and over again. Once they became lovers, those dreams had heated up even more. He couldn't seem to get enough of her.

"Would you care to talk about it?" she asked, but when he hesitated, she persisted, "It might help."

He paced for a time, unaware that his nudity was a definite distraction. She could barely take her eyes off him. Eventually, he said, "Nothing helped until recently."

His response served to remind her that she'd spent much of

the night awake concerned about her own place in his life. Damn him! He was shutting her out, again! "Excuse me for wanting to help. Next time I'll know to mind my own business," she said, jumping to her feet.

"What? Where are you going?"

"Do I have a reason to stay? Everything I do to try to help seems wrong."

"Anthia?"

"Don't 'Anthia' me. Dex, I'm tired of throwing myself at you. Last night we made love, tonight you can't stand the sight of me. Forgive me for sounding a bit upset, but I have feelings, too."

"You sound as if you think I'm pushing you away."

"Aren't you?"

"No! Where did you get that idea?"

"From you, you big jerk!" Her hurt was in her beautiful sad eyes.

His long ground-eating strides made short work of the distance between them. He held her at arm's length. "I never said I didn't want you or want to be with you tonight, baby. Give me some credit. What I didn't want to do was to take advantage of our situation. If I came to your room tonight, I would have wanted to make love to you again and again. Hell, I've been in a lousy mood since I spoke to my father." When she remained silent staring back at him, he said, "Baby, give me a break here. Neither one of us got much sleep last night and we both came in late tonight. I just didn't want to impose myself on you."

"Why don't you just admit it? You don't want a relationship with me. Last night was my fault. I didn't even have sense enough to remind you about the condom."

"Girl, what in the hell are you talking about?" Was she questioning his sincerity? "Anthia, I know I messed up last night. I will marry you if you're pregnant. I take my responsibilities seriously."

He still could not believe that he had been that reckless. He had been incredibly selfish, putting his own needs ahead of hers. Deep inside he admitted to himself that he had not wanted anything between them, not even a rubber. He treasured each delicious stroke of her feminine heat. Dexter knew he had it bad. He was nuts about her.

If he was not extremely careful, he would end up deeply in love with her. It was something he had sworn to himself he would never let happen again. All he had to do was look at how badly his marriage ended. His late wife would rather kill herself and their unborn child than continue being married to him.

"I didn't ask you to marry me. Besides, if I'm pregnant then I will simply have another child. It won't be your concern."

"Like hell! It has everything to do with what we shared," he snapped, his temper flaring. His nostrils expanded as he filled his lungs with her sweet scent. He was very conscious of her soft breasts against his bare chest, veiled by that annoying layer of silk.

She glared up at him.

"Why are you so mad at me? Your encouragement had nothing to do with what happened in my father's office tonight. He has taken a coldhearted approach to life, leaving no room for errors."

"That's not it . . . well not entirely."

"Anthia, if I had come to you tonight, it would have been a repeat of last night," he said somewhat impatiently. "Honey, I knew you have to be tender considering the way I took you so many times. Or did you think I could sleep with you without wanting to be inside of you?" His voice was husky with desire.

She could feel his heavy sex against her. She closed her eyes thrown off balance by her sudden change of emotion. She was dizzy from pure longing. "I didn't think of that."

"You're so small, so tight. I don't want to hurt you. Nor do I want to shock you because of my appetite."

"Appetite? What are you talking about?"

Dexter chuckled. "Sexual appetite," he clarified still chuckling. She socked him in the stomach. He really laughed then. He caught her close so she couldn't hit him again. Her closeness caused his body to harden even more. She was driving him wild with desire.

She fought the impulse to press herself even closer to him. She wanted to rub herself against him, beg him to ease the ache

he alone created. There was not one doubt in her mind that he
was man enough to eliminate that aching need.

"To hell with it," he mumbled as he swung Anthia off her
feet and moved with her to the large bed. He came down with
her on his chest, his mouth greedily ate at her sweet, full lips.

"Stop it!' she said, although her small hands clung to his
neck as her soft curves nestled against him. "How dare you
make fun of me!"

"I can't help myself," he said as he kissed her. He plunged
his tongue into her mouth, seductively stroking her tongue with
his. "How is it possible . . . a woman with a nearly grown son
can be so naive? Baby, you're as tight as a virgin," he said
between hot kisses, "you feel so good, I can't get enough of
you. I want to make love to you all night long."

"Oh . . ."

"Why baby? Why haven't you wanted to be with a man?"

"We talked about this," she whispered, hiding her face where
his neck and shoulder joined.

"No, we didn't, sugar. You have not told me why. Jeff is
nineteen years old."

"I know when my son was born. I was there remember?"

"Yeah. You weren't alone, were you?"

"My mother was with me," she admitted, touched by his
concern. "I was with Jeff's father because I thought I was in
love with him. I could not have been more wrong." She whispered, "I've been careful not to make that same mistake. I suppose I hadn't met a man I felt I could trust and care about that
way." Until Dexter she had never been in love. The problem
was she clearly wanted him so much more than he apparently
wanted her. And there was nothing she could do but ride out
this emotional storm.

He nodded. "It's been quite awhile for me, too. Why do you
think I stayed away from you? With the least bit of encouragement from you, I'm as hard as a rock. The timing didn't seem
to matter. I've had more erections around you than I care to
count. There's something about you that keeps my hormones
hopping," he said softly, then surprised them both when he admitted, "No other woman has ever affected me that way."

She couldn't help asking, "Are you saying you haven't had sex since your wife died?"

He admitted, "A few empty times after I was paroled. I'm not one for casual sex, never have been. I never considered having sex outside of my marriage, even when we were having problems."

She couldn't believe it. A man sexually abstinent for years? It did not seemed possible. Yet, how could she doubt him when she was no different herself? She thought she had been in love with Jeff's father and that was what made it right for her at the time. What she felt for Dexter went far beyond what she once felt. There was no comparison.

"Anthia?" he persisted.

"I don't know what to say."

Dexter rolled over taking Anthia with him. He lay between her thighs, his sex pressed against her silk covered mound. He moved against her, groaning at her softness. He could feel her heat even through the cloth. He was painfully ready for her sweetness.

He kissed her silky throat. "From the first time we met, I wanted you. I just refused to let you guess." When his lips found her luscious mouth, he licked her lips before he slid inside and rubbed his tongue against hers.

When their mouths eventually parted and they both could breathe again, he said, "What about Doug Henderson? He had it bad for you for a while there." Her long-standing friendship with Henderson had annoyed the hell out of him for some time. "You and Doug are still friends, aren't you?" he asked sharply.

"Friends, nothing more," she kissed him deep and long. "I've never felt about him the way I feel about you, honey."

Dexter sighed as he moved down trailing kisses to the tiny pearl buttons on her lacy bodice. "You don't need this." His hands dropped to the knee-length hem and began pushing it up until he could toss it over her head.

Once her lush breasts were bare for his touch, to his mouth, he didn't hesitate. He pressed soft, butterfly kisses over the full top swell before moving to the bottom swell. Her moan was so seductive, erotic to his enflamed senses. He covered her sweetly puckered nipple with his lips, licking repeatedly. When he lifted his head to look at her, her lovely breasts were wet from his hungry exploration.

"I love the taste of you. Your nipples are the color of bitter-sweet chocolate, so dark and so sweet." He licked the pouting peak again and again until her entire small frame trembled in reaction. "You like that, don't you, baby. You like my mouth on your breasts." He lowered his head, only this time, he sucked the aching tip until it stood out like a plump berry.

Anthia was moaning, restlessly moving her head from side to side rubbing her soft mound against his muscled thigh. "You are wet for me, aren't baby, I can feel you against my thigh." Dexter returned his mouth to her nipple and concentrated on pleasing her. Just when she thought she could bear no more he moved to the other nipple and performed the same sweet service. Anthia whimpered from the delicious sensation as he thoroughly enjoyed her. He laved her until she cried out his name a heartbeat away from climaxing when he stopped.

"Dex . . ." she moaned.

He pressed his mouth against hers.

Anthia was beyond speech, she lifted her hips and rubbed her wet mound against him. Her hands caressing down his spine, loving the supple feel of his bronze skin.

"Anthia . . ." he crooned throatily as he moved to separate her plump womanly folds using one finger he slid deeper still to apply a tender friction. Dexter took his time, ignoring her urging to hurry. He stroked her again and again before he moved to the highly sensitive nub at the top of her mound. His seemingly relentless caresses sent her over the edge. She cried his name as she gave in to the endless delight as white hot pleasure overwhelmed her . . . consumed her.

As she rested against his chest, Anthia marveled at his capacity for giving. She stroked down his chest pausing to worry his small nipple. At his groan, she smiled. "Now it's your turn," she whispered.

"I had my turn." Stroking her arm, he said, "That was what I was talking about when I spoke of appetite . . . mine for you." He enjoyed her innocent blush.

Anthia didn't know what to say. She didn't have the experience that he had. But she desperately wished to pleasure him as thoroughly as he had satisfied her. She ran her caressing hand over his flat stomach, pleased by his deep sigh as her hand neared the thick crisp hair surrounding his sex.

Dexter held his breath as she slowly stroked her fingertips along his pulsating shaft. He almost came off the bed as she smoothed over the crown of his sex at the same time her wet tongue flicked over his nipple. He gasped out her name in a hoarse whisper.

"What are you doing?" he groaned thickly when she replaced her soft hands with exquisite heat of her tongue. Over and over the damp caresses continued, nearly driving him past his endurance, pleasure built to such alarming proportions that he had to grip her shoulders, pulling her up into his tight embrace.

His tongue-plunging kiss was sizzling hot. "No more baby. I need you now. I need to be inside of you."

She pressed her breasts into his chest, rubbing her hard nipples against his skin. "Dex . . . please. Hurry."

Dexter tingled from the sweetness of the invitation as she moved against him. Not once did he even consider resisting her. He had to have her . . . had to know her sleek heat. He paused long enough to rip open a condom and prepare himself.

On his back, he encouraged her to straddle him thus allowing her to take as much or as little of him as she could handle. Her body's hot, wet caress along his length was nearly his undoing. His masculine instincts demanded he take control . . . give her firm, deep thrusts of his steel hard manhood. It took all his willpower to resist as she gently rocked against him slowly sliding until finally she encompassed his entire length. He let out a deep, throaty groan.

"Oh, Dex . . ." she whispered as a burning fire built inside of her. She instinctively tightened around him giving him the internal caress he craved. Again and again, she moved over him stroking him like a silk-lined glove until he groaned into her ear, how badly he wanted her . . . needed her while his large hands cupped her breasts worrying her hard nipples before he moved to her clitoris, to give her the delicately sweet caresses she adored. She wanted to scream out her enjoyment, but she desperately wanted to please him even more.

Anthia opened herself, offering even more of her sweet fire to him, relishing the powerful thrusts of his body. "Yes . . ." she shuttered as he moved insistently, steadily against her. When he began the exquisite torment of stroking her ultrasensitive feminine nub with his shaft, Anthia tightened around him then convulsed into a unbelievably sweet release. Her climax triggered his, he voiced a deep, throaty shout as the numbing pleasure caused his large frame to shutter from the powerful force of his release.

She clung to him, not willing to entertain the idea of letting him go . . . he was her heart. She was deeply in love with Dexter Washington and had been so for a very long time.

"You okay?" he murmured, his voice heavy from the lingering pleasure. His hand caressed along her spine, their bodies still comfortably joined.

"Mmm . . . you?" she whispered lazily.

"Yes . . ." he sighed.

There was so much left unsaid between them, yet, her eyes had drifted closed. Tonight had proven to him that Anthia made a keen difference in his life. It was quite simple. She made him happy. Could he do the same for her?

Could she accept him even though he could not give her the love that another man would be able to offer? Only this morning he found himself wishing that he had made her pregnant and that they would have to marry. There was no other way to justify the deed in his mind. Even though she deserved better, their child would be raised with two loving parents. They would be a family. He'd do everything within his power to make her happy.

Even tonight, he had been so desperate to have her that for a moment he had hesitated before reaching for the condom. It was only then that he fully realized how badly he needed her.

The idea that she could belong only to him gave him a deep sense of masculine satisfaction. No other man would enjoy her sweet loving. Yes, he found the idea tremendously appealing.

"Anthia?" he said softly. But her soft, even breathing confirmed that she was getting some much-needed sleep. She had been very upset with him. And he couldn't blame her.

He had been withdrawn when he left her earlier, determined to keep his hurt and disappointment to himself. She evidently found his natural inclination to not share painful emotions hurtful. How could he make her understand?

Goodness everything was all so complicated. He had gone against his better judgment and brought Anthia into his troubled world. He knew better than anyone else that she deserved love and devotion. She needed a man without so much emotional baggage. "Damn!" he whispered aloud. He was no champion.

He was too damn selfish to even consider letting her go. He found he needed her in his life. Needed her to get through the endless hours of the night. Only Anthia brought in the sunshine. By holding her against his side, Dexter was able to sleep soundly.

Anthia woke to the warm brush of Dexter's mouth against her throat. She blinked in surprise as the sweetness of the night before came into focus. She had come to him and he had made such exquisite love to her.

Her voice was husky from sleep when she said, "Hi. What time is it?"

Dexter gave her one of his slow, sexy smiles that made her heart race. "Hi, yourself." His dark eyes stroked the thickness of her lashes, the smoothness of her cheek, the succulent fullness of her beautiful lips. "After nine. Mmm, this is nice way to start the day." The more he thought about it, the more the idea of spending the day here with her appealed to him.

"Nine. Why didn't you wake me? We have so much to do." She pushed back the comforter, then pulled on her gown. But before she could hurry away, he held her hand.

"Not so fast," he was not ready to let her go.

"Dex . . ."

"I want to thank you." At her obvious puzzled frown, he elaborated, "I needed you last night. Yet, I couldn't to ask you to come to me."

Anthia's thick lash lids dropped as she recalled her own anguish and self-doubt. Her sweet smile warmed him, then she said, "There is no need to thank me. We care about each other."

"Yes," he said, looking into her eyes. His concern was evident in his voice when he asked, "Is that enough for you?" He would not hurt her. She meant far too much to him to even consider it.

"For now, yes," her voice was so soft that he had to strain to hear her.

Dexter nodded, accepting that he had no choice. He wanted things to be good for them. He intended to give her the world, but how could he ask her to be his wife? How could he give her the commitment he suspected she wanted when he was so uncertain of his future. He was a man with a horrendous past.

"Care to share a shower?" he asked, still reluctant to let her go.

"You go ahead. I have to finish packing before I can dress for the wedding." She kissed him before she hurried out.

Anthia found she was just as eager to leave this house as Dexter. She shook her head sadly as she worked. Dexter had no real family here. He had not been made to feel welcome by anyone other than his sister. It was a miserable situation, but it helped Anthia understand him better.

When Anthia was made up and fully dressed except for the pink suit, she threw on her robe and hurried down the hall to Stephanie's room. It was a beehive of activity. Maids were rushing around and her mother was smoothing out the lovely wedding gown spread across the bed.

Anthia knocked softly on the open door. "May I come in?"

"Of course. Do I look as nervous as I feel," Stephanie asked with a huge smile.

"Of course not, darling. You are beautiful and you are going to make a lovely bride," Marion said, giving Anthia a curious look.

Stephanie sighed. "Naturally, you think that way, Mother. I'm so nervous. What if I forget my vows? What if I trip and make an utter fool of myself."

"Not you. Everything will be perfect," Anthia soothed. She squeezed Stephanie's cold hands.

"What can we do for you, Anthia?" The older woman asked, her tone far from welcoming.

"I just wanted to have a word with Stephanie. See, if I can do anything to help."

"Thanks, Anthia. I'm glad you came. Sit down, please," Stephanie said, motioning to the armchair beside the skirted makeup table. "Mother, will you please excuse us while we indulge in a little girl talk."

Marion's nose jutted into the air as she said, "Of course. Naturally, I have last minute details to see to. Don't forget Marilyn will be here shortly to help you dress."

Stephanie nodded, her smile warm. Once they were alone, she asked anxiously, "How is Dex? Is he very upset with Daddy?"

He had been badly hurt, but there was no point in upsetting this lovely young woman before her wedding. "Dex will be fine," Anthia smiled.

"I wanted to warn him when you two arrived, but Daddy insisted I stay out of it. I'm so sorry. Kenneth and I both tried to change Daddy's mind. Buying Dexter's share of the company was not our idea. Dexter is Daddy's only natural child. He deserves better. I was lucky when Mother married Daddy and he adopted me as his legally." She paused, before she said, "Oh, Anthia, sometimes Daddy can be so stubborn. It's useless trying to talk to him. I keep praying that the two of them can someday set aside the past. Daddy may not know it now, but some day he will need Dexter's love."

"I agree. You're stuck in the middle because you love them both."

"Yes. For years, I have tried and tried to change Daddy's mind." A frown pleated her smooth brow. "I'm just so glad Dexter came for my wedding. And I am grateful to you, Anthia. It has been wonderful seeing him smile. He has been through so much."

"Grateful to me? Why?"

"For the first time in a long time he has someone to care about him, someone he cares about as well," she squeezed Anthia's hand.

Anthia did not know what to say. Finally she admitted, "Dexter and I have been friends for years. It's only recently that our relationship has deepened."

"You're good for him. He has been treated so badly. I just don't understand how anyone could think for even a minute that he could have harmed Christine and their baby. He loved her and was so looking forward to being a father."

Anthia's own tender heart ached, even though this was not new information. She had known all along that Dexter had been in love with his Christine. The trouble was Anthia believed he was still in love with her. After what they shared this weekend that knowledge was even more painful.

Anthia had to swallow the lump in her throat before she could say, "I'm so glad he has a sister like you, one who believes in him."

There was a knock on the door before Stephanie could respond her best friend and maid of honor, Donna Holmes rushed inside. "Time to get shaking!" Donna giggled. She was followed by three other bridesmaids.

Stephanie laughed and hurried over to hug her friends.

Anthia, having met them last night, excused herself but did not leave before she hugged the bride and wishing her well.

It did not take long to change into her suit and tidy up the room.

"Ready?" Dexter asked from the connecting door. He looked so handsome in a three-piece, dark gray suit that he had teamed with a pristine white shirt, and burgundy and gray striped tie.

"You look very nice." She straightened from securing her make up case that along with her garment bag was packed.

"Thank you. He walked across to her and placed a soft kiss against her lips careful not to smear her deep rose-tinted mouth. "You are beautiful. Are you sure you're not the bride?"

His warm gaze slowly moved over her petite length in the lovely two piece pale pink suit with gold trimmed pearl buttons at the sleeve and down the front of the jacket. She wore gold and pearl swirl earrings along with a pearl, set in gold, bracelet watch. Her shapely legs were enclosed in ivory hose and she wore high ivory stack-heeled pumps.

"You are so sweet, but I saw the bride. She is breathtaking. Wait until you see her," Anthia laughed.

He smiled. "All set? Should I take these down?"

"Yes. Thanks." Anthia tried not to react to his masculine charm. He was just so handsome and despite their problems, she longed to claim him for her own. She picked up her small ivory purse with its gold-chained shoulder strap.

Dexter stored their things inside the trunk of the rental car. They would not have to bother anyone to take them to the airport after the wedding reception.

Stephanie was a beautiful, yet elegant bride. Her parents had spared no expense, giving her an elaborate send-off. The church was bursting with flowers. As Anthia sat beside Dexter, she marveled at the elaborate cream-and-peach satin-trimmed decorations.

Marion's family and many of Houston's dignitaries, as well as Damon's business associates were in attendance. The church was overflowing with people. Dexter held Anthia's hand throughout the ceremony. She could see that his emotions were close to the surface as he watched his beloved sister take her vows. He was so proud of her.

The wedding reception was held at the Four Seasons in one of the huge ballrooms. Champagne flowed freely and the array of food was spectacular. No detail had been overlooked. Before it was time to cut the wedding cake, Anthia and Dexter had a private moment with the newlyweds. Their flight time was fast approaching.

"I am so glad you could come." Stephanie kissed and hugged her beloved brother while tearfully trying to tell him how much his being there and sharing this special day meant to her.

Dexter was all choked up with emotion but he did manage to say, "I love you and I want you to be happy. If you ever need me, you know I'm only a phone call away."

Stephanie nodded before she turned to Anthia and gave her a warm hug. "I am so glad you came. It was wonderful meeting you, Anthia." She whispered into Anthia's ear, "You're perfect for him. Don't let him get away."

Anthia hugged her back, "Thank you. I wish you both a long

and joyful married life." It was evident that Stephanie was the sole member of Dexter's family who truly loved him.

Dexter and his new brother-in-law shook hands. "Take good care of her. She deserves only the best." Then he said, "You two must come to Michigan for a long visit. And soon."

The two women smiled fondly at each other. They were on their way to becoming friends.

NINETEEN

"Did you give your father an answer?" Anthia asked as they waited for their plane.

"No. Right now, I don't have one. I've owned that stock for many years. After I went to prison, it became my only link to my father. I never considered severing that final tie." He stared at his hands, scowling when he eventually said, "I don't know how I feel. The income along with wise investments have kept me financially sound."

He did not need what he made from the center, more often than not he funneled that money back into the center. They needed a security guard so badly that he had hired the man and was paying his salary himself. It was not a first for him.

Anthia could only imagine what he had gone through. He'd lost his mother, then his wife and child and now finally his father. He had moved on intellectually and spiritually, but not emotionally. Even after all these years, he hadn't sold the home he had once built and shared with his wife. Dexter had not been able to put his loss behind him and move on with his life.

Where did that leave her? How long could she live on the hope that someday he might come to care for her as she cared for him? Was she leaving herself open for disappointment and heartache?

Dexter was the one who broke the silence. "I know this was not an enjoyable weekend for you. I want you to know how glad I am that you came with me. It means more than I can express," he said quietly. "I just hope it didn't put you behind schedule with your work. Do you have dolls due out soon?"

Anthia was amazed at how much his appreciation meant to her. Unfortunately, she could not turn her feelings for him on and off like a light switch. They went too deep. "Not until the next week. I enjoyed meeting Stephanie. She was a beautiful bride. The wedding went so smoothly."

"For Stephanie's sake, I'm glad. It was worth it to see her so happy. Kenneth seems to love her as much as she loves him."

"That's what matters."

Dexter frowned, there was a time when he also felt that way, Yet, time had changed all of that. At least it had for him and Christine. "Love is not always enough."

"You don't believe that, do you?"

The announcement for their flight intruded, leaving Anthia disappointed that she did not get an answer. It wasn't until they were strapped into their seats that she asked, softly, careful that her voice would not carry, "What did you mean when you said that love isn't enough?"

Dexter had been staring broodingly out the window. He did not respond for so long that Anthia wondered if he had not heard her question. When she repeated his name he looked into her pretty dark eyes.

He said, "I can't speak for anyone but myself. When I married Christine, it was because of how we felt about each other. The problem was it didn't last. Love was not enough to keep our marriage going nor was it enough for her. We grew apart, Anthia. I ended up spending too much time at the office while she consoled herself with alcohol. We were on a dangerous path even before that last night."

If Anthia was shocked by his candor, he was unable to detect it. He was not concerned because with Anthia he could be himself. He didn't have to sugarcoat his thoughts or feelings. There was never a need for pretense.

Anthia's small hand slid into his and she squeezed it. She managed to hide her surprise. It was the first time that he had ever even hinted that there had been problems in his marriage. She said, quietly, "Nevertheless, how can you not believe in love? How is that possible when you could see the deep love your sister had for her husband. You've seen what Charles feels for Diane. You've seen the beauty of it firsthand."

He shook his head. "I never said I didn't believe. I'm hoping and praying that Stephanie and Kenneth's love will last a lifetime. I want no less for her." Yet, that part of his life was over. It ended when Christine died. It was nothing he could explain, it was simply how he felt. Although, he believed Anthia was entitled to the best . . . that included love, nonetheless he was selfish enough to admit he was not about to give her up.

It was early evening when they reached Anthia's home.

"Hungry?" he asked after carrying her luggage inside.

"Not really." She wanted him to stay, but she wasn't about to ask. She was not up to begging for anything that should be given freely. She loved him so much but she was not going to cling to him.

He stood near the mantel watching Anthia flip through her mail. Finally he broke the silence when he asked, "Too tired for company?"

Anthia's eyes went wide at the question. Her smile was soft, beguiling to his hungry gaze. "You're always welcome, if that's what you're asking."

He clasped her hand urging her toward one of the armchairs near the window and onto his lap. Dexter released a deep breath, one he did not realize he had been holding.

The ticking of the clock on the side table was the only sound in Anthia's living room. Anthia relaxed against him, not allowing her thoughts or worries to intrude. There would be enough time for that later. Her cheek was on his chest, her arms around his waist.

"Comfortable?"

"Mmm. You?"

"Oh, baby," he said, pressing his mouth against her lips ever so briefly, making no move to deepen the kiss and seek the honey within. They were together and that was enough for now. Slowly his own tension eased. They had both been on edge the entire time they had been away.

"It feels so good to hold you," he said, close to her ear. He couldn't resist pressing a tender kiss below her ear on the highly sensitive place on her neck. He was rewarded by her tiny shiver of awareness.

All her defenses melted away as the evening slipped away. She told herself that the here and now was all that mattered as if there was only the two of them in the entire world.

She snuggled even closer. Neither were cognizant of the heavy shadows filling the room. Anthia slept with her head resting on his shoulder. Dexter was not about to complain. The last two nights, he enjoyed the pleasure of sleeping with her against him. He told himself that tonight should be no different, but he knew he was only trying to console himself.

They were back home . . . back to the world of responsibility and stark reality. They had learned so much about each other because of what they shared. Things could not go back to the way they had once been. He was too hungry for her. His need went too deep.

It was late when he carefully lifted her and carried her into her bedroom. When he put her down on the side of the bed, her lashes fluttered open.

"Hmm," she mumbled, her head rested on his shoulder.

"You're exhausted, aren't you baby? Let me help you get ready for bed."

She nodded, leaning back against him. He brushed a kiss against her temple then he opened her blouse and slipped it down her arms. The lacy bra, skirt and pantyhose were a little more difficult to maneuver without her help. He was relieved when he found her gowns neatly folded in the top bureau drawer.

Once he had her covered, he pulled back the comforter and sheet then placed her beneath them. Anthia didn't do more than offer a sleepy murmur as she settled against the pillow.

As he stood looking down at her, he knew he should go. He had not been invited to stay. Yet, as he looked longingly at her, he could think of nothing he wanted more than to stay with her . . . each and every night.

He had no idea how long he watched her with indecision before he silently undressed. Although he rested beside her, he was not content until she turned and positioned her back against his chest, her soft bottom snug against his sex. He exhaled slowly as he held her close with one arm around her waist. Anthia let out a soft sigh, but she did not wake. Her breathing slow and even.

Dexter was not as lucky. He replayed the disagreement with his father. It had been bitter and angry, nothing good had come of it. It had managed to put even more distance between them.

He was thankful that he had not endured it alone. Anthia had been right by his side. Her quiet strength had stiffened his spine and kept him from being hurt more than he already was. This time his father had not done any significant damage and he had Anthia to thank for that.

Was he taking advantage of her by staying? Who was he trying to kid? He was where he wanted to be. His place did not provide the warmth and peace that he found here. Anthia alone did that for him. He felt more at home here surrounded by her things than he did at his own house.

There was no competition where she was concerned. Without even trying, she soothed him, filled his nights with sweet magic. She alone filled the empty place inside of him. When he was with her, he found himself doing and saying the unexpected.

He certainly had not planned on showing her the house he had once shared with Christine. It had just happened. He wanted her to see, wanted her to know, wanted her to understand it all.

When he was with Anthia, nothing else mattered. She filled his days with thoughts of her and his nights with sexual fantasies about her. What was happening to him? What was happening between them? She was so damn good to look at. There was no doubt in his mind that she could have any man she chose. She was not only a talented woman but she was also intelligent enough to turn a natural flair into a profitable business.

She was incredibly desirable. Her soft, petite frame was small, yet packed with seductive curves. Oh, she knew how to pleasure him, and keep him coming back for more. He could not seem to get enough of the feel of her small-fingered hands on his body, her deep feminine voice or her seductive scent. She aroused him seemingly without effort. All he had to do was look at her and he was as hard as steel, ready to make love to her.

It had been like that from the very first. After more than two years, he was even more fascinated with her now, than ever before. There had been nothing holding him at her side but her sweet allure. When had it gotten so bad? How had he lost control? Always in the past, he kept a firm grip on his emotions.

He had steadfastly kept himself on an even course, concentrating on the community center and the children they serviced. It had been his top priority, everyone and everything else had ranked a poor second. The community center was his world. At the end of a day he felt good because he knew he had done his very best, knew he had done everything within his power to change the negative spiral so many of the kids' faced. What he did mattered more so than any house or shopping complex he was capable of designing.

He had turned his life around for the better. He now had purpose, direction and he was respected. He had invested wisely, so even after years in prison, he was financially sound. Why had he allowed his father to hurt him yet again? Why at this late date did it matter what the man thought of him?

Had he been hanging on to the past? Was that why even after he had moved to Detroit, he had not been able to put the old house on the market? It wasn't as if he ever planned on living in it again? It was time. Anthia's response had forced him to take a long look at what he had been hanging on to. How difficult would it be to resign his position in the company? Even if he kept the stock, he was never going back to the company.

He did not need to remind himself that his future was here in Michigan. If the truth be known he had gotten so much more from the center and the kids than he could ever give back. He needed to feel valued and the community center filled a deep void in his life. No, he would never go back. He couldn't if he wanted to . . . but he did not want to. It was time to go on with his life. Time to put the past entirely in the past.

He hadn't told Anthia but he had seen his former brother-in-law at his sister's wedding. It had been such a shock that he had not been able to say a word to the man, not that his comments would be welcome. They had stared at each other for a time and then looked away. It had brought back the guilt. Anthia had eased his discomfort without even realizing it, for she had turned to him, smiled then whispered in his ear. He couldn't even remember what she said but suddenly all his attention was on her.

"Can't sleep?" Anthia murmured, pressing her soft lips to the base of his strong brown throat.

"Just thinking," he said, his hand caressing down her spine, lingering on her soft bottom.

She pushed a thick wave of hair away from her face. "I fell asleep on you, didn't I?"

He chuckled. "Something like that. Go back to sleep. You haven't gotten much rest this weekend.

She smiled, her dark lashes rested against her cheeks. "You undressed me?"

He lifted a brow. "Somebody had to do it."

She giggled, snuggling even closer to him. She didn't ask him why he was still here. She was too happy that he was to question it, she decided as she moved her hand over the muscled plane of his chest. Her nails explored his flat nipple.

He shivered from the contact, filling his lungs with her scent. "What woke you?"

"You," she whispered pressing her lips where she had caressed moments before. Her soft hands moved steadfastly down his flat stomach.

Dexter sucked in his breath, shuddering in reaction, a deep throaty sound. "How?" was about all he could manage at that moment. His sex thickened and lengthened.

"You're so sexy, Mr. Washington." She licked his bottom lip again and again. "I want you . . ."

He groaned heavily, holding his breath waiting with the keen expectation as she neared his sex, wondering if he could bear the exquisite torment. She was killing him. Impatient, he took her hand and placed it where he needed it most. He did not stop until he curled her fingers around his throbbing shaft.

"Anthia . . ." he groaned. "Help yourself." His tone was rough from the searing heat of his arousal as she stroked him from the thick base to the broad crown. Anthia enjoyed handling him as much as he seemed to enjoy her velvety strokes. Unable to tolerate more, Dexter lifted her hands to his neck and plunged his tongue deep inside her mouth. He parted her thighs and palmed her, squeezing her wondrously soft mound.

Anthia quivered as Dexter deepened the kiss while tantalizing her clitoris with gentle but consistent strokes. "Dex . . ." she whimpered. It felt so good, but it was not nearly enough. She needed his long, hard strength deep inside . . . now.

Dexter obviously was of the same mind-set when she reached into the nightstand and handed him the foil packet. He accepted it without comment. He did not hesitate to reposition himself between her soft, dewy folds Carefully, he filled her creamy, tight sheath. They moved together naturally as if they were on the dance floor but this dance of love was incredibly erotic and gloriously intoxicating.

Anthia matched each of Dexter's insistent thrusts without reservation. Following his lead, she opened herself to his irresistible masculine strength. All too soon, they both felt the scorching heat flair out of control as she claimed her release an instant before he took his own, their shouts of triumph blended as they held on to each other.

He cradled her against his heart while his breathing slowly returned to normal.

"Oh, Dex . . ." she said around a tender sigh.

He whispered close to her ear, "You make it so good for me, baby . . . every single time."

Anthia shivered, knowing he gave her pleasure without fail. Her lips were sweet against his when she teased, "Better than a sedative?"

He chuckled, although his lids were so heavy he could barely keep them open. "Mmm . . ." he mumbled as he relaxed into a deep satisfying sleep.

Anthia smiled, she was where she wanted to be most—in his arms. Her body was tight against his. Somehow, she had to convince him that what they had did not have to be a temporary thing. They not only needed each other but were good for each other. She did not know how much longer she could keep her feelings to herself. Her love for him grew with each new day. And she was no different than any other woman. She wanted her man's love.

"Be patient, girl," she mumbled softly. It had taken her years to find this special man. Wasn't he worth waiting for? The lure of sleep proved to be irresistible.

Dexter was rudely awakened that morning by the insistent ringing of the telephone. He automatically reached for it, his voice thick with sleep, "Hello?"

Jeff was so taken aback at the sound of a man answering his mother's telephone that it took a moment to recognize the male voice. "Dex?"

"Yeah," he said, suddenly wide awake. "Jeff?"

There was a prolonged silence as the two accepted the significance of Dexter being with Anthia that early in the morning.

"Yes. Things have evidently changed between you and my mom." Jeff did not have to be told how his mother felt about the man. She was in love with him. He said firmly, "I don't want her hurt."

Dexter felt Anthia stir beside him, but for the moment he concentrated on her son. "I care for her." He also cared for her son. He wanted Jeff to accept their new relationship and accept him as an important part of her world.

"You would not be there if she didn't want you there. Treat her well."

"Absolutely," he said, looking down into her beautiful dark troubled gaze. "Hold on," he said into the telephone, "It's Jeff. Sorry, I shouldn't have picked up the phone."

She soothed, "He had to know eventually. I don't keep secrets from him. I'm not ashamed of your being here." Having disengaged herself from Dexter's arms, she accepted the receiver, "Morning, baby. How are you?"

Dexter let out a heavy sigh as he swung his legs down to the floor. He grabbed his slacks from the chair and pulled them on before he went into the bathroom, intent on giving her some privacy.

He swore softly as he ducked his head under the spray of the shower. Why had he answered her telephone? What had he been thinking? That was the problem, he hadn't been thinking at all. He'd been roused from a deep, satisfying sleep. He let the hot water pound his body, clearing his head. He felt good. His body was loose, no longer strained from the prolonged sexual frustration he normally dealt with. His thoughts were not clouded from being sleep deprived. No nightmares, never when he was with Anthia. It was as if he had no room in his head for any thoughts but of her.

He understood Jeff's caution without question. In fact, he respected the young man's deep concern for his mother's well-being. Jeff knew his mother did not fool around with men and that his being there with her had to mean something. Yeah, he thought with pride, Jeff had grown up. He was no longer a boy any more, he was a man.

"I'm all right. More important, how are you?" Jeff held on to his uncertainty, needing to know she was okay.

"Still asleep. I'm not used to traveling. Texas is beautiful this time of year. It's strange to see so much green grass and flowers. And it's so big. Goodness . . ."

"Ma! What's going on between you and Dex? I was a little shocked to hear his voice on the telephone this time of morning. It's barely eight."

They both knew that the time of day was not the issue. "Why are you so surprised? You've known how I've felt about him for some time," Anthia said evenly, her eyes on the closed bathroom door.

"And?" he prompted.

"Son, does it bother you knowing that he and I are together?"

Jeff sighed loudly. "Kinda. It takes some getting used to. This is the first time I can recall you being with a man. If it's happened before you certainly kept it from me."

"It's the first time. Honestly, I have nothing to apologize for except that I intended to be the one to tell you about the change in our relationship. For that I apologize. You should have heard it first from me."

There was an awkward silence. Finally he said, "You don't owe me an apology. If I had called at a decent hour it wouldn't have happen this way. I didn't mean to embarrass you or Dexter. I just wanted to make sure you were home from your trip and safe. I left you a message on your machine when I hadn't heard from you by this morning I got worried."

"Sorry, baby. I was so tired when we came in that I didn't even check the machine. Tell me about you?"

Dexter chose that moment to return, a towel slung casually over his wide bronze shoulders. He was whistling softly as he smiled at her, before he retrieved his shirt and left the bedroom.

"Everything is fine. School will be over before long and I'm trying to figure out what I should be doing this summer." He didn't tell her he was considering asking Cora Denton out this weekend. He longed to spend some time alone with her. He'd been concentrating on building his confidence . . . trying to prepare himself for the possibility of rejection. If he didn't ask, he would never know what she thought of him. Wheelchair or not, he had to find out one way or the other.

"Are you thinking of staying on during the summer? Taking more classes," she asked amazed at how badly she hoped he would say no. Even though she missed him terribly, she really wanted him to do what was best for him.

"Haven't decided yet."

"Have you thought more about speaking at the center?"

"I've tried not to think about it," he said candidly.

Anthia refused to go into the lengthy lecture that was burning in her throat. She said softly, "Just don't forget you did not get to that college by yourself. You had some help along the way. Others might also benefit from your helping hand." She left it at that. "Will you be home for the weekend?"

"Not this weekend."

"Okay. Something going on at the college?"

"There is always something going on. Look Ma, I know you have company so I'll let you go. Talk to you soon."

"Love you."

"Be careful," he said before he hung up.

Anthia had just pulled on her robe when she heard Dexter's shout.

TWENTY

Jeff grabbed his books, and notebook and stuffed them into the backpack that hung on the back of his wheelchair. He maneuvered himself and his crutches out the door. Even though Paine was small, he needed the chair to get across campus. He reminded himself to concentrate on moving, he was already late. He used powerful shoulders and forearms to control the speed.

He assured himself that he did not need to worry about his mother. For years he'd hoped that Dexter and his mom would get together. He had seen the tender feelings in her eyes when she spoke of his mentor and friend.

The only unknown in the puzzle was Dexter. He was not the kind of man to take advantage of any woman. Come to think of it, women had been notably absent from his life. He had asked him about it once, and Dexter said something about unless a man was able to commit there was no point to it. Just how serious was Dexter about his mom?

For the first time in Jeff's memory, she was in love. He did not want her to be hurt. She is entitled to some happiness. She had sacrificed so much over the years for him. And the last few years had been rough for both of them.

"Hey, watch it!"

Jeff blinked in surprise stopping instantly. "Sorry. Are you all right?" His voice was huskier than he would like but the pretty young woman always had that affect on him.

Cora Denton scowled at him. "I know you don't like me, but

it never occurred to me you'd try to run me down." She stood near the entrance of the library. Her soft dark brown skin was smooth and flawless, her features were small and very feminine. Her slim figure was covered in jeans and dark green sweater. Her brown hair had been styled in a close-cut natural.

"How can you say that?" He frowned as he watched her rub her leg. "It was an accident. I didn't have my mind on what I was doing. Are you hurt?"

"Not really. Just a little bruised. Geez, don't worry about it. I'll remember to keep my distance. You don't have to run me over to make a point."

She would have walked away if he hadn't caught her arm. "I was not trying to hurt you, Cora."

"Look, Jeff. We both know you don't like me. Why pretend?" She had felt his angry glance on more than one occasion. No matter what she told herself it still hurt. In spite of his reluctance to have her tag along with him and Cynthia, she still enjoyed his smiles. Why did she have to have a crush on one of her gorgeous roommate's boyfriends? It didn't make a lick of sense.

Jeff's handsome amber tone features were marred by a scowl. He could not take his eyes away from her lovely face. "That's not true." He unwittingly smoothed his thumb over her petal soft skin. "Besides, what difference does it make? Cora, you have enough guys chasing after you without me making a fool of myself over you."

Cora shook her head not believing this conversation. "What are you talking about? We both know you hate it when Cynthia drags me along with the two of you. Evidently, I cramp your style, brother-man." She jerked her arm away unaware of the way he flushed with embarrassment.

"Cynthia and I are only friends." Jeff shrugged, before he admitted, "Her dad helped me when I got myself into a stupid situation."

"Yeah, she told me. I'm glad you're okay," she said softly.

"I'm not exactly okay," he said, gesturing to the wheelchair and crutches.

"You will be," she smiled at him.

His breath caught in his throat at her beauty. "You busy on

Saturday night? *Amistad* is playing." His heart raced with a combination of wild anticipation and dread.

"I'd like that," she whispered, softly hugging her books close to her small, perky breasts.

Jeff forced himself to look away from their softness. He's heart hammered with excitement. "I don't have a car." He laughed, then said, "I couldn't drive if I did have one."

She shrugged. "I have one. I'll pick you up. Is there a problem with that?"

"Not for me." He grinned. "Mind if I give you a call this week?"

"Nope. 'Bye," She surprised him by leaning down and pressing her soft full lips to his cheek, before she whispered, "Took you long enough." Then she dashed away toward the student union.

Jeff roared with laughter. He didn't stop until he reached his class.

"Dexter? What's wrong?" Anthia was breathless from running. He sat at the kitchen table, staring down at the open Sunday morning edition of the newspaper. An untouched steaming coffee mug stood nearby.

He swore heatedly. "I don't believe this!" He pointed to the headlines.

Puzzled, Anthia read the glaring words plastered in big bold letters on the front page, "Convicted Murderer Who Heads Local Black Youth Center Is Accused Of Sexual Harassment By Female Employee." Anthia could not believe what she read. "Who could have done such a hateful thing?"

His troubled eyes locked with hers. "I suppose it had to come out eventually. But, damn it, not like this."

"What are you saying? I know you have not touched anyone at the center." Anthia was livid. She knew better than anyone that it had taken years before he had finally given in to his desire for her.

"No! I'm talking about the prison thing," Dexter said, in a shocked whisper as he envisioned all that he had worked for dissolving like sand through his fingers. He had struggled to gain the boys respect, something he valued above all else. It was all gone because of a partly true statement.

"Who are they talking about?"

"Reporter is Jason Madison. The woman's name was not mentioned in the article," he said tightly.

"I don't believe this! Why would someone try to ruin your reputation this way?"

Dexter paced the confines of the kitchen, feeling as if the walls were closing in on him. When he slumped against the counter, he snapped, his voice edged with bitterness, "It's all over. Everything I worked for is over. After this, I won't have a reputation to salvage. Everything I've worked for the last few years is gone."

Anthia stared at him. Suddenly, her legs were so weak that she had to sit down or fall flat on her face. Sinking into a kitchen chair, she insisted, "You can't just give up, honey. You have to fight this. It's a terrible lie!"

He studied her with sad, tired eyes. He fought his need to hold her. "What have I ever done to deserve having you in my life? Not even for a single moment have you doubted my innocence," his voice cracked from the force of his emotions.

Anthia blinked, astonished. "Why should I doubt your innocence? I know you. I know how you've closed yourself off to tender emotions. I know what it took for you to even kiss me that first time. How could I even think that promiscuity is part of your character?"

He signed heavily, "Why would she do this? Why does she want to destroy the little I have left to value in this world?"

"You think it's Tina, don't you?"

"Yes," he said gruffly. "It couldn't be anyone else. We have less than a handful of woman who actually work or volunteer at the center. I know it wasn't Mrs. Ramsey, the cleaning woman. And it certainly wasn't you, baby. It has to be Tina Douglas."

Anthia shook her head as if trying to clear it. This was not making a bit of sense to her. "Did you have an argument with her?"

"About what? A forgotten telephone message?"

"About her interest in you."

"Oh that," he dismissed.

"Obviously, you haven't taken it seriously, but she clearly has. Why else would she do something so destructive?"

"It is ridiculous! The girl is barely twenty years old. I'm too damn old for her."

"Apparently, she doesn't think so. Did she say something to you about her feelings?"

He looked decidedly uncomfortable, when he said, "She was waiting for me after work one night. She was upset because you and I have been seeing so much of each other. She wanted me to know that she was interested in me romantically. I told her as clearly as I could that it was impossible. It was late. I took her home and that was the end of it."

"Was there anyone else around?"

"No, it was after hours."

"So it will be your word against hers. Oh, Dex, this is terrible," she said unhappily brushing her hair out of her face. "Men always seem to come off so unfavorably in these things. So many people almost automatically believe the female."

"With my past, I don't even have a leg to stand on. No one will believe me."

"I believe in you. Our friends are bound to believe in you."

His eyes locked with hers. Then he walked over to her, pulled her up and into his arms. He rocked her, needing her warmth, her assurance as much as she seemed to need him. "It has taken so much hard work to establish that community center and keep it going. I'll walk away with out a backward glance before I let all that be destroyed."

"No! You love that place and those kids. Why aren't you fighting mad?"

"I've been down this road before, baby. People prefer to believe the worse. After Christine and the baby died, none of our so-called friends supported me," he said tightly. "You saw for yourself that my own father didn't believe me. Anthia, without the boys and the community's respect, I might as well give it up. Hell, I can't do a thing to make them change their beliefs and follow their hopes and dreams, if the trust is broken. Trust is paramount to what I'm trying to do at the center."

Anthia vehemently shook her head. "I won't let you give in to her lies. Her little stunt to gain your attention could send you back to prison. This is no game!" She shuddered at the thought.

Dexter did not need the reminder. He thought of all the new friends he'd made since he'd moved to Detroit. People he respected and valued. Charles Randol had been willing to give an ex-con a chance. In the three years he'd been at the center, Dexter had done nothing to jeopardize that faith. What would Charles think? Would his best friend believe the worst? What could he say? How could he explain something he didn't understand himself?

How could he fight this? He had no idea how to even start. Hell! He didn't see how anything positive can come from this. He would be lucky if he had not already lost his job.

"After John Poindexter the founder of the community center died, his daughter, Margaret, took control of managing the foundation. She isn't about to stand back and let everything her father worked for be destroyed. The community center must stay open regardless of the personal cost to any one man," he insisted.

What was best for the center must come first. For so many of the boys, it was their only link to a better life. The boys were what mattered.

"The truth will come out. You'll see," Anthia insisted, running a soothing hand over his chest.

"Always the optimist," he said, caressing her cheek.

"Absolutely. In fact, I think we'll both feel better after some breakfast. What would you like?"

Food was the last thing he wanted, but he didn't want her upset anymore than she already was. "Why don't you get showered and dressed while I make breakfast."

"Okay," Anthia brushed her lips against him. Reluctant to leave, she asked, "You all right?"

"Yeah," he shrugged, feeling as if his life was once again crumbling around him. Damn it! He had not touched that girl.

Now all he had to do was prove it. What if he lost his job? More importantly, what if he lost Anthia?

Dexter quickly pushed that thought away knowing he was on very shaky ground and couldn't handle it. Instead, he busied himself looking for the makings of an omelet.

Neither one of them had much of an appetite and were almost grateful for the interruption when the doorbell rang. Anthia and Dexter exchanged a look before she rose to answer it. He was only a few steps behind her.

"Hey, sugar," Charles Randol filled the doorway, He leaned down to kiss her cheek. At six four he towered over most people, the petite Anthia was no exception. His dark handsome features were set. "Is Dexter here?" Before she could answer he shoved a rolled copy of the newspaper forward. "Have you seen this?"

"Mornin,' " Dexter said having heard the other man's voice. He steeled himself not to so much as flinch as he looked his friend and mentor straight in the eye. "Yeah, we've seen it."

"Well?" The two large men filled the small foyer.

"Well what? Are you asking if I hit on the kid?"

"Hell no! What do you want with that baby when you have a lady like Anthia? What? Do I look stupid?" Charles demanded.

"Never that," Dexter's eyes twinkled.

"What did you say to tick the kid off? I assume we are talking about Tina Douglas?"

"Hell, I don't know anything for sure. From the newspaper article it certainly sounds like her. Who else could it be?" Dexter scowled.

"I wouldn't put it passed her. That little girl has been after you for months. And what in the hell are we going to do about this mess?"

"Charles, have a seat. Let me take your raincoat."

"Thanks, Anthia. Diane sends her love. She would have come with me but the baby has a slight temperature and we thought if best if she stay with her," he said as he handed over the wet coat and dripping umbrella. He settled on the sofa while both Dexter and Anthia shared the loveseat.

"You knew she was interested?" Dexter asked, beginning to feel like a fool. Where was his mind? He hadn't noticed a thing.

"Everyone knew but you. It was no secret, my man. But I never thought she was vindictive enough to take it this far. How could she play with your life like this?"

Dexter was having difficulty handling his good fortune. He rose and paced in front of the picture window. He didn't even see the beads of water running down the glass. He was so choked up with emotion that he was close to embarrassing himself. He blinked the tears away. First Anthia's show of support, now Charles' . . . it was too much for him to handle easily. He had no comparison.

"Dex?" Anthia said softly stepping in front of him. "Honey," she said, sliding an arm around his waist. "You all right?"

His eyes locked with hers before he bent and kissed her pretty mouth. "I'm okay," he said.

Once they were seated side by side, he cleared his throat, then he said, "Before we left for Texas, Tina tried to tell me how she felt. She was upset about my relationship with Anthia." He swore impatiently, "I really tried not to hurt her feelings. But come on. Not for a moment, was I willing to let her believe that I wanted her. It was out of the question. Hell, it had never occurred to me that she wanted a relationship with me. It was crazy."

"Where did this talk take place? Was there any witness?" Charles asked pointedly.

"No. She was waiting for me after the center closed. She said what she had to say, then I gave her a ride home. That was the end of it. I can't believe she would go to the police or the newspaper with these lies."

"She apparently knew she didn't have a case or she would have pressed charges against you," Charles said dryly.

"Thank goodness for that," Anthia whispered.

"What I can't figure out is how she knew about your past?"

Unable to remain seated a second longer, Dexter paced the length of the fireplace. "It's certainly not something I would discuss with her. As far as I knew only you, Anthia and Mrs. Poindexter knew my personal history. That was until this hit the fan," he gestured toward the newspaper resting on the coffee table.

"How could the newspaper print something like that? They have no proof that you ever touched her," Anthia exclaimed.

"They don't need proof. All they need is an accusation. The part about my past cannot be disputed, which is more than likely why they went with the story. Like you said before, Anthia, it will come down to her word against mine."

"This is no lightweight accusation. This affects everyone connected with the center," Charles hissed impatiently. "It jeopardizes all our goals!"

Dexter swore heatedly. "I know that! Do you want me to quit?"

Charles rose to his own superior height to glare down at his friend. "Don't be a complete ass. What I want is to see that you are protected and get to the bottom of this mess as quickly as possible. Have you spoken to Quinn?" he asked referring to their mutual friend and prominent attorney Quinn Montgomery.

"No. I've been too busy trying to decide what is best for everyone concerned. Man, I've even thought about just walking away. I don't want to do anything that will harm the center. The kids are what matters. The new projects have to go on no matter what," Dexter sighed wearily.

Although Charles was just as determined as Dexter was that nothing jeopardize their funding, Charles was not about to stand back and let Tina Douglas destroy his friend. Charles said roughly, "If you walk away she wins! Can't you see that?"

"Sit down, both of you. I'll make some coffee. You two put your heads together and figure out what needs to be done," Anthia said before going into the kitchen.

Even though, both had reclaimed their seats, they were clearly shaken by this very real threat to the community center.

Charles eyed him thoughtfully before he said, "You've invested too many years and comprised your personal safety too often to just walk away from the center." Charles wasn't even willing to entertain such a thought. "You're a good man, Dex. You don't deserve this."

Dexter was moved by the other man's faith in him. Charles

Randol was a man he both admired and respected. Charles was a wealthy man who did not have to devote himself or his time to this cause. He did it because it was something he wholeheartedly believed in. The male mentoring program had been his idea from the very beginning. He had put everything that was needed into place. Expanding the center to all parts of the city was another goal that they were determined to find the needed funding for.

"I mean it, man. I won't let my past overshadow what we're doing at the center. It isn't that I don't appreciate your support because I do."

The center must remain the number one priority. There was nothing Dexter was more proud of in his life than the work he had done at the center. Even if he left tomorrow, the center would stand alone as his single greatest triumph.

Charles said, "Let's take this one step at a time. When Ms. Poindexter couldn't reach you at your place, she called me. She wants me to let you know that she's calling an emergency directors meeting Tuesday morning. She would like you to be there. She also thinks it would be best if you waited until after the meeting before you resume your duties at the center."

"Okay," was all Dexter was able to say. His eyes spoke of the anguish he held deep inside.

"We'll go together."

"That's not necessary. I've inconvenienced you enough."

Charles looked at the man who had stood up to him when his marriage had been falling apart and told him the unvarnished truth that he needed to hear. Charles was not about to walk away because this situation was messy. True friends were rare. Dexter was just such a friend. He was not influenced by Charles' social standing in the community or his personal wealth.

Their friendship was based on mutual respect. It was something they both could count on. Besides, they had been in some tight spots together up against gang members on more than one occasion. Dexter had never failed to stand with him when it came to what they both believed in . . . the community center.

"I'll be there." Charles' chin jutted stubbornly. "Quinn is due in court tomorrow but he said to tell you he'd be available to talk to you Tuesday afternoon after two."

Dexter's brows shot up. "It pays to have friends in high places." Dexter was choked up. He had no experience with this degree of support and trust. His past had taught him that when he stood up for himself he stood alone. With a history like his, this tremendous show of support from first Anthia, then Charles and now Quinn . . . it was too much for him to grasp easily.

The doorbell sounded suddenly. Dexter glanced out the front window at the squad car parked out front. He swore heatedly, his face a cold mask of fury.

"I don't believe this!" Charles was on his feet, his hands balled at his sides.

"What's wrong?" Anthia looked anxiously from one man to the other.

Dexter was stiff with fury as he reached for the doorknob. "Detroit's finest. Who else?"

Charles caught her before she could reach Dexter's side. He shook his head, forcing her to stay where she was. "Let him handle this."

Dexter faced the two plainclothes officers on the threshold. "Hey, Maxwell," he acknowledged the man by name. He was a regular volunteer at the community center, which was no doubt how they knew how to find him. Maxwell was aware that he was seeing Anthia.

"Sorry, man. But we'd like to take you down to the station for questioning."

Dexter didn't bother to ask why. "I'll get my coat."

"You can't do this! He hasn't done anything wrong! Tell them, Dex," Anthia pleaded.

Dexter went to her, whispered close to her ear, "Calm down, baby. The man said questioning, nothing more. They can't hold me without charges."

"I'm going with you," she insisted, glaring at the officers. "You have the wrong man. He hasn't done anything to that girl. He wouldn't! He's not like that!" She struggled not to cry.

Dexter squeezed her hand, kissing her gently. "I want you to say here. You can't do anything at the police station but wait."

"Dex is right, Anthia. I'm going with him. Call Quinn. Tell him to meet us at the precinct," Charles said tightly.

Anthia was trembling all over, but she lifted her chin regally and said to Dexter, "I'll call right now." She couldn't seem to move as she watched Dexter file out along with the others. It was only when the police car and Charles' car had disappeared down the block that the tears filled her vision.

Forcing herself to inhale deeply, she brushed furiously at her damp cheeks. She didn't have time for this. She had to get help for Dexter. In her opinion Quinn Montgomery was the best criminal attorney in the country. All she had to do was stop shaking long enough to make the call.

TWENTY-ONE

Dexter was so furious he could barely speak. This was going a bit far, but then what had he expected? He was still a black man and an ex-con, the combination was deadly. It was something that was not going away.

Sexual harassment was certainly nothing to play around with. It had brought some very powerful men some nasty consequences. Yet, he was thankful that it was not child molestation. He would not have had a prayer of proving himself innocent. What was he thinking? Most people were going to take Tina's word over his. That was just the way this society functioned. Why in the hell would Tina do this to him? What did she hope to gain?

"Mr. Washington . . . Dex. Let's go over this one more time."

"No!" he barked. "I will tell you for the last time, I did not say or do anything remotely sexual to anyone who works at the community center or who volunteers at the center for that matter. I'm not into children, man. I have a woman in my bed, not a youngster."

The men were seated around a long table, closeted away from the hustle and bustle of the police station.

"Damn straight," Maxwell put in.

His partner glared at him.

"You've had him here long enough. Either charge him now or let him go," Quinn Montgomery put in smoothly. Everything about the highly successful black attorney was smooth from his long muscular body to his dark brown skin. He knew his business. There was no inflection in his voice just a flat statement. He had allowed Dexter to be questioned only because Dexter insisted. It did not mean he liked it.

The two detectives looked at each other. It was Maxwell's partner who said, "You can go now, Washington. But don't think this is over. We won't let you get away with this. Just because you have some big-shot attorney doesn't mean you're gonna walk."

"Come on, Dex. Let's go," Quinn said coldly.

Charles was waiting for them. Dexter was clearly enraged by the accusations thrown his way.

"It went well," Quinn said as the three men left together. He quickly brought Charles up to date on what happened. "They were hard on him but we expected that. He has a record and it's not working in his favor." They paused on the sidewalk. Ignoring the steady downpour, Quinn went on to say, "Dex, I'll get my investigator on this. We've got to get to the bottom of this and quickly. We have to find out what she is getting out of this, before this thing goes any further."

"That's what I've been asking myself. Having me locked up is not going to help anyone. What in the hell did she hope to gain? Is she planning a civil suit?"

Quinn patted him on the back. "Don't worry. We'll get to the bottom of this. We'll talk more on Tuesday. Good luck with that meeting at the community center." He paused, "Oh, do me one favor, stay the hell away from Tina Douglas."

Dexter offered his hand, "Thanks. I appreciate your help. I know how busy you are."

Quinn shrugged. "Give Anthia my best. See ya, Charles." The two men shook hands before he hurried off to his car.

"Ready?" Charles asked.

"Yeah." Dexter was so coldly furious, he could hardly speak. The idea of having to deal with the criminal justice system again held no appeal. He was so quiet on the drive back to Anthia's place that Charles did not try to force small talk.

It wasn't until Charles had stopped in front of the house that he said, "Man, it's going to work out."

Dexter made an impatient sound in his throat, before he said,

"If it were not for you and Quinn, I'd probably be behind bars right now."

"They don't have enough to hold you."

"Thank the Lord for small favors," Dexter said as he got out of the car. He glanced back at the other man, "You coming in?"

"No, I should be getting back home. Want to check on my baby girl, make sure she is all right. Give Anthia my love. And I'll see you at the center on Tuesday. And Dex, keep the faith. You've done nothing wrong."

"Look, Chuck, I appreciate your . . ."

Charles cut him off, saying, "There's no need. We're friends." He knew Dexter's family history and thought it was a real shame that he had to come so far to learn what love, true friendship and support meant.

" 'Night," Dexter said. He stood staring after Charles even after he had driven away. No there had been nothing in his past to prepare him for the warmth and acceptance that Anthia, Charles and Quinn offered unconditionally. The necessity for that support was eating away at him. Trying to get his deep-seated anger under control, Dexter slowly made his way to Anthia's door and let himself inside.

"Hi," she said, from where she sat in an armchair. She quickly put down the doll dress that she'd been embroidering flowers on, before making her way over to him. "Where is Charles?"

"He had to leave," Dexter said softly, indulging himself by holding her close for a moment. He hated the fear and anxiety he saw in her lovely eyes. She was entitled to so much better than what he had to offer . . . so much better. Like her doll business, she was special . . . one of a kind.

"Diane called. She sends her love. She was very upset that she could not come today with Charles."

"They're good people."

"You hungry? I made dinner . . ." she said softly, avoiding the obvious—what had taken place at the police station. She was dying to ask but she did not want to do anything that might upset him.

"You really didn't have to go through so much trouble for me."

She shook her head. "No trouble. Did Quinn make it?"

"Yes."

"Are you okay?"

He shrugged, the last thing he was was all right. Too much had happened in the last few hours to destroy all that he had worked for since he'd been back in Detroit. The trouble was he would not be the only one hurt if he had to leave the community center. So many of the boys he mentored had come to depend on him to be there for them. How could he turn his back on them and just walk away? What choice did he really have? Leave before they put him out?

Restless, he walked over to the mantel and stood staring at a black ballerina doll that Anthia had designed. Every few weeks she changed her doll displays. As he absently fingered the doll's toe shoes, his anger mounted.

Tina Douglas with her reckless act was destroying his life bit by bit. How long could Anthia or even Charles believe in him considering the amount of controversy this accusation would create around them? More importantly, how could he expect them to stand by him? Anthia was clearly suffering. It was in her troubled dark eyes.

Anthia stood where she was longing to help but not knowing how. It was all so horribly unfair. "Dex, please. Honey, talk to me."

What could he say? How could he explain what it had been like during those painful years in prison. He had learned to protect himself as well as to depend only on himself. He had known the darkest kind of despair. It had taken so long to pull himself back from the edge. He had turned his life around. Why would this silly child try to take it away? No! He would not go back there.

"Dex . . ."

He stared at her unable to bear the suffering on her face. He could not ignore that he was the one responsible for putting it there. Hell no!

His voice was gruff with anguish when he said, "I can't hurt you this way. I'll see you later." He did not wait for her response, but moved steadfastly toward the door, then closed it quietly behind him.

Anthia had watched in disbelief. Evidently, he felt there was nothing more to be said. Or rather he was not willing to share it with her. She blinked back tears, refusing to give into the keen disappointment building inside of her. She reminded herself that this was not about her . . . it was about Dexter.

He had made some mistakes in his life, serious mistakes. He had paid for those mistakes with his life. His world had not been the same since he struggled to take the gun away from his late wife and failed. He had done the time and come out on the other side a better man. He had devoted his life to helping others. Now he faced the challenge of his life. But the fact that he preferred to face this alone was what hurt her to the core.

He was a strong black man with a generous and kind heart. He was also a stubborn fool. He was more concerned about her well being than his own.

There was no doubt in her mind that he had not said or done anything improper to Tina Douglas. Other than to try to help guide her the same way he had with all the youngsters that he came into contact with, he had done nothing. Anthia knew Dexter.

Yes, he was a deeply sensuous man. Dexter could be wildly seductive. Even if he was attracted to Tina, which she seriously doubted, he was not one to cross the line. It would go against his strong sense of right and wrong.

How well she knew that he was a man of his convictions. He simply was not the kind of man to act on his sexual impulses. It had taken years for Anthia to get next to him because he had fought against his own desire for her. Talk about self-control . . . he took the word to new heights.

Tina's actions were reckless and vindictive. Did she honestly think that this was the way to make him change his mind about her? Why couldn't she see that he would never risk all that he had accomplished at the center for the sake of a girl more than half his age? He had worked too hard and for too long to make a go of the center to take such a chance.

Anthia shivered as an icy cold chill of fear ran up her spine.

What was he going to do? Why must he face this alone? Why couldn't he let the people who cared about him the most and believed in him support him against these false charges? More importantly, how could he shut her out like this? Why couldn't he see that she didn't need his protection? What she needed was his love.

It had only been recently that he had opened himself up to her, shared that dark part of himself with her. "No way!" She didn't want to go backward. She could not bear for the closeness they were just beginning to develop to disappear. It just was not fair! They needed each other too much.

Refusing to give in to the need to cry, Anthia went into her studio determined to escape her troubled thoughts. She simply could not think about how he was pushing her away, yet again. She would not worry that this time he might succeed. She busied herself by setting out and then preparing peach-lacquered tissue lined boxes for the nearly finished dolls. The last thing she tucked in was the One of a Kind certificate of authenticity that she always shipped with her dolls.

It was very late when she finished dressing two dolls and carefully packing them for shipment. Still there was no sign of Dexter.

Anthia hoped to ease the tension in her body and soothe taut muscles by taking a long fragrant bath. When she eventually emerged some time later, she toweled off and smoothed on her favorite scented lotion. The ringing telephone had her hurrying across the bedroom while covering herself with a ivory silk lace-edged bathrobe. She caught it on the third ring, "Hello?"

"Ma! What is going on? I heard that Dexter has been accused of sexual harassment and that he's a murderer. What is this?"

"Calm down, son." The story had apparently been picked up by the wire services across the country.

"Ma?"

"Yes, it's true. Tina Douglas has taken her accusation to the media. I'm sorry you had to hear about it this way. I should have called you right away. It was headline news in the morning paper here," Anthia said as she sank down to the edge of the bed.

"You mean to tell me this is not some mistake?"

"No, it's real."

"Dexter is not involved with Tina. Even I know better than that several states away."

"No he isn't. But it will be her word against his," she sighed unhappily.

"It's not surprising. She's had a thing for him for a long time. All the fellows knew because a few tried to hit on her. I never thought the girl was stupid. How could she go so far as to try and ruin his reputation? It isn't right." Jeff's indignation came across the line with crystal clear clarity.

"No, it isn't. It has created a terrible mess for him."

"Ma, what about him being an ex-con? Is that true?"

"I'm afraid so, son. Dex served five years of a ten-year sentence for manslaughter in the death of his wife and unborn child."

Jeff's disbelief was in his voice. "How is that possible? He could not have killed anyone . . . certainly not someone he loved."

"It was a horrible accident, honey. He was trying to take a loaded gun away from his pregnant wife. She was trying to kill herself. The gun went off and he was charged and convicted."

Jeff gasped. "How could they convict him when he was only trying to help?"

"It happens every day to black men. I think that's one of the reasons he's so self-contained."

"How is he, Ma? If he needs me, I can come home."

Anthia's heart swelled with pride. "Thanks, honey. Although, I'm not sure there isn't much any of us can do right now. Quinn has taken his case. And so far he hasn't been charged with anything. That has to be a good sign. I'll be sure and tell him what you said."

"Thanks. Whatever I can do. Dex has been there for me. I want to be there for him. If he still needs me to talk at the center, I'll do it."

Anthia sniffed, wiping at the tears that filled her eyes. "I am so proud of you."

"Aw, Mama. Don't start. This isn't about me, but helping Dex."

"You're absolutely right, son. We had better hang up now. We've already talked this morning."

"Okay. Give Dex my best wishes. You'll tell him what I said?"

"I promise. Love you. 'Bye." She had just returned the receiver to its cradle when the doorbell chimed. "Now what?"

Certain that she was not in the mood for company this late at night, she flicked on the porch light recognizing the lean, broad-shouldered man instantly.

"It's me, Anthia."

She quickly unlocked the dead bolt and the locked screen door before she opened the door. She stepped back giving him room to enter.

"Hi," he said cautiously unsure of his welcome. "May I come in? Or would you rather I stayed at my own place?" He had a garment bag strapped over one shoulder.

"You know the answer to that. I didn't ask you to leave in the first place. That was your idea, remember? What's going on with you, Dex?"

She looked at him with large, troubled eyes. She had done everything short of begging him to stay. He was the one who was constantly pushing her away, not the other way around.

He dropped his bag on the carpet, closed and locked the door, before he reached for her. "I'm sorry, baby," he whispered close to her ear, pressing his lips against that tender spot behind it. "I didn't mean to upset you. I needed some time . . . needed to get my head together."

She trembled in his arms determined not to give in to the tears that were so close at hand. "I feel as if you are always pushing me away."

"No, baby. Never that. I'm just so afraid of hurting you. I come with so much emotional baggage," he confessed unhappily. "Besides, I didn't like what all this was doing to you. This whole day has taken on nightmarish proportions."

Anthia let herself sag against him for a few moments allowing herself the luxury of his male strength. She needed him so much. Was she being weak to give all her love without the assurance of ever having it returned? When had just being with him stopped being enough? No matter how vehemently she denied it, knowing he could never love her as she loved him was like pouring salt in an open flesh wound.

His stomach chose that moment to growl, easing the tension between them. They both laughed.

"Sorry about that," he grinned.

"I think I can do something about that problem," she said moving toward the kitchen. She had not bothered to eat either, she been too upset to even think of food.

"Let me put my things away, then I'll give you a hand."

When he returned, she was busy at the counter. "Can I help?" he asked a few steps behind her.

"Nope, just sit . . . relax." She already had the table set and was finishing a tossed salad that she had to go with the grilled chicken and scalloped potatoes she had prepared earlier. As she worked, Anthia could feel his dark, thoughtful gaze.

Once she had placed everything on the kitchen table, she asked, "Iced tea?"

"I'll get it," he said. "Looks good."

"Thanks." Her gentle smile went a long way toward easing his tension. Once the edge was off his appetite, he squeezed her hand. "What have you been up to?"

She smiled, soothed by his touch. Little things like that meant so much to her. "I did some work in the studio. Packed two dolls, getting them ready for shipping. That sort of thing. I don't know if I'm just hungry or this is really good."

"It's good," he said, content to do nothing more than watch her enjoy her meal.

"Oh, Jeff called. He'd heard the news."

Dexter's brow creased into an immediate frown. "He was disappointed."

"He was shocked as we all were. Why would he be disappointed, honey? He didn't believe a word of it. If anything he was outraged on your behalf."

"Loyalty must run in this family," he sighed gently.

"Absolutely. He sent his love and best wishes. He said if you need him he'll come home. He also agreed to talk to the boys at the center. Dex, he's willing to do anything he can to help you."

Dexter nodded, deeply touched. "He's a fine man."

"Where did you go?"

"Drove around town," he said quietly. Everything he had worked for these past few years would mean nothing if he didn't stop this runaway train. All his efforts would be destroyed because of the doubt and mistrust that was bound to sweep through the community. All because of one young girl's need for revenge.

"Finished?"

"Yes, thanks, baby." When she would have rose to clear the table, he said, "Let me take care of the cleanup. Relax."

She sat watching him, perfectly at home in her kitchen. She could feel his self-absorption. Unfortunately, there was nothing she could say that would make things better. "That didn't take long."

When he bent to take her glass, she lifted her face toward his and brushed her lips against his. That brief contact quickly changed as he thrust his tongue deep inside her mouth, pulling her up against his long length. He rubbed against her, finding her soft petite frame irresistible. Her sweetness was a seductive lure that had him quivering with burgeoning need.

"Let's go to bed," he groaned.

Anthia looked into his eyes and saw the hunger reflected there. Yet, she didn't need to look for it . . . she could feel the proof of his desire . . . his erection was thick and long, pressed insistently against her. She ached with desire for his hot kisses and intense lovemaking.

She nodded, taking his large hand in her own. Her bedroom was lit by a night-light. Neither noticed as they quickly undressed. Her eyes hungrily met his from the opposite side of the bed.

They met in the center of the bed. Their arms locked around each other as they shared one hot kiss after another. There was no hesitation for either of them. Anthia loved Dexter with all her heart while he was in desperate need of her love.

"No," she whispered when he would have covered her body with his. "Let me pleasure you."

She bent to give him the ultimate caress, using her velvety soft tongue down his chest, laving each flat nipple in turn. His shudder gave her the courage to continue on down his trim stomach, passed the thick crisp strands of black hair surrounding his sex. She slowly laved the length of his heavy shaft, taking time to circle the highly sensitive peak over and over again until he groaned deeply and quickly moved her away.

"Feels too good," he whispered, his mouth hot and hungry over hers.

His hands were not idle as he squeezed and caressed her plump breasts before moving to her lush hips. When he parted her soft womanly folds, he found her sweetly wet, ready for him. He whispered her name throatily. Then, he quickly reached for the foil packet on the nightstand and prepared himself for her.

Before she could catch her breath, he stretched out on his back and lifted her up and over his hips. He closed his eyes as her wet heat slowly encased his steel hard length, taking every aching inch of him deep inside.

Dexter could not contain the fire racing through his system. His strong, powerful strokes quickly establishing an exquisite rhythm that thrilled them both. There was no turning back as the delectable torment went on and on until they both were in such perfect accord that they lost control and reached completion as one.

They slowly recovered while holding on to each other, their uneven breathing the only sound in the room. Gradually as their bodies cooled and breathing calmed Anthia shivered.

"You're cold," he said, then reached for the sheet and comforter to cover them. "Better?"

Anthia snuggled deep into his arms, "Yes," her voice revealed how tired she was.

"Sleepy?"

"Mmm," she said around a yawn. "How about you?"

He was feeling no pain. "Yes." Being with her filled all his dark, lonely places. Anthia touched places deep inside that no woman had ever come close to reaching, not even Christine. It had been difficult for him to admit to himself, but recently he faced some hard facts.

Things had not been peaches and cream for him and Christine. They had been vastly different people. When they first met and later married those differences seemed so small that they were overlooked. It was only as time went on and the sexual tension eased that he began to take notice of the sheer enjoyment Christine found in partying and drinking.

It was a lifestyle that had quickly gotten old for him. He wanted a real home and he wanted his wife home with him at night. He didn't need a room full of people to be happy. He had grown fed up with the constant string of parties she dragged him to weekend after weekend.

"Mmm," Anthia sighed.

His caressing hand cradled her nape beneath the fall of her thick, cotton, soft curls. He relished the silkiness of her supple brown skin. There was something so soothing about her that eased his tension and male hunger.

He had been away only a few hours, trying to get rid of his anxiety and fears. It was his need for her that had brought him back tonight. What was happening to him? Was it because she had first been his best friend and was now his lover that made her so essential to his well-being?

"What time do we have to leave for the center?" she asked sleepily.

"The meeting's on Tuesday."

Dexter's heart pounded with gratitude. It was the kindness of the offer that was so overwhelming . . . comforting. He thought he'd reached heaven a few moments ago when he'd lost himself within her feminine heat. He was floored by her incredibly sweet spirit. What had he ever done to be on the receiving end of such genuine warmth?

"Dex, I plan to be with you." When he didn't answer she repeated his name.

"I heard you, baby. I just don't know what to say. I hadn't realized how badly I wanted you with me . . . until now." His voice was thick with emotion. His large hand smoothed down her back, as he eased her onto his chest.

His kiss was filled with warmth and building male hunger. He paused at the small of her back just above where her womanly hips flared alluringly.

"I don't want to wreck your schedule, baby. If you have to work, I will understand."

"Nothing is more important than being with you."

Dexter groaned, smoothing his hand over her sexy behind. "Forgive me, baby . . . but I need you now," he whispered, cupping her softness with both hands while moving the crown of his sex against her mound, parting the plump folds. Anthia trembled, pressing down as he slowly, steadily entered her. The loving continued late into the night and it was very late when they gave in to their need for sleep.

TWENTY-TWO

"You look nice," Anthia said, straightening Dexter's tie. He was so handsome in a dark blue suit, pale blue shirt, and blue and cream patterned tie. "You okay?"

Dexter was anything but okay. It had been a rough couple of days. He was raw and on edge. It took all of his willpower not to let it show. He felt as he had that day when he faced the jury to learn his fate. It had been the most difficult moment of his life, waiting to hear if he had been found not guilty or convicted of manslaughter for his wife and child's deaths, while still grieving their loss. It wasn't over. He felt as if he were on trial now, only this time in the court of public opinion. Yet, he had no choice but to face this head-on.

"Honey?"

"I'm fine. I'd rather spend the day making love to my lady," he said kissing her cheek.

Anthia smiled, "Good answer." She suspected it had been designed to distract her.

He gave her a rare smile, the first for that day. His bold gaze moved over her. She was dressed in a slim beige dress and matching waist-length jacket accented with sterling-silver buttons. She wore heart-shaped, diamond studs in her ears and a sterling-liquid-silver bead necklace. Her hair was brushed up into puffy curls on top of her head, her long bangs swept to one side while soft curls framed her small amber tone face.

"You look good, baby. Ready?"

"Yes." She had to work to keep the smile in place, determined to hide her own reluctance. She had spent time on her knees this morning praying for God's help. Anthia knew this was one of those times when she had to let her faith see her through. She knew deep in her heart that Dexter had done nothing to deserve this.

Anthia was unsure what to expect when they reached the community center but certainly not the media circus that greeted them. They were swamped by press and television news crews almost as soon as he helped her out of the car.

"Lisa Green, Channel 7 News, Mr. Washington. You've been in Detroit for several years now. Why would you choose to be involved with a young woman barely out of her teens rather than a woman your own age?"

"Brian Gordon, Channel 4 News. Have you been charged yet?"

"Brenda Hawthorne, Channel 62 News. Mr. Washington, is it true that you would be willing to take a lie detector test?"

"No comment," Dexter said tightly as he escorted Anthia through the media crowded on the sidewalk leading into the community center. They barely had time to take note of the community members walking along the front walkway for suddenly they were flanked by Charles Randol on the left and Guy Malone on the right. Both men had the advantage of above-average height and were using their broad shoulders, as well as their arms to clear a path so that Anthia and Dexter could enter the facility. The newly hired security guard let them inside, then quickly relocked the doors.

Anthia was thrilled to find Diane Randol waiting inside for them. Diane gave both Dexter and Anthia a hug and kiss.

"Oh, I am so sorry about this. It's just not right," she said emphatically.

"I'm so glad that you're here," Anthia said squeezing her hand gratefully.

"I had to be here. I had to show how much I support Dexter. Charles and I have been so upset by this. Don't you two worry, we're going to straighten this all out."

"Thanks, Diane," Dexter said quietly unable to take the Randols show of support for granted. It meant too much. When his gaze moved to Anthia, he realized she was trembling. "You okay, baby?"

"I just don't understand how they can take her word over yours. They have no proof!" she referred to the media frenzy.

"What she is is a nasty little girl who refuses to take no for an answer," Charles snapped impatiently. "First they pull you in for questioning and now this. How much do you want to bet we'll be on the evening news?" Evidently he expected no response for he went on to say, "It's undermining what we're trying to do here. We don't need this kind of publicity. It's destructive!"

Diane stroked her husband's arm. "They can't win."

Dexter was holding Anthia's hand so tightly she cried out at the pressure. "I'm sorry, baby. I didn't mean to hurt you."

"No harm done." She leaned close to whisper, "Stop worrying. We are all on your side. Did you see the boys and their families marching in front of the center? They're here to support you, honey."

"Really," he hadn't noticed. He'd been too distracted by the television cameras. He took a deep, fortifying breath while trying to ignore the way his stomach was a mass of nerves that he couldn't seem to get rid of.

"Ready?" Charles prompted.

"Yes," he said gruffly with Anthia at his side. For once, he did not need to remind himself that he was not alone . . . not this time. No matter what happened this day, he had that to remember . . . to savor.

Margaret Poindexter, along with the executive board, was already seated around a long table that had been set up in the community center gymnasium. There was a sudden hush as Dexter walked into the room, and he along with his supporters took their seats at the table.

Ms. Poindexter opened the meeting, "Good morning. Shall we get down to the business at hand?" She did not wait for a response but went on to say, "We were all disturbed by the newspaper account in yesterday's paper. Suddenly, we have media attention, but the wrong variety," she paused for a breath.

"This is not about the media. It's about Washington," interjected Morgan Smith, a board member and outstanding community activist.

Anthia could see the way Dexter's mouth tightened into a hard line.

Ms. Poindexter went on as if he had not spoken. "Mr. Washington, your integrity and sincerity have never been in question by myself or this body. Now suddenly we're forced to confront some very disturbing issues that are directly linked to you, which in turn links them to the community center."

"Why couldn't you keep your hands to yourself, Washington? More importantly why didn't you tell us you were a ex-con," Thomas Templeton interjected hotly.

Charles, also a board member, could not sit still a moment longer. "I think you've said quite enough, Templeton. You have no way of proving those accusations. Until you know the truth, I suggest you keep your mouth closed."

"Gentlemen! Let's keep this orderly. Mr. Washington has been very forthright about his past. It isn't an issue here today," Ms. Poindexter insisted.

"Like hell, it isn't!" Morgan Smith interrupted yet again.

"Thank you, Ms. Poindexter, but I can speak for myself," Dexter said as he came to his feet. "I have nothing to apologize for. I never said or did anything improper to that young woman. I dare any one of you to bring me proof that I did otherwise." Every eye seemed to be on him when he said, "I hired Ms. Douglas to work in the center's office. I encouraged her to finish school and go on to college. That is the extent of my involvement with her." A muscle jumped in his cheek as if he were trying to hang on to his temper.

"She approached me not the other way around. As far as I was concerned that was the end of it. I have no answer as to why she went to the press with this."

Ms. Poindexter said, "Thank you, Mr. Washington. You may be seated."

"I don't see the pro . . ." Charles was interrupted.

There was a commotion in the hall before the door was pushed open. All heads turned toward the noise. Dexter dropped into his chair, shocked by what he saw. The sheer numbers of the young men filing into the room, black males that he had worked with during the three years he'd been at the center was heart warming. Some were accompanied by a parent or grandparent; some came alone.

"What is the meaning of this?" Ms. Poindexter was on her feet.

"We'd like to speak on Mr. Washington's behalf," Josh Underwood, a twenty-year-old college student at Michigan State University approached the founder's chair.

Anthia couldn't stop the tears that welled in her eyes, she blinked them away. Now was not the time to lose control. She had to remain focused. As she stroked her fingertips over the back of Dexter's hand resting on his lap, she could feel his tension.

"Mr. Washington?" Ms. Poindexter asked.

Dexter nodded, trying to believe this was for him. He was floored by the wall of emotions threatening to fill his throat and eyes. He took comfort from Anthia's touch.

"Mr. Washington has made an impact on all our lives. That's what we're here to address. Both my parents died in a single night inside a drug house. My mother by an overdose, my father by a junky who felt he'd been cheated. I had no one. I was thrust into foster care at fourteen. Nobody was interested in adopting me. I was a kid with a huge chip on my shoulder. I met Mr. Washington while I was at Martin Luther King High School. He spoke to a group of us boys but I felt as if he was talking to me. He talked about the community center. Afterward, I went up to him and asked him questions. He not only took time to answer all my questions, but he was not afraid to look me in the eye while he did so. He sat down with me and we talked. For the first time that I could remember an adult listened to what I had to say."

Josh paused, his dark brown face intent as he look at Dexter. "It was because of Mr. Washington that I took three buses every day after school to get here to the center. It was because of his faith in me when I didn't have faith in myself that I finished high school and earned a four-year scholarship to Michigan State." He paused, then said, "He showed me by example what it is to be a man. Someday, I will be an engineer. I have one man to thank. Thank you, Mr. Washington."

Dexter nodded, swallowing with difficulty.

An elderly woman stepped forward. "My name is Ella Hunter. I also have Dex to thank. My grandson here didn't have no man to guide him the right way. But Dex and Charles Randol spoke at my church about this here community center. I knew right off, that it was the answer for my Clarence. My boy will be starting community college in the fall. He'll be the first of our peoples to graduat' from high school and go on to college." She wiped tears away from her cloudy brown eyes, before she said, "No matter what some silly fool girl says, Dex ain't no child molester. He may have made some mistakes in his life but he done made up for it. He ain't no criminal. One thing I know is that Dex Washington is a good man. It would be a big mistake for you all to keep him from helping these youngun's who out here. A big mistake."

Each story was an individual one with one single overwhelming theme: Dexter was clearly highly respected and appreciated in the community, and the center's executive board members would be making a huge error in judgment if they let him go.

Charles was on his feet with the others when it came down to the vote. Eight to four in favor of Dexter remaining on the job while the sexual harassment accusation was being investigated.

Dexter's heart was full as he, with Anthia at his side, thanked each and every person who had spoken on his behalf. He was so choked up by their show of support that by the time they reached the car, he was barely aware of the cameras or microphones stuck in their faces.

"Oh, honey. It was so wonderful. I still can't believe it. What a surprise," Anthia gushed once they were in the car and underway.

While she chatted with excitement Dexter on the other hand was quiet and deep in thought. In fact, he was absorbed for so

IN

long that Anthia grew concerned. She quieted, reframed from
intruding on his thoughts. He parked in front of her house rather
than the driveway.

"You're not coming inside?" she asked

"No, remember I have an appointment with Quinn."

"Yes, of course," instead of getting out of the car, she placed
her hand on his sleeve. When his gaze met hers, she said, "That
was a great show of support. It was totally unexpected," she
wanted to add that it was no more than he deserved for giving
so unselfishly of himself, but she didn't want to embarrass him.
She had seen the sheen of tears glistening in his eyes before he
blinked them away.

"Yeah. It was overwhelming."

"How are you?"

"I don't know. Anthia, I never expected . . . never dreamed
of that kind of response."

"People care about you because you have given so much of
yourself for a long time. That kind of positive energy can't be
ignored." Her eyes suddenly filled with tears, "I almost stood
up and told my story. You have been there for me, so many
times."

Dexter was deeply warmed by her high regard but he was
also embarrassed. She was the wonder. And she cared for him,
deeply. What had he ever done to merit such a woman's tender
feelings?

"Anthia," he whispered throatily. She had so much to offer
a man. It was so unfair that she was now suffering along with
him. He had tried to fight her sweet appeal the other night when
he had walked out.

But he had not been able to stay away for long. All he knew
for certain was that she was critical to his well-being. He had
to resolve this mess and quickly. He would not allow her to
suffer anymore than she already had because of him. She was
precious to him.

He caressed her cheek. "Why don't you get some rest? You
didn't sleep very well last night."

"Neither one of us got much sleep," she said remembering

how he had tossed and turned after they'd made love. She had been equally as restless.

"I don't like the strain this has placed on you. I care about you," he brushed her lips ever so briefly with his. "Take a nap for my sake, okay? I'll see you tonight. Would you like to go out to dinner?"

She shook her head, trying not to be disappointed that he had not said the one thing that she longed hear: He had never told her that he loved her. Now was not the time to dwell on it. There was so much still to be done to clear his name. Once that was taken care of then they would talk, really talk. She made that promise to herself. She could wait.

"Anthia?"

"No. I'd rather stay in."

"Okay, baby. I might put in a few hours at the center."

"This is not my scheduled night but I can come in, if you need me?"

"What I need is for you to be all right. I hate what this is doing to you . . . to us. Somehow, I have to prove the truth to you," he insisted.

"You don't have to prove a thing to me. I know you never put your hands on that child."

"How did I get so lucky to have found a woman like you?" he whispered. Nevertheless, he needed to prove it to her for his own peace of mind. He did not want this accusation to ever come between them. He had to make certain it didn't. "Get some rest, baby. 'Bye."

" 'Bye," she said as she stepped out of the car. It wasn't until she was inside the house that she realized he had not kissed her. When she relaxed in the chair behind her desk, she mumbled aloud, "Please, don't let us be slipping backward." That was something she could not bear. They had faced so much together. What if . . .

"Calm down," she told herself. It was perfectly natural for him to be self-absorbed. For heaven's sake, his whole life had turned upside down by this thing with Tina. What did she expect? He was under such tremendous pressure right now.

It would be wrong to make demands on him now. She would

not be another problem for him to solve. There was no point to dwell on the fact that only the other night he had walked out of her house without explanation. Nor would it do her any good to recall that because he had made love to her, it did not necessarily mean that he loved her. He claimed to care about her, not love her. There was a distinctive difference.

"Enough!" She was being incredibly selfish. It was time to stop thinking of her own needs and desires. They were together, they had been so since their trip to Houston. It would all work out for the best. She just had to keep reminding herself of that. The question that she could not answer was would it be to her liking.

Dexter was going through a personal crisis that could very well change his life. It would not be easy for him to get through this. He had strong opposition. Those four board members who had voted against him today could quite possibly sway the others against him. This thing was far from over. What if he lost his position at the community center? What then?

Anthia hung her head wearily. She didn't have to be told that the center meant the world to him. Without it, he would be like a ship sailing aimlessly through life. He needed to help those boys just as much as they needed someone to care what happened to them. Things simply had to work out in his favor. They just had to.

Dexter nodded to Quinn's secretary when he was told to go on in. He didn't bother to knock but walked in and to his surprise found Quinn Montgomery seated behind his desk with a lovely, woman on his lap wrapped in his arms.

"Excuse me," Dexter said with a grin.

"No need," the petite beauty said with a giggle. "It's all his fault. I stopped in to bring lunch to my husband and look what happened," Heather Gregory-Montgomery said with a smile. The golden tone beauty had a flawless, creamy complexion, shoulder-length hair that had been braided into tiny individual braids. She shook her finger at her husband. "Your lunch break is over, let me up." On her feet, she said, "Dex, I'm so sorry about what happened with that ridiculous story that appeared in the newspaper. You know you have both Quinn and my support. How are you?"

"Thanks, Heather. It's good to see you, again. I really appreciate your vote of confidence."

Dexter had met the Montgomerys through Charles and Diane Randol. Long before Charles and Diane married, Charles, Heather and Diane had at one time worked in a privately funded high school in Detroit. Charles at the time was coaching, while Heather was the counselor and Diane taught business classes.

The community center had since profited from all their expertise. Not counting the fund-raisers both the couples supported, Heather was on call for private counseling at the center when needed, while Diane taught computer classes at the center when she could. Quinn could be called on for legal advice. Charles remained the most actively involved in the center.

"How did the board meeting go this morning?" Quinn asked, wiping lipstick from his mouth with his napkin. His lunch forgotten on the desk.

"Much better than expected." He quickly recounted the surprising testimonials by the kids and their families, as well as the eight-to-four vote.

"Well, I am not surprised. You have done a wonderful job with those kids. It would be tragic to lose you now," Heather insisted. "Well, I really should be going. I have to pick the twins up from preschool." She gave her husband a quick kiss. "See you tonight," she said with a smile, before she walked over and gave Dexter a hug. "Take care. And give Anthia my love."

Dexter smiled, "Will do. He didn't have to ask how she knew he was seeing Anthia. Diane and Heather were close friends.

Once they were alone, Quinn indicated the empty chair in front of his cluttered desk. "Have a seat. Then we can get down to business." He reached for a file from one of the stacks piled on one corner of the desk. "Got the investigator's report. He did go over to Tina Douglas' place and question both the Douglas girl and her mother. . . ."

* * *

Dexter left more frustrated than he had been when he arrived. He had walked out shouting that if Quinn's investigator was not competent enough to find any answers than he would do it himself.

It was his life, his problem. He was determined to get to the bottom of it. Tina had created these lies. She was the only one with the answers. Even with Quinn's warning to stay away from her, nothing was going to stop him. Dexter moved purposefully toward his car.

The way he saw it, he could not make things worse. What more could she do to him? What more could she accuse him of? Hell! She had already destroyed his reputation and brought his past out into the open. It was time Dexter did what needed to be done. He was going to have it out with Tina before this day was over.

TWENTY-THREE

Anthia worked at keeping herself busy. She scrubbed the kitchen before she started on the bathrooms. It was late afternoon before she took time to eat. The most she could get down was part of a sandwich before she went into her studio.

Several days' worth of mail that had been stacked neatly on corner of her desk did not hold any appeal to her. She needed the soothing feel of clay against her fingertips to ease the tension in her body. The amount of stress that had accumulated from when they were met by reporters—an experience she didn't care to ever repeat—to the board meeting and the final vote had been tremendous. It was all she could do to hang on to Dexter.

He had been so strong, so determined. She had been so proud of him. Realizing that others might actually believe the media hype, Anthia was disheartened. He had been through so much, enduring the loss of his wife and child, and then having to pay for something he had not done with five years of his own life, should have been enough. It didn't end there. And then he had come home after the confrontation with his heartless father to these public lies. It was just too much. She wiped at tear, impatient with herself. It would work out . . . it had to.

It was nearly dark when she covered the doll head she had been working on, washed up and then moved over to her desk. One letter in particular caught her eye. It was from a large at-home shopping network. Naturally, she had seen the popular cable channel but that was as far as it went. Curious, she broke the seal.

Anthia was shocked when she read that one of their buyers had seen one of her dolls in a New York City art gallery and was impressed. The at-home shopping network were wondering if she would consider designing and producing a limited edition collection of dolls for its upcoming Collectors' Day in November.

"I don't believe this," she exclaimed. Her hands were actually shaking as she punched in the community center's telephone number, then quickly pushed the disconnect button. No, she wanted to tell him this news face to face. Instead she punched in Dana's number.

"Hi, it's Anthia. You will never believe this. Are you going to be home this evening? No. I can't tell you over the telephone. You have to read this letter yourself. Okay," she giggled. "I'll be over as soon as I freshen up. Yes, I'll hurry if you let me get off the phone. 'Bye."

Anthia was laughing as she showered, then changed into a black silk sweater and jeans. She hurried to find her purse and keys. She remembered Dexter's warning as she was backing out of the driveway. Perhaps, she should leave him a note but decided against it. She would be home hours before he finished at the community center. Dana was going to be thrilled. Showing her dolls on national television was something that had never entered Anthia's mind.

She sobered as she wondered how Dexter's meeting with Quinn had gone. She reminded herself as she made the trip into Detroit that Quinn was the best. Dexter's future was in capable hands. Quinn had not only gotten Jeff out of the armed robbery charge, but had won his civil trial against the convenience store owner thus securing Jeff's financial future.

Dana opened her apartment door before Anthia could knock more than once. "Get in here, girl. What took you so long?"

Anthia couldn't help chuckling at her friend's enthusiasm. "Sit down. I want you to read something."

Once they sat side by side on the sofa, Anthia handed over

the letter. Dana quickly read it and her dark eyes were shiny with tears when she met Anthia's twinkling gaze.

"Congratulations! You have made a name for yourself in the business. New York gallery. What an accomplishment. Now a network shopping channel! Wow!"

The two women laughed, cried and hugged each other all at the same time.

"I'm so happy for you," Dana said.

"Me, too," Anthia was beaming. "Oh, Dana! I can't believe it. I certainly could not have done it without your expert help. The dolls have really turned out more beautiful than even I could ever imagine."

"I thank you for seeing potential in me. Remember, you're the genius behind One-of-a-Kind Dolls. They're your designs from the skillfully sculptured faces, unique natural-looking wigs to the embroidered hems. Well, boss, are we going to do it? Are we going to create a collection for this Collectors' Day?"

"I don't know. I've been so excited I really haven't thought this thing through. I honestly don't know if I want to do a limited edition of any one doll. That is not exactly one of a kind, now is it?" Anthia was on her feet, pacing the length of the living room. "The work involved will be almost impossible to do in such a short time. We have enough orders to take us into the new year as it is."

"Designing a half dozen dolls? A piece of cake for you, girl."

"If only it were that simple. Molds would have to be made in order to reproduce the dolls even in a limited collection. That's more than five hundred dresses, slips, shoes and pantaloons and accessories for each doll. It's a tremendous amount of sewing and stuffing."

"We can do it if you want. We just have to have help."

"What I would have to have would be a doll manufacturing company. Oh, Dana, I don't know. Making one-of-a-kind dolls has been so important to me. It was what I wanted to do, their uniqueness makes them so special. Every one of your girls has her own doll that look just like they did as babies. I have a doll that looks like my own son when he was a baby. It's so dear to me. Diane loves the Madelyn doll she gave her mother. The dolls mean so much."

"You, my friend are what makes them special. They all have your talented, loving touch."

"Thanks." Anthia found herself blushing.

"Just think, Anthia. More and more people will be able to enjoy the dolls."

"Our dolls must have the hand-painted eyes and embroidered yokes, hems or slips. Then there's the custom-made shoes and lace details. They will be very costly to reproduce. What about the fabric?" She paused thoughtfully. "The natural, African-American skin tones we are known for will be very difficult to duplicate, especially in porcelain. I'm not sure about vinyl. Hmm? Can any factory duplicate those added touches that make our work unique?"

Dana was forced to ask, "How can you even consider turning this down? It can launch your new limited editions line of dolls."

"Maybe, I won't have to turn this down. Maybe, they will be happy with fifty or so individually designed dolls. What do you think?" Anthia asked, hopefully.

Dana clapped her hand excitedly. "If anyone can convince them, it will be you, my dear. Remember, you're living your dreams. You're able to create your dolls in your own studio. It's all about you . . . enjoy."

Anthia's eyes went wide and then she laughed for the sheer joy if it. "It's been wonderful. This is a big boost to the business and would offer a tremendous amount of exposure. I'm thrilled by the pleasure One of a Kind Dolls have given to so many others." And she had been in the black, something that rarely happened with a small home-based business, since that first year.

"You put so much of yourself into your work. You okay?" she asked while Anthia wiped her tears away.

"Just happy. Thank you, Dana." Anthia went on to say, "We haven't talked for several days. How have you been?"

"We're fine. More important, how are you and Dex? I flatly

refused to believe that trash I read in the newspaper. Where did that come from?"

"Tina Douglas, she works at the center. She has a thing for Dexter and was a little upset when he didn't return her feelings."

"A little?" Dana huffed. "She must be vindictive."

"Very. She's barely out of her teens." Anthia said wearily, "Thanks, Dana. Dex and I both appreciate your faith in him. This has been so hard on him." She shook her head in disbelief. "I still can't believe the number of television news cameras that greeted us this morning at the community center. It was like a circus."

Anthia went on to explain, "We attended the executive board meeting. I was so nervous. I tell you, if I never see another television news camera it will not be too soon for me."

"Well, thank goodness it's over," Dana said, patting Anthia's hand. "How did the meeting go? They weren't looking to fire him, were they?"

"He had some opposition, but the boys he has helped over the years came, some with their families to speak on his behalf." She went on to retell their individual testimonials.

"That's fabulous. I can't imagine where they could have gotten such a wild story that Dex had been convicted of manslaughter."

Anthia met her friend's gaze head-on. "It was not made up. That part is true. Dexter did time for manslaughter in Texas. It was an accident. He was trying to stop his wife's suicide attempt when the gun went off. His wife and their unborn child were killed."

"How tragic. It must be terribly painful for him to relive it publicly."

"Yes, it has been." She looked around, "It's too quiet in here. Where are the kids?"

Dana forced a smile as she glanced at the wall clock. "They're with their father, visiting his grandmother."

"What!" It popped out before Anthia could stop it.

Dana was immediately on the defensive. "If I can understand why you support your man, why can't you see why I support mine?"

"What did I say? For heaven's sakes, Dana! I was just surprised. I've never known you to leave the kids with anyone outside of your own family."

"Are you implying I don't trust Jerome's people? Or Jerome for that matter with his own kids?" Dana persisted.

"Excuse me, but I thought we were talking about your babies?" Anthia knew better than to get into any kind of discussion with Dana about her lover. He could do no wrong in Dana's view.

Dana was so upset, she was shaking. "This is about Jerome and we both know it! You don't like him. Oh, please! Girl, don't you think I know you can't stand my Jerome?"

"And why is that Dana? His brother is in jail for armed robbery and my son would be in the next cell if it was left up to Eddie." Anthia fumed, as the painful memories washed over her. "Besides, Dana, you know that Jerome makes no secret of the fact he can't stand me or mine. He resents me because my son didn't do jail time. You were here when he threatened me."

"He has never threatened you," the younger woman insisted, close to tears.

Anthia sighed heavily. This entire conversation was pointless. Dana's love blinded her to the man's faults. All she saw when it came to her lover was what she wanted to see.

Anthia said, "I apologize if I upset you. Can we please drop this right now?"

"Hello, Mrs. Douglas. I'm Dexter Washington. I'd like to speak to Tina."

She had apparently just gotten out of bed. Her hair had not benefitted from a comb and she smelled of stale beer. She swore heatedly. "After what you put my baby through? No way! The police been here trying to trap her. And that investigator you sent to shake us up. Well, it didn't work! Them damn reporters camped outside the front door all morning, trying to get in to talk to Tina. Enough! Now, get the hell out of my face!"

"I have no idea how the reporters knew that Tina is behind the story in the newspaper. I certainly am not responsible."

ally attracted to children, Mrs. Douglas. In my mind Tina is a child. She knows how I feel."

Mrs. Douglas stared at him, suddenly remembering how upset Tina had been with him because he had been seeing someone at the center. Was that what changed her attitude toward him?

Did she think she could force him into wanting her? Had Tina decided that a man was the answer to her problems, like so many woman these days? Hadn't she learned anything from her own mother's mistake? Tina's father had walked out on them because he couldn't handle the responsibility of a family.

She only had to look at him to see why. Dexter was a tall, good-looking brother. He was all that and then some. But to do something so evil as to lie about the man. Was that why she had not wanted to go to the police?

Janet Douglas walked into the hallway and screamed at the top of her lungs, "Tina! Get dressed and get your behind out here, girl!" When she didn't appear fast enough to suit her, she screeched. "Tina!!"

"What?" Tina yelled back.

"Get the hell out here. I want to talk to you now!"

"What!" Tina snapped, entering the room while rubbing sleep from her eyes. She was dressed in leggings and long T-shirt. She stopped abruptly, then asked with agitation, "Why did you let him in?" She didn't wait for an answer but walked over to the front door to fling it open. "Get the hell out!"

Her mother was fuming as she walked over to her and slapped her. "Shut the damn door! Then take your narrow behind over to the couch and sit down!"

Angry tears filled Tina's eyes as she poked out her lips like a small child, but she did exactly as her mother demanded.

Mrs. Douglas folded her arms across her frail body, before she said, "Why did you lie?"

"I didn't!"

As her mother approached Tina, she swore long and heatedly. "I don't have time for this. We both know you had a thing for that man. So why did you lie?"

"I did not lie. He touched my breasts and he forced himself

on me," she said glaring at her mother. "Why don't you believe me? Why don't you ever take my word for anything!"

"When and where did this happen, Tina?" Dexter said rising slowly to his full height.

Tina looked away unable to even look at him. "You had no business coming here. Haven't you done enough all ready?"

"What have I done, Tina? What have I done to make you so angry that you had to get back at me this way?"

Tina shook her head, covering her ears as if she could tune him out. "Leave me alone!"

Dexter paced the length of the room before he turned back to face Tina and said, "You went to the newspaper with this story to hurt me. We both know that. What I want to know is why? I have never laid a hand on you in a sexual way. Nor have I spoken to you out of turn." He was holding on to his temper by a solitary thread. Maybe Anthia and Quinn were right? Maybe he was making things worse by coming here.

"I hate you! Do you hear me, I hate you!!" Tina yelled, jumping to her feet and screaming the words at him.

"Sit down, Tina." He spoke with quiet authority, his voice tinged with frost.

She sank onto the sofa. "I want you out of my house."

"Girl, you don't pay nothing up in here, so shut your mouth."

"I don't have anything to say to him."

"You had plenty to say the night you waited for me after closing. The night I drove you home. You made a play for me that night. Did you tell your mother about that? Did you tell her how I turned you down?" He came right up to her. "Why can't you look me in the face? This all started when I began seeing Anthia, didn't it? You have resented her since she first started volunteering at the center."

He should have seen the trouble coming. But no, he had been so caught up in his feelings for Anthia and in his work at the center, that he had not noticed Tina at all. As long as she did her job, he had not had a problem. How could he have been so blind?

"You overheard me asking her to go away with me for the

weekend, didn't you? Was that what made you try to hurt me? You couldn't stand the idea of our being together?"

"Tina? Is what he says true? Did you throw yourself at him? And when he said no did you make up a story? Did he or did he not fondle you?"

The girl could not meet her mother's pain-filled eyes or Dexter's dark, angry ones. She had never expected the newspaper to take such an interest in the community center. Who could have guessed it would blow up into the media circus, it had become. It had turned into a nightmare, with no end in sight.

The worst had been when the police had come to question her. She had been terrified. She tried to say as little as possible. She did not want to go to jail. She did not want him to go to jail either. Why couldn't they see that she was the one who had been hurt?

When Tina looked at him, her hands were balled into fists while tears ran down her face. She hissed, "What did you see in her? I did everything right. I never worked so hard at anything as I did at the center." She sniffed, wiping at the tears that she couldn't seem to stop.

"I really liked you from the very beginning. I did everything you wanted me to do. I worked hard and I went to school." She hesitated, wiping at her tears. "I always took time with my hair, my nails, my clothes. I did all that! But you never even noticed me! You saw me as a little kid. And I wasn't. I was all grown up! But you never even looked at me, not like you look at her!" Glaring at him, Tina asked belligerently, "What was so special about Anthia? She's old. She has a grown kid! What did you see in her?"

"I love her," Dexter said quite openly, suddenly realizing it was the simple truth.

He had been in love with Anthia for a very long time. She had won his heart by the courageous way she would not give up on her child when he was lying shot in hospital bed in critical condition. She never, not once gave up on Jeff. Dexter's admiration for her only seemed to grow over time.

"I'm just as pretty as she is!"

"It has nothing to do with her looks, Tina. Her beauty comes from inside." Suddenly Dexter wanted nothing more than to be with Anthia and be able to give her the good news. It was nearly over.

The girl's mother was near tears herself when she said, "I'm sorry, Mr. Washington. I'll make sure that Tina does the right thing."

Dexter nodded, yet he took no pleasure from Tina's mistake.

"About the lawsuit, we don't have no money," Mrs. Douglas whispered fearfully.

Dexter said, "All I want is my good name back. Or as much of it as I can have. My lawyer will be contacting you about a press conference to straighten this all out."

Mrs. Douglas wept as if her heart were broken. Dexter felt sorry for her, for both of them. Tina in her efforts to get back at him had not only hurt him, but her mother and even more importantly . . . she had hurt herself. The hurt was something she was just beginning to understand.

She heard the anguish in her mother's sobs. "Oh, Mama. I'm so sorry. I didn't mean it to turn out like this."

Dexter rose saying, "Thank you, Mrs. Douglas. Good-bye."

TWENTY-FOUR

As if she were unable to remain seated a second longer, Dana moved back and forth to the door several times before she stopped abruptly and said unhappily, "You're my friend. Doesn't that count for something?"

"Yes, it does." Anthia nodded, "Don't I have to be honest with you? Dana, you are a wonderful person. I think you deserve so much better than Jerome." Anthia hated the way the man treated her friend and that was all she was focusing on when she went on to say, "He lives here but, can you honestly say he even takes care of his kids financially?"

Dana looked away. "I never asked you how many nights Dexter spends in your bed."

Anthia answering truthfully, "As many as possible. I'm not ashamed of how I feel about him. But there is a difference in our situations. I don't support him. And I don't have his babies, although, I must admit I would like nothing more." She did not add that if Jerome would even look after his own kids, then Dana would be able to work a few hours outside of her home.

"You would consider having a baby with Dexter?"

"Absolutely. I just don't want to have to raise another child alone. It's too hard. Dana, honey, I'm older than you. I know what I'm talking about."

"I know you only want the best for me. But I love him, Anthia. I can't help it." Her unhappiness was evident in her eyes.

"Love should not hurt so much."

"You don't know him like I do. He has a sweet side, a tender side that he doesn't show anyone else but me. Sometimes a black woman has to go beyond the norm to keep her man."

Anthia did not know what to say, did not know why she was even arguing the point. This was Dana's life, she could not live it for her. But she could not stop feeling as if Dana were making some really bad choices.

"You have more than yourself to think about. You have those four beautiful babies. You have to do what is best for them."

Dana sank back down beside Anthia. "Yes, I know. Right now they have to come first. They're still so young and totally dependent on me."

"Girlfriend, I was lucky. Although, I got pregnant way too young, I had my mother to help me and guide me."

After Dana's parents divorced, she lost contact with her father. Her mother was a very religious woman and she strongly disagreed with Dana having children without marriage.

"You have accomplished a great deal on your own."

"Thank you, but so can you. You're very talented, Dana."

She was only half listening. Every few minutes, she stared at her watch then ran damp hands down her pant legs.

"What's wrong?"

"They should be back by now. It's past my girls dinnertime. Where could they be?"

"Perhaps, you should call Jerome's grandmother?"

"I'll give him another half hour," Dana said, refusing to verbalize her fears. Jerome could be responsible, if he were sober. And he had been straight when he left with the children, otherwise she would have not let them go. The question was, was he still in control of himself? What if he ran into some of his boys? Surely, he would bring the babies home to her before he took off with them.

Anthia felt helpless as she watched Dana move restlessly from the living room into the dining room and back again. "If you don't want to call, let me."

"No! I don't want him thinking that I don't trust him with the girls or that I'm checking up on him." Dana shuttered at the thought of unleashing his temper. He was not always an easy man to live with, although he had never hurt her.

"My car is right outside. Why don't I take you over to his grandmother's?"

The other woman shook her head. "No, it's only been a couple of hours."

Just long enough to drive a young mother out of her mind with worry, Anthia fumed. "Why don't I make us some coffee? That might calm us both down."

"Please," Dana said trying to smile, but failed.

While Anthia worked in the small, but spotless, kitchen she thought of Dexter. He would be upset with her. She had stayed much longer than expected. It was after nine. Picking up the extension, first she called the community center. When she didn't receive an answer, she called her own number and left a message for him on the answering machine.

When Anthia returned with the coffee mugs she heard a key rattle in the lock before the door was pushed open and the children rushed forward to greet their mother.

Dana's eyes briefly locked with Jerome's before she looked away. He'd been either drinking or using. She was infuriated that he could be so reckless with the children. He was supposed to know better.

"Mommy! Mommy!" The girls exclaimed, giving out hugs and kisses. "We missed you."

"Hi babies," she giggled, holding them close. She checked each one in turn, assuring herself that they were safe and well. "I expected you hours ago. Did you guys eat?"

With four little girls all talking at once, it was hard to decipher the information from baby talk. Gina, one of the older girls said, "We ate at Granny's house." Then noticed Anthia looking on with an affectionate smile. "Auntie!" she called. Soon Anthia was on the receiving end of all those hugs and wet kisses.

"What's this 'B' doin' in my house?" Jerome said, insultingly. "I told you before I didn't want her up in here!"

The kids stiffened, wide eyes moving to their mother. Dana said, "Go ahead, girls. Time to go change into your pajamas.

I'll read your story before you go to bed. Go on." She urged them out, then she closed their bedroom door.

The tension was so heavy, it was like a thick fog murking the atmosphere.

"I asked you . . ."

"Look, it isn't necessary for you to go there Jerome. I'm leaving." Anthia began collecting her things. "Dana, I'll call you soon," she said, having placed the important letter in her purse.

"Not so damn fast!" He stood glassy eyed, leaning against the door. "I have a few things to say to you. And you are going to stay and listen!"

Dexter was so excited by the time he reached Anthia's place he was almost bursting with good news. He had considered going in to the center to get in a few hours' work, but the anticipation of seeing Anthia's face wreathed in smiles proved to be irresistible. This experience with Tina had been difficult for Anthia. She was so special to him. She had not jumped to conclusions or believed the worst of him. She believed in him.

He could not suppress a chuckle. He was looking forward to her sweet kiss of congratulation. He was worse than a green boy with his first serious crush. He had to see his lady.

Damn straight! That was exactly how he felt about her. The lady was his from her soft dark curls to her small red-painted toenails. It was way past time he told her how he felt. He hesitated staring out into the seemingly cloudless sky.

Was he rushing things? Was he pushing her into a relationship that would possibly result in disillusionment and hurt for both of them? It was one thing to know about his past, it was quite another to actually live with it day in and day out. And that was what he wanted from her. He would be lying to himself if he didn't admit the unvarnished truth to himself.

The full disclosure of his past had very nearly cost him the only job he valued. He had become an architect to please his father. He had headed the community center to please himself.

He felt a keen sense of accomplishment that he had not come close to duplicating while he worked in his family-owned firm.

What he did at the center made a difference in this troubled world. Plus, it was like a cool balm that soothed his painful past and thus allowed him to go on with his life. The community center had done more to help him than he had ever done for anyone there. It gave him focus, direction when he needed it the most. It validated his worth as an African-American man.

"Anthia," he said aloud. A slow smile graced his strong bronze face. It drew the corners of his mouth up and caused his eyes to sparkle. As he parked his car in her driveway he forced himself to face his own difficult situation.

Even though, he could not offer her his name, he did not want to ever let her go. He loved her too much. The weight of his own selfishness had him swearing beneath his breath. What he was asking was ridiculous. He wouldn't be surprised if she turned him down flat. She had a right to expect the man who claimed to love her to also be willing to marry her. It wasn't like she didn't know his situation. Surely, he could coax her around to his way of seeing things?

Dexter was disappointed when he discovered that Anthia was not at home. He walked around to the back of the house, dropped down to search in the flowerpot beside the rear door for her spare key.

He grinned with satisfaction when he found it and unlocked the door. He quickly disengaged the alarm in the rear hallway outside the kitchen. He grinned when he didn't see a single pot on the stove. The kitchen was squeaky-clean. Were they eating out, or was he supposed to be bringing their meal? He didn't have a clue.

He had been distracted when they last talked. There were no messages on the message board in the kitchen, only the beginning of a grocery list. In her studio, he glanced around but found no indication as to her whereabouts.

Returning to the kitchen, he got himself an ice-cold beer then settled in an armchair in the living room. He made a quick call to Quinn and explained what happened with Tina. The longer he waited for Anthia the more he brooded, wondering if she were all right. Surely, she hadn't gone over to Dana's, not after he had warned her about that place after dark? She could have stopped by to see Diane? Or gone shopping?

Suddenly remembering the message light blinking on the answering machine, he retraced his steps. Perhaps, she have called and left a message for him. The telephone rang just then, he practically snatched it off the hook.

"Jenkins' residence?"

"Dex?"

"Yeah. Jeff?"

"Yes, how are you?"

"Better. Your mom passed along your message. Thanks. Your support means a lot to me," Dexter ended quietly.

"It's how I feel. I'm hoping everything works out in your favor. I can't believe how Tina has been jerking you around," Jeff growled in disgust.

"Yeah, but I think I've gotten it settled. She admitted the truth to me this evening in front of her mother. I think they're willing to do the right thing without having to go to court."

"Hey, that's great!"

"Yeah. Look, I'm grateful for your faith in me. I know you love your mother and are concerned about her welfare. Now that you know the truth about my past, you have every reason not to want me with her," Dexter said guardedly.

"Hey, hold up! This is Jeff you're talkin' to, man. I've known you longer than a few days. Ma explained about the manslaughter conviction. I agree with her. It was an accident. Dex, you are not a killer," he paused as if struggling to keep his emotions in check. "How can I ever forget that you stuck by me when I was at the lowest point in my life? How could I do less for you?"

Dexter had trouble swallowing the lump forming in his throat. "Anthia, has done a good job with you, kid. By the way, she isn't home. But I'll tell her you called."

"Thanks. Aw . . . by the way . . . I aw . . . have gotten past the problem we talked about."

"Huh? I'm drawing a blank here."

"I was concerned . . . aw . . . about a personal problem."

"Oh, yes. I remember."

"I didn't think I'd ever find someone who didn't have a problem with my limitations," he laughed. "I was wrong."

"Oh?"

"Yeah. Her name is Cora. She's Cynthia Montgomery's roommate. She has agreed to go out with me this weekend."

Dexter grinned, imagining he could hear the smile in Jeff's voice. "That's the way, my man! Good luck."

"Thanks. I must admit I'm a little nervous. We've talked a couple of times this week on the phone. That's helped keep me calm."

"You have nothing to worry about. Have you considered talking to your doctor about that other concern?"

"Sexual?"

"Mmm-hmm."

"No . . . but I'm sure I won't have a problem if the situation presents itself."

"Tested yourself?"

Jeff laughed. "Something like that. The usual way. She kissed me and while she was close I responded immediately. Oh, man, it felt good."

Dexter cautioned, "Don't rush it, kid. You're there to get a degree, not get laid."

They both chuckled.

"I'll remember that. Got to go. Tell Ma, I called. See ya."

After Dexter replaced the receiver, he pressed the play button on the answering machine. Anthia's voice was soft and sweet to his ear. "Hi Dex. If you're listening to this then I know you are worried. Sorry, honey. I stopped in to visit with Dana and have stayed longer than expected. I hope you've brought dinner, I'm starving. See you soon."

Dexter ground his teeth in frustration. "Hell!" That woman could be so stubborn! Why didn't she realize that just because he had taught her a few self-defense moves, she was no expert. She could not protect herself against the thugs that liked to hang out around that building. This was not a play thing. Her safety was at stake. "Damn!"

Grabbing his jacket, then fishing his keys out of his pocket, he muttered to himself, "I don't care if she does get mad, I'm going after her."

"What's wrong with you Jerome? Anthia wants to leave." Dana put herself between the two of them.

"You think I don't know what you two were talking about? You think I'm stupid," he said glaring at her. "She doesn't think I'm good enough for you." His words were somewhat slurred. To Anthia, he snapped, "What you tryin' to do? Ruin my life like your precious son ruined my brother's?"

Anthia stiffened, her back straight as if trying to make herself taller than five-one. "My son is not responsible for Eddie's troubles. Eddie holds that honor. You know that's your problem. You're always blaming someone else for what goes wrong in your life, rather than looking at yourself for not trying hard enough."

Dana looked anxiously from one to the other. She didn't need this, especially since Jerome was not sober. She could smell the liquor on his breath. To be honest, she was relieved it was alcohol and desperately hoped it was not drugs. She said, "Anthia don't. Let me handle this."

But Anthia was not listening. All she could see was how this young man was carelessly hurting someone she cared deeply for. Her tone was sharp when she went on to say, "You're right, Jerome. I don't think you're the right man for Dana. She's too good for you. But I would be the last person to tell her to leave your sorry butt. That's her decision, not mine."

"Shut up! Shut the hell up!" he yelled at her, moving his shoulders and flinging his arms menacingly. "I don't like you, lady! I want you out of my house . . . now. Out of our lives. Dana's not going to be doing anymore work for you."

"What!" Both women said at the same time.

"You heard me! I don't want you near her! Don't come back here!"

Dana was shaking, but she did not offer a word of protest.

"Dana, are you going to let him decide for you? Dana?"

Dana looked away, unwilling or unable to meet Anthia's eyes.

Anthia was so upset she, too, was trembling. As she looked from one young face to the other, she fully accepted that when it came to this man, he could do no wrong from Dana's viewpoint.

"Dana, if you are not careful this man is going to take over your entire life. Are you going to let him do your thinking for you?" Anthia wished she could call back the words the instant they left her mouth. It was the wrong thing to say.

No matter how truthful those words were, she had to face the fact that Dana was not ready to hear them. Those hasty words could also serve to drive a wedge between Dana and Anthia. It was possible that Dana may not ever be ready to believe them.

"How could you?" Dana whispered, blinking back tears.

"I'm sorry, Dana. I shouldn't have said that. Please, can you forgive me?"

Dana nodded, but she failed to look at Anthia. Her arms were crossed tightly against her body as if she needed to protect herself.

Jerome snarled, "Get out!"

Anthia shook her head. "Not until I've talked to Dana, privately."

"I said get the hell out!" he shouted, moving threateningly toward her.

Instead of retreating, Anthia braced herself. "Don't touch me."

"Open this door before I break it down," Dexter said, from the other side of the door.

Dana was shaking from head to toe as she hurried to do just that. "Thank goodness."

"Amen to that," Anthia mumbled.

Dexter's tall frame filled the doorway. His dark eyes immediately going to Anthia and quickly moving over her. She was pulled against his side. "You okay?" he asked softly, his gaze on the other man.

"Fine. What are you doing here?"

"You're here. That's good enough for me. What was all the yelling about? I could hear your voices all the way down the hall."

"I want her out of here, man. She was trying to turn my lady against me."

Dexter's eyebrows arched inquisitively. "How could she do that?"

Anthia open her mouth to speak but quickly decided to keep quiet. She had already said too much by suggesting that Dana leave the man in front of him.

"Dana listens to her. Believes everything she tells her. How can I compete with that," Jerome said bitterly.

"You don't have to. Anthia loves Dana like a sister. She isn't trying to run your life," Dexter said reasonably. "As long as you're the man in your own home, what difference does it make what anyone says? By being the man, I don't mean how many babies you've fathered. I'm talking about taking care of your children and keeping a roof over their heads. A man always takes responsibility for his actions . . . good or bad."

Jerome stared at Dexter. "That's easy for you to say. You don't know what it is to be out here! You got a good job, man. And a woman who respects you!"

"You can have those same things. But first you have to start respecting yourself and your body. How the hell can you function without being sober? Is the liquor doing the talking for you, my man?"

"Hell no!"

"Then be a man without it! There's nothing to keep you from making something of your life . . . nothing but your pride."

The two stared at each other for some time without speaking, one enraged and the other cool and composed. The younger man was the first to look away.

"You have no idea what I am up against."

"Man, have you read the paper lately? I know what it is to be a black man. But I also know that if you want your lady's respect and your children's respect you have to earn it. That means leaving the streets alone." Dexter paused, hoping to give his words time to sink in.

"I can help you find a job. I can help you improve your educational skills. That's my job, man." Dexter shrugged, then said, "Whether I can point you in the right direction, is up to you. Your choice, my man. Come by the center. We'll talk."

Both Dana's and Anthia's eyes were on the younger man. Dana was too afraid to hope while Anthia was filled with pride for Dexter.

Jerome nodded, before he said quietly, "Okay." The two men shook hands.

"Ready?" Dexter asked Anthia.

"Almost." To Dana she said, "I'm sorry Dana. Please, don't hold what I said against me."

"I can't," she whispered, her throat filled with tears, "I love you." While the two hugged each other, she whispered urgently in Anthia's ear, "Please, don't let Dexter stop trying to reach him. Promise?"

Anthia nodded, kissing her cheek. "Shall I come by next week for the new doll clothes?"

"Yes, please. I'll have them ready and will be ready for more. Good night."

" 'Night."

Anthia was downright weary with relief as she walked into the hallway with Dexter at her side. They were nearly to the elevator when she said, "Thanks for coming. It was getting a little rough there for a while."

Dexter did not comment as he pressed the button to summon the elevator. One glance at his set features told it's own tale. He was not happy with her.

"Honey . . ."

"Don't even try to get around me."

"I'm sorry. I know you asked me not to come in the evenings. But it was important that I see Dana, right away."

"Evidently, what I asked didn't matter," he snapped, holding the doors open so she could proceed him inside.

"That's not true. If you just, let me explain . . ."

As the elevator descended, Dexter maintained his silence. A muscle flexed in his jaw as if he were clenching his teeth.

"Dex . . ."

"We'll talk about it later," he said as they exited the building. "My place is closer. Let's go there."

Although surprised, Anthia nodded her agreement. "That's fine."

He did not leave until she was strapped in her seat with the doors locked. Only then did he jog to his own car. He drove slowly, checking in his rearview mirror to make sure she was right behind him.

TWENTY-FIVE

Anthia had been racking her brain for an explanation that might ease his mood. She had barely stepped out of the car when he walked up behind her. Without so much as a word, he reached for her bringing her against his chest. His mouth open and hungry over hers. He was not satisfied with a simple kiss, but took her mouth in a deep, drugging exchange that left her weak in the knees, her body aching for his.

"Let's get inside," he said roughly guiding her along the sidewalk. He unlocked the door then stepped aside, allowing her to enter first. He flicked on the hall light. "This way." He guided her into his sparsely furnished front room. "I'm not much of a decorator."

The room held the basics, a big black leather easy chair positioned in front of the television set, a black leather sofa against the wall, floor-to-ceiling bookshelves on either side, and a single floor lamp. There were no pictures on the walls, no plants, no rugs on the hardwood flooring, nothing to soften the area.

"Should I apologize?"

"Absolutely not. You're comfortable here. That's all that matters." She put her arms around his trim waist, saying huskily, "Evidently, I missed something between there and here. Why did you want to come here tonight?"

"You've never been to my place. I thought it was about time you saw where I live," he said simply. His feelings were so jumbled where she was concerned, so complex and intense.

There was nothing easygoing about what he felt for this beautiful black woman.

"I thought you were angry with me?"

"Not angry, infuriated. I don't like you putting yourself at risk. Dana's apartment is safe enough during the day, but at night . . . it's out of the question."

"What is safe, Dex? Even your precious community center has had to hire a security guard."

"Shut up and give me some of that sweet sugar," he growled, lifting her until her mouth could meet his without strain. His mouth was insistent as he stroked her soft tongue with his own. He groaned heavily, sucking her tongue.

Eventually he said, "You know damn well what I mean." He head was filled with his need for her. "Oh, baby . . ." he moaned floored by her sweetness.

"Dex!" She was thrown off balance as he spanned her waist when he whirled her around, laughing deeply.

"Baby, you're not going to believe what happened."

Anthia's black eyes locked with his deep brown ones. She saw none of the disappointment or disillusionment that had lingered there since reading the newspaper accounting on Sunday.

"What happened?"

He chuckled giving her a tight squeeze. "I can't believe it."

Impatient, she insisted, "Honey, tell me what happened." He was not the same brooding man who had dropped her off earlier that day.

"It's over baby. We can finally put this whole miserable experience behind us."

Anthia's small palms cradled his hair-roughed jaw. "What are you talking about?"

"Tina confessed. She admitted in front of her mother that she lied. It's over, Anthia."

She shook her head, unable or rather unwilling to get her hopes up only to have them crushed later. "How did this happen?"

"I was so ticked after I left Quinn's office that I decided to go over to the Douglases' place and talk to Tina."

"Dex! You took a terrible risk. You could have made things so much worse. I know Quinn didn't agree to this."

"He didn't know," he said, taking her hand to guide her over to the sofa. Once they were seated side by side, he looked pointedly at her. "I had to do it."

"I can't believe it. The risk you took . . ."

"Something like you did tonight."

"That wasn't nice."

"It wasn't meant to be. Do you want to hear what happened or not?"

"Yes," she said earnestly, her hand clasped in his. "How did you get inside?"

"I talked my way in. Her mother, Mrs. Douglas, eventually agreed to let me talk to Tina. She was very defensive but I managed to keep at her until Tina broke down and admitted that she lied. Her mother was there to hear her confession."

"Mrs. Douglas and I agreed that if Tina makes a statement to the press and tells the truth, I won't press charges against her." He stopped, watching Anthia closely, finally he said, "Anthia, I couldn't let her get away with destroying my life. It took years to get to the point were I've been able to regain my self-respect."

"Oh, baby," Anthia said her arms around his neck. She kissed him over and over. "That's wonderful. I just hope they keep their word. So you've told Quinn?"

"Yes. Like you, he did not agree with my method but he is pleased by the end result. He's arranged the news conference for tomorrow at the community center. It's going to happen."

"Yes. It's really over." She shared his deep sense of relief. He had been through so much. This latest revelation had stripped him of his highly valued privacy. How would he manage from now on? He had the community's support but she suspected he would not be content until he was fully reinstated as the director of the center.

"Almost. Tina is a very troubled girl. She's going to need some counselling to get herself straightened-out. I'll talk to Quinn to make that a condition of our agreement. What do you think?"

"I think you are wonderful!"

He couldn't help smiling, but said thoughtfully, "Even after the news conference, I know there will be people who won't ever believe that I didn't touch that girl, but . . ."

She finished for him, " . . . that's their problem, not yours."

"Exactly," his hungry gaze lingered on her exquisitely shaped mouth. "You have been so wonderful through all this. Tell me, what I have ever done to deserve your faith in me?"

He'd never been on the receiving end of such unconditional support. What did it mean? Was it love? Was she in love with him?

He didn't give her time to form an answer for his mouth quickly covered hers. He sponged her lush bottom lip before slipping inside to savor the sweetness within.

Whatever her response, it would have been lost beneath the onslaught of his hot kisses. Anthia could not gather her thoughts, all she could do was feel as Dexter waged a one-man attack on her senses. She had no protection from his masculine appeal. Did he have any idea that he owned her heart forever more?

She had given it to him long ago. She had been in love with him for some time. Once they became lovers, Anthia found she loved him even more. He was everything she wanted in a man. His compassion and generosity touched her tender heart. Perhaps, it was time she told him how she felt.

When Dexter lifted his head to looked deep into her eyes, she whispered his name. Her eyes searched his hoping to read his thoughts. Uncertain of what she saw beyond the unmistakable proof of his desire for her, she smiled up at him.

"I am so glad for your sake. I was so worried. I know it didn't seem that way with me going over to Dana's but I had such exciting news that I had to share, since you weren't around I called Dana. She and I have grown close over the last year that we've been working together."

"What news?"

He watched as her lovely brown features glowed with an inner radiance that was reflected in her smile. Dexter found that he could not look away as he acknowledged that he had been fighting his feelings for her for a long, long time. How could he have been so blind?

She giggled like a schoolgirl as she searched for the letter in her purse. "Here it is. Read it," she said, giving it to him.

He studied the envelope. "The network shopping channel?"

She nodded, her excitement building. "Hurry." When he didn't comply fast enough to suit her, she pulled the letter free of the envelope and held out to him. "Can you believe it?"

His generous lips formed an indulgent smile before he quickly scanned the letter. When he looked at her he said, "Yes. I can believe it. You're very talented. Why are you surprised?" He leaned forward to brush his mouth against hers. "Congratulations, baby. We're going to have to go out to celebrate. I knew you could do it."

Happy tears filled her eyes. Swiftly, she brushed them away. "Thank you. I appreciate your belief in me. What a wonderful end to very long day," Anitha sighed, looking into his eyes. "I'm proud of you. You stuck to your guns and refused to back down. The board members have to be out of their minds if they let you get away. Just look how well you defused the situation with Tina."

"The meeting could have gone either way. I was just plain lucky."

"Nope. You've earned the community's respect. Don't ever forget that. You have put your life on the line time and time again all for someone else's kid. There is nothing you won't do to save a child. You are such a very special man." She squeezed his hand recognizing she loved him so much.

"Girl, you know how to make me feel good."

They sat grinning at each other quite pleased with each other.

Dexter thoughtfully studied her, wondering how he had gotten so lucky, considering his past, to have a wonderful woman like Anthia care for him. How deep were her feelings? Was it even within the realm of possibility that she could someday love him as he loved her.

"What is it?"

"Nothing," he shook his head as if to clear it. "Care for something to drink? Coke or beer?"

Anthia immediately felt a mixture of anger and disappointment. She said quietly, "Coke, please."

"Be right back."

She was grateful for the time alone in order to pull herself together. It hurt knowing he still did not feel as if he could share his thoughts with her. Anthia did not have to be told that something more was bothering him. She despaired that things would ever significantly change between them.

"Here you go," he said passing her the ice-filled glass of cola before settling beside her.

She happened to look up once more to find his dark, brooding gaze on her. Unable to remain silent, she blurted out, "Haven't we been through enough together? Must you continue to doubt me?"

Shocked, he said, "I have no doubts where you are concerned."

"Then why do you continue to shut me out?"

Carefully, he put his beer bottle down on the coffee table, then he said, "Anthia, what are you talking about?"

"You don't trust me with what's bothering you. Don't say I'm imagining things. It has happened too many times in the past for me to be making it up."

He looked away, unsure if he could offer the candor she required.

When he hesitated, she said, "Look, it's late. I think it's time I went home." She picked up her purse, trying to not to notice the way her hands trembled as she searched the bottom of the bag for her keys. She could not bear this pretense. They had been through too much.

"Baby," he said, blocking her path. When she didn't even look at him, he cupped her shoulders. "What's wrong?"

"What could be wrong? I'd like to go home, that's all," she bit her lip to keep from crying.

Exhaling heavily, he ran his hand over his natural agitatedly. "Damn it! I don't know what you want from me?" How could he explain the relentless hunger inside of him that he so recently discovered? He had lost so much over the years. He was only just beginning to understand how terrified he was of opening himself up to the possibility of yet another loss. If she left him, he knew he could never survive it. His feelings for her ran too deep.

As she stared at him, she was forced to acknowledge what she wanted most in the world was his love . . . nothing more and nothing less. In spite of her best efforts the tears spilled from her eyes. She tried to turn away from him in hope of hiding her grief. She was mourning what she could not have. Love had to be given freely, never taken upon demand.

In desperation, he pressed his mouth to that soft, tender place where her neck and shoulder joined.

"No, baby," he whispered, his throat thick with emotion. "I am not letting you go. I can't . . ."

Cradling her chin, he lifted her face toward his. He studied her face. "Look at me . . . please." When he saw how her dark, velvety eyes were washed with tears, he insisted, "Baby, we can work it out . . . whatever it is."

Anthia's small frame shook from her sobs. She tried to catch her breath but couldn't. Speaking coherently was out of the question. Tears rolled down her cheeks as she fought to hold in a sob.

He pulled her against his chest. "Don't . . . please . . . baby." Dexter murmured close to her ear. When she tried to free herself, he tightened his hold. "No, don't ask it of me. I can't let you go . . . not ever. I love you too much."

Uncertain if he had said what she wanted to hear most or if she had just imagined it. Struggling to catch her breath, she said, "What?"

"I'm in love with you, Anthia. I have no life without you," he said gruffly, his chest tight with a combination of fear and need.

"Oh . . ." was all she could manage to say. She had been hungry for those words for so long that she was momentarily uncertain. She finally asked, "Do you mean it?" She blinked trying to clear her vision so that she could see him.

He dropped his head so she could see his eyes and he could see hers. "I mean it." His heart beat so loudly it seemed to drum in his ears.

"Dex . . ." she whispered, lifting up on tiptoes to encircle his neck. "I've waited so long to hear you say that."

Their lips touched softly then more urgently as the kiss deepened into an intoxicating exchange. He crushed her to him, unable to let her go. Anthia clung to him, needing his support for her legs were trembling badly.

Dexter felt as he had that first night they made love . . . he had unknowingly claimed her as his own. Grateful. Ravenously, he thrust his tongue against hers, his throbbing penis thickened and lengthened in anticipation of bolder, deeper thrusts. He wanted to make love to her . . . needed her lovemaking.

"Dex . . ." Anitha moaned losing touch with everything but him.

"Hmm," he groaned, pressing his open mouth against the tender underside of her chin before moving down her sensitive throat to the fragrant hollow. "Let me . . . let me make love to you, baby."

Anthia was beyond coherent thought as she pressed her body against his long male length, rubbing the sensitive peaks of her breasts into his chest. She ached so, for his attention. She trembled against the insistent pressure of his erection. She knew from experience he would fill her to bursting and pleasure her to the point of madness with his intense brand of lovemaking.

The all-too-brief contact was not nearly enough for either of them. He wanted the skin-to-skin contact from her soft hands, her plump, pretty breasts, her damp, tight sheath.

"Touch me," she whispered urgently. Anthia shivered at the wonder of his hands cupping and squeezing her breasts. She nearly cried out when he stopped and systematically stripped her clothes. She sighed when he returned to her breasts to caress them before he tongued each large chocolate-brown nipple in turn. When he lifted his head, she was breathless from the heat of his mouth.

Longing to give as well as receive pleasure, she moved her hand along the prominent ridge of his heavy sex, caressing from the wide base along the shaft to the ultrasensitive tip. He was all man and she shivered, thrilled that she could give him so much enjoyment.

When her soft hands moved to his waist to release the restriction of his slacks, he held her still. When she lifted her face to question him, he kissed her hard, then to her surprise lifted her up until she was balanced over a wide broad shoulder.

"What are you doing?" she laughed, grabbing the back of his shirt trying to steady herself.

Dexter gave a deep throaty laugh, his long legs taking the stairs two at a time. His room was at the top of the stairs on the right. He moved purposefully through the dark room before he put her down across the king-size bed. The moonlight spilled in through the open drapes.

"What did you think I was going to do, darlin'?" he teased as he pulled off his clothes. The shirt went first then he peeled down his slacks and briefs until he stood on the side of the bed looking down at her. She lifted her arms to him. She didn't have long to wait for he quickly dropped down beside her and covered her mouth with his.

She nearly forgot to breathe as his slow, sweet kisses inched down her throat to linger in the sensitive hollow before he gently cupped her breasts, luxuriating in their cushiony softness before dropping his head to tantalize her with the warm wash of his tongue. He licked the entire globe before he moved to concentrate on the engorged nipple.

Anthia could not muffle her pleasure as he applied the most delectable suction, taking it deep into his mouth. She cried out his name cupping the back of his head as if to keep him there. He stroked down her thighs before he moved to the softer inner skin to cup her sex, squeezing the plump feminine folds. He was rewarded by the dewy, slickness he found inside.

Thrilled that she was so ready for him, Dexter moved to give her left breast the same sweet attention that he had given the right. Yet, he continued the deep caresses within her sizzling heat with a long blunt finger. Anthia cried out, needing more . . . wanting him.

"Now please . . . Dexter . . . now."

He deepened the suction while intensifying his strokes as he used his thumb to worry the tiny center of her desires.

"Dex!!" she screamed his name as she climaxed, ripples of

sheer pleasure flooding her senses. He held her close, cradling her against him. She lifted her tear-dampened face to his, giving him kiss after sweet kiss. "I wanted to wait," she managed to say somewhat breathlessly. "I wanted to wait for you, honey."

There could be no doubt about the commitment they saw in each other's eyes. He stroked the soft curves of her brown face. One gentle kiss led to another and another until they became deep and hungry . . . unmistakably needy.

"All in good time," he said huskily as he moved his mouth slowly, tenderly from her lips to her throat, then down the center of her chest planting kiss after kiss. When he reached her soft stomach she whimpered with delicious expectation.

"No . . . you can't want to . . ."

"Yes, let me." Dexter's eyes locked with Anthia's as he waited for her consent.

There was no question about what she saw, his gaze was not without longing.

"Don't you enjoy the feel of my mouth on your sweetness? Oh, baby, you are sweet, so sweet. Let me taste you."

Anthia melted unable to marshall any resistance. "Yes . . . please," she whispered her breath quick and uneven from the sizzling expectation.

By the time Dexter kissed her feminine mound, Anthia gasped out his name. He moved lower still, parting her silky thighs even more and raising them to his shoulders. There was no hesitation on his part, Dexter caressed her slick folds then parted them in order to lave her feminine essence. He gloried in her womanliness, relishing her soft whimpers from sheer pleasure as he plied his hot tongue concentrating on her clitoris.

Dexter took his time, making slow, drugging love to Anthia with the wet, hot wash of his tongue. Anthia cried out as the whirling pleasure completely shattered her control and sent her hurling toward completion.

When she recovered enough to speak, Anthia said caressing his hair-roughened cheeks, "I need you, baby, deep inside of me. Please."

He required no further urging. Dexter rose until he could give them what they craved, the joining of the steel-hard strength of his body with the dewy heat of hers. His control had nearly vanished when Anthia reached that last release.

"Baby . . . hurry."

Pausing only long enough to prepare himself, Dexter carefully filled her, forcing back the natural urge to thrust deeply. He let out a deep shuddering breath when she lifted her legs to encircle his waist, opening herself even more to his deep, slow penetration. The burning heat seemed to build very quickly . . . higher and higher the flames seemed to shoot through their systems as they clung to each other. Dexter's breath was quick and uneven as he closed his eyes focusing on the overwhelming sensual pleasure Anthia gave him while his penis throbbed relentlessly.

"Anthia . . . Anthia," he groaned heavily as he rocked his himself against her, quickening his thrusts. "Love me . . . love me,' " he crooned in her ear.

Instinctively tightening her inner muscles around him, she stroked him in such a highly erotic way that soon had them both crying out from the pure beauty of it.

"Oh, yes . . . yes," Anthia moaned.

Dexter's large frame quaked in response, unable to hold back any of himself from her. He gave her the full force of his masculinity. She gasped her appreciation. Her soft hands stroking down his back, squeezing his buttocks. He knew he could not last much longer, yet he also wanted them to experience the wonders of a shared climax.

He reached between their bodies to caress her clitoris as he moved insistently inside of her. His open mouth tongued the sensitive spot on her neck. Anthia felt as if her world had turned upside down. The deep thrusts along with his tantalizing caresses caused her to shatter like glass into a million shards of exquisite pleasure while his hoarse shout of exaltation blended with hers as they reached that ultimate pinnacle of pure bliss together.

Dexter was the first to move, dropping down to lay on his back beside her. He was not content until she was cradled on his chest. Anthia took note of the masculine glint of satisfaction

in his dark eyes. She laughed softly to caressing his hair-roughened chin.

"I love you," she whispered.

Dexter's arms tightened around her as he stared down into
her velvet darkness of her eyes. Desperately wanting to believe,
he finally managed, "Are you sure?"

"Absolutely."

He closed his eyes as he tried to compose himself. A single
tear slid pass his black lashes. His voice was ragged with emotion when he demanded, "Why?"

She laughed, "What do you mean?" then realized he was
very serious. His eyes spoke of his inner turmoil.

"Love won't change how others view me. In time, you may
have regrets. I was convicted of manslaughter, Anthia. I have
to live with that for the rest of my life. It's not a small thing.
It's not going . . ."

Anthia pressed her lips to his, stopping the flow of his words.
She said without hesitation "I know you too well to ever believe
it was anything more than a terrible accident. Dex, you are what
matters to me . . . only you."

He nestled her cheek, afraid to hope while needing to believe.
"Anthia, I love you so much."

She blinked as her eyes filled with tears of happiness. Brush-
ing them quickly away, she said, "You have no idea how long
I've waited and hoped that you might someday say those words.
I nearly gave up on it ever happening."

"No longer than I have waited to find you, my love. Oh,
Anthia, I wish I had met you first," he confessed. "I know now
what had always been missing from my life. It's you and your
unselfish love."

Their kiss was as deep and tender as their love. Her leg was
thrown over his hips while his hand moving lovingly along her
thigh.

"Was that why you wanted to leave? You didn't think I was
in love with you?" he made himself ask.

"Mmm-hmm," she said. "It hurt so much thinking you did
not return my feelings."

"I'm sorry, baby. I never want you to be hurt and certainly not by me."

"So many times I almost told you how I felt, especially when we made love that first time," she confessed as she stroked his chest.

"Why didn't you," he asked, knowing how much the knowledge would soothe that deep and pain filled ache in his heart.

"I didn't want to burden you. I knew you were troubled by your past. I knew you were still in love with Christine. I couldn't tell you. You were so determined to keep our relationship platonic."

"I wanted you, in any and every way I could have you. I just didn't think I was good for you."

"How can you say that? You make me so happy."

"I hope so," he said, pressing his lips to her forehead. "You were wrong. I'm not in love with Christine. My feelings for her died the night she tried to destroy our child along with herself. That I could not understand or forgive. Because of my own involvement, I could not handle my feelings. I felt such incredible guilt."

"You never told me. You've kept this inside all this time?"

"Yes. It was more from habit than needing to keep secrets. I'm not used to sharing my thoughts. You are the only one who cares what's going on inside of me."

"More people care about you than you realize. This incident with Tina should have shown you that."

He nodded. "Yes. And I am thankful. It was a humiliating experience. One that I don't want to ever repeat. But most important, my love, you always believed in me. Never once did you doubt my innocence. I've never known anyone as unselfish and generous as you are."

He was wrong about her feelings for him. Anthia was extremely selfish where he was concerned. She wanted all his love. She wanted a future with him.

"When did you know how you felt about me? And why didn't you tell me the instant you realized?" she demanded.

Dexter grinned roguishly. "Baby, I was halfway in love with you that first night when we met at the charity dinner-dance.

You were so beautiful that I think my heart stopped beating when I first saw you. I wanted you even then."

"Stop teasing me," she said around a grin.

"I'm serious, my love. It was that long, awful night that Jeff was shot that you took my heart away," his voice was deep and husky.

She shook her head, her soft hair caressing his throat. "I was a total mess."

"You were so determined, yet, so scared. Most of all you were courageous. You fought and prayed for your son's life. You were not going to let him go easily. Not once through that entire night did you stop believing in or loving Jeff. That was the night you claimed my heart because of your unfailing devotion. I knew then you were one of a kind and I could not help wanting you for myself."

"Oh, honey," she whispered, pressing her lips where his neck and shoulder joined. His body began to swell once again, acutely sensitive to her softness and her feminine scent. He chuckled. "See what you do to me," he said, placing her hand over his hardening manhood for only an instant before he moved it to his chest. He knew how shaky he was when it came to her. It would not take much of her attention to arouse him to the point of madness. "Tell me when you knew how you felt about me, baby."

She had to force herself to focus on their discussion rather than her need to once again be one with him. His hard, male length had her instantly aware of his keen masculinity.

"Stop teasing me," she scolded, feeling him flex against her thigh. Her smile so sweetly alluring.

"Tell me."

"I fell in love with you while Jeff was recovering from the injury. I was overwhelmed at your generosity to us both, Dex. First, you stayed all through that agonizing first night with me in the hospital. Later, you were so kind and thoughtful. You were constantly feeding me, coming over after the center closed to spend time with me, knowing I wasn't comfortable being in the house alone. You were there for both my son and me throughout his entire recovery. How could I not fall in love with you?" she said, pressing her lips to his throat. She relaxed against him enjoying the feel of his hands smoothing down her back.

"Do you love me enough to marry me?"

"What?"

"You heard correctly. I didn't think I could ever do this again, but Anthia I want you to be my wife. Will you?"

He was trembling as he waited for her answer, needing so badly for her to say yes. How could he accept anything less from her? He wanted her so badly he had seriously considered getting her pregnant in order to keep her in his life.

"Yes, Dex." There was no hesitation on her part, just a breathless whisper. She refused to let her fears intrude. He said he loved her. She would not to voice her lingering doubts because he had not put his part in Christine's death behind him.

He kissed her deeply. When he finally allowed her the luxury of breath, he asked "Soon? Baby, don't make me wait."

"Yes . . ." she smiled into his eyes.

"Thank you," he said softly, his lips were warm and insistent over hers. Only when he had gotten his fill did he say, "There's something I would like for you to see." He flicked on the bedside lamp before he reached into the nightstand and removed a letter.

When she raised questioning eyes to his, he explained, "It's from Christine's brother. Please, read it aloud."

"Dear Dexter, I was shocked to see you at Stephanie and Kenneth's wedding. I suppose I should have been expecting it but I didn't. It has been a few years since we've talked—not since the trial. It seems according to your sister you have built a new life for yourself up North. I know you may not believe this but I'm relieved. For too many years there has only been bitterness and blame between us. I, too, have gone on with my life. And my wife has convinced me that it is long past time to let the past go. Nothing can bring my sister back . . . punishing you can only keep the pain inside of me. I am doing this for my sake, not just yours."

When she paused, Dexter insisted. "Please finish."

". . . I have enclosed the letter Christine sent me the day

before her death. I have finally accepted that she did what she wanted to do. I'm sorry that you were punished for it. And I deeply regret that I did nothing to help you. Perhaps this will give you some measure of comfort. John."

Dexter handed her the second letter addressed to John Barns. "Go on, please."

"Dear John, I'm sorry. I know you won't understand what I'm determined to do. I'm sure you will see it as a coward's way out, for me it is the only way. As much as I love Dexter and I know he loves me, things are bound to change once he knows the truth. I never wanted this baby. I got pregnant for his sake. It was wrong of me. I know that now. The baby is not developing as it should and it's my fault. Dexter thinks I've stopped drinking, but I haven't. I can't, not even for him. He knows about the drinking, but not about the drugs. The doctors have warned me that our son will be extremely deformed. I can't live with that . . . I just can't. There is only one way to solve this. Please, help Dexter through this. And please, forgive me. Love, Christine."

Anthia's eyes went to his. "Oh Dex . . ." she finally said, unable to express her own shock and disbelief. "She was determined to die."

"Yes, she was and she intended to take our son with her."

Anthia could feel his anguish. "I'm so sorry."

"So am I."

"Was this letter used as evidence during your trial?"

"No. This is the first concrete proof that I have of what her intentions were. I am grateful that after seeing me my former brother-in-law decided to send it."

"It could have helped your defense tremendously."

He shrugged, "Possibly." Anthia watched the way his eyes filled before he blinked them away. "I'm just so glad it came when it did. It helped me accept that it is long past time I let it go. Finally, I feel as if I have the right to go on with my life, to seek my own happiness."

Anthia's eyes also filled with tears from a mixture of both despair for Christine and what she had lost, and tremendous joy for him. Dexter truly believed that finally he had a right to be happy. For that, Anthia was deeply relieved and grateful.

"It was kind of him to send it. He wanted your forgiveness for not helping you sooner."

"It's over, baby." He gave her a hard, hungry kiss. "I'm ready to make a new life with you."

"I'm so glad," she said, thrilled by the happiness she saw in his strong angular face and the depths of his dark eyes. Her smile of happiness matched his as she smoothed her hand over his hair-roughened bronze chest.

"So . . ." he drawled. "When do we drive down to Augusta? Day after tomorrow too soon? I assume we want to tell Jeff in person?"

Anthia laughed delighted by his impatience. "He'll be home at end of the semester for a few days before summer school starts."

"Can't wait that long. Don't you realize yet, my love, I've waited as long as I'm prepared to wait to make you my wife. I know you're going to want him at our wedding as much as I do. So, is this weekend too soon to get married?"

"No," she whispered against his mouth. "Yes, I'll marry you as soon as we can arrange it."

He chuckled. "We don't want our friends counting the months before our baby is born."

She giggled. "Oh, you still think I might be pregnant?"

He laughed. "If not now you will be. This was the last time I plan to use protection, that is if you have no objections."

Anthia laughed, her heart filled with pure joy. "Not a single one." There was nothing she wanted more than someday having babies with him. "Love me," she whispered, pressing her lips against his.

EPILOGUE

It was a bright, brilliantly clear day. Dexter and Anthia sat side by side out in the sunshine waiting for Jeff to take his turn across the stage.

Dexter held their oldest daughter, Lynette, in his lap. At three and half, she considered herself a big girl. Although, she clearly resembled her mother with her petite stature, pretty features, amber skin tone and thick black braids, her dark brown eyes and stubborn little chin came from her father.

Anthia held their baby girl, Chanette, who sat sucking her thumb. At eleven months she like her big sister, favored their mother and like her sister she was a daddy's girl.

"Da-da . . . Da-da," she chimed, leaning over to pat Dexter's bronze cheek.

Dexter laughed, giving her a kiss on her baby soft cheek. And he chuckled even more when Lynette insisted on having a kiss. He easily complied. His gaze caressed his lovely wife. Like their girls, she was dressed in pale pink. He marveled at her beauty as he wondered if he could possibly by happier. She had given him more joy than he could ever imagine. He worked to keep her happy.

He had no idea how she managed their home, the girls, appearing regularly on the network home-shopping channel to show her dolls, yet always making enough time for the two of them. Anthia had gone on to start her own small doll manufacturing company in Detroit.

As far as he was concerned, Anthia had managed a miracle

by bringing himself and his father together. Although Dexter and his father hadn't totally reconciled, his father was a loving and doting grandfather to Dexter's daughters.

It was impossible for him to believe, but Dexter knew he loved Anthia more now than the day they married.

"Dex! Oh, honey look. Here he comes!" Anthia exclaimed. Tears of pure joy ran down her cheeks as she watched Jeff walk unaided across the stage to receive his engineering degree from the Georgia Institute of Technology. She had thought she could not have been prouder when he graduated from Paine at the top of his class. She had been wrong.

"Jeff!" Lynette bounced on her dad's lap.

The baby waved her chubby little arms and cooed her enthusiasm.

"Oh, Jeff!" Cora Denton Washington, sitting on the other side of her mother-in-law, clapped and cheered for her husband.

Anthia turned wet eyes up to Dexter's. The caress of his mouth against hers was both tender, as well as comforting.

"He made it," she whispered.

"Yes." Dexter was choked up with pride and love. Jeff was the son he had always longed for. He had been deeply touched when Jeff had decided to take his name. They were a loving family in every sense of the word.

Dear Readers:

One of a Kind is a result of your kind and loving letters requesting Anthia Jenkins and Dexter Washington's story. The two first appeared in *Forever After* which is Diane Rivers and Charles Randols' love story. I hope you feel this one has been worth the wait.

I would like to thank you for your love and support. I do so enjoy hearing from you. Please keep the letters coming. I admit to being slow in responding when I am on deadline but I promise to answer all letters.

I am also a bit old fashioned, I do not care for email. You may write me at PO Box 625, Warren, MI 48090-0625. Please include a self-addressed stamped legal size envelope.

God Bless

Bette Ford

ABOUT THE AUTHOR

Bette Ford grew up in Saginaw, Michigan, and graduated from Saginaw High School. She obtained her bachelor's degree from Central State University in Wilberforce, Ohio. Bette began her teaching career in Detroit and completed her master's degree from Wayne State University. She has taught for the Detroit Public Schools HeadStart program for many years.

COMING IN MARCH . . .

OPPOSITES ATTRACT   (1-58314-004-2, $499/$6.50)
by Shirley Hailstock
Nefertiti Kincaid had worked hard to reach the top at her company.
But a corporate merger may change all that. Averal Ballentine is the
savvy consultant hired to ensure a smooth transition. Feeling as though
he is part of the threat to her career, she hates him sight unseen. Averal
will convince her he's not out to hurt her, but has *all* her best interests
in mind.

STILL IN LOVE   (1-58314-005-0, $4.99/$6.50)
by Francine Craft
High school sweethearts Raine Gibson and Jordan Clymer pledged to
love each other forever. But for fear he would be a burden to Raine,
Jordan walked out of her life when he learned he had a debilitating
medical condition. Years later, Jordan returns for a second chance. In
the midst of rekindled passion, they must forge a new trust.

PARADISE   (1-58314-006-9, $4.99/$6.50)
by Courtni Wright
History teacher Ashley Stephens ventures to Cairo, following her love
for archaeology, hoping to escape her boring, uneventful life and enter
an adventure. With her mysterious guide, Kasim Sadam, she is sure
to get her money's worth . . . and a little something extra.

FOREVER ALWAYS   (1-58314-007-7, $4.99/$6.50)
by Jacquelin Thomas
Carrie McNichols is leaving her past to be the best mom to her son.
A lucrative job in L.A. offers her the chance to start over, but she runs
into someone from the past. FBI agent Ray Ransom is her new neigh-
bor and her old lover. He can't believe fate has given him a second
chance. Now he will do all in his power to protect their love . . . and
her life.

---

*Available wherever paperbacks are sold, or order direct from the
Publisher. Send cover price plus 50¢ per copy for mailing and handling
to BET Books, Arabesque Consumer Orders, or call (toll free) 888-345-
BOOK, to place your order using Mastercard or Visa. Residents of New
York and Tennessee must include sales tax. DO NOT SEND CASH.*